TO MAKE MEN FREE

wm

WILLIAM MORROW
An Imprint of HARPERCOLLINS*Publishers*

TO MAKE
MEN FREE

A Novel of

THE BATTLE OF ANTIETAM

RICHARD CROKER

HarperCollins books may be purchased for educational, business, or sales promotional use. For information please write: Special Markets Department, HarperCollins Publishers Inc., 10 East 53rd Street, New York, NY 10022.

FIRST EDITION

DESIGNED BY DEBORAH KERNER/DANCING BEARS DESIGN

Maps designed by Robert Croker

Printed on acid-free paper

Library of Congress Cataloging-in-Publication Data

Croker, Richard, 1946–
   To make men free : a novel of the Battle of Antietam / Richard Croker.
      p.   cm.
   ISBN 0-06-055908-X
   1. United States—History—Civil War, 1861–1865—Fiction.   2. Maryland—History—Civil War, 1861–1865—Fiction.   3. Antietam, Battle of, Md., 1862—Fiction.   I. Title.

PS3603.R636T6   2004

2003059254

04   05   06   07   08   WBC/BVG   10   9   8   7   6   5   4   3   2   1

As always
For Terry and Amanda

For Joel Westbrook, who made the words better, and
Robert Croker, who helped me keep the facts straight

With gratitude for the genuine scholars, particularly
Stephen W. Sears,
the world's foremost expert on
George B. McClellan and
the Battle of Antietam

For the living historians and the volunteers who serve
our precious National Battlefield Parks,
particularly Walter Smith

And for a man who has inspired hundreds of would-be
Civil War novelists . . . myself included,
Michael Shaara

CONTENTS

Abraham Lincoln

Robert E. Lee

CAST OF CHARACTERS

ARMY OF THE POTOMAC • USA
Maj. Gen. George B. McClellan, *Commanding*
Brig. Gen. Randolph Marcy, *Chief of Staff*
Brig. Gen. Alfred Pleasonton, *Chief of Cavalry*

JOSEPH HOOKER, FIRST CORPS

1st Division, Brig. Gen. Abner Doubleday
1st Brigade, Col. Walter Phelps
3rd Brigade, Brig. Gen. Marsena Patrick
4th Brigade, Brig. Gen. John Gibbon
    The "Black Hat Brigade"
    Battery "B" 4th U.S. Artillery
    Pvt. Johnny Cook

2nd Division, Brig. Gen. James B. Ricketts
1st Brigade, Brig. Gen. Abram Duryea
2nd Brigade, Col. William Christian
3rd Brigade, Brig. Gen. George Hartstuff

3rd Division, Brig. Gen. Geo. G. Meade

FITZ-JOHN PORTER, FIFTH CORPS

AMBROSE BURNSIDE, NINTH CORPS
    Brig. Gen. Jacob Cox

1st Division, Brig. Gen. Orlando Willcox

2nd Division, Brig. Gen. Samuel Sturgis
2nd Brigade, Brig. Gen. Edward Ferrero
    51st N.Y., 51st Pa.

3rd Division, Brig. Gen. Isaac Rodman
    11th Conn.
    Col. Henry Kingsbury

EDWIN SUMNER, SECOND CORPS

1st Division, Maj. Gen. Israel Richardson
Brig. Gen. Winfield Scott Hancock
2nd Brigade (The Irish Brigade)
    Brig. Gen. Thomas Meagher

2nd Division, Maj. Gen. John Sedgwick
3rd Brigade, Brig. Gen. N.J.T. Dana
    20th Mass.
    Capt. Oliver Wendell Holmes, Jr.

3rd Division, Brig. Gen. William H. French
2nd Brigade, Col. Dwight Morris
    130th Pa.
    Cpl. John Strickler

3rd Brigade, Brig. Gen. Max Weber

WILLIAM FRANKLIN, SIXTH CORPS

MAJ. GEN. JOSEPH J. K. MANSFIELD
BRIG. GEN. ALPHEUS WILLIAMS
TWELFTH CORPS

1st Division, Brig. Gen. Samuel Crawford
    3rd Brigade
    27th Ind.
    Sgt. John M. Bloss
    Cpl. Barton W. Mitchell

2nd Division, Brig. Gen. George S. Greene

UNION GARRISON
AT HARPER'S FERRY
Colonel Dixon Miles • Cavalry: Col. Arno Voss, *Commanding*
Brig. Gen. Julius White • Col. Benjamin Franklin Davis

ARMY OF VIRGINIA • USA
(SECOND MANASSAS)
Maj. Gen. John Pope, *Commanding*

FIRST CORPS, MAJ. GEN. FRANZ SIGEL

THIRD CORPS,
    MAJ. GEN. IRWIN MCDOWELL

1st Division, Brig. Gen. Rufus King
2nd Brigade, Brig. Gen. Abner Doubleday
4th Brigade, Brig. Gen. John Gibbon

FIFTH CORPS,
    MAJ. GEN. FITZ-JOHN PORTER*
    *Detached from the Army of the Potomac

SECOND CORPS,
    MAJ. GEN. NATHANIEL BANKS

THIRD CORPS,
    MAJ. GEN. S. P. HEINTZELMAN*

1st Division, Maj. Gen. Philip Kearny

NINTH CORPS, MAJ. GEN. JESSE RENO*

IN WASHINGTON

John Hay, *Personal Secretary to President Lincoln*

Wm. H. Seward, *Secretary of State*
Edwin Stanton, *Secretary of War*
Salmon P. Chase, *Secretary of the Treasury*
Edward Bates, *Attorney General*

Gideon Welles, *Secretary of the Navy*
Montgomery Blair, *Postmaster General*
Caleb Smith, *Secretary of the Interior*
Maj. Gen. Henry Halleck, *General in Chief*
Clara Barton

THE NEW YORK TRIBUNE

George Smalley, *Chief Correspondent*

Nathaniel Davidson (Nat), *Reporter*

ARMY OF NORTHERN VIRGINIA • CSA
Robert E. Lee, *Commanding*
Col. R. H. Chilton, *Asst. Adjutant*
Col. Walter H. Taylor

CAVALRY
Maj. Gen. J.E.B. Stuart, *Commanding*
Lt. Col. William Blackford
Maj. John Pelham • Artillery

JAMES LONGSTREET'S CORPS
Maj. Moxley Sorrell, Chief of Staff

Maj. Gen. Lafayette McLaws's Division

Maj. Gen. Richard Anderson's Division

Maj. Gen. D. H. Hill's Division
Garland's Brigade,
    Col. D. K. McRae, Commanding
Brig. Gen. Roswell Ripley's Brigade
Brig. Gen. Robert Rodes's Brigade
    6th Ala.
    Col. John Brown Gordon
    Sgt. Edward & Pvt. Joseph Johnson

Brig. Gen. G. B. Anderson's Brigade
Brig. Gen. Alfred Colquitt's Brigade

Brig. Gen. John G. Walker's Division

Brig. Gen. D. R. "Neighbor" Jones's Division
Brig. Gen. Robert Toombs's Brigade
Col. Geo. T. Anderson's Brigade

THOMAS J. "STONEWALL" JACKSON'S CORPS
Capt. Henry Kyd Douglas, Asst. Adjutant

Brig. Gen. John Bell Hood's Division
Col. Evander Law's Brigade
    Col. S. D. Lee, Artillery

Maj. Gen. A. P. Hill's Division
Brig. Gen. Maxcy Gregg's Brigade

Richard Ewell's Division
Brig. Gen. A. R. Lawton, *Commanding*
Brig. Gen. Jubal Early's Brigade

Jackson's Division
Brig. Gen. J. R. Jones, *Commanding*
Winder's (The Stonewall) Brigade
Col. Arnold Grigsby, Commanding

CITIZENS OF SHARPSBURG

Samuel Mumma
Henry Mumma
Jane Mumma
Ada Mumma

Joseph Rohrbach
Henry Rohrbach
David Miller
Mary

N O T E :

"The New York Rebel," Joel Westbrook and
Donald McGuire are fictitious names,
but not fictitious people.
Their stories are generally true
but their names are
lost to history.

These are only the persons
and units highlighted in
To Make Men Free

For a full Antietam
"Order of Battle" see:
The Gleam of Bayonets by James V. Murfin

TO MAKE
MEN FREE

PROLOGUE

A wagon filled with dismembered men rolled gently down Pennsylvania Avenue, the driver trying desperately not to jostle his fragile cargo. For Abraham Lincoln it was agonizing to watch but he couldn't turn away.

A "meat wagon," they call it. Heartless.

More wounded men limped along behind as the wagon eased its way toward the Capitol. A sad parade of crippled heroes. McClellan's mutilated army being shipped back from Virginia one pitiful boy at a time, broken beyond repair and of no further use.

Lincoln glanced out the window to the lawn below and the more pleasant sight of Tad in his wagon being pulled around by Nana the goat, but even this rare smile was all too brief. Too bittersweet to see Tad playing alone. Without Willie. The beautiful boy, his playmate, gone now. Forever. Mary had ordered his room closed and sealed, untouched, and then took to her own bed. Jailed by grief in her own dark cell, suffering beyond endurance. *Like so many others*, he thought, as the meat wagon thankfully, finally rolled out of sight.

Lincoln turned his gaze back into the room, and to the document that still lay on the table. The Emancipation Proclamation. His advisers sat in stunned silence around the table. All shocked and some appalled by what he had just announced. Only the Navy Secretary, Gideon Welles, remained standing. He leaned against the mantel, under the portrait of Andrew Jackson, observing the others like the good newspaperman that he was. Lincoln knew full well that "Father Neptune" was anxious to get the deed done so he could get back home to write it all down. He had often imagined Welles's diary, immaculately kept, religiously updated. A pang of jealousy always struck the President at the thought of keeping journals. No time.

Like all the others, Welles had spoken his piece about emancipation. A New Englander, Welles was a practical man and argued in favor of the proclamation on practical grounds. The Negroes don't bear arms against us, but they do build the forts and dig the trenches and harvest the food that keeps the Rebels strong. They are contraband. Just like guns and horses.

Around the table sat the rest of the cabinet. Montgomery Blair was the son of one of the country's most powerful and respected families and was absolutely certain that the document would bring a quick and painful death to the Republican Party. Blair and Smith, as usual, sat together. They were both from slave-holding Border States and passionately opposed. Smith now sat red-faced and angry and deep in prayer; while directly across the table sat Edwin Stanton, also pleading with God, begging for precisely the opposite.

God's dilemma, Lincoln thought. Only one of their prayers can be answered. God's dilemma, but my decision. God cannot be for and against the same thing at the same time. Unbearable burden.

Stanton struggled for a breath, fighting off another asthma attack. Along with Chase and Seward, Stanton was a longtime advocate of abolition. He saw the document as too little and too political. The exceptions were tantamount to an actual endorsement of the vile institution. Border States could keep their slaves. Counties currently under Union occupation could keep their slaves. Yes, setting free the slaves in Maryland might well send her headlong into the rebellion, but so be it. Free them all, Stanton had said, and let us put this whole, sorry episode behind us.

Finally, Lincoln turned his gaze on Seward. The last to speak, the Secretary of State had given the President a reason to wait. England and France were chomping at the bit to get this thing over with. Both wanted an end to slavery on moral grounds, but both economies were starved to death for lack of cotton. It could not be known which way the proclamation would tilt those critically important scales. But this Seward did know: we are losing the war and, if announced at this desperate moment, an emancipation proclamation will be nothing more than a worthless scrap. A cheap and tawdry act of political desperation. Lincoln remembered the exact words: ". . . The last measure of an exhausted government, a cry for help . . . our last shriek on the retreat.

"Wait for a victory."

With those words, the room had fallen totally silent, allowing the distant groans of a dying army to enter from the streets. That's when Lincoln had gone to the open window to look out again on the sights of defeat. The meat wagon had echoed Seward's words.

Taking yet another small moment to consider his course, the President could not resist one more glance out the window. Another small group of wounded men made their own way up the avenue as best they could. One, Lincoln saw, was armless but walking tall. Almost marching. Almost proud. These same men had marched in the other direction down the same street just five months before. Straight and whole in their clean blue uniforms, they had been escorted then by magnificent bands and beautiful flags, marching in precision, rifles at right shoulder shift. Proud again, brave again and "on to Richmond" at last. They had fought their way close enough to the Confederate capital to hear the church bells ring when a random piece of flying metal disabled the Rebel commander, Joe Johnston. It was then, in desperation, that Jefferson Davis realized what Lincoln had suspected from the start: that Robert E. Lee was the best military mind in the nation. Since Lee had assumed command of the Rebel army, Lincoln had stood at this window every day to watch this endless stream of wounded men flowing by the thousands back into Washington.

Jeff Davis had found his general.

He turned his attention back again to the document still on the table where he had left it.

Wait for a victory, he had said.

Jefferson Davis had found his general, but Abraham Lincoln had not. Wait for a victory.

Unable or unwilling to speak, the President looked at Seward and nodded. He gently rolled the Emancipation Proclamation into a scroll, placed it in his right coat pocket and left the room without another word.

CHAPTER 1

"FLAT TREASON, BY GOD"

JULY 23RD
NEW YORK CITY

George Smalley stood on the aft deck of the ferry and looked back at the most beautiful sight in the world: New York City growing continually smaller. He imagined that the city was leaving him instead of the other way around.

This town gives me the hives, he thought. He remembered his lawyer days and thanked God that he had found his calling. Horace Greeley was a pain to work for, but all in all the *New York Tribune* was a fine place.

He found a rear-facing seat and unfolded the latest copy of the paper. They say that only cub reporters lovingly read their own work in its finished form, but George loved his words. After years of reading and writing legal documents, fighting off the muses in favor of legalese, it was a joy for him at last to set them free. Of course his New York readers cared little about the war. The rich looked for society news, financial data and the like. Only the poor rushed out to pore over the latest casualty lists. It was *their* sons who were dying. Agate type. Alphabetical. Black on white. Careless columns of names in neat, even lines, like a banker's ledger, under the headings of "Killed" and "Wounded."

The question of the day in Smalley's report was, "Where is Stonewall?" Here was a question that enticed even the rich, and for very good reason. Jackson's reputation by now was so grand that his movements were charted not only on Pennsylvania Avenue but on Wall Street as well. Each day that passed without action brought rumors and uncertainty. As anxiety rose the stock market fell.

As the ferry docked in New Jersey, Smalley glanced back up at The City and smiled. *Off to answer my own question.* "Where is Stonewall?" Off at last to cover the war from the battlefield. *To do the work that real reporters do.*

Where is Stonewall? Greeley wanted George to find him where the entire *Grande Armée* of the Republic could not.

The long train ride gave Smalley his first opportunity to think it all the way through. Stonewall Jackson had been hugely successful in the valley, constantly threatening the capital and keeping "Old Abe" as nervous as a fawn in a forest fire. Jackson had been called south only when McClellan's army had clawed its way to within sight of Richmond. Seven consecutive days of horrendous fighting had followed and Jackson was involved. There were too many sightings and reports in the Rebel papers to doubt it. *But now McClellan's been whipped,* Smalley thought. *He's licking his wounds and waiting for reinforcements. If you're Bobby Lee, what do you do now?* You would try to make certain that those reinforcements are not forthcoming, and the only way to do that is to send Stonewall back north to rattle his saber at Washington. In this way a couple of thousand men can keep hundreds of thousands of men at bay. *Stonewall is headed back north.*

Smalley nodded his head as though agreeing with himself. His first stop in Washington would have to be at the War Department and a meeting with Secretary Stanton, but his next stop would be at John Pope's door. *Northern Virginia is where the next action will be.*

WASHINGTON

A single carriage moved against the flow of wounded men, headed toward the docks on the Potomac. The day was oppressively hot even for Washington, making the ride as uncomfortable as it was awkward. Henry Halleck wiped the sweat from his balding head and complained about the heat before broaching the subject.

"I need your help, General Burnside, more than I can say."

You need someone's help, Ambrose Burnside thought, and more help than *I* can give you. *General in Chief* will look nice on the door, but *Edwin Stanton's Errand Boy* might be more accurate. Burnside nodded and said nothing.

"I arrived in Washington this morning from the West. I have not so much as unpacked my bags and now it's off to the Peninsula for what I am certain will be a very pleasant meeting with your old friend George McClellan." Both men smiled. Both knew the meeting would be anything but pleasant. "So I appreciate you accompanying me on such short notice."

"You are the General in Chief, General Halleck, and I am only a soldier."

"General in Chief, indeed. It is my job to stop our generals from fighting each other and try to make them fight the enemy!"

Burnside thought of McClellan and Pope, both brilliant, at least in their own minds. Each disdainful of the other. Nice choice of words, Burn. They *hate* each other. The difference is McClellan *is* brilliant and Pope is nothing more than a pompous . . .

"What will I get from George?"

"Resentment. A demand for more men."

"Lincoln and Stanton have already told me that."

"You'll get the same from Pope."

"Wonderful. Simply wonderful."

HEADQUARTERS,
ARMY OF NORTHERN VIRGINIA
OUTSIDE RICHMOND

General James Longstreet visibly shivered in the wet heat as he walked slowly toward General Lee's tent. Moxley Sorrel noticed but said nothing. Longstreet was a different man since the winter. Not a family in Richmond had been untouched by the winter's plague, but my God . . . how did he endure it? His children. Every one of them, one at a time lowered into the grave. He is a different man now. Who wouldn't be?

Another breath. Another shiver.

"You all right, General?"

"Yes, Moxley," he said to his Chief of Staff, "I'm only a little worried about what might come next."

"Beg your pardon, sir?"

Longstreet considered whether he should reveal his concerns to his friend or be a good soldier and keep them to himself. Lee was well on his way to becoming a national hero and no good could possibly come from a public debate with the man on strategy, but Longstreet's cautious demons demanded to be heard. "Lee worries me sometimes, Moxley. I thought early on that he would put up a defensive fight, back when he was digging trenches . . ."

" 'The King of Spades,' " Sorrel said with a smile. "The men hated him for it. Didn't think ditch digging was appropriate work for white men."

"The men were wrong, Moxley!" Longstreet's outburst startled Sorrel. "Digging entrenchments is most appropriate work for soldiers, and work that will save their lives if done well. But no sooner were the fortifications done than he sent the men out, I believe recklessly, and on to the offensive. We lost twenty thousand men in seven days, Moxley, and I'm not at all certain that it was necessary."

"You can't argue with the results though, General. We pushed McClellan right off of Jeff Davis's doorstep and back into the swamps. And the morale of the army has never been better. The men quit calling him 'Granny Lee' and now he's 'Marse Robert.' " After two or three more steps, Sorrel stopped, and in a whispered tone he said, "Have you noticed that some of the men don't cheer for him anymore when he rides by like they used to? They take off their hats like they was going into a church or something and just stand there looking at him. It's the darndest thing I ever saw."

Longstreet *had* noticed and that concerned him as well. A general on a battlefield has enough power without being endowed with godlike qualities as well. He took a deep breath and the shivers hit him again. "But McClellan's still out there, Moxley, not fifteen miles from Richmond. And John Pope's got another army fifty miles north." He was so intent in his thoughts that Sorrel had to stop him from walking past Lee's tent.

Lee's back was to the door as Longstreet entered, and he didn't even look up from his map before he spoke. He began the conversation in the middle, just as though they had been talking for hours.

"The arithmetic is against us, General, but we must accustom ourselves to that." Now he turned and looked "Old Pete" Longstreet directly in the eyes and Longstreet shivered again. "All that we learned at West Point and in Mexico is useless to us here. The tactics that we have spent our lives learning are the very tactics we must now learn to defeat. That is why I have sent General Jackson back north." Lee was answering Longstreet's questions even before they were asked.

"We must keep the pressure on Washington. As long as Lincoln believes his capital is threatened, Pope will remain exactly where he is and the two armies will remain apart." Longstreet saw the logic but feared the consequences. "If we are to win this war, we must do it on the flanks. United we fall, Pete, to the sheer weight of numbers."

It took a moment to register that Lee had called him by his nickname. The new commander was rarely so informal.

"Not if we fight a defensive fight, sir. Dig in and let 'em come, General. Wave after wave of 'em. And they will come, General. You know that as well as I. Those are the tactics you spoke of—the ones we learned at The Point. Mass your fire. Mass your men."

"No, General. Not yet. If Pope and McClellan come together we would never be able to survive a siege. We must be aggressive. We must strike them where they are weak. We must force them to divide their armies even further and defeat them in detail, one corps at a time."

Or be *defeated in detail*, Longstreet thought. One corps at a time.

"And to do that, we must divide our own army. It is the only way for now."

Longstreet waited for Lee to continue, but he did not. The commanding general appeared older to Pete already. The striking brown eyes seemed tired after only a month in command.

Finally, Lee spoke: "And there is more intolerable news from General Pope. He has issued new orders, General. John Pope is an offense to civilized man." Longstreet steamed as Lee told him about Pope's latest atrocity. "Male civilians will be arrested and compelled to swear allegiance to the Union. Should anyone refuse, his property and lands will be confiscated." He paused for effect, allowing Longstreet's blood to rise for a moment before driving home the other point of Pope's abominable order. "And there's more. Civilians behind their lines risk a firing squad for attempting to communicate with any Confederate soldier. Mothers writing letters to their sons can be shot as spies." By now Lee's own disgust showed clearly on his face, but no hint of it appeared in his voice. "John Pope is a miscreant, and ought to be suppressed if possible." Lee said these words without emotion as though he were telling Longstreet he had a bug on his sleeve.

"This is an offense to manhood, sir! Uncivilized!" Lee let Longstreet rail on for a moment, but soon brought him back to the practicality of the matter.

"Be that as it may, General, we are caught in the jaws of the Federal army. And I must reject the notion that we can sit here and wait like a fly in a web." Longstreet bristled for an instant, taking it as a personal affront to his earlier comments, but Lee moved on. Apparently no reprimand intended. "We must move against one or the other, and in his present position McClellan is too well defended. But he can be held where he is. It *is* George McClellan, General. In some ways he is a fine general—he proved that here. We would have destroyed a lesser man, but his retreat was well ordered and masterful. But he lacks tenacity. He is . . ." Lee's eyes darted randomly around the tent while he searched for the appropriate word; a kind euphemism for "cowardly," ". . . reluctant on the offensive. If we send ten men against him, he will see a hundred. That is what we must do. We must hold McClellan in place and move against Pope."

Longstreet remained silent, still enraged by Pope's orders.

"Think on it, General Longstreet. But Pope is our next target."

After their meeting ended Longstreet and Sorrel walked in silence back through the camp, the dark cloud almost visible over the general's head, until suddenly he stopped dead in his tracks and began to laugh. Sorrel was confused, to say the least.

"I just got outflanked!"

"I beg your pardon, sir?"

"That old man just pulled me into a trap. He made me angry, sucked me in with a classic feint and when I fell for it, he slammed the trap shut!"

"And you find this amusing, sir?"

"Moxley. If he can do it to me, he can sure as hell do it to John Pope."

JUNE 24TH
HEADQUARTERS, ARMY OF THE POTOMAC
HARRISON'S LANDING, VIRGINIA

George McClellan stood ramrod-straight on the pier, pulling himself up to his full five feet seven inches, as he waited for Halleck to disembark with his staff, but the first face he recognized was that of his old friend Ambrose Burnside.

For an instant he was glad to see the affable old cuss, with his floppy hat and ludicrous whiskers. The sight of "Old Burn" always made him smile. But only for an instant this day. Burnside and Halleck on the boat together gave him another thought, and not a pleasant one.

He felt the heat in his face as every muscle tensed up in anger. He turned suddenly and stormed back up the hill.

"If they come here to take my command then *by God* they can come to me!" he told a junior staff officer. "Tell them I am occupied."

He tornadoed into his headquarters where his chief of staff and father-in-law, General Randolph Marcy, waited. McClellan threw his gloves onto his desk and shouted loudly enough for the army to hear, "E. M. Stanton is the most unmitigated scoundrel I ever knew! His treachery would have made Judas raise his arms in holy horror! And if Lincoln isn't worse it's only because he's weaker!"

Marcy knew his son-in-law well enough to avoid any intrusion on his rampages.

"First he talks that baboon of a president into promoting Halleck over me, even after I have saved the Republic against certain defeat, and now it appears Burnside, of all people, is to take my command from me entirely!"

The shock registered on Marcy's face, but he continued his silence.

"If what I fear is true, the war is lost. You know Burn. He's a fine man. He's a good friend. The last time they offered him my army he turned it down and came directly to me to tell me. But, God help us, he's a terrible general."

A knock.

"Enter!"

The young officer McClellan had left on the dock cautiously stepped in. "Sir, General Halleck sends his compliments and begs to inform you that the men are assembled for review."

McClellan rolled his eyes, defeated now by protocol. "Very well, Major. Send him my apologies and tell him I am coming forthwith."

He kept his guests waiting just long enough for them to know that they were being kept waiting. It was a tactic not wasted on Halleck. The first words he spoke were, "I am not here to relieve you of your command, George. Nor am I here to challenge your authority. My business is to hear your intentions and to provide you with whatever you may need to crush this rebellion. But you must know that I cannot condone any further hesitation. Tell me the situation as you see it and let us get on with it."

A huge burden was lifted from George McClellan's soul. *It isn't over. Not yet. We'll see. Halleck is an inferior officer, but a West Point man at least. So maybe there's hope. Maybe.*

Burnside went out to interview the corps commanders and some of the other officers while McClellan took Halleck into his office in a commandeered plantation house to explain his plan. McClellan unrolled his map. "Lee has concentrated his armies on the north side of the James, so we shall cross the river here and move up the southern bank to Petersburg. Here we will cut off Lee's supply lines from the south and either force him to attack us on our ground or abandon Richmond without a fight."

In an instant McClellan's freshly elevated spirits fell back to the floor as Halleck shook his head, giving this masterful plan no more consideration than a child's request for a too expensive toy. "No. This plan is far too risky. The Rebels could bring reinforcements up from the south by the trainloads and catch you in between. No, George. It risks too much on a supposition."

Nothing had changed. Halleck was corrupted by a single day in Washington.

"General Halleck, I am here with fewer than ninety thousand effectives. Lee may have as many as two hundred thousand in and around Richmond. I do not expect you to provide me with greater numbers than the enemy has at his disposal, but surely with adequate numbers to fight him with some chance of success."

"And what number do you consider 'adequate'?"

"With thirty thousand reinforcements I can storm Richmond on *either* side of the James. If Pope's entire command could be shipped here for another try on this side of the river, success would be assured."

"General McClellan, you know full well that that is not possible. It may be possible to release twenty thousand to you, but no more exist. And furthermore, if you find this number inadequate, then the entire operation will be reconsidered." He saw the anger in McClellan's eyes, but better to press on and say what must be said. "And as to the shipping of Pope's command south, the President would never risk leaving Washington so unprotected. The Rebels would trade Richmond for Washington like a rook for a queen."

Now he did give McClellan an opportunity to speak, but it was missed. Halleck softened his tone to try to make the blow a softer one. "And George, if there is to be a merger of your command with Pope's, it will be in *northern* Virginia, with Washington at your backs." McClellan looked as though he had been struck in the stomach with a rifle butt. The color was gone from his face and his eyes watered.

"Allow me, sir, to consult with my staff. I have arranged quarters for you for the night. And if you'll excuse me, sir . . ." The General in Chief was dismissed.

Ambrose Burnside was as kind and as generous a man as could be found. His courage and his honor were questioned by none. He was loyal maybe even to a fault, but he was not a military genius. He owed all that he was to George McClellan. And now, under orders, he had to go behind the back of his closest friend in the world and pass judgment on his competency.

McClellan's corps commanders mealymouthed their way around the question of going or staying, but the division commanders weren't nearly so timid.

"General, if we remain through the rest of the summer this army will die of malaria. The swamps are vaporous and poison the air with an enemy we can't even see, much less fight. We *must* move, sir, either back to Washington or on to Richmond or we shall die here one man at a time."

"We prefer, or at least I prefer," another said, "that it be on to Richmond. Go back to those imbeciles in Washington and get Mac what he needs or by God, sir, we will move this army *against* Washington, remove those old women in the government and run this war as it *should* be run!"

If the shock at hearing these words from a single officer wasn't enough, Burnside was dumbfounded by the reaction of the others. "Amens" and "hoorays" rose up from the group like an angry wave from still waters. Burnside was stunned.

"I don't know what you fellows call this talk, but I call it flat *treason*, by God! You are an *army* and not a mob! You will take your orders and you will take them from *civilian* authorities." Burnside stopped for a moment to try to regain his composure. He failed. ". . . And you will obey them to the letter or I shall personally see each and every one of you court-martialed! You disgust me."

It was not a figure of speech. Burnside was nauseated by what he had heard.

JULY 26TH
HARRISON'S LANDING

McClellan felt the early signs of the old ailment coming on again. A sleepless night. Anxious. Angry. Frightened. Frightened of what? Losing his army? Losing the battle, the war? Losing his command and prestige? To Lincoln and Stanton. Losing to that pompous idiot POPE! *I'd rather lose to Lee than the whole lot of them!*

Marcy entered with a steaming cup of coffee.

"What do you make of it all, Mac?"

"It's beyond comprehension. I managed to get only twenty thousand additional troops out of Halleck, who should know better. He actually threatened me with using *my* army to reinforce that moron Pope."

Marcy opened the drapes, and the soft morning sun blazed into

McClellan's brain like a branding iron. He winced visibly and Marcy closed the drapes tightly.

"Sorry, George. The neuralgia again?"

McClellan shook his head, more hopeful than confident. "Just a headache for the moment." He lay back down and covered his eyes with his arm, but continued the conversation.

"It took me months to train the officers and men of this army and now Pope's told them to forget about their lines of retreat and bases of supply. He told them that 'success and glory are in the advance, disaster and shame lurk in the rear.'" McClellan closed his eyes tightly as a sharp pain began in his right temple and shot down his neck and into his shoulder. "Our old friend John Pope is about to learn that disaster and shame may well lurk wherever he goes, and if he should pretend to command *my* army, he'll do it, by God, with no help from me! I shall have Mr. Pope's job *and* Mr. Halleck's, and even perhaps Mr. Stanton's. I need but one victory, General, but there is little chance of that as long as they keep me poor. We must convince them to send more men. There must be a way."

McClellan still lay on his cot with his eyes tightly closed against the pain. Then, as quickly as it had come, the pain was gone. He sat upright, his eyes darting around the room as though looking for something.

"Send Pinkerton in here, and anyone who's even had a peek at the Rebels in the last day or so. And send Hooker out to poke around. Find the spots where the enemy has strengthened his positions."

McClellan shot out of bed, pulled back the drapes and began to dress.

"This battle is not lost yet."

The moment Halleck entered his office an aide handed him a wire sent only hours after he and McClellan had parted company. He looked at his desk and realized that he had yet to sit at it.

. . . Reinforcements are pouring into Richmond from the South.

Now Halleck sat.

. . . from 7,000 to 8,000 troops en route to Richmond. . . . Can you not possibly draw 15,000 to 20,000 men from the West to reinforce me temporarily? They can return the moment we gain Richmond. Please give weight to this suggestion—I am sure it merits it.

Halleck left his office in the War Department to walk the two blocks to the Executive Mansion. Only now did the burden of his impossible office dawn on him. *Mac outranks me and hates the politicians,* he thought, and the politicians outrank me and hate McClellan and I am caught in the cross fire. So deep was Halleck in thought that he failed to notice the government buildings and monuments being draped in black until he reached the President's house and had to skirt himself around a ladder.

"What is the occasion for the mourning?" he asked a worker.

"President Van Buren has passed away."

Halleck shook his head and said, half to the workman and half to himself, "As though this poor nation doesn't have enough reason to mourn already." He put aside any further thoughts of the deceased President and went to the desk of the living one.

"If you could send him a hundred thousand troops today, he would report to you tomorrow that Lee now has four hundred thousand and that he could not move an inch without a hundred thousand more," Lincoln said. "It is a flaw in his nature like the scorpion that begged a ride across the river from a horse. Halfway across the scorpion stung the horse, and as they were both going down to their deaths the horse asked the scorpion, 'Why?' and the scorpion replied, 'It's just my nature.' That's the way McClellan is, General, it's just his nature."

Halleck stopped paying attention with the beginning of the scorpion story. A decision must be made as to what to do with the Army of the Potomac.

If McClellan's numbers are fabrications, then no number of reinforcements will appease him as Lincoln had said. But if his numbers *are* correct and the Rebels outnumber McClellan and Pope combined, then it is folly to keep these armies separate where they can be defeated in detail, first one, then the other.

George McClellan had sprung a trap on himself. Either way, the Army of the Potomac would have to be joined with Pope's Army of Virginia. It was time, Halleck knew, to start over.

July 31st
McClellan's Headquarters
Harrison's Landing

The quiet night exploded suddenly into a never-ending, deafening roar. A tremendous fire, courtesy of D. H. Hill's artillery, startled the Army of the Potomac awake.

McClellan and Marcy listened for a moment. The fire showed no signs of slacking off.

"They wouldn't stage a general assault in the middle of the night, would they?"

The thought had never occurred to McClellan. He started to say *of course not*, but then he remembered Malvern Hill and all of the other things Lee had done lately, all the things that went against the book, and suddenly he wasn't quite so sure.

"I'll tell you this, if Halleck had listened to me, none of this would have happened. If any lives have been lost tonight the guilt is on *their* shoulders." Marcy busied himself with the chore of waking up and forcing his feet into his boots. He had memorized the diatribe by now. "I am sick and tired of serving such a set of incompetent . . ." He struggled to find a word and thought it better to move on. "I do not believe that any nation was ever cursed with worse leaders than we have today!"

The explosions came louder now as McClellan's gunboats returned fire. George raised his eyebrows and smiled. "Every family should have a gunboat," he said with a laugh.

The duel lasted for ninety minutes. One leg wound was the result.

August 3rd
Washington

Clad as always in black, Clara Barton moved about the chambers of the United States Senate like a tiny dark dot, flitting from one wounded soldier to another until Charles Mason, her friend and mentor from the Patent Office, found her to deliver an important letter.

"It's from the Surgeon General, Clara, so I thought you would want it brought to you."

They shared a knowing look before she tore it open. She read only the first paragraph before wadding it into a ball and parading out of the Senate. Almost at a run she marched to the Surgeon General's office, demanded an immediate audience, seated herself in the waiting room and didn't budge for two solid hours.

"I don't think that woman's going to go away, General."

The Surgeon General looked up from the stack of requisitions on his desk. "Woman?"

"Yes, sir. Miss Barton. She's been sitting out there all morning long, bolt upright and looking straight ahead. I don't think she's even blinked in the last two hours."

Bill Hammond closed his eyes and sighed. "Very well, Major. Express my apologies for the wait and send her in." He stood and buttoned his collar button and waited to receive the wrath of God.

He stood over six feet tall, and she stood barely five, but she lit into him like a badger attacking a bear. She opened her tiny fist to show him the wadded-up letter.

"I will *not* accept this as a final answer."

He smiled his most gracious smile and nodded at the little lady. "Now, Miss Barton, I'm sure you understand . . ."

"I understand only this . . ." She took a tiny step closer to the general. ". . . I understand that our wounded men are being poorly cared for." Another step closer. "I understand that those poor boys have more to fear from your 'doctors' than they do the Rebels!" Now she stood so close that the Surgeon General of the United States looked down his nose at her. Like a cobra at a mongoose. "I further understand that, because I am a woman, regardless of my proven abilities to care for these men, you have determined that my presence at the battlefield is 'inappropriate.'" She held the tiny paper ball under his nose. "Well, General Hammond, you are not the first pigheaded bureaucrat who has stood in my way and you will not be the first to be gotten around."

Hammond finally exploded. "Let me assure you, Madam, that the battlefield is *no place* for a woman!"

"And let me assure *you*, General Hammond, that the battlefield is no place for a *man*!" Hammond, left without an argument, looked genuinely wounded. Barton eased up on the rhetoric. "I have seen the results here in Washington, General. I have been caring for the boys from Massachusetts since the war began."

"And for all of that the government is grateful, Miss Barton, but you have had no medical training . . ."

"No offense, Doctor . . ." The word dripped with sarcasm. ". . . but your profession is not nearly so perfect as you think. My training is as good or better than many of the men you've got out there."

After a long pause and a struggle to find the appropriate word to use in the company of a woman, Hammond spoke softly. "Are you not concerned, Miss Barton, that a single woman traveling with an army might be thought to be a . . . camp follower?"

Clara's face blushed beet red and her knees weakened at the thought. She responded with a whisper.

"It is not important what might be thought, General. It is a risk I am prepared to take."

"Very well, Miss Barton. I shall reconsider and inform you of my decision."

After she had left, the general's aide returned to find out what all the ruckus had been about. "Whew. That's a lot of powder in a very small shell."

WHERE IS STONEWALL?

Smalley had set up camp on a long line of seekers of Stanton's attention. He spent his days at the War Office waiting to see the secretary and his evenings at the Willard Hotel drinking the nights away. By the time the door to Stanton's office was opened to him, he was steaming mad and brought his attitude in with him.

"I've been waiting for over a week simply to hand you a letter so I could get on with my job. I hope the rest of the effort flows a little more efficiently."

Stanton was stunned by Smalley's outburst. Not so much as a "howdedo" from another scrawny, pencil-shaped scribe with glasses so thick a bullet couldn't pierce them.

"The rest of the effort has a significantly higher priority than dealing with every scribbler who fancies himself the next Dickens. Now tell me what you want."

Smalley adjusted his tone. "I have a letter of introduction addressed to you from Mr. Greeley at the *New York Tribune* and a request that I be allowed access to General Pope's command."

"Very well," Stanton said after a time. He began to write. "This note will introduce you to General Pope as a fully authorized representative of the press. And I will ask you to deliver to him another letter as well." Another piece of paper and another note that Stanton made very certain that Smalley could not see. He folded it, sealed it and wrote across it "For General Pope's eyes only!" and handed both letters to Smalley. The Trib man thought he saw a glint of humor cross the secretary's face, but he couldn't be certain.

Halleck read the latest of McClellan's endless pleas, each one more desperate than the last. A withdrawal of his army would be "fatal." It would result in demoralization of the army and the recognition of the Confederacy by England. "These appear to me sufficient reasons to make it my imperative duty to urge in the strongest terms afforded by our language that this order may be rescinded, & that far from recalling this Army it be promptly reinforced to enable it to resume the offensive."

AUGUST 5TH
HEADQUARTERS, ARMY OF THE POTOMAC

What progress is Hooker making?"
"He reports that Malvern Hill seems only lightly defended. Odd, after all the pain you inflicted on them in their effort to take it, but nonetheless that is what it seems."
"We may be saved yet, General. If Pope's reports are correct and Lee is moving north, then Richmond may be left to us for the taking. Order Dan Webster saddled up for me will you? I'll ride up and see for myself. Just the taking of the hill may be enough to cause Halleck to think again."

HEADQUARTERS, ARMY OF NORTHERN VIRGINIA

Lee could see in Longstreet's eyes that his best officer was troubled. Longstreet always thought the worst and the sad, deep eyes always showed it.
"The Yankees seem to be on the move, sir, back to Malvern Hill."
"In what numbers, General?"

"Our best guess is twenty thousand men or fewer. McClellan probably knows that Jackson and Powell Hill are gone north and sees an advantage."

"You forget again, General, that it is McClellan over there. He has yet to see an advantage even though ample advantages have been offered him." Lee removed his glasses and rubbed his tired eyes too hard. "No, he won't move on Richmond unless we leave it to the women and children, but here is our best chance to find out for certain. Go shake your sword at him. My supposition is you'll chase him off without a fight. He's testing us, but I think it won't be too difficult a test."

"With your permission, sir, I intend to treat it as a general assault and answer division for division and then some. Apparently Burnside's corps has sailed but he's still near a hundred thousand strong down there. If Burnside has joined Pope this could well be the first movement of the coordinated north/south assault and it must be handled quickly."

"Very well, but leave Harvey Hill where he is. Don't forget that it could also be a feint to draw us north while George crosses south. I suppose anything is possible."

MALVERN HILL

What Joe Hooker found on Malvern Hill were not defenses at all, but an outpost that was easily dispatched from the summit. McClellan witnessed the fight in which his army lost three killed and eleven wounded, but to his way of thinking, Bull Run had been avenged.

Sitting astride Dan Webster, as though he had no time in the heat of battle to dismount, McClellan scribbled an "urgent" communiqué to Halleck. "We have re-taken Malvern Hill. If we are adequately reinforced . . ."

AUGUST 6TH

Dawn found "Fightin' Joe" Hooker astride the massive white stallion looking through his field glasses down the slopes of Malvern Hill. "Goddamn 'em all to hell! Lee has no more moved his army north than . . . Send a message to McClellan. Tell him that we're facing three divisions or more. Prepare to repel an assault."

As Hooker looked down the hill at Longstreet, Longstreet looked up at Hooker. There wasn't a snowball's chance in July that Longstreet would attempt another assault up Malvern Hill. It had been attempted once before and while the hill was taken, the cost was appalling.

The two armies spent this steamy hot day simply watching each other while Hooker tried to find out what Mac had in mind. That took him all of the day and well into the night. It was near midnight when Hooker received instructions. "I find it will not be possible to get the whole Army in position before sometime tomorrow afternoon, which will be too late to support you . . . Abandon the position tonight, getting everything away before daylight."

When first light shone on Malvern Hill on Thursday, August 7th, all that remained of Hooker's command was a handful of scarecrows, stuffed with grass and dressed in blue. George McClellan's grand campaign to save the Union, after a year's worth of planning and tens of thousands of dead and wounded, had ended, at last, with this . . . a handful of scarecrows stuffed with grass and dressed in blue.

Redheadedness is a curse. If it isn't true that redheads have shorter tempers than other men, it is at the very least true that they are the worst at concealing their anger, and there was no concealing Ambrose Powell Hill's ferocity at his latest commanding general. His face, already red from Virginia's summer sun, now glowed with blood as he finally surrendered to his rage.

"I pledge you my word . . . I do not know whether we march north, south, east or west, or whether we will march at all." He slapped his thigh with his gloves. "General Jackson has simply ordered me to have the division ready to move at dawn. I have been ready ever since, and have no further indications of his plans. That is almost all I ever know of his designs."

"Well, sir, it looks as though you are about to find out."

"Little Powell" looked off in the direction indicated by the young officer to see Stonewall himself approaching at a run and obviously in very much the same frame of mind as Hill.

"Why have you not begun the march, sir?"

"I have no orders to march, General!"

"You have been under orders to march at dawn since midnight last night."

"My orders, *sir*"—Hill made no effort to conceal the distaste with which he used the respectful term—"were to follow Ewell, and there has been no sign of him."

"Those orders were rescinded. It was your division that was to lead. Now, move on!"

"Move on *where*, sir?"

"North, General Hill—across the Rapidan, and quickly. The *other* generals managed to understand the change of orders and Ewell has taken another crossing and is now well out ahead—and alone! Now you shall have to follow Winder!"

Without offering any further details or even waiting for a response, Stonewall dug his spurs into Little Sorrel's flanks. The creature reared and turned and headed back the way she had come at a run, leaving A. P. Hill spitting dust and spitting mad.

The army marched from "can" to "can't." From can see to can't see and from can walk to can't take another step. Every man in Jackson's corps was absolutely exhausted except for one young man from Maryland who loved every second.

Kyd Douglas was the youngest officer on Jackson's staff and he lived his life at a gallop. On this night he huddled with his newly arrived friend Joel Westbrook and a gaggle of other men from Jackson's staff, who quietly gambled away next month's pay on a friendly game of poker. Or is it month-after-next? They played quietly because Jackson would be furious. It's against God's will to gamble. Douglas was doubly guilty. If his hellfire-and-brimstone father found out, he'd take a strap to him, even to this day. But this is part of it. Part of the adventure. Man stuff. Army stuff. Cussing and laughing with the boys. Telling stories. Westbrook was new, and had to hear 'em all. Like that one time back in the spring, in the heat of one of the earliest battles, a bunch of cavalrymen charged right out into the middle of the field and started chasing down the most terrified fox in the Commonwealth of Virginia, and the battle just stopped while both sides watched and laughed—and bet. Douglas bet on the fox, but all bets were off after the damned Yankees started the darned battle back up again. To hear Douglas tell it it was the greatest fun ever had. Of course some men died. Lots of men. But that's the only bad part.

Westbrook didn't know how much of this malarkey to believe, but Douglas was so innocent-looking and honest-sounding. His dad was a preacher, so lying wouldn't come easy. But still, the rules against lying don't count for much around a campfire. And braggin's what war's all about. The men around the fire were laughing just as though they had never heard the tale before, but they just liked the way Douglas told it. Big-eyed, bouncy, can't stand still, bragging like he'd just beat up the school bully and can't wait to tell it again!

AUGUST 9TH
CEDAR RUN, VIRGINIA

The roads were bad. The heat was stifling. The air was thick with pale red dust and Jackson's army was further slowed as men and animals fell, suffering and dying from the effects of the heat alone. Three days of hard marching under the relentless heat of an unmerciful Virginia summer made his strongest men suffer; and none suffered more than Brigadier General Charles S. Winder. In addition to the heat and dust that suffocated everyone, Winder was ridden with fever. He led his brigade while flat on his back and confined to the "comfort" of an ambulance—confined at least until the first sounds of battle woke him from fever's sleep.

Ewell, marching in the lead, encountered the Yankees first as he came under fire from artillery lined up along Cedar Run. Winder escaped his mobile deathbed and ordered his infantry to establish Jackson's left flank while he personally took command of the artillery. Winder loved the big guns. Artillery is a much more civilized way to war than the close-up savagery of muskets and bayonets. As wet with sweat as he would have been in a downpour, he struggled to focus all of his attention on the enemy's big guns. So intent was he on the job at hand that he could not be distracted by anything or anyone other than Stonewall himself.

"You are our left flank anchor, General. If they attack our center you will turn on their right. Understood?"

"Yes, sir. It's your old brigade, sir," Winder reminded the general unnecessarily. "The Stonewall Brigade. You can rely on us, sir." Secretly he had hoped for a smile from General Jackson. He should have known better. "I think a few well-placed rounds might silence those guns."

"Do what you can, General Winder. It is already late in the day. This battle might well be fought tomorrow. God be with you, General Winder."

"And with you, sir."

With those words, Stonewall rode to the rear to await developments—and to take a nap.

There would be no nap for Winder. He returned his attention to the gunners across the way who had spotted the conspicuous Jackson on horseback and were finding the range on Winder's position.

First an officer on his left went down with a shell fragment in his brain. Blood and brains and little pieces of bone splattered into Winder's face and clung to his chin whiskers. Seconds later another man went down with a splintered spike from a fence rail lodged in his gut like a spear and still Winder held his field glasses high and barked out corrections as his own guns returned the fire. An unexploded ball caught another of his officers square and lifted him high and laid him down again, badly hurt but living, and still Winder called out his commands. He discarded his tunic as a concession to the fever and the heat, and his white shirt, while dirty and wet, made a beautiful bull's-eye for the gunners on the other side of the field.

The six-pound ball struck him solidly in the left shoulder. It took with it his arm and most of the ribs on that side of his chest.

"General," his staff physician yelled over the perpetual thunder, "lift up your head to God."

"I do," Winder whispered back. "I do lift it up to Him. How are my men?"

"They fare well, General."

The final words Winder heard on this earth may have been comforting, but they were far from true. The Union assault did not wait for tomorrow nor was it directed against the center. It came as the general's mangled body was laid back in his ambulance, and it came against the left. Union General "Commissary" Banks was bound and determined to regain his reputation lost at the hands of this army, and he'd be damned before he'd wait till tomorrow.

Kyd Douglas found Jackson napping on the porch of a nearby farmhouse, oblivious that his army stood on the verge of collapse.

"Winder is dead, sir, and the enemy is breaking through between his brigade and Early's!"

Jackson was up and aboard Little Sorrel in the beat of a heart, riding hard to the sound of the guns.

He arrived as the Stonewall Brigade turned its back to the onslaught. He rode headlong into the proud unit that bore his name and ripped the colors from the hands of a retreating soldier. He had not had time to belt his saber, but had brought it with him and waved it in one hand, still in its scabbard, and the flag in the other. His men were astounded and stopped stone still.

"Rally, brave men, and press forward! Your general will lead you! Follow me!"

The line commanders took up the call and the men turned as one, as though ordered to "about face" on a parade field for the amusement of the ladies in the stands.

The Federals had already begun their victory celebration when out of nowhere the Rebels turned and counterattacked. They simply stopped in midflight and came back screaming like banshees.

Jackson had his blood up like never before. The famous blue eyes flashing like beacons, he pulled his saber and discarded the scabbard, fully prepared to lead his men directly into the heart of the Union guns when Kyd Douglas rode up next to him and parked his horse between Jackson and the receding blue line.

"Your work is done here, General. Look to your rear. Here comes Hill."

A. P. Hill had continued to struggle on the march. The roads and the air had been made even worse for him by the very nature of being last in line. But he was here now. He parted his ranks just long enough to allow Winder's wounded to pass through to the rear. During the delay he opened his saddlebag and took from it the red shirt he always wore into battle—his "hunting" shirt. His men cheered at the sight, and A. P. Hill's "Light Brigade" launched an assault that sent Banks's men reeling.

So quickly and totally had the tables turned that Jackson ordered the pursuit continued into the night under a clear sky and the light of a full moon turned red by the dust of battle. Only when he received word that Banks was being heavily reinforced did he finally order a halt.

The men would sleep on their arms in the line of battle and wait to see what tomorrow would bring. Jackson tried to find a home in which to stay the night, but all were full to overflowing with wounded soldiers from both armies.

Finally, he dismounted and lay down in the grass.

"Would you care for some food, sir?" Douglas asked.

"No. I want rest. Nothing but rest," he said and, in an instant, Stonewall Jackson resumed his interrupted nap.

On the Federal side of the line, Private Barton Mitchell of the 27th Indiana Volunteers fell exhausted under a tree and remembered the horror. As they had turned to run, a Rebel ball ripped through the cloth of his coat directly between his left arm and his heart. The bullet drew no blood, but a letter from his mother that he had read only twice was ruined by it. Mitchell froze in his tracks, as still as Lot's wife. Astounded to be alive and angry at his loss, he could not move until his sergeant and friend from home, John Bloss, grabbed him by the shoulders, turned his back to the screaming gray hordes and physically pushed him from the battlefield.

An inch more in one direction would have cost him an arm. An inch in the other would have cost him his life. As it was, he had lost a jacket, a letter and his pride. The jacket and the letter were gone for good, but he vowed in his heart to get back his pride.

AUGUST 10TH

It was Sunday morning and both sides woke to the sounds of agony: cries for help and pleadings for water. As neither attempted to resume hostilities at dawn, an unofficial cease-fire tacitly fell upon the field to allow doctors from both sides to care for the wounded. Both sides observed the Sabbath all day long.

Jackson was a Christian so devout that he was reluctant even to read his mail on Sunday. He preferred to spend the day in prayer as God intended, and while he would fight on the Sabbath if need be, it was sacrilege to initiate a battle on that Holy Day, even in the name of the Lord.

The afternoon brought rain, and both sides thanked God for it.

August 11th

Sigel and McDowell were up in support of Pope, and Stonewall knew he was outnumbered now by three-to-one. On this Monday morning, Jackson expected nothing less than a full frontal assault at dawn, but what he saw instead was a small detachment of Union cavalry approaching under a white flag of truce. There were only two possibilities: they would either demand surrender or offer another reprieve to bury the dead. They offered the latter, and after pretended consideration Jackson agreed.

"Douglas."

"Sir."

"Order burial detachments onto the field and have the men prepare for a full withdrawal under cover of darkness. Each man will build a fire at sunset and another one hour later and another before he leaves the field."

If ever anyone "looked his part," James Ewell Brown Stuart looked his. Everyone but his men called him "Jeb," and among this army of mismatched men, uniform only in their lack of uniformity, shoeless, frayed and worn, Jeb Stuart was a resplendent prince amongst retched paupers. He wore polished boots to the knee, highlighted on occasion with spurs of gold. His tunic was trimmed with garish amounts of garland and brass, and the full thick beard and mustache were always elegantly curled and groomed—even in the heat of battle.

But the vanities of vanities were the hat and the cape.

Pinned up on one side and plumed on the other, the broad-brimmed hat was always noticed first, at least while he was standing still—which was seldom. But the cape—the exquisite gray cape, trimmed with gold and lined with blood-red silk—that was the grandest touch of all. It flew behind him like a flag unfurled and told who saw, "This, by God, is a cavalryman. And a hell of a one at that."

He took his greatest joy, after an evening with the ladies, in circumnavigating the whole damned Union army, stealing supplies, cutting telegraph lines, burning bridges, attacking rear detachments in the dead of night and vanishing as suddenly as he had appeared back into the darkness.

His men called him "Beauty."

General George Hartstuff stood on the Union lines casually surveying the activities of the burial details when he saw a lone horseman in gray approaching under a white flag. A broad smile bent the sun-baked lines of his face when he recognized his garish old friend and classmate.

"Welcome back to the Union, Cadet Stuart."

"And welcome to Virginia, Mr. Hartstuff. How goes it with you?"

"It goes well, but it could go a damned sight better if you would quit circling our armies like a bunch of goddamned carrousel horses."

Jeb dismounted with a flourish and acknowledged the compliment with a giant smile and a cavalier's bow. "That performance gave me a major generalcy and my saddlecloth there was sent from Baltimore as a reward by a lady whom I never knew."

"I didn't know that there *were* any ladies you didn't know."

The men laughed and embraced, as happy to see each other as two men could be. They shared some wonderfully disgraceful memories.

By now Hartstuff's staff had begun to gather round to catch a glimpse of the famous Jeb Stuart and to enjoy the banter. An assistant surgeon even produced a pint of whiskey for the two men to share.

"You damage my reputation, sir. No man ever born was more faithful to his wife than am I—but"—Stuart smiled his best mischievous smile,— "it never hurts to be friendly!"

"*Major* General, huh? Not bad for a plebe. The last I heard you were still a *lieutenant* for crying out loud."

"Strange as it may seem, you can hop on a carrousel, ride a horse around in circles and *still* pass your upper classmen!"

Hartstuff sucked hard on the flask and immediately went red in the face and began to cough uncontrollably. Jeb remembered that he still carried a ball in his chest from an unpleasant encounter with some angry Seminoles down in Florida. Damn near killed him, but it'll take more than a bullet . . .

"How's the old wound, George?"

"Damned nuisance is all," he said after he caught his breath at last. "Hasn't killed me yet." He coughed again. "But it's damned still trying," he said with a laugh.

Finally, his breathing returned to normal and the friendly smile came back to his face. "Whew. Can't drink like the old days anymore, Jeb."

"Nobody can drink like the old days."

The two generals studied each other for a minute, each picturing two younger men, boys really, sneaking off post, chasing after girls and accumulating demerits at a record-setting pace.

"Take care, Jeb. I hope—well—Just quit being so goddamned reckless, will ya?"

Stuart raised the flask. "Here's to you, George. May we meet again in peace, in heaven or not at all."

As night fell, General John Pope himself came forward to assume command of the Union army at Cedar Run. A giant of a man with a swagger to match, Pope was prepared to meet his destiny. Tomorrow John Pope will destroy Stonewall Jackson, and next week, when the story hits the papers, every man, woman and child in America will know his name.

He came forward to observe the preparations being made on the other side of the field. It was dark but a good general can look and listen and figure out all he needs to know. There were sounds of movement all night long and the number of fires increased hourly.

"Send a wire to Halleck," Pope ordered. "Enemy being strongly reinforced. Tell McClellan to do something. Anything."

"The usual salutation, sir?"

Pope nodded and the adjutant wrote, "Headquarters in the Saddle, John Pope, Maj. Gen'l Commanding."

The morning sun revealed an empty field.

"Where the hell is he? Where the hell is Jackson now?"

Pope could yell till nightfall, but, once again, no one could answer the question "Where is Stonewall?" The man and his army had simply vanished. Again.

AUGUST 12TH
WASHINGTON

Charles Mason left the Patent Office with yet another letter for Clara Barton. All the way to Capitol Hill he felt misgivings. He was somehow deathly afraid of this piece of paper, but he wasn't sure why. It was either another rejection by the Surgeon General, which would be a disappointment to Clara—if not a defeat—or it was an approval for her to attend the wounded on the battlefield, which would take her away from him, possibly forever. Sweat dripped off his chin as he climbed the steps toward the Senate chambers where he knew she would be working.

"Clara!"

She looked to see him at the top of the aisle, and he lifted the letter for her to see. They weren't that far apart, but every empty space was claimed by a wounded soldier. She wiped her hands on her dress and maneuvered as best and quickly as she could to the spot where he held her future in his hand. She grabbed the document and tore it open. After only a second she looked up at her old friend with a tear in her eye and a smile on her face.

AUGUST 14TH
THE EXECUTIVE MANSION

John Hay had never seen anything like it before. Nor, for that matter, had anyone else. It had never happened before. Negroes in suits—not slaves or servants, but colored men wearing suits, parading themselves into the Executive Mansion like honored guests. Invited! By the President of the United States!

The President's secretary escorted the five men into the office and sat them all down, poured water for them and then informed the President that the delegation was seated. Lincoln entered, nodded and sat down behind his desk.

He looked into the black faces and wondered how he would be received by these leaders of the Negro community. He thanked them for coming, and before he began to speak he looked down for a moment to compose his thoughts. He involuntarily glanced at the drawer in which the Emancipation Proclamation secretly rested.

There will be hell to pay when that weapon is fired. Only God may know what will happen. Insurrection. Rape. Murder, some men thought. Haiti all over again. White men rioting in the North and a black rampage throughout the South. Slaves demanding to take up arms for the Union.

The five men sat quietly, politely, and waited for the President to begin.

Cushion the blow, Lincoln thought. An alternative. A middle ground. It's the only real hope.

"Gentlemen, I need your help."

No movement. No recognition. He moved on.

"You and we are different races. We have between us a broader difference than exists between almost any other two races."

State the obvious and move on.

"I think your race suffer very greatly, many suffer the greatest wrong inflicted on any people, while ours suffer from your presence."

Now there was movement from the delegation as several glanced around to see if they had heard right, but still no one spoke. Lincoln continued.

"We should be separated. Equality for the black man is not possible in this country and, in my view, never will be."

Still no one spoke, but the indignation on their faces spoke eloquently for them all. These are men, Lincoln knew. Black men to be sure, but men nonetheless. They have overcome so much that they believe they can overcome anything. But they are wrong, and they must be made to see that.

"This is something that I cannot alter. I cannot alter it if I would. The fact is that were it not for your race among us there could not be war, although many men engaged on *either* side do not care for you one way or the other."

The indignation he had seen before on their faces now was gone.

Subtly it changed to anger, but still no one spoke. Anger and something else.

Abraham Lincoln then made the men an offer—"on behalf of the white race." In his view he offered them a veritable Paradise compared to what awaited them here. Free or slave, your lives will be better elsewhere, he told them. Here they would never be equal to the ruling classes. Or, for that matter, equal to any white man. But in the tropics an entire colony of people of African descent can be provided. You can work the coal mines there and your race can live equal to each other, and maybe some day you may even be able to govern yourselves.

The men continued to listen without interruption. Backs straight. Heads high.

"And you, gentlemen, must take the lead. Avoid the selfish view and take the lead for the benefit of your race. For the benefit of mankind. It is exceedingly important that we have men at the beginning capable of *thinking* as *white* men, and not those who have been systematically oppressed."

By the looks on the faces Lincoln could see that his best hope had failed. They apparently took some offense in the offer, or in something he had said. Now Lincoln recognized what he read on their faces. Not only anger. It was pride.

AUGUST 15TH

An hour before the dawn Stonewall Jackson's tent glowed like a lantern as Lee and Longstreet finally arrived. Stonewall had pulled back across the Rapidan River and the entire Confederate army now hid behind Clark's Mountain.

Stonewall opened his map and pointed. "Here is the confluence of the Rapidan and the Rappahannock." He pointed inside the ">" of land between the two rivers. "Here is Pope."

James Longstreet went slack-jawed. Lee's eyes opened just a touch wider and he turned his head slightly and adjusted his spectacles as though a different perspective might improve his vision or offer some explanation either for his failure to understand what Jackson had said, or for Pope's incredibly stupid blunder.

Pope had positioned his entire army with its back not just to one river, but to two.

"If we move quickly we can seal off Pope's only dry avenue of escape across the river, here at the rail crossing at Rappahannock Station. Generals, this is too golden an opportunity to delay. Anyone who does not see the hand of God in this is a fool. I suggest we move at first light."

"My men have only just arrived, General," Longstreet said, "and as that beast Mr. Pope seems in no hurry to go anywhere, a single day's delay would do no harm and may do considerable good."

Lee considered both arguments for a moment and said, "I would love nothing better, General Jackson, than to move quickly, but the remainder of our cavalry has not yet arrived from Richmond and Stuart will need to burn that bridge before general operations can begin. When the bridge is gone we will move."

AUGUST 17TH

Fitzhugh Lee was another of Marse Robert's nephews. His orders to join Stuart indicated no urgency. His most direct path was lightly guarded, his horses were in need of grazing and his men in need of supplies. Fitzhugh Lee was in no hurry at all. Stuart and his staff rode ahead to meet him, but midnight came and went with no sign of him. They took up residence in an abandoned farmhouse, caught up on their sleep and waited.

At last the sound of horses rousted this handful of men from their light sleep, and two rode out to greet the commanding general's nephew. Stuart himself stepped out onto the porch so that he could begin dressing Lee down for his tardiness the moment he came into view, but he was still half asleep and having trouble screwing up his anger.

"Yankees!"

A spattering of gunfire, and a blur of motion and Stuart and all of his men save one were mounted and gone.

It happened in a gasp and was over. Abandoned on a table in the farmhouse sat a broad-brimmed hat, pinned up on one side and plumed on the other. On a peg by the door was an elegant silk-lined cape, and on the floor, under the bed, was Jeb Stuart's adjutant general grasping a dispatch book containing orders outlining the disposition and intentions of the Army of Northern Virginia.

AUGUST 18TH
CLARK'S MOUNTAIN

The following day, Lee and Longstreet climbed to the top of the observation tower Jackson had constructed on top of Clark's Mountain, and it became very apparent that Stonewall had been right. Thousands of wagons kicked up mountains of dust and the forest of tents that were awaiting destruction yesterday were being felled and folded for the move north—north across the river.

Lee saw the chagrin in Pete's face. After the confrontation with Jackson that had almost come to blows or worse, the shame of being wrong was painfully multiplied.

Lee lowered his glasses and heaved a sigh. "General, we little thought that the enemy would turn his back upon us this early in the campaign."

WASHINGTON

Our President is a *fool*, sir. And a *blind* fool at that!"

Salmon Chase looked across the table at the Secretary of War as Stanton continued his months-old diatribe. The man was in a constant state of agitation, his asthma making it difficult for him to yell. He would explode if only he could catch a breath.

"Can he not see that McClellan is a traitor? Can he not see what is happening directly beneath his ugly old nose?" It took him three full seconds to refill his lungs before he launched into his tirade again. "It is obvious to every educated man in this city that he has no desire to make any gains whatever until after the November elections. A victory by the army would mean a defeat of the Democrats and that little pip-squeak of a general knows it." Another few seconds of air sucking and beard pulling. "That, by God, is what *I* think, and if old honest Abe had any wits about him at all, that's what he would think as well!" His lungs wholly empty now, he struggled once again to fill them, like a man who had just run up a hill. In a softer tone he continued. "All he ever says about McClellan is that he has 'the slows.' Ain't that Western quaint?"

Chase waited a moment to make certain the storm had calmed before he ventured out. "Maybe McClellan's waiting for Pope to get into trouble so he can ride to the rescue and assure himself of a statue. At any rate, we have all told the President how we feel. He *must* know that the man is dangerous."

An idea hit Stanton in a snap. "No! We haven't *all* told him how we feel. Not all of us. Seward is never around and Welles just sits off to the side with that ridiculous gray wig and that holier-than-thou expression pretending to be smarter than all of the rest of us together. But if we *did* tell him how we feel, all of us, together and in writing, then he would *have* to act!" Stanton pounded the desk so hard that Chase feared the inkwell would overturn. "He can't go against the wishes of his *entire* cabinet. Something must be done. McClellan must be brought up on charges. There is no doubt in my mind that he would be found guilty of treason and shot! Then, when that is done, maybe the President will go about his business with the Congress and let us run the war."

A knock on the door interrupted Stanton's speech. "Secretary Welles is here to see you, sir."

"Gideon! A pleasant surprise," Stanton shouted with a knowing glance at Chase. "Your name just came up in our conversation—please come in."

Welles's face was angry, but his voice was calm. "Was my name mentioned in the context of telling me that the Peninsula campaign has been aborted?"

"I beg your pardon?"

"Were you planning on informing your navy or did you suppose that we would find out in our own sweet time, or perhaps read about it in the papers?"

Stanton stroked his beard. "I'm certain you were informed, Gideon."

"Yes, I was. Last night at Willard's Hotel by an inebriated Member of Congress." Welles waited for an apology long enough to be certain that none was forthcoming. "No harm has been done to the moment," Welles said, "as I strongly believe that at least the gunboats should remain on the James for the protection of the withdrawing forces and even thereafter to continue applying some pressure on Richmond to hold at least some of the Rebel army there and away from the capital. We are fortunate this time, Mr. Secretary, but in the future, please remember that we do, in fact, have a navy."

With that, the Secretary of the Navy nodded, about-faced and left the room without a good-bye.

AUGUST 22ND
CLARK'S MOUNTAIN

Where's your hat?"

The next man who asked Stuart that question would be about the ten thousandth to do so and would risk a firing squad at Jeb's whim. He had been hanging around Lee's headquarters like a camp dog waiting for scraps and begging for a chance at "that beast," John Pope.

"I intend to make the Yankees pay for that hat."

On this day Lee gave him the opportunity—and it was made to order.

"Pope is using the river as a defensive line, General. A crossing in force is impossible, but the cavalry may be able to cross upstream. Cross the river. Get behind him and try to draw him backward. Find a spot where infantry might cross undetected. If you are successful, Jackson will follow."

Along with his best officers and 1,500 of his finest men, Stuart rode off in search of a crossing, in search of revenge and in search of a hat.

All that considered, Jeb Stuart was not one to have his judgment clouded by personal vendetta—he was far too good an officer for that. One quick look at his map and there was no question in his mind as to where Pope would be found—at Catlett's Station, on the direct rail line between his massed army and his main supply depot at Manassas Junction. Far to the west of both armies he crossed the Rappahannock unopposed and rode without pause.

Darkness and rain fell together. One of those events alone is normally reason enough to halt operations. The confusion of the battlefield is enough to reckon with in the daytime, but nighttime could have your men warring on each other, and rain flooded creeks into rivers and rivers

are traps. Stuart and his officers were ready to call a halt when a trooper
reported in with a black man in tow, a slave who had known Stuart for
years, and who agreed to show them where the Yankees were.

The sound of their movements was covered by the pelting rain, steady
wind and almost constant thunder. The sounds of nature were so loud
and so unending that the staff had to yell to be heard.

"You gonna take the word of a nigra, General?"

"I know him. I doubt that he has the nerve to lie to me."

Again, Stuart's instincts were correct, and in the frequent flashes of
lightning he was able to see into Pope's headquarters encampment. Dead
in the middle was the largest of the tents, capped boldly with the Stars
and Stripes. Pope had marked his own tent like the bull's-eye on a dart-
board, and Stuart couldn't wait to see what was in it.

Safe and sleeping in their tents and accustomed to the noise of the
storm, many of the Union troops didn't even awake until they felt pistol
barrels planted deeply in their ribs. Others scurried to find safety in,
under or behind wagons. Others fled into the woods and three hundred
were captured. Pope, unfortunately for the Rebels, was not at home.

The rain showed no signs of abating, and crossing the swollen streams
before a pursuit could be mounted was Stuart's highest priority. Inventory would have to wait.

It was midmorning before the exhausted troopers were able to stop
and examine their booty. The rain too had finally exhausted itself and it
was time for a rest—and for an accounting.

In addition to the three hundred prisoners, Stuart made off with some
of the finest horses the Union army had to offer and a significant amount
of Federal dollars.

"This should please General Lee significantly," Stuart said.

"And this, my dear General, should please *you.*"

Fitzhugh Lee stepped out from behind a tree dressed in a too big
broadcloth Union blue overcoat that hung over his hands and reached
nearly to his feet. It had an elegant velvet collar emblazoned with the
insignia of a major general. Down almost over his eyes sat a huge blue
hat—complete with two gold stars and a lovely collection of vibrant
plumage. Lee looked like a child playing soldier, and 1,500 men, from
Stuart on down, rolled in uncontrolled laughter not only at the sight of

Fitzhugh Lee so ludicrously attired but at the ironic form of justice God had brought.

As the men regained their composure, Stuart called for his adjutant.

"Send a dispatch to Major General John Pope, U.S. Army. My dear General, you have my hat and plume. I have your best coat. I have the honor to propose a cartel for a fair exchange of the prisoners."

Three deserters had been caught and court-martialed.

Three graves had been dug.

Stonewall ordered his entire corps assembled for a lesson in discipline.

The deserters were marched to their unmarked graves. Standing at the foot, facing the head, they were shot in the back—an appropriate way for a coward to die. Each fell forward into his coffinless grave so as to lie face down for eternity.

Stonewall's divisions marched by to view the remains before the bodies were covered, and only then was the somber army dismissed.

"OH, MY GOD, LAY ME DOWN"

AUGUST 24TH
THE GEORGIA COAST

James Wilson was one of the *wunderkinds* of the West Point Class of 1860. He graduated sixth in his class and, like most of his class-mates, was already a major and looking for his first regimental com-mand. Brash, enthusiastic and cocky beyond belief, he firmly believed that if he were in charge the war would have been won by now. But due to some oversight, he was most definitely not in charge. He was stuck in the backwaters of Georgia and South Carolina swatting mosquitoes and drawing maps.

Every night his dreams were filled with visions of himself transformed into the grand paintings that lined the walls at The Point. Every night he charged the ramparts on a gigantic black stallion with Old Glory in his left hand and a pistol in his right, firing into the face of some poor, terri-fied Rebel. But that was only at night. During the day he sweated buck-ets, complained endlessly and read the papers from up north that told him about the real war: "On to Richmond" was all the people wanted to hear about. He read about the Young Napoleon. Now there's a soldier! Class of '46. Richmond was surrounded, the month-old papers said, with Pope on one side and McClellan on the other. The Rebel capital was about to fall, and when it did the war would be over and the chance of his lifetime missed. He was so miserable and such a pest that when he requested permission to go to Washington to apply for a command in person his superiors happily let the arrogant little bastard go.

HEADQUARTERS, ARMY OF NORTHERN VIRGINIA

A long table sat in the middle of a field, looking like a church picnic for a tiny congregation. There was not another soul within five hundred yards as Lee, Longstreet, Stuart and Jackson planned their next course of action.

"Pope is far too strong and far too secure to be attacked from the front," Lee told his generals. "If we pull back, the siege of Richmond will be resumed. If we hold fast here, McClellan will join with Pope and against such numbers all hope will be lost. Stuart's success in getting into Pope's rear is our only positive sign. So I propose, sirs, to divide our army once again."

Lee looked at each man in turn and saw exactly what he expected to see. Jackson and Stuart were elated, and the ever-cautious Longstreet was concerned.

"General Jackson, you will move out and around the enemy's right as Stuart did." Lee looked back into the famous blue eyes of Stonewall Jackson. "You will have no specific objective. With his supply and communications lines down and with a strong force at his rear and again threatening Washington, Pope will be forced to pull back most, if not all, of the army facing us here."

This was Lee as none of the others had seen him before. This was Robert E. Lee seizing the initiative, planning his first campaign. He no longer looked tired and old, and even Longstreet could not challenge this plan. "If he moves, as I believe he will, it will be with his entire force against you, General Jackson, placing General Longstreet at his rear."

Now Lee's gaze shifted to Longstreet. Pete rocked slightly back and forth in his chair. His jaw was set and his eyes darted around the table, carefully looking at no one. But he didn't need to speak. Lee was fully aware of his concerns and spoke them for him. "I understand that we are already outnumbered and that I am taking a risk in making two small armies out of one of only moderate size to begin with. But our only other option is to retreat, allowing their two large armies to join together as one totally invulnerable force. Our sources inform us that the lead elements of McClellan's army have already joined with Pope. We must act before more can join. It is our only chance at victory. It must be done and it must be done now."

This time there was no conversation. No opinions were sought or offered. Stuart stood and joined Jackson at the head of the table. The two men saluted and turned and walked quickly back toward their units, leaving Lee and Longstreet seated alone.

"It truly is the only way, General."

Through his mind quickly ran a thousand options. A thousand objections. But none made better sense given the situation. Besides, the decision was made and in motion. Good little soldier. Longstreet said simply, "Yes, sir."

August 25th

Stuart took Jackson to the fording point he had selected across the Rappahannock. The two generals looked out over the river at a point where the waters were so swift and the opposite bank so steep that no sane man living would ever consider a crossing there. A single observer posted on the Union side could sound an alarm and a single division could stop the entire movement before it ever began.

"But no one's there, General."

Jackson shook his head. "And there ain't gonna be neither. What darned fool general would waste a perfectly good sentry on a crossing as bad as this? It's perfect."

An hour later and as quiet as a breeze, Jackson's army moved once again to the Union rear.

Stonewall rode to the front and found a boulder on which to stand from which he could encourage his men with his persistent urgings. "Close it up now, men. Close up. Keep it moving. Close it up."

The first units to see him lifted their voices for the obligatory cheer and Jackson shushed them. "Quiet, now. The Yankees will hear you. Close it up."

The word passed back through the ranks, "Quiet. The Yankees'll hear." So as the men passed Jackson striking his heroic pose atop his gigantic rock, they contented themselves with a silent salute. They raised their hats and waved them in the air in tribute to the mighty Stonewall.

By the time the later units passed, Stonewall was content that no Federals were near enough for it to matter or surely they would have made themselves known by now. The rear guards either had not gotten the word or simply couldn't contain themselves, for last in line was the Stonewall Brigade. They bore his name and they bore it proudly. A cheer rose up at the sight of him that the line commanders tried to squelch, but could not. Even Jackson's own raised hand failed to quiet the roar.

"It's no use, General," Douglas yelled, grinning like a jackass, "not even you can stop them."

"Back in Romney they called me 'lunatic.' I would hear them yell it as I rode by." Then, speaking so softly as to be heard by himself and God only, Stonewall Jackson said, "Who could not conquer with such men as these?"

Twenty-six miles they marched this day. Not until midnight did they fall from their ranks to sleep where they had fallen and before even a hint of dawn kissed the sky, Stonewall's army was up and on the move again.

GENERAL POPE'S HEADQUARTERS, CATLETT'S STATION, VIRGINIA

Catlett's Station wasn't exactly a hotbed of activity on this day and George Smalley had little trouble getting in to see the commanding general. He presented his letter of introduction from Secretary Stanton, which Pope simply glanced at and tossed aside.

"Okay, so the revered *Tribune* is now keeping an eye on me as well. Not the best news I've ever had."

Smalley had had time now to think on his blunder with Stanton and had totally revised his plan of attack.

"We're only here to do our jobs, General, and I know you don't think too highly of the estate. There's no reason why you should." A smile to warm the moment. "We are pests, we are liars and we are spies."

Pope burst into a belly laugh that could be heard in Washington. "Well, at least you are honest about it, young man."

Now—attack the Achilles' heel—an ego the size of Montana. "But we can be helpful if you let us."

"Now that's a rare notion."

"Listen, General. The whole world right now is keeping its eye on McClellan." He rolled his eyes to emphasize the feigned sarcasm. "The Young Napoleon. I believe that he is on his way to exile and the spotlight is about to fall on you. This is why I requested to be sent here—to be the first to tell *your* story."

Pope had had smoke blown in his face before and recognized it for what it was, but he liked it nonetheless. He made no attempt to stop the flattery, but he did take time to open the "For General Pope's eyes only" letter that Smalley had handed him. While Pope read, Smalley continued. "I believe that Jackson has returned north and that it may come down to a fight between Pope and Stonewall."

"Well, God help him if that's so. I want that bumpkin bastard so bad I can taste it."

"Is it so, General? Is Jackson facing you now?"

"Oh yes. He's out there somewhere. And Stuart too. It's only a matter of time before I brush those gnats off of my ass."

A big, friendly smile now, to let the bombastic general know he was deliberately kissing his ass. "Well, I want to be here when you do, and I want to tell the world about it."

Pope smiled a big smile too, but not at anything Smalley had said or done. He finished reading Stanton's letter, and the irony was not lost, even on Pope. "Maybe you will be, and maybe you won't."

He handed the letter to Smalley, who felt instantly ill as he read an order that all newspaper representatives be banished from access to all armies. It specified that reporters were to be denied access to telegraphs and were not even to be allowed to mail letters. And Stanton had used him as the courier to deliver his own death warrant. Nice touch.

Pope enjoyed the young reporter's discomfort. This was perfect. The kid had volunteered to be Pope's advocate, and here was the perfect tool delivered at the perfect time to guarantee the boy's allegiance. The fight between Pope and Jackson was coming and, by God, Pope wanted the world to know about it. But he wasn't ready to let Smalley off the hook just yet.

Finally, when he could remain silent no longer, the reporter decided that this was a battle to be fought on higher ground. "Very well, sir. If this is your order I have no choice but to take my leave."

A huge smile now from Pope. "Don't be too hasty, young fellow. No such order has been issued, and for as long as you and your confederates behave yourselves none will be." Smalley saw no need to disguise his relief.

"Go on about your business, Mr. Smalley, but pass the word along to your colleagues that this weapon is pointed at your heads. One missed step and it will be fired. Do you understand?"

"Yes, General. You make yourself quite clear."

HEADQUARTERS, ARMY OF THE POTOMAC
FORTRESS MONROE, VIRGINIA

It looks to me as though they may have come to their senses, George."

McClellan smiled. "They have no senses to come to, Father-in-Law. I am only their whipping boy at this point."

He looked again at the telegram from Halleck and tried to read into it whatever might be there. "They're only scared. Jackson may be on the loose again. Pope is drawing back toward the capital and they feel threatened. They want me there to take the blame when Pope fails."

"But George . . ."

"I'm tired of it all! It matters not a lick to me which way it goes at this point. I almost look forward to the end of this thing for me."

"But George! If Pope *does* fail . . ."

"And he shall."

"And he shall. To whom must they turn?"

McClellan didn't respond as he tried to catch up with his father-in-law's characteristically positive train of thought.

"They will turn to you, George. They must. There simply *is* no one else. They have ordered you to Washington, where we can sit, and wait, and"—with a smile and a flourish—"ride to the rescue!"

AUGUST 26TH
MANASSAS, VIRGINIA

Day two of Jackson's march was no less rigorous and no less dangerous than day one. Between himself and his goal lay Throughfare Gap, where again a single Union division could have halted the maneuver dead in its tracks. Again, not a single Yankee was there. Once through the gap, all hell could break loose for all Jackson cared. He would be alone again, taking orders from no one. In his mind Lee's words remained. *"He may turn his entire force against you,"* Lee had said.

"So be it," Jackson said, aloud and to no one.

Jackson's first target was Bristoe Station, hub of Pope's line of supply, retreat and reinforcement. After two days and fifty miles of marching, Jackson's lead elements arrived just before sunset, and no Rebel soldier, no matter how exhausted or footsore, could pass an opportunity to attack and derail a Union locomotive. It was simply too damned much fun.

Following a skirmish during which the lightly guarded depot fell to the Rebels, an empty northbound train approached. The Confederates rushed to throw the train from the tracks. Some tried to loosen the rails from the ties. Others threw lumber onto the tracks, but it was too little, too late. The train tore through the barricade like toothpicks, survived a pelting of small-arms fire and continued northward to spread the alarm.

No harm. Another would be along soon enough and this time they would be prepared. The Rebel infantry posted themselves to add mayhem to the chaos and there they waited for the one that wouldn't get away.

Only a couple of miles away, Kyd Douglas got word of the goings-on at Bristoe Station. By now, he and Westbrook were inseparable. Laughing, joking and cutting up like boys playing hooky from Sunday school.

"You ever seen a train going fast as hell go flying off the tracks, just one car after another, people jumping off in every direction and the whole damned thing blowing up?"

"Can't say as I have."

Douglas grinned. "Neither have I." They sped away from the column hellbent for leather, damned to hell before they'd miss this party. They arrived on the scene just in time. The sight of the billowing smoke and the sound of the screeching whistle brought smiles to the dirty faces of the waiting Rebels, suddenly not quite so tired anymore.

Horrifying sounds and wondrous sights came together as the flag-draped engine left the tracks, pulling behind it half of its cars. The gigantic machine hurled itself down a steep embankment into a ravine. Even over the horrendous racket of crashing cars and iron grinding against iron at breakneck speed, one man's death scream was clearly heard as the furnace threw white-hot coal into his face just before the boiler burst and spewed boiling water and scalding steam on him. The earth quaked on impact and the thirty-two-ton smoke-belching monster finally came to rest in a massive shroud of steam and dust. An ominous moment of silence was only a prelude to the explosions of a hundred muskets fired on a single command. It was a garish display of fire and thunder, and Douglas and Westbrook and about a thousand other Rebels loved every second of it.

The tracks were now so ruined that the ecstatic Rebels had only to sit and watch as first one train and then another collided into the wreckage of the first. By now Jackson himself was on hand to sit and watch and enjoy the show.

After three more trains plowed into the wreckage, the mountain of smoke billowed so high that approaching engineers saw the danger in advance and were able to brake and reverse direction. The initial train that had escaped the trap carried word of the raiders northward to Manassas, and Alexandria, and on to Washington, and by now word would be en route southward to Pope as well.

Among the unfortunate passengers was a civilian whose ankle had been broken in one of the wrecks.

"Who are you? Where did you come from?"

"We're with Stonewall," Douglas boasted. "Now that I think about it, so are you. That's the general himself standing there."

"Jackson is here? Lift me up. I must see this man."

His captors were glad to accommodate and helped him to his feet.

The magnificent Stonewall sat astride his ugly little horse wearing the unassuming garb of a private soldier—a frayed and dingy gray uniform left over from his days at V.M.I. and a ragged cap, the standard issue kepi, pulled down almost to his nose. Over his uniform he also wore the filth of a fifty-mile march. In the North, maybe even more than in the South, Stonewall was a mystic conqueror. He was Caesar, Alexander and Napoleon all rolled into one, but this sad example of a soldier was certainly none of these, and still the greatest Union generals and the grandest Union armies couldn't defeat this ragamuffin god. Most of the time they couldn't even find him.

The man was mortified for his country. "Oh, my God," he said, "lay me down."

August 27th

General Isaac Trimble, a hard-nosed and ambitious officer, was the first to arrive at Manassas Junction, and he easily brushed off sparse Union defenses. His men arrived tired and hungry to find a city made of food and shoes and blankets. Heaven on earth. Gigantic warehouses contained enough bounty to feed, clothe and equip almost 200,000 men. A full mile of railroad spurs held hundreds of cars loaded with massive amounts of food and equipment ready to roll south at a moment's notice.

The capitals of Europe would have been proud to serve the contents of this depot for the entertainment of visiting royalty. It was grand—and it was off-limits. Even among these incredible riches Trimble forbade his men even to enter the bakery. Not a loaf could be taken until authorized by Jackson.

The pilfering began with small bands of adventuresome men sneaking around the grounds to fill their canteens with molasses and their cups with coffee beans. Soon A. P. Hill's hungry division arrived and were in no frame of mind to be denied by Trimble's halfhearted guards. The pilfering ended and the plunder began. It was a scene of joyful chaos. The manna included cigars, honey, flour, canned fruits and mustard.

A scarecrow of a man, whose diet for the better part of a year had consisted of what he had stolen or picked from a tree, sat in the dirt leaning against a flour barrel eating lobster salad with filthy fingers. He washed it all down with a fine Rhine wine earmarked for Pope's own table and wiped his chin with a linen napkin.

"You look to be a contented soldier, Private," one lieutenant said.

He showed a yellow-toothed grin and said, "Shittin' in high cotton today, sir."

The Rebels were in heaven. The Yankees were in trouble.

The bold brigade of Union troops, oblivious to the numbers aligned against them, marched smack into the heart of Jackson's army. A squad of mounted men rode forward under a white flag and were greeted by Kyd Douglas.

"What is the purpose of your visit, sir?"

"We are a full brigade with cavalry and artillery and to avoid any unnecessary effusion of blood we demand an unconditional surrender."

Douglas tried desperately not to laugh out loud.

"I beg your pardon, sir."

"You heard me, Captain. Now please give my compliments to your commanding officer and deliver my message. Tell him if he doesn't reply within one half hour we will assume that he has determined to fight. Now ride."

Douglas bristled at the arrogant Yankee's tone, but couldn't wait to deliver the message to Stonewall. With a gigantic grin he said, "I shall be happy to, sir."

Everyone but Jackson was amused and anxious to dispatch the bold blue-bellies straight to hell. "No, gentlemen," he said, looking down the hill at the pitiful handful of men aligned against him. "Those are courageous soldiers down there who are badly led. Arrange an artillery demonstration that will show our strength. Do not be too careful in rounding them all up. It may serve my purpose to allow a few to escape and tell what they've seen here."

Artillery fire poured down on the boys from New Jersey from three directions, and in a scant five minutes the white flag came out again. The arrogance, however, was gone.

Jackson ordered the huge stores at Manassas Junction put to the torch and the quiet town became a burning city. The glow from the flames was visible for miles.

* * *

"General Pope, sir. We have reports from several quarters that General Jackson's entire command is to our rear. The supply depot at Manassas Junction is burning and some of our soldiers say it's the whole damned Rebel army."

"We know full well that it's not, but my guess is that it is the bastard Jackson. And now he's wandered in between me and our other army up in Washington. I want that son-of-a-bitch and now's my chance to get him. Wire Washington. Tell 'em at the earliest blush of dawn, we shall bag the whole crowd. Instruct all divisions, north and south, to move quickly toward Manassas. We'll get the bastard this time."

John Pope was not a shy man and anything worth saying was worth saying loudly. Sitting twenty-five yards from Pope's tent, George Smalley heard the whole exchange as though he'd been invited in. He'd been hanging around Pope's headquarters like a lapdog waiting for a table scrap and this was one hell of a scrap.

Smalley knew the Federal troop placements probably better than Pope did, and it didn't take him long to figure out who would have to take the lead. King's division. Probably Gibbon's brigade. Just geographically this unit was the best situated to move out first, and Smalley got there before the orders did.

WASHINGTON

Washington, D.C., teetered on the edge of panic. The President, the cabinet, the Congress and the people all now knew of the massive strike on the supply depot at Manassas Junction. Bull Run. The name alone brought back shameful memories to the entire city, like some kind of appalling recurring nightmare. Dreams of Rebels marching through the streets, torching, or worse yet, *occupying* the Capitol and the Executive Mansion. Rebels. Rebels in Manassas. Less than a day's march away. Again! The army was spread all across Virginia from hell and gone and the hordes were at the gates.

Halleck and Chase sat in Stanton's office reviewing the current disasters.

"Prying soldiers away from McClellan is like pulling nails with my teeth," Halleck said. "Some units have moved to Pope's aid, but precious few at this point."

Stanton resumed the tugging of his heavily perfumed beard and said, "The man is perfectly willing to fiddle while Washington burns. It is time, Sal. We must put our plan into effect. General, if you will excuse us . . ."

AUGUST 28TH

For over an hour the President stood at his window watching his worst nightmare unfold before him. Wagons sped by, loaded with household goods and headed north at a run, while somewhere just over that hill Lee's army stood poised at the gates, bent on killing the Republic. Hay had never seen him so despondent.

"Oh. John. How long have you been standing there?"

"Just stepped up, sir."

Lincoln took one more glance out at the street. "Now that's a sad sight, John. We have two armies—two generals—out there, hopefully between Lee and Washington, and still the people are packing up to go. They have less faith in our generals than I do."

"No more news from Pope, sir?"

"The lines are still down the last I heard. It's the news from McClellan that concerns me most though."

"McClellan?"

Lincoln took his time in responding. He considered it carefully before allowing the thoughts to become words. Not until a thought is spoken or written down does it become genuinely real. Irretrievable. Public property.

"I'm afraid that he is playing a different game from the rest of us, John."

"How so, sir?"

"Pope is in trouble. How much trouble, no one knows. Pope himself probably doesn't even know. But mark my words, John . . . McClellan knows. He knows full well." Lincoln looked back out toward the Lee house, but not at it exactly. At the hill. Over it. Beyond it. Through it to

Manassas, where he could see the armies lining up on the same ground as last year to go at it again. Bull Run. It *has* to be different this time.

"Sir?"

John. The President had to bring himself back. Finish his thought.

"He has been ordered to send every corps of the old Army of the Potomac to join Pope as quickly as possible, but 'quickly,' I'm afraid, means something quite different to George than to the rest of us. He tells us that Franklin's corps lacks cavalry, and Sumner's lacks artillery, so *neither* can move. The thought of hooking Franklin's artillery with Sumner's cavalry apparently has not occurred to him, and two corps now sit in Alexandria drinking coffee and playing cards."

Another long pause. Another debate. Another private thought made public. "I am afraid, John, that Mr. McClellan is . . ." No. Not yet. Keep it private for as long as you can. ". . . playing a different game."

"That is without a doubt Jackson's corps down there, sir," a young staff officer told Pope.

The bombastic general swelled with anticipation. "McDowell and Sigel are approaching from the south with thirty thousand men and Heintzelman, Porter and Reno are approaching with an equal number. Franklin and Sumner are available if that little jackass will ever send them to me. No matter which way the son-of-a-bitch moves, we've got him, by God. This time, we've got him!"

"What about Longstreet, sir?"

"Longstreet be damned. We'll take care of him in due time. Right now, we've got that bastard Jackson right where we want him. Hell, I couldn't have placed him better myself. Send out to all commanders— come quickest. And inform Washington that we have Jackson trapped. I see no possibility of his escape."

"Escape" was the last thing on Jackson's mind. Stonewall the puppeteer had pulled the proper strings and Pope the marionette had leaped to do his bidding. *"His entire force . . ."* All that remained was Longstreet.

With some trepidation Longstreet's men approached the dangerous, narrow passes of Throughfare Gap. General James Ricketts of McDowell's corps did his best to slow the advance. He requested assistance, but everyone else was headed toward Jackson like horses to the barn and John Bell Hood took care of Ricketts.

"General Lee, sir. General Jackson sends his regards, sir, and informs you that he has reached Groveton Woods on the old Manassas battle-field. The enemy is not fully joined yet on that field, but Stuart informs us that as many as four corps are approaching."

"Very well, Captain. Tell General Jackson that we are clear of the gap and that we will be on our way at first light tomorrow."

"Tomorrow, sir?"

"That's what I said, Captain. First light tomorrow."

The courier turned to ride the eight miles back to where Jackson lay in wait for John Pope.

"What are you thinking, General Longstreet?"

"Tomorrow is good, sir, but first light may be too early." He knew that Jackson would soon be heavily involved and his losses would be large, but by arriving too soon the entire plan could turn to disaster. "We don't want to arrive ahead of the Yankees."

BRAWNER'S FARM, VIRGINIA

George Smalley had done his homework as usual, and knew more than a little something about the unit he'd joined up with.

This was a unique brigade that John Gibbon commanded, two times over. It was composed entirely of Westerners. Three regiments from Wisconsin and one from Indiana. They were Yankee farm boys and not too far removed from their pioneer stock. When Gibbon had taken over the command, he had found them ragtag and undisciplined. He drilled them mercilessly, punished them heartlessly and enforced regulations relentlessly. In short, he whipped a thousand independent and strong-willed farm boys into a single proud and cohesive unit. The second way in which they were unique was in their appearance. He had required them all to use their clothing allowance on new and highly distinctive uniforms. The Union blue frock coats reached almost to the knees and the trousers were light blue, highlighted by white leggings. Gibbon replaced the standard-issue kepi caps with black full-brimmed Hardee hats festooned with pins and plumes. Now only one thing was lacking: only one of his regiments had ever seen battle.

Smalley rode alongside the Union army's tiniest soldier, little Johnny Cook, the bugle boy for the 4th U.S. Artillery. He was fifteen, going on twelve by the looks of him. He could tiptoe and stretch his way up to five feet tall. Everything about him was frail and small. Everything but his head, which was about the size of a Wisconsin pumpkin. Everyone had adopted young Johnny and looked out after him in the hard times. General Gibbon himself had taken a liking to the boy. The 4th U.S. had been his old command back in the regular army, about a million years ago back in Utah, so Gibbon was partial. The little fellow played his horn well enough. He marched like a veteran and enjoyed his role as unofficial mascot of the boys with the big guns. They complained about his sour notes and yelled at him to shut up halfway through Reveille every morning, but it had become a unit tradition to pat him on the head for luck. His job was to remain always at the side of Captain Campbell, and the men said it was funny that such a large man should cast such a tiny shadow.

Gibbon's men were experienced marchers by now so they were accustomed to being shadowed and observed by the occasional Rebel scout. To them the lone Rebel horseman barely got noticed. Back and forth he rode along the ridge, watching them like the sole observer of a grand parade. Only Smalley saw something odd about the man. Neither grandly garbed nor mounted he might have been a private trooper, but there was something else. Something familiar. But Smalley was distracted by another thought. Why don't they just shoot the bastard? He's not a hundred yards away.

The scout rode along the ridge, up and down their flank. He stopped and gave his horse a tug on the reins and a touch of the spur and the animal reared and turned and galloped forward for a view from the front. Another turn and back down the flank.

Sergeant Herzog rode up alongside of young Johnny Cook and poked him in the ribs and pointed up at the lone Rebel.

"Quite a horseman," he said with a laugh.

"He's got an ugly little horse, though."

On the other side of the hill no one spoke, no one whispered, no one breathed. On this side of the hill as on the other, all eyes were now on the horseman.

His officers sat mounted at the bottom of the hill and watched more intently than most, each trying to detect from some gesture or expression what to expect. Slowly and calmly he guided Little Sorrel down the slope and approached the officers at a walk. With a casual salute Stonewall Jackson simply said, "Bring up your men, gentlemen."

Herzog said to Cook, "Well, now the Rebels know where we are. I wonder if *our* generals have any idea."

"I wonder if they have any idea how bad my butt hurts."

White-hot iron from Confederate cannon suddenly exploded into the heart of Gibbon's untried brigade. George Smalley had found Stonewall Jackson.

The 4th U.S. unlimbered their guns, loaded and fired back at their Confederate cousins and the artillery duel was on. They took the heat and stood their ground and reloaded and fired again.

The Union's brigade commanders began desperately looking for some guidance from their division commander, but General Rufus King was stricken with an epileptic seizure the moment the very first rounds were fired, and his four brigades were left very much on their own.

Gibbon found Abner Doubleday positioned safely to the rear.

"What do you think it is we're facing here, John?"

"It's really hard to tell, but it could be Jackson's main force, I suppose."

"Twenty-five thousand men against one division scattered along five miles of bad road? I don't think so. If that's the case they probably would've come screaming over that hill all at once." A Rebel round overshot the Black Hats and landed a little too close to the generals for comfort. It startled their horses and threw a little dust on their boots, but no harm was done. "My guess is that it's Stuart's horse artillery, and that Jackson is at Centreville. Hell, John, that's where Pope's sending us. He must be at Centreville."

"Horse artillery, huh?"

Both men sat still for a minute to see if the situation changed, but the artillery duel continued.

"Well, Abner, we can't go forward, and we can't stay here, so I guess I'd better just head up that hill and see if I can't take those guns."

"Well, Godspeed, John. And I guess we're about to see how Westerners fight."

"I guess we are."

Gibbon selected the 2nd Wisconsin for the job. They were the only unit he had with any battlefield experience whatsoever. It had been a year, a month and a week before when the 2nd Wisconsin had stormed Jackson's brigade in the first fight fought on this field. They had been pushed back by the boys from Virginia who had simply refused to run. These were the men who were in disordered retreat when some Rebel yelled over the sound of the fighting, "Look, men! There stands Jackson like a stone wall!" From that day to this, these boys from Milwaukee, Madison, Racine and Oshkosh had not fired a shot in anger; and from that day to this, they carried with them a festering shame that today, by God, they intended to shed.

They moved quietly through a stand of woods so as to come up to the right of the Rebel battery. Out of sight they formed in lines of battle and moved forward in good order. They crested one hill and prepared to fire on the battery when suddenly the Rebel artillerymen ceased firing, limbered their guns and sped off toward the rear.

Gibbon knew immediately that something very bad was about to happen, and, at that instant, out from another stand of woods came Rebel infantry, seemingly by the thousands and at the double-quick. This was *not* Jeb Stuart's cavalry.

Some of Gibbon's men fired at the Rebs even though they were still well out of range.

"Hold your fire, men!" he yelled. He walked slowly and tall—the picture of perfect calm. The wasteful firing stopped and his lines became eerily quiet. Gibbon heard one man whisper, "Come on up, God damn you."

The Rebs were now two hundred yards to the front. Almost there, but not quite, when another Black Hat hissed, "Damnation!"

"What?"

"It's them again!"

"Who?"

"See that flag there?" He pointed. "It says 'Second Virginia.' I tell you it's them again. It's the goddamned Stonewall Brigade!"

"Hold it," Gibbon said as the most famous military unit in the world was now 150 yards away.

"Hold it . . . hold it . . . FIRE!"

At 100 yards all 450 muskets exploded in a single instant, but the Rebels kept on coming until finally they fell in behind a rail fence only about 80 yards to the front. The firing now was constant, and Gibbon knew that his men were outnumbered and outclassed by Stonewall's veterans.

At the same moment both commanders glanced up at the sun and Gibbon prayed for it to hurry the hell up while Stonewall prayed for it to stop dead in its tracks.

Like boxers in a ring the two generals began exchanging punches.

Gibbon called in the 19th Indiana and Jackson countered with the 60th Georgia.

The 7th Wisconsin joined the fight and the musket fire continued at a constant roar.

While Jackson commanded over 25,000 men, they weren't all massed at Brawner's Farm. He was frustrated and angry, first at A. P. Hill (again), and then at his artillery units, which were grouped almost five miles away, but he was perhaps most angry at the sun. The day, it seemed to him, was hellbent for darkness and he just couldn't get his men into the fight quickly enough to overwhelm Gibbon's piddley little brigade.

Finally, he found an entire brigade—four regiments, which outnumbered Gibbon by themselves, and sent them into the heat, and they arrived just as Gibbon's last reserves came up as well and the battle just grew louder and more deadly.

In the Rebel ranks General Taliaferro was carried from the field only after being shot three times. Dick Ewell, one of Jackson's brightest and most reckless officers, saw his men bogged down in a gully and rode headlong into the fight. "Here's General Ewell, boys!" shouted a Rebel at the very instant the Yankees rose to fire, each one it seemed taking sight at the gallant mounted general. His men watched in horror as blood and bone exploded from Ewell's knee. Ground was given and his men were forced to leave him on the field, not knowing if Ewell would be numbered among the dead or wounded.

For two and half hours they stood and fought, and screamed and died. Abner Doubleday brought his brigade forward in support of Gibbon and the blue lines stiffened. Only as darkness approached did both sides begin to fall back—slowly and well ordered.

There would be no back wounds on either side this day.

As quiet followed darkness, litter bearers moved out among the dead and dying and found General Ewell unconscious but still gripping his left thigh. They brought him back behind friendly lines where surgeons sawed off his leg.

Bugle boy Johnny Cook lay down in the darkness to sleep and to try to erase from his mind the bloody visions of this brutal day. He put down his head on an inviting mound of leaves only a little too high and hard to form the perfect pillow. He brushed away the top layer of leaves and blanched in horror to find the bleached white skull of a soldier left on the field a year, a month and a week before.

AUGUST 29TH

The field at Brawner's Farm had been quiet for several hours before General King recovered from his seizure, shocked to see the carnage from the battle he had missed. Informed that it was the main body of Jackson's force that he faced, he made the decision, frankly, to get the hell out of there. At 1:00 A.M. the officers began rousting the exhausted heroes from their sleep with orders to move out. The wounded that could be carried were carelessly tossed over the backs of horses or carried by their comrades, and the brave and proud Westerners of Gibbon's Black Hat Brigade crept off the field in the dead of night.

Pope ordered King to hold his ground, but by the time the orders arrived King had already retreated to Manassas Junction. General Phil Kearny's orders were to advance on Jackson in darkness, "drive in the enemy's pickets tonight and at early dawn attack him vigorously." Kearny had received too many such orders from Pope directing him to hurry nowhere for no reason. "Tell General Pope to go to hell! We won't march till morning." To Fitz-John Porter, newly arrived from McClellan's army, Pope said, "Be expeditious or we shall lose much." After consulting with General McDowell, Porter too delayed, awaiting clarification, and worrying about Longstreet.

While waiting for McDowell and Pope to figure out where the hell he was supposed to go and when, Porter scribbled off a private and ill-considered note to another of McClellan's allies, Ambrose Burnside. "I hope Mac is at work and we will soon get ordered out of this." The Rebels, he said, seem to know what they are doing, "which is more than anyone here knows." Ever the dutiful soldier, Burnside sent the message forward to General Halleck in Washington.

Porter finally moved out at 10:00 A.M. and very quickly fell under the watchful eye of Jeb Stuart, who didn't like what he saw—an entire corps of Union infantry on a collision course with Longstreet's advancing army.

"Cut every low-hanging limb from every tree you can find, tie them to the backs of your horses and raise a dust cloud big enough to look like an advancing corps, and then dismount a regiment to greet him as he comes up." Stuart looked much more confident than he was, but even if it didn't work, or even if it delayed the Yanks for an hour or less, at least nothing will have been lost.

Porter fell for the ploy, and his already tardy corps stopped dead in its tracks.

Jackson had brought his men together and placed them in the relative safety of an unfinished railroad cut. All around the old battlefield the Union troops began arriving piecemeal, trying to figure out precisely where Jackson might be hiding. Pickets engaged whenever one side or the other drew too close, but neither would commit to a general engagement as both were waiting for friends.

By 10:30 the armies started to get a little feisty, and some fairly serious skirmishing broke out. A Confederate general saw movement to his right and sent a scout to find out who it was. He took only moments and returned with the answer to 25,000 prayers—"It's Longstreet!"

Quietly and patiently, Lee and Longstreet moved 25,000 men to support Jackson's right flank.

"Is it not time, General?"

"I think not, General Lee. The trap is baited, sir, but the bait is not yet taken. Jackson holds good ground down there, sir, and eventually the Yankees are going to wear themselves out."

"There are more Yankees on the way, General."

"That is true, sir, and that is what concerns me most. An entire corps is being held up only a few miles from here, but they won't be held in place for long. Our people in Washington tell me that Franklin and Sumner are still in Alexandria and showing little signs of life. But Porter and McDowell are definitely nearby. Stuart says they may come up soon on our right and if we move now they could well gain our rear. If that happens, General, we will have sprung our own trap on ourselves. We need to wait, sir, and see what comes next."

While Lee and Longstreet debated the proper tactics, Jackson's men came under ever heavier attack. Piecemeal though it may have been, Pope continued to send in brigade after brigade, and Stonewall watched as assault after assault approached his lines only to be pushed back. At the center a Union captain grabbed up his regimental colors and rallied the bloodied remains of his command to another attempt. With the flag in one hand and his pistol in the other, he rose and yelled and his men came forward over a hill where twenty bullets took him down before his soldiers finally fled. It almost brought Jackson to tears. He rode forward to see what remained of his center and heard a captain chastising the troops.

"A man as brave as that should be spared and taken prisoner. His death is a shame."

"No, Captain, the men are right," Stonewall said softly. "Kill the brave ones—they lead the others."

"General Pope, sir. General Reynolds begs to report, sir, what I have recently seen for myself that a fresh Rebel force, many thousand in number, sir, has pulled up along the Rebel right flank."

Pope just smiled at the young officer as though he were an ignorant child.

"You are simply excited, young man. Those flags you see are Porter's men and I'm glad to hear of it."

"Begging your pardon, sir, and with respect, but I've been there myself, and I am certain that this is an entire Rebel corps."

Pope just smiled again and said, "I'm sure you are, my boy," and turned away.

Pope firmly believed that he had Stonewall trapped and desperately continued his attempts to prevent his escape, and finally it was Kearny's turn to move against Jackson's exhausted left.

Phil Kearny's left arm was buried in a ditch somewhere in Mexico, so it looked awkward to others to see him on horseback with the reins clenched tightly in his teeth while he scanned the enemy lines through his field glasses. It may have appeared awkward to others, but by now it was perfectly natural to him. One of the finest horsemen in the Union army, he was in total control of the animal this way, even at a full run. Shifting his weight in the saddle, or tightening the pressure on one side or the other with a gentle nudge of the knee, or a touch of the spur, told his spectacular black thoroughbred all he needed to know. But now he sat tall at a dead standstill, peering through the smoke. Old Jack was over there somewhere and probably hip-high in the action. The two had been odd friends in the old days; the country cousin and the New York millionaire who used three different forks to eat soldiers' food. But each admired the other's courage and tenacity. Finally, he caught sight of a mounted officer with a kepi pulled too far down over his eyes. He wanted it to be Jackson and he wanted it not to be Jackson, Kearny's *aide-de-camp* spotted the same distant silhouette.

"Is that him, General? Is that 'Stonewall'?" He tried to make his pronunciation sound sarcastic, but on this field, on this day, the effort rang hollow.

"Maybe." Kearny struggled to return the glasses to their case so he could take the reins out of his mouth to speak more clearly. "You know, I remember a time when that man stood next to me—right *next* to me— and saluted the Stars and Stripes. I remember when he would personally kill any man who tried to take her down!" *It wasn't so long ago*, he thought. One more glance up the hill at a man who might or might not be Jackson before he said, ". . . And I still will."

Quiet and invisible, Kearny's men sneaked into the woods, where they prepared to attack Powell Hill again between brigades where his lines were weakest. His men looked and listened as their one-armed general, as calm as a Sunday morning, quietly reminded them of what they were about to do.

"The events of this day will turn on you, men."

He took a pause and looked up and down his lines. "Remember: one volley and then like demons up the hill."

Another long pause, and then, not as a shouted order, but casually and with a nod he said, "Fix bayonets."

On the other side of the line, on Jackson's left flank, stood Maxcy Gregg, a South Carolina lawyer and gentleman—a well-bred son of the South. His men had been fighting and holding their own for several hours, and in the quiet before the storm they thought their day was done. Gregg checked his pistol for the tenth time just to make sure it was still fully loaded when his pickets opened fire on the advancing Federals.

"Here they come, boys!" He rushed forward to observe and shouted, "Let the pickets back in—let the pickets back in. *Now! Fire!*"

Just as they had been told, Kearny's Yanks fired a single volley and then came screaming up the hill. Gregg's Rebels held and then wavered. The Yankees broke through and for a crucial moment things looked grim for the gray. The South Carolinians stiffened and rejoined their broken lines and the bluecoats hesitated, halted and fell back to regroup.

"General Hill sends his compliments, sir," a courier informed Gregg, "and inquires if you will be able to hold your position."

"Inform General Hill that we shall make every effort. Inform him also that our ammunition is almost expended, but we still have our bayonets."

A. P. Hill received the response grimly. "Ride to General Jackson and tell him the situation here" he told Kyd Douglas. "Tell him that we are pressed and low on ammunition and tell him that the future of his left is in serious question."

Douglas didn't have to ride far. "Tell General Hill if they attack him again, he must beat them!" Jackson told him. "Wait. I shall tell him myself."

Jackson and Douglas rode off together to met Hill, who himself was riding to consult personally with his commanding general.

"Your men have done nobly, General Hill; if you are attacked again you *will* beat the enemy back!"

Before the final words had passed his lips, the fresh sounds of battle drew the attention of both men, as Kearny had rallied his men to try it again. "Charge, boys! Charge, you sons-of-bitches, and I'll make every one of you a major general!"

"Here it comes!" Hill shouted over the din. He turned without waiting and spurred his horse back toward the battle.

"I'll expect you to beat them!" Jackson shouted after him.

The boys from South Carolina stood and fought again. With every man who fell, the Rebels backed up a step, and another, and another until, without even knowing that they had given any ground, they found themselves atop a hill. Gregg knew too well that if they fell back another step they would then be on the downside and would lose any small advantage they had.

He drew his sword, his grandfather's scimitar that had cut British flesh back in the first Revolution. He stood behind his lines and shouted, "Let us die here, my men. Let us die here!"

No more of Gregg's boys would die this day, as up the hill stormed Jubal Early with the last of Hill's reserves. The Yankees recoiled and withdrew, giving up their hard-earned ground with the same grudging, bloody resistance as had the Rebels.

Exhausted, Gregg's men yielded gladly to the newcomers and fell instantly to the ground, but their duty wasn't wholly done.

"Form a line and lie in it, men. If they come back this way rise up and give 'em the bayonet."

Douglas approached Jackson with a cloud of dust and a crisp salute. "General Hill presents his compliments and says the attack of the enemy was repulsed."

Jackson smiled. He actually smiled and said, "Tell him I knew he would do it."

Dr. Hunter McGuire, ever at Stonewall's side, heard the conversation.

"General, this day has been won by nothing but stark and stern fighting."

"No. It has been won by nothing but the blessing and protection of Providence."

* * *

So close had the fighting been to the capital that on occasion the cannon fire could be heard on Pennsylvania Avenue. President Lincoln had not left the telegraph office all day and the information that was his life's blood flowed ever so slowly in. Desperate, Lincoln wired anyone and everyone who might be able to tell him anything.

What news from the direction of Manassas Junction? he wired McClellan. *What news generally?*

To his enemies, McClellan's reply was telling.

I am clear that one of two courses should be adopted—1st To concentrate all of our available forces to open communication with Pope—2nd To leave Pope to get out of this scrape & at once to use all our means to make the capital perfectly safe. No middle course will now answer. . . . It will not do to delay longer.

As the darkness ended the fight, John Pope finally had to concede that Longstreet might possibly be nearby, but in his mind it changed absolutely nothing. Stonewall Jackson was still a stone's throw away, and while his lines might be strengthened by Longstreet's arrival, it remained Pope's only goal to "bag the whole crowd." He would have done it today had it not been for McClellan's boy, Fitz-John Porter. Pope was in the process of telling everyone in hearing range—hell, even some Confederates might have been close enough to hear—that Porter was an idiot and probably a traitor when an unfortunate soldier arrived with a dispatch from Porter himself. "Please let me know of your designs, whether you retire or not . . ."

Pope exploded. "I'll arrest him," he shouted and actually began to dictate the arrest order when General McDowell calmly suggested that now might not be the best time to arrest a corps commander.

For once on this entire day, Pope yielded to the advice of another, but the order he did send to Porter left no doubt about the commanding general's frame of mind.

"You will immediately march your command to the field of battle of today and report to me in person for orders!"

After the unfortunate courier had left the room, Pope's tirade continued. "I should arrest him, and Franklin, and Summer and even that little bastard McClellan! We might have won the *war* today if those bastards had just bothered to show up!"

AUGUST 30TH

Saturday morning dawned lazily, with each side again watching the other. That's all—just watching. Pope's spirits had improved overnight, still totally convinced that Jackson was desperate to "escape" and only by his own brilliant plan had the Rebels been held in place.

"Take down what I say, young man," Pope said through a cloud of blue smoke from his celebratory cigar, "and send it off to the gentlemen in Washington." Then, with an arrogant smile, "I should send a copy to Mr. McClellan as well, but he'll hear of it soon enough."

Another pull on the cigar and a thoughtful glance at the ash. This was not a dictation. It was a recital. A performance on the stage of history. "We fought a terrific battle here yesterday. The enemy was driven from the field which we now occupy. The enemy is still in our front, but badly used up. We have lost not less than eight thousand men killed and wounded . . ." To the men in the room it sounded like a boast. As though Pope would have been happier had the number been larger. ". . . but from the appearance of the field the enemy lost at least two-to-one. Our troops behaved splendidly. The battle was fought on the identical battle-field as Bull Run, which greatly increased the enthusiasm of our men."

A courier barged in and handed him a written dispatch, which interrupted the soliloquy but gave him an opportunity for another loving draw on his costly cigar.

"The news just reaches me from the front that the enemy is retreating toward the mountains. I go forward at once to see. Headquarters in the Saddle, et cetera."

The morning sky was cloudless and the air was hot and still. The Federals poked around in front of Jackson's lines, which were now only a few hundred yards rearward of where they stood yesterday. A sparse line of pickets remained on the old lines just to raise a ruckus in case the Yankees got frisky, but no one was in much of a mood for a brawl. Spatterings of small-arms fire interrupted the quiet from time to time. The dry grasses of summer ignited from the sparks and a hundred little fires filled the air with smoke and haze, and still the day dragged on. So slowly was the day progressing that men of both sides dozed in line of battle like hounds under the porch waiting for the hunt.

It was midmorning before the prodigal Fitz-John Porter finally arrived at the head of his 8,000-man corps and reported, as ordered, directly to the commanding general. Porter informed Pope, in no uncertain terms, that Longstreet had pulled up alongside of Jackson's lines, doubling their length and more than doubling their numbers.

"I have been receiving reports all morning long that elements of the Rebel army are pulling back in large numbers." He had also been receiving reports to the contrary, but chose to believe only the ones that indicated withdrawal. "If Longstreet is up in force, which I seriously doubt, his sole responsibility will be to cover the retreat."

"They are *absolutely not* in retreat, General! They are up and in large numbers, and if you fail to guard your left flank then it is *you* who will be in retreat!"

John Reynolds joined the verbal battle on Porter's side. It was, after all, his division that guarded the left. It was his men who would die if Pope screwed this up.

But Pope would have none of it.

"The Rebel army is retreating, sirs, and it is my intention to pursue them all the way to Richmond! Now—report back to the head of your units and await my orders—orders that you *will* obey immediately! Understood?"

"Understood."

"You are dismissed."

A flurry of orders from Pope went out throughout the morning ordering his generals to "pursue" the fleeing Rebels, but each pursuit came up against a wall of determined resistance. It was well after noon when Reynolds rode up to Pope's headquarters at a gallop, his horse frothing from the two-mile run.

"General, the enemy is turning our left!"

The conversation got heated and Pope again refused to take the advice of "a McClellan man." But very soon the same reports began coming in from "Pope men," like Franz Sigel and Irwin McDowell, and finally, reluctantly, he sent a brigade—a single brigade—to help Reynolds protect against Longstreet while he continued obsessively to focus on Jackson's line that had been so tested yesterday.

As the concept of "pursuit" was gradually replaced with the concept of "attack," it was Porter who got the call. By the time he got himself untangled from the pursuit orders and prepared for the attack, it was after three o'clock. Then, at long last and against his own better judgment, Porter finally moved and the pent-up calm of the day exploded into chaos.

Porter's first challenge was to move his corps over seven hundred yards of open fields that lay under the muzzles of S. D. Lee's massed artillery, and thousands of Porter's men never laid eyes on Jackson's lines. Those who did found that Stonewall still had the protection of the unfinished railroad cut and the Yankees who survived the artillery now had to storm uphill against entrenched infantry.

One Federal colonel, fearlessly or stupidly, led his men on horseback, inspiring them onward until a bullet caught him square in the jaw, but failed to dismount him.

"Colonel! You're hit!" shouted a major.

"To your post!" the colonel shouted back.

It was the next bullet that killed him.

The Confederate lines had fought off assault after assault yesterday, but never one as relentless as this. Never a full corps.

"We are under a continuous and determined assault, sir, and need immediate relief!" a young officer reported to Jackson.

"What brigade, sir?"

"The Stonewall Brigade."

"Go back. Give my compliments to them, and tell the Stonewall Brigade to maintain her reputation."

Captain Stickley hesitated before returning to the fight, his disappointment showing on his face.

"Tell them to hold at all hazards, Captain, and that reinforcements will be quickly sent."

But Stonewall could easily see that a bold reputation and a brigade of reinforcements would not be enough to save his line. Not this time.

"Douglas!"

"Sir!"

It was against the grain of Stonewall's soul, what he was about to say, but there must come a time.

"Ride to General Longstreet and tell him we need help, and we need a full division." There was the sound of grudging defeat in his voice. He felt like a pauper pleading for a handout, but it had to be done.

It wasn't only the Stonewall Brigade that faced a desperate fight. To their immediate left stood Stafford's brigade taking every bit as much of the heat, but they had it even worse . . . they were out of ammunition.

It is every soldier's nightmare to reach into his sack for one last desperate round and find nothing there. The bravest man will awaken from exhausted sleep, wet with sweat and trembling in horror, just from the dreaming of it.

A long-faced Virginian, too young to grow a beard but with splotches of blond chin fuzz, fired his final round. In panic he searched through the cartridge boxes of fallen Rebels all around him but could not find a single round to fire. In desperation, he looked around on the ground for a .58-caliber rock to force down the muzzle of his rifle. He couldn't find one small enough to shoot, but he found one, by God, big enough to throw. "Give 'em the rocks, boys," he yelled as he took sight on a man just as though he were aiming his musket and hurled the primitive weapon with all the force his aching body could command. It struck the Yankee square in the face and down he went to his knees—blood pouring from his nose. The Rebel was astounded to be alive, and more astounded yet to hear the yipping of the Rebel yell behind him as his comrades followed his lead and a hailstorm of rocks came hurtling into the Union lines. He was more astounded when the ground shook and fire erupted from the earth in the midst of his enemies and those who weren't maimed or killed by this God-sent hellfire turned and ran and never came back.

High on a hill just off to the right, James Longstreet lowered his field glasses and turned to his chief of artillery, and said, "Very nicely done, sir. Very nicely done."

Porter had more men he could send in—over the seven hundred yards of deadly ground and up the hills against the stubborn Rebel lines, but

SECOND BULL RUN/MANASSAS
AUGUST 28–30, 1862

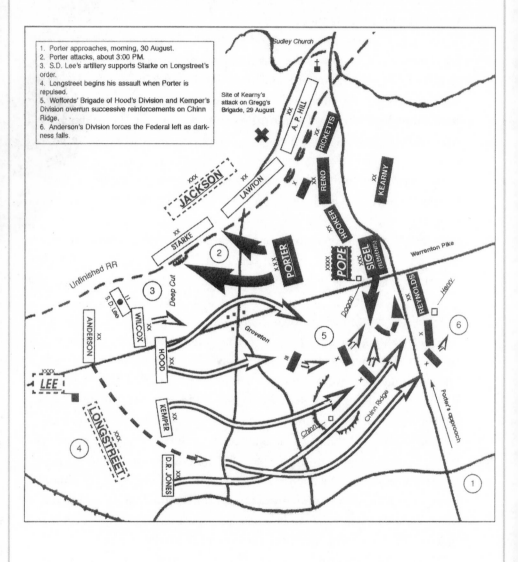

1. Porter approaches, morning, 30 August.
2. Porter attacks, about 3:00 PM.
3. S.D. Lee's artillery supports Starke on Longstreet's order.
4. Longstreet begins his assault when Porter is repulsed.
5. Woffords' Brigade of Hood's Division and Kemper's Division overrun successive reinforcements on Chinn Ridge.
6. Anderson's Division forces the Federal left as darkness falls.

Sudley Church

Site of Kearny's attack on Gregg's Brigade, 29 August

A. P. HILL

RICKETTS

RENO

KEARNY

JACKSON

LAWTON

HOOKER

STARKE

POPE

SIGEL

CLEMENTS

Warrenton Pike

Unfinished RR

S. D. Lee

WILCOX

Deep Cut

ANDERSON

HOOD

Groveton

REYNOLDS

Henry

Doson

LEE

LONGSTREET

KEMPER

Chinn

Chinn Ridge

Porter's approach

D. R. JONES

PORTER

there was a law every West Point man knew to be absolute: never reinforce failure.

Of course the problem was that the retreating troops had to cross back over that same hellish seven hundred yards. The fire on the retreat was no less brutal than it was on the attack, but this time they had to leap over the bodies of the dead and wounded they had left behind only an hour before.

On Chinn Ridge, off to the Union left, General Irwin McDowell could clearly see the chaos of Porter's retreat. He was so certain that the entire Rebel army would pursue them over that field that he ordered his entire corps, Reynolds included, to the Union center to help prevent the disaster, and in so doing he left only 2,500 men to guard the Federal left flank while in the woods and behind the hills only a stone's throw away lurked the 25,000 men of Longstreet's corps—well rested, well fed and spoiling to get into the fight.

"Courier! Locate General Longstreet and tell him that the time is . . ." Lee's trailing words were covered by the sounds of Longstreet's attack.

"I beg your pardon, sir."

"Never mind, Captain. Never mind."

Longstreet and Lee recognized the opportunity the moment McDowell came forward and without any need for consultation they ordered the charge at the very same instant.

Safely away from the heat of battle, in a meadow at the base of Chinn Ridge, stood the 5th and 10th New York Zouaves. They were magnificent soldiers and magnificent-looking as well. Crimson trousers cut so full they might appear to be dresses were bloused at midcalf by wedding-white spats. Their blue jackets were cut with the sharp, wide lapels and garnish of the Revolutionary style, and many wore red fez-type hats complete with yellow-gold tassels. They looked more like a dance troupe than the hard and proud soldiers of New York's finest militias.

McDowell had left the brave Zouaves behind at the bottom of the hill just in case of an emergency. The emergency was 490 New York militiamen swinging rifles like clubs against 25,000 screaming Rebels. Against even these odds the Zouaves chose fight over flight, and in only a matter of moments 347 lay dead or wounded on the hillside. The tidal wave of

Longstreet's army poured over them and passed on with hardly a pause, leaving behind them a sight that might have been lovely if viewed from afar—a pleasant Virginia hillside spotted with vibrant shades of red and blue "as though carpeted in the spring by wildflowers," one Texan thought as he looked back over his shoulder at the Yankees he had killed.

There was fighting left to do. Many who lived to see the sunset died before the dawn, but the battle was decided hours ago. The moment the Rebel forces rose up from the valleys and charged over the hills, crushing the bulk of Pope's army between them, John Pope had lost the Second Battle of Bull Run. Only courageous stands by individual regiments saved the Union army from total destruction. Longstreet's assault was delayed just long enough to allow the Federals to save the high ground at Henry Hill and preserve those "lines of retreat" that Pope had ridiculed only a few weeks before. "Disaster and shame lurk in the rear," he had said on the day he took command.

There was not the panic that had so humbled the nation following the initial conflict here—the retreat was slow and well ordered. These were soldiers now, where before they had been only boys, but they were in retreat nonetheless, and it was a disaster for the army and a disaster for John Pope. The army knew it—Pope did not. Not yet.

"General Lee, here is someone who wants to speak to you."

Into the opening of his tent stepped a filthy artilleryman, his face blackened with powder, his hair plastered with sweat.

"Well, my man, what can I do for you?"

"General, don't you know me?"

General and soldier laughed aloud and Robert E. Lee hugged and kissed Robert E. Lee. When they stepped apart, the general's always immaculate dress-gray uniform was smudged with soot. He wiped his son's face clean and said, "Write to your mother, son, and tell her we're both well."

WASHINGTON

It was late in the day when Navy Secretary Gideon Welles was approached by his secretary and told that Secretary Chase was waiting to see him.

Welles approached with caution. The time of day was well past normal calling hours, so the news could not possibly be good.

"Good evening, Mr. Chase, and welcome. How stands the nation's treasury?"

"Good evening to you as well, Mr. Secretary, and like everything else, the nation's treasury is a shambles. I regret the lateness of the hour, but as you must have surmised, I have pressing matters to discuss."

"I had, indeed. Please be seated."

Chase refused Welles's invitation to sit so as to take advantage of his full six feet. "Gideon—the time is long since past when this government should be rid of General McClellan. The events of the past several days have only served to verify that Mr. McClellan is incompetent, politically motivated and can be proven by his actions—or lack thereof—to be a traitor to the cause of the Union." Chase took only half a breath, as he didn't want Welles to interrupt before he had reached his point.

"The President is unwilling to act on his own, for reasons of his own. Only he and God may know what those reasons may be, for I certainly do not. Nor does Secretary Stanton."

Now the Treasury Secretary hesitated for a moment to offer Welles an opportunity to interject, but saw by his expression that he was not about to be lured untimely into dialogue, so the monologue continued.

"The Secretary of War and I have therefore prepared a document." He took a seat on Welles's sofa and removed a single sheet of paper from his valise and handed it to Welles. "A document that will *coerce* the President to act if signed by most, and preferably all, of his cabinet. Any political repercussions can then be deflected off himself and onto us, but most importantly we shall be done with McClellan and a Union man can be put in his stead."

For the most part, the charges contained in the document were retellings of McClellan's never-ending delays, or flat failures in carrying out orders, but there were some new ones that caught the eye of Secretary Welles. For the three days most recently past, General McClellan had held back over 20,000 men who had been ordered *posthaste* to General Pope's assistance. McClellan's own phrase, "to leave Pope to get out of his scrape," was damning to be sure, but even more so was a refusal to send ammunition and supplies to an army engaged with the enemy unless a cavalry escort could be provided *by the general engaged.*

"I know nothing of this charge here, Mr. Chase."

"Oh, it is all too true. General Pope requested the supplies which were *already loaded* at Alexandria and ready to roll to the troops at Manassas. McClellan informed Pope that he had no available cavalry and that he would not release the trains to roll unless Pope dispatched units of *his* cavalry as an escort."

Chase's words came faster as he became angrier. His face was red and he had trouble keeping his seat.

"Cavalry escorts are not even *required* for rail movements and to demand that Pope, whose cavalry was, needless to say, otherwise occupied, provide one . . ." He shook his head in disbelief. "Another obvious effort to *assure Pope's defeat.*" The last three words were spoken slowly. Deliberately. Ominously, to make absolutely certain that their full meaning would be known.

"General Porter even refused direct orders issued by Pope, and we have correspondence sent from Porter to Burnside stating flat out that McClellan should be 'at work' to unseat Pope! It is treason, sir, and nothing less!" Chase realized he was shouting now, and took a deep breath to regain his composure.

"So, you see, Gideon, we must take it upon ourselves to relieve our Young Napoleon, to see him dismissed from the military and placed on public trial. We cannot wait another day for Abe to act . . ." His tempo slowed and his tone lowered; he nodded his head in the direction of the cannon fire and said, ". . . the Union may not last that long."

At the bottom of the document were two signatures, Stanton's and Chase's, and the printed names of the other members of the cabinet.

"Secretary Smith has seen the document and agreed to sign, but as

Secretary of the Navy, you are next in line and he deferred to you. When you sign, he'll sign."

Welles took his time in answering. He looked at the paper and pretended to read it while he considered his response.

Deplorable. *Yes, McClellan's actions could be seen as treasonous,* he thought, but so can this document. Perhaps even more so. There is more to this. More than bickering over who will command the army. Palace coup. That's what this is. An effort by Stanton to establish himself as *de facto* Commander in Chief. Far from protecting the President politically, this is deliberately designed to weaken him. Politically, practically and every other way.

"Mr. Chase. I may agree with your goals, but I simply cannot accept your methods. While I too believe that General McClellan has been dilatory to say the least, I doubt that he is motivated by treasonous intentions. I agree that his removal is demanded by public sentiment and would be in the best interest of the country—but Abraham Lincoln is the Commander in Chief—not you nor I"—he raised his ample eyebrows and leaned slightly forward in his chair to emphasize his point—"nor even Secretary Stanton."

Chase began to resume his argument, but Welles raised his hand and continued. "Should the President request my opinion I will happily offer it to him. Perhaps I should offer it even without his seeking it, however for the cabinet to attempt to act as a body in what is wholly a military matter is well beyond our mandate."

"Our mandate, Mr. Secretary, is to protect and defend the Constitution. It would be a violation should we *fail* to act with energy and promptitude. The choice, sir, is not between propriety and impropriety—it is between McClellan and the Constitution—for one or the other must go down."

"Certain of the charges contained here are beyond my personal knowledge. I do not consider General McClellan a traitor. I believe that a general meeting of the cabinet for the purpose of openly discussing the matter to be a mandatory precursor to any overt actions."

Chase did not respond, so Welles decided to probe into the extent of the revolt.

"What has been the response of the Attorney General and Postmaster General?"

"They have not yet been consulted. We have not reached their turns on the list."

"Even should I be inclined to attach my name to so radical a document, I would never do so without consultation with them. Frankly, the getting of signatures without an interchange of views is repugnant to my ideas of duty and right.

"Again, Mr. Chase, I have no hesitation in saying to anyone at the proper time and place that McClellan should be removed from command, however I cannot . . ."

"Excuse me, gentlemen."

Chase and Welles looked to the doorway and there stood Postmaster General Montgomery Blair. Chase couldn't conceal his surprise and discomfort at the President's friend appearing out of the blue at this most inopportune moment. He looked at the petition that was still in Welles's hand and beads of sweat appeared instantly on his brow.

"General Blair! Please come in."

"Thank you, sir, and a good evening to you both, if a good evening can be had with the Rebels on our porch."

"The same to you, sir, and what brings you here so late in the day?"

Chase heaved an audible sigh upon realizing that Welles would not bring up the matter at hand.

"Concern for the capital. There are signs of panic in the streets here, gentlemen, if you've not been out today. The army is keeping order so far, but the people are loading their belongings and the northbound roads are already clogged. Pope seems optimistic, but the citizens, it seems, are not."

"Frankly, nor am I," Chase said. "Arrangements are being made at this moment to ship the entire treasury of the nation on boats to New York for safekeeping. Another setback and it will be afloat."

"Gideon. How is the navy preparing? The President wants to know."

"At the moment, the gunboats that had been left on the James River are en route to the Potomac. Beginning tomorrow or Monday, General Lee will have a difficult time should he attempt a crossing. It is also my understanding that General McClellan has prepared the Chain Bridge as well as some others for demolition should that become necessary. The capital is safe, I believe, at least for the moment."

"Be aware, sirs, that the city is rife with spies and could soon be in the grip of panic. The President is anxious that we all take the proper precautions."

"Assure Mr. Lincoln that we shall," Welles said as Chase nodded agreement.

"Thank you, sirs, and again"—he indicated the sounds of battle that seemed closer now than when he arrived only minutes ago—"have as good an evening as possible, and pack a bag."

Blair took his leave and after he was out the door, Welles said, "Don't you think that we should call him back in and consult him now on this?"

The sweat reappeared and Chase quickly said, "No! Not now. For the present it is best that he should know nothing of it."

"He has the ear of the President. And beyond that, he is the only one among us with a military education. Were I in your place General Blair would have been the *first* man I would have consulted."

"It is not yet time to bring him in. And his politics, I might add, do not differ that greatly from McClellan's own."

Politics. Welles let that be the period at the end of the conversation, as though Chase had proven his own argument for him. He shook his head and returned the petition.

"Please, Gideon, do not mention this matter to General Blair or to anyone for that matter. I shall express your concerns to Secretary Stanton."

Welles nodded and Chase left.

The Navy Secretary stood alone in his office, looking after his departed guests and wondering what tomorrow would bring.

A long gun from the city's defenses exploded so loudly it seemed next door and startled Welles from his thoughts.

I'd better go down to the telegraph office and check on the President, he thought, *and the war*. Then he spoke aloud, though still to himself, "This is going to be a very interesting week. An interesting week, indeed."

JOHN POPE'S HEADQUARTERS

George Smalley rushed to the telegraph office with his notes on the battle ready to send to the *Tribune*. The story would be significantly less than flattering for Mr. Pope. *"We have been whipped by an inferior force of inferior men, better handled than our own."*

Smalley knew the risk he was taking. Pope would not view this report lightly and might well shut down the telegraph for use by him or any other reporter, but this was a disaster of monumental proportions and no amount of rosewater would make it taste any sweeter. He needn't have worried about being the man to shut down the press—someone had already beaten him to it. By the time he arrived, the office was closed to all reporters and the race was on to Washington.

CHAPTER 4

A TOTAL ABSENCE
OF BRAINS

AUGUST 31ST
SHARPSBURG, MARYLAND

Sunday morning brought a chance of rain to Sharpsburg, Maryland. David Miller observed the Sabbath by looking out over the most beautiful stand of corn he'd ever seen and thanked God for the harvest he would reap within a month unless some disaster should befall him.

The German Baptist Brethren moved their services away from their tiny church so that this week's moderator and a parishioner could stand in the waters of Antietam Creek to perform the sacrament of Baptism in the manner that had earned them their more commonly used name— The Dunkers. Today one of Samuel Mumma's sixteen children stood waist-deep in the Antietam to be immersed three times in the soul-cleansing waters. Once for the Father, once for the Son and again for the Holy Ghost. Later they would return to the humble, white, steepleless church across from the Mumma farm to discuss among themselves the evils of war.

Kyd Douglas's family rode down the hill where they lived so that "Father" could deliver the sermon at the Reform Church and to pray for the safety of their son and his mentor, Stonewall Jackson, while the Rohrbachs attended with the Lutheran congregation to ask God's guidance for Old Abe Lincoln.

After church six-year-old Ada Mumma will join all the other little Mummas and Rohrbachs down on the creek. The family was so huge that every week, it seemed, brought another birthday, but it will be her turn next. Her turn to stand out. Her turn to be the center of everybody's attention. Seven years old. Time goes so slow when the special days are coming.

It was a beautiful, peaceful Sunday morning in picturesque Sharpsburg, Maryland.

CHANTILLY PLANTATION, VIRGINIA

Just like at Cedar Mountain, Second Manassas was followed by a rainy Sunday. References to God's tears came easily to the poets of both sides. The soggy clothes and muddy boots only added to the despair of America's army as it slogged back toward Washington in degrading retreat. They had marched straight and proud onto yet another field of battle, and once again had left the field miserable and ashamed.

WASHINGTON

President Lincoln knocked on the door of John Hay's private chambers in the Executive Mansion early on that Sunday morning. He often sought out his young private secretary when he needed someone to talk to. Six months after her son's passing, Mary had finally been tempted out of her seclusion and lured to New York, but he rarely confided in her anymore anyway. Hay knew the instant he saw the "Tycoon's" face that this was one of those moments. Lincoln handed him a dispatch.

"I received this from Pope yesterday." Hay read: *We have had a terrific battle again today . . . Under all the circumstances thought it best to draw back to this place at dark. The troops are in good heart. Do not be uneasy.*

John looked up and into the President's eyes. He saw another dispatch in Lincoln's hand and knew the President would not bother him with good news.

"And I received this one today." *Our troops are much used up . . . and worn out . . . I should like to know whether you feel secure about Washington should this army be destroyed.*

"Well, John, we are whipped again, I am afraid. The enemy reinforced on Pope and he has retired to Centreville, where he says he will be able to 'hold' his men." Hay thought for a moment that the President was on the verge of tears. "I don't like that expression. I don't like to hear him admit that his men need 'holding.'" He looked at his feet for a while and added, "The bottom's out of the tub, John. The bottom's out of the tub."

MANASSAS JUNCTION

Back on yesterday's battlefield, Lee stood alongside his proud silver stallion with the handsome black mane. He and Traveller together were one, and were thought of that way. The men of his army never pictured in their minds one without the other, for that was the way they most often saw their commander—astride Traveller, atop a hill, looking out for them all.

Lee absentmindedly patted Traveller on the nose as he spoke briefly with some reporters who had come up from Richmond to file reports on the glorious triumph. When Lee had assumed command three months earlier, Richmond was on the brink of disaster, McClellan was to the east and Pope to the north; and now, almost suddenly, both were whipped and gone. For the first time in a year Virginia was virtually free of Yankees. With the invasion repulsed, Lee was a national hero, and the people of the land were anxious to know him. But a few modest remarks thanking God and praising the men, dead and living, were all the reporters would get from Lee before he had to return to the business of war.

He grabbed Traveller's mane, placed his left foot in the stirrup and just as he lifted his right foot off of the ground a nearby artillery piece fired and the giant horse startled. Lee's wet-bottomed boot slipped and down the great man went, falling hard on both hands. One wrist was badly sprained—the other badly broken.

WASHINGTON

McClellan and Marcy sat down to breakfast in the pleasant, warm drawing room of his home in Washington. Coffee, eggs, sausage and fresh-baked bread. White cloth over a mahogany table, set with china and silver. He admired the delicate and elaborate art of Mary Ellen's silverware. "When we're finished here, wash these up," he told a servant, "and ship the silver off to Mrs. McClellan in New Jersey." In a resigned and frustrated tone he told Marcy, "It would be a horrid shame if something so elegant were to end up on the table of some vulgar boor like Jackson."

The food was wonderfully prepared and exquisitely served, but the vague and distant sounds of artillery, real or imagined, killed his appetite. He gazed out the window, as though he could see through the city, through the rain, through the hills. He closed his eyes to imagine the calamitous scene or to hold back tears.

"My boys."

That was all he said as he stared blankly out at the rain. "My boys."

A young lieutenant, drenched from the deluge outside, brought the general his morning copy of the *Washington Chronicle*, and a bad day became suddenly worse.

"The Secretary of War reports that General McClellan commands that por-tion of the Army of the Potomac that has not been sent forward to General Pope's command."

"Which means I command nothing!" he shouted at his father-in-law. "I'm sitting here sucking my thumb and doing nothing!"

With that, at least, John Pope would eagerly have agreed.

By the time Stonewall Jackson got to his tent that night he was bone-weary. Jim had the cot set up and covered with clean, dry sheets. How does he do it? Stonewall wondered. There isn't a dry sock within twenty miles, and Jim provides me with sheets. Sheets with the smell of home ironed into them. And the damned Yankees would have me give him up. The idiot Yankees just cannot understand that Jim would never be able to care for himself.

But Jackson still had work to do before he could take advantage of Jim's hard work. He sat at his field desk and opened one of his official journals—the one in which he kept track of A. P. Hill's marching transgressions. He leafed past his entry on the incident on the banks of the Rapidan, where he chastised his red-haired general for marching late and slow, and on a clean page entered that today, in the rain and muck, he had marched too fast, encouraging stragglers and outpacing the following units. "It is no less a sin to march too fast than not to march at all," he wrote.

He strained in the lantern light to focus on the words. He rubbed his aching eyes, and as he looked around the tent his attention focused once again on the cot, but he still had another duty to perform before he could lie down. He closed the journal and returned it to its proper place and then, by his cot, on his knees, like a child, he prayed. Only then did he enjoy the sheets Jim had ironed dry for him and before he slept he said one more, brief prayer. *Thank you, God, for Jim.*

WASHINGTON

James Wilson's trip from hell lasted almost five days. He had to wait for a steamer out of Fort Pulaski that chugged its way north along the coast. A well-manned canoe might have passed her at any moment. They wouldn't drop him at Washington like he requested and he had to catch a train south from Baltimore to Washington. But the trip was near its end and his life as a real soldier was finally about to begin. Surely there had been some serious fighting down around Richmond recently and McClellan was bound to be in need of some replacement regimental commanders. A good fight always opens up some quality positions. Just not too good a fight, Wilson prayed. Please Lord, don't let it be over. He knew it was wrong to pray for a war to go on, but he couldn't help it. He had to get into the fight. He had to lead that one, gallant, desperate assault. He had to. His worst nightmare along the way was to get off the train at Washington and be greeted by victory parades where he could only stand on the side of the road and watch the real heroes, McClellan and the others, being showered with the adoration of a grateful nation.

But what greeted him in Washington was anything but a celebration.

What greeted him bordered on sheer panic. He had trouble getting off the train for all the people clamoring to get on. Once he pushed and shoved and elbowed his way out of the station and onto the street, the sights there were even worse. Wagons were piled high with the stuff of everyday life, all tightly tied down and bound for points north. That wasn't the worst of it. The worst part was the soldiers. The wounded were bad enough, but he was disgusted by the cowards. Men in filthy, disheveled uniforms aimlessly wandered the streets, still wearing the stale stare of fear.

Wilson found a man—one man—who still seemed to have his wits about him.

"What in God's name has happened here?"

"Pope's been whipped," the man said. "Lee's done busted out of Richmond and you can bet your momma's housecat he'll be here by tomorrow."

"What about McClellan? Where's he?"

"McClellan? My guess is he's sitting up on H Street somewhere havin' a cup of tea while the darkies load his wagon."

Wilson by now was so thoroughly confused that he had to start over.

"Did he take Richmond already?"

The man was flabbergasted. "*Take Richmond?* Where the hell you been, young fella? This fella Lee's done kicked McClellan out of Virginia weeks ago and now he's done kicked Pope's butt out too."

"Oh, my God." Wilson had to get to the War Office. He had to get his regiment. It wasn't only about him anymore. Suddenly James Wilson's war became more than a painting on the wall at West Point. Suddenly the war that was supposed to be so much fun and so easily won had turned into a desperate, frantic struggle for survival.

The man started to turn away, but Wilson grabbed his arm for one more question. "Where is the War Office?"

The man laughed and shook his head. "My guess'd be it's in Philly by now."

SEPTEMBER 1ST

The rain continued to fall hard and the roads quickly clogged with stuck wagons and mired artillery. Teamsters whipped horses and mules without mercy and when that didn't work they commandeered exhausted troops to pull the damned things out of the mud. The troops had just fought three hard days of vicious combat. They were tired and hungry, footsore and wet, but on Monday morning, Jackson's men were once again astride the Union lines—lying in wait for Pope's poor army.

Pope ordered Phil Kearny ahead to deal with the threat on the grounds of a mansion called Chantilly. In the midst of a violent thunderstorm, the two armies joined one more time.

It was a truly bizarre spectacle, this battle of Chantilly. The rank and file of both sides knew it was nothing more than a period on the end of Manassas. The Yankees just wanted to go home, and the Rebels saw no harm in letting them. That was, after all, exactly what they had been fighting to get them to do.

By afternoon the storm had become so fierce that thunder was indistinguishable from cannon fire. Lightning bolts and artillery rounds took limbs from trees and the rain blew across the field in blinding waves. Visibility was nil and running in the ankle-deep mud next to impossible for men and horses too weary even to walk.

Someone sent a messenger to Jackson requesting permission to withdraw his men "because all my ammunition is wet."

"Tell him the enemy's ammunition is just as wet as his!"

Even as bizarre as this battle was, it was a battle nonetheless. Gallant men died, and the wounded fell again under the care of Clara Barton.

The floor at her feet was pink with the mixture of rain and blood as more and more arms and legs were thrown carelessly onto a pile.

"Miss Barton, can you ride?"

She looked up to see a mounted lieutenant. His words were spoken calmly, but the look on his face betrayed the panic in his heart.

"Yes, sir."

"But you have no ladies' saddle—could you ride mine?"

"Yes, sir, or without it if you have a blanket and surcingle."

"Then you can risk another hour," he said and turned and galloped off.

General Kearny was angry. He was less angry with the Rebels than with his own superiors and his own men. One last attempt had to be made to halt the Confederates here. Franklin and Sumner had finally reached the field from Alexandria, and if order could be maintained here, and panic averted, then Washington might yet be saved. But his men would fire and reload on the run, and turn and fire and run again.

Kearny put the reins of his horse in his mouth so that he could use his only hand to draw his saber to rally his troops. It was either a lightning strike or an artillery burst that made his horse bolt forward, for both exploded all around him, and in a flash the hero of the Mexican War found himself totally surrounded by a drenched pack of unhappy Rebels. They shouted for him to surrender. He offered his captors a textbook-sharp saber salute, snapping the blade to touch the brim of his hat, pointing to heaven. Then, with a twist of his butt in the saddle, he turned and spurred his mount to a run.

No fewer than ten balls struck him—all at once, all in the back, and all in full view of his regiment. The battle was over and the rout was on.

"Now is your time, Miss Barton," the young lieutenant said. "The enemy is already breaking over the hills. Try the train. It will go through unless they have flanked and cut the bridge a mile above us. In that case I've a reserve horse for you and you must take your chances to escape across the country." He saluted Clara Barton and turned and vanished again into the deluge.

She didn't want to leave. She hated the thought of leaving these boys behind. But the army was in retreat. She could see them already, coming over the hills in huge numbers. She gave one more wounded boy one more sip of water and headed to the platform to get on the train.

WASHINGTON

We have rewritten the document in a way that you might find more palatable, Gideon. Secretary Stanton is most insistent that you reconsider."

Welles scanned the new version of Stanton's treachery and noted that this version was in the hand of the Attorney General rather than the Secretary of War, and carried Blair's signature as well. Four names were missing—Smith, Bates, Seward and Welles.

"Bates has not yet been approached and Seward, once again, is absent. It seems always to be so when there is an emergency—'Seward is absent.' "

"It's amusing to me, Mr. Chase, that in this instance our roles have so drastically reversed. Nine months ago I was telling you that McClellan was devious, and a poor choice to lead our armies. You, however, were on the bandwagon and quite certain that our Young Napoleon would end the war in only a matter of days."

"I recall, sir, and the only objection I have now to *your* objections of that time is that they weren't stated strongly enough."

"They were stated as strongly as I could, but that is no longer the issue today. The issue today is *ultimata*. We are called together by Abraham Lincoln to be his friends and advisers, perhaps too informally at times, but that is, in fact, our purpose. I am sorry, Sal, but I shall not be a party to this."

Henry Halleck, General in Chief of the United States Army, looked for all the world like a spanked child. He approached the President timidly. Whipped. He wiped the rainwater from his face and said, "These two wires arrived at the War Office within minutes of each other. This one is from McClellan."

The road is filled with wagons & stragglers coming towards Alexandria. We were badly beaten yesterday & Pope's right is entirely exposed. . . . To speak frankly, & the occasion requires it, there seems to be a total absence of brains & I fear the total destruction of the Army. It is my deliberate opinion that the interests of the nation demand that Pope should fall back tonight if possible and not one moment is to be lost.

I shall be up all night & ready to obey any orders you give me.

G B McClellan

When Lincoln had finished reading he said nothing, but only held out his hand for the other telegram.

"And this is from Pope."

I think it my duty to call your attention to the unsoldierly and dangerous conduct of many brigade and some division commanders of the forces sent here from the Peninsula. Every word and act and intention is discouraging, and calculated to break down the spirits of the men and produce disaster. My advice to you is that you draw back this army to Washington. You may avoid greater disaster by doing so.

John Pope,
H'Qtrs in the Saddle

Lincoln held both dispatches. "At long last," he said, "my generals have found one thing upon which they can agree. We are whipped, and must retreat back to the very point from which we started a year and a half ago."

Halleck and Lincoln sat in the President's office awaiting George McClellan's arrival. The general had sent for McClellan as ordered, but had no idea as to the President's intentions. As they waited, Halleck took the time to consider the man. He is only comfortable while standing, Halleck observed. Chairs aren't made for men so tall. He looks like a grown man sitting in a child's chair with his knees tucked under his chin. He watched the lanky Westerner fidget and tap his toes and check the wall clock about twice every minute. The President of the United States is as nervous as a cat, Halleck thought. And then it dawned on him. The Commander in Chief, in time of war, hates confrontation! He can deal with it on a grand scale, and from a distance, but not one-on-one, face-to-face . . .

The thought was interrupted by the sounds of a small army marching down the hallway. And then another thought struck Halleck like a bullet.

He remembered his meeting with Burnside back on the Peninsula just a few weeks ago. Fragments of the conversation rushed back into his mind . . . *march on Washington . . . replace the government . . . capable of it.* And then two more words, maybe more ominous than all the rest . . . *Julius Caesar.* And suddenly, in Halleck's mind, the footsteps in the hallway became the sounds of an approaching enemy. *The Potomac—The Rubicon.* Without thinking, the general touched his hip, where his revolver would have been when he commanded armies in the field, but now he was unarmed and more than just a little bit embarrassed at having such thoughts. Still, he was relieved when the sounds of twenty pairs of feet stopped, and only one continued.

McClellan marched into the doorway, unarmed.

Absolutely confident that he was being called upon to save the Republic yet again, he literally swaggered into the office; pulling his short frame as tall as he could, he was fully prepared to accept the apologies of the President of the United States, demand the firing of Halleck and Stanton, instruct the Commander in Chief that he should stop meddling in military affairs and proceed from this moment forward to win the war on honorable terms. Back to the Union as it was. Back to Mary Ellen in New Jersey.

"General McClellan," Lincoln began without so much as a 'hello,' "we have called you here to discuss some very serious allegations that have been brought against you and your subordinates." McClellan's arrogant posture vanished in an instant. He wouldn't have been more surprised to walk into the office and see Jeff Davis himself. Prepared to attack, the Young Napoleon found himself suddenly on the defensive. "General Pope has accused elements of the Army of the Potomac of everything short of treason." McClellan puffed himself back up, his face flushed, but before he could speak the President stood and towered over Little Mac like a tree. *Comfortable when standing,* Halleck thought. "We have received confirmation that various commanders formerly of your command have responded slowly or not at all to orders issued by the general commanding in the field. It is the belief of much of the government that this is being deliberately done, frankly, to assure Pope's defeat and the return of the command of the combined armies to you. Certain dispatches have come to our attention, particularly from General Porter, highly critical of General Pope. Dispatches that take a very dangerous tone, George—a tone that suggests insubordination." Lincoln put up his hand to forestall McClellan's objections. "Be this true, or be it not true, it now falls upon you to prove to the nation otherwise."

Lincoln took one step closer until he stood toe-to-toe with McClellan, looking directly down on the little general. "General McClellan, the success or failure of the Republic cannot depend upon jealousies and envy among generals. Your friends in the field today must cooperate in every way with General Pope or the entire cause may be lost. General Halleck and I have called you here to urge you to communicate with your former commanders in the field and to inform them that the future of the Republic depends upon their cooperation. Will you do this?"

McClellan now had to choke down both his pride and his rage and neither was a small bite. Insulted by imbeciles. Scurrilous and totally unfounded lies, spread by idiots and believed by simpletons. From what McClellan knew, Porter had *saved* the army from total destruction. The man deserved a parade!

Halleck stood aside and studied both the men and the moment. Lincoln was perfectly calm. The tone in his voice held only an ominous hint of what might come should McClellan handle this badly. Halleck could see that McClellan was fighting a war within himself. His blood was up, but he would not look up into the President's face. He could not allow himself to assume such a subordinate posture to this man.

McClellan snapped to attention, looking straight ahead at the frayed and dirty collar of Lincoln's shirt. "Mr. President, I assure you that I have in no way encouraged any insurrection within the Army of Virginia. It is impossible for me to conceive that General Porter or any other of my former command would behave in any manner that would jeopardize their men or their nation."

"Nonetheless, the appearance of it is there, and the appearance of it is no less jeopardizing than the actual design. Will you now, this instant, communicate with them and urge their cooperation?"

A long hesitation made Halleck very uncomfortable. McClellan's entire body was clenched. His jaw. His fists. And then, "At your request, sir, of course I will."

As Halleck made his way back to the War Office, he was still as tense as a bowstring. His heart pounded and his nerves were at the snapping point. McClellan had behaved well, or at least as well as could be expected, but Halleck still couldn't escape the sense of dread. What he remembered most from this incredibly bizarre meeting was his own fear of what McClellan might do.

He reached the entrance to the War Office and found his way blocked by a young major he'd never seen before.

"General Halleck?"

"What do you want, Major?"

"A regiment, sir."

The brand-new insignia of a major's rank did little to compensate for James Wilson's boyish appearance. What Halleck saw was a little boy with peach-fuzz chin whiskers, pumped up like a peacock and dressed up like a soldier.

"A regiment? Oh, of course, I'm sure I've a spare around here somewhere."

Wilson was unimpressed with the general's sarcasm, and equally unimpressed with the man. He had expected a strong, bold, towering man. A "command presence." What he found was a flustered, fat, balding, disheveled, scared little bureaucrat.

"Sir, I'm James Wilson, Class of '60 . . . ," as though that should mean something to Henry Halleck, Class of '39, ". . . and I was given permission to come here and apply to you directly for a regimental command, and it looks as though you could use some good officers right now."

"We could always use good officers, Major Wilson," Halleck said as he finally managed to push past the impetuous young officer. "Give my clerk your name and where you can be found and if something comes up we'll find you."

September 2nd

Johnny Cook would play no Reveille today, as "quiet" was the attitude on the retreat. No one was in the mood for joking, and the fifteen-year-old bugle boy and mascot of the 4th U.S. Artillery got no good-luck head pats today. They had fought their guns at Cedar Mountain and yielded under A. P. Hill's assault, and again at Bull Run, where they fought well, but again in a losing cause. Twice they had been in the front of the action with eternal glory only seconds away, and twice the tide of battle turned against them. Little Johnny Cook assisted in limbering the pieces, mounted his milk-white pony in silence and rode a full length behind Captain Campbell so no one would see the tears.

His friends came together to pay their respects over the body of Phil Kearny. The empty sleeve of his Union blue uniform remained neatly pinned within the buttons of his tunic in the Napoleonic pose, but the rest of him was a mess. Someone had made some effort to wash the mud off his face and out of his hair, but he had fallen forward off his horse and had landed on his face. His nose was grotesquely broken and bent, and there was little skin left on his right cheek. The mud couldn't be gotten out of his uniform. Some of the bullets had passed clean through him and the blood around the holes seemed still wet from the rain and mud.

"Poor Kearny. He deserved a better death than that," A. P. Hill whispered to Longstreet.

"Send his remains forward—it may be some consolation to his family," Lee said.

"Use my personal ambulance," Jackson added.

"General Lee?" He looked over and saw Stuart with Kearny's horse. God, what a beautiful animal. Black as pitch. Strong and proud and uncontrollably defiant, even under Stuart's masterful hand.

"Send the horse too."

The entire group turned as one, astounded at Lee's order. "I'll pay for him," Lee said. "But this is Kearny's animal. Look in his eyes." Lee stroked the stallion's snout. "No other man can ever master this one."

They watched as their friend's body was placed in the ambulance, each man saying his own prayer. Only after the wagon had pulled away did Lee speak.

"This must end, gentlemen. We have fought a dozen battles in which more men have died than in all of our previous wars combined. Good men." He nodded toward Phil Kearny's hearse still bouncing slowly off through the mist, the black stallion, empty saddle, trailing behind. "Good men on both sides. Officers and men."

The four leaders of the Confederate army, Lee, Longstreet, Jackson and Stuart, walked their horses slowly back up the hill toward Lee's tent. Lee had discovered too late that he could not mount Traveller without assistance because his wrists hurt almost to tears.

"Virginia is safe at last, at least for the moment. The cotton embargo is doing its work in England and France. Their economies are dying things, and their governments must join us soon or die with them. It is only the slave issue that keeps them away."

He looked at the three for a moment. He knew almost everything about these men. It was his job to know their abilities and temperaments, to know when they would fight and how. It struck him now, though, that he had never discussed the Ethiopian question with any of them and did not know where they stood on the issue. It just wasn't important.

"Slavery is not the question here, sirs. It cannot be permitted to be. If that is the issue for which we fight we will surely lose. We will lose because . . ."

He caught himself and stopped in midsentence. His lecture on the evils of slavery might be wasted on these men and cause a breach between himself and any who felt strongly on the matter. Politics must be put aside among military men, but the point had to be made to put the strategy in perspective.

". . . We will lose because the world will align itself against us. Europe, Russia, all modern nations have banned the practice and will not come to our aid if they see it as the issue. I am deeply afraid, sirs, that unless we win a decisive victory soon that Mr. Lincoln will seek to make it the issue." Only Longstreet responded, and he did so only with a nod of approval.

"Maryland is the key," Lee told his generals. "She is Southern and is being held in the Union against her will." He paused to think it through once more. The grand strategy. While Virginia is safe, we must take this war north, through Maryland and into Pennsylvania. The people of the United States have long since tired of this struggle, and if the trials of war can be brought to bear on the populations of *Northern* states the elections may well go our way. "If Maryland can be encouraged to secede, if Washington falls, then England will lend us her navy to break the blockade. We must take this war north, gentlemen. Only then will the will of those people to fight be broken and we will soon be able to get on with the work of building our new nation."

"We must look closely after our supply lines."

This time it was Jackson who expressed concern, and Longstreet was pleased to be relieved of his duties as Chief Naysayer.

"Our supply lines will be no longer than theirs are now. It is my hope, General, that the people of Maryland will welcome us—open their stores and homes and fields to us. They will accept Confederate scrip and provide us with the bounty of their harvest. But you are correct, General Jackson. I believe that we will be welcome there, but it cannot be assured, and this must be made perfectly clear. No plunder or pillage will be allowed. This will be a liberating army, and not a conquering one. Looters and thieves will be shot." That was Lee's plan. That was his hope.

"Consider please, sirs, what I have said. Tomorrow offer me your advice and concerns—and be prepared to move north—into Maryland."

After his generals had left him, Lee wrote out a personal voucher—to reimburse the Confederacy for the loss of Kearny's horse.

Another dispatch came into the President's hands from Pope, today's more disconcerting even than yesterday's.

Unless something can be done to restore tone to this army it will melt away before you know it. Lincoln was forced to agree. Once again he sought out John Hay.

"We no longer have an army, John. It is demoralized and disorganized. A decision must be made and command placed in the hands of a single man."

"Is that man not Halleck?"

"Halleck is wholly for the service. He does not care who succeeds or who fails so the service is benefited, but he is little more than a first-rate clerk. We must use what tools we have." The thought had been in his head for days, but he had dared not speak it to anyone until now. "There is no man in the army who can man these fortifications and lick these people of ours into shape half as well"—he hesitated, almost afraid to hear himself speak the words aloud; he closed his eyes as he spoke them—"as McClellan."

"But your War Secretary will bust a gut if command reverts back to McClellan! Half the nation, most of the Congress and virtually all of your own cabinet think him guilty of treason. You told me yourself only yesterday that you feared it may be true and last night Stanton expressed his views clearly enough at dinner."

"You may add *Mrs. Lincoln* to that list," the President said with a weak smile and shake of the head. "She writes me from New York that relieving McClellan should be my first priority." Another shake of the head and a moment of silence while the President thought. "Perhaps McClellan is slow, John, but I doubt that he is a traitor, and if he can't fight himself, he excels in making others ready to fight."

Lincoln considered making the trip alone, but he simply could not. For lots of reasons. He needed a witness. He needed a military presence. He also needed moral support, but that would not be available anywhere. Stanton was obviously out of the question, so he left the mansion in search of General Halleck to make another call on George McClellan.

As they walked, they didn't speak. Lincoln bristled the whole way. There was no purpose to his stride, like walking to a deathbed. This is all so very hard. George McClellan. What is it about this man that he should intimidate the President of the United States? It's not only his arrogance. They're all arrogant. But the Young Napoleon is arrogant on a grand scale. The Emperor of Arrogance. He flushed with anger, remembering the incident from last year, back before the Peninsula campaign ever began, when he had made this same walk down H Street to call on his top-ranking officer and found him not home. The President had waited in the parlor for His Majesty to return and when he did, McClellan walked right past him, without so much as a word, leaving the President of the United States sitting, hat in hand, in the parlor. Lincoln remembered the attitude of his manservant when he came downstairs later. Arrogance, it seems, is contagious. "General McClellan begs to inform Your Excellency that he has retired for the night."

It was the memory of this affront, this humiliation, this insult to the office more than anything else that made the President hesitate before knocking on the door, hat in hand, once again. If only there were an alternative.

McClellan was taking breakfast.

"Mr. President—General Halleck. Please enter and have a seat. May I offer you coffee?"

"Thank you, no. Obviously, we come on urgent business. General Halleck has recently met with members of his own staff who were sent south into Virginia in order to ascertain the true condition of our army. We are informed that it is worse than even we had imagined. We have ordered General Pope to march as quickly as possible to within the confines of Washington and we have come here, sir, to ask that you assume command of the returning troops as they enter the city and to be responsible for the defense of the capital."

Stanton's long, perfumed, brown beard was streaked with gray from the lower lip down. In the best of times those whiskers were constantly tugged and groomed, but today he pulled them so hard his chin hurt. He ordered the cessation of liquor sales in the city and that government clerks be drilled and armed. He ordered the capital's armories emptied and their contents prepared for shipment to New York—and then he left his office on his way to a scheduled meeting of the cabinet. He looked forward to it. Even though he and Chase had been successful in gathering only the four signatures, his petition to dismiss and court-martial McClellan was powerful enough. Today, the President's folly would end, and the Secretary of War would finally take charge of the war effort— as it should have been all along.

He was early, or at least not late, so he decided to stop by Halleck's office on the way. It was here, hours after the fact, that he found out about the morning meeting on H Street. Immediately there was no air left in the room as an asthma attack hit him like a hammer to the chest, but he forced himself to run toward the Executive Mansion. His body screamed for air and his starving lungs pleaded with him to stop. Halfway up the stairs his lungs won out and he had to lean against the wall for a moment to concentrate entirely on breathing. When he finally stepped into the doorway of the meeting room, Gideon Welles thought for a moment that the War Secretary had been shot. His face was pale and panicked and wet with sweat. His lungs rattled with every breath as he screwed up all the indignation he could muster to announce that the President had reinstated McClellan.

"This cannot be allowed to happen!" Chase shouted. "Pope has failed, but mostly because of McClellan! Pope may not be the answer, but McClellan *surely* is not." The room nodded agreement, but the next voice heard was that of Lincoln, who had eavesdropped from the doorway.

"May I ask then, 'Who is?' "

Four men tried to speak at once, but with Stanton still struggling for each breath, it was Chase whose persistence and volume demanded final attention.

"Mr. President, giving command to McClellan is the equivalent of giving Washington to the Rebels."

"Gentlemen, no one is more aware of McClellan's shortcomings than am I. He has the slows, and is good for nothing in an offensive campaign and his actions toward Pope over the past week have been unpardonable. But I *must* have him to reorganize the army and bring it out of chaos . . . There has been a design—a purpose in breaking down Pope, without regard of consequences to the country. It is shocking, but there is no remedy at present. McClellan has the army with him. I should gladly appoint someone else were there another general capable of performing the miracle needed now, but there is none."

Silence.

"The order is mine, and I shall be responsible for it to the country."

Even the finality of Lincoln's last statement failed to halt the debate. Chase railed on, but to no avail. Stanton pulled the petition out from his pocket and took a step forward toward Lincoln, determined to end this madness now and forever. This man had no business being President and had even said so himself. *Now*, Stanton thought, *I must take charge of the conduct of the war and leave the President to his speechifying*. Stanton's face reddened and his hand shook. He opened his mouth to speak and felt a firm hand grasp his arm. He turned to the right and looked square into the face of Gideon Welles, who pulled Stanton back a step and placed himself forcefully between him and Lincoln. A stern expression said loudly without words what had to be said. Producing this document after the fact would be nothing short of mutinous, and would accomplish nothing more than the firing of the Secretary of War. Stanton's initial response was to pull away from the pompous Welles and deliver the ultimatum, but Welles stood firm and at that moment the President's voice rose above the clamor and said, "The decision is *made*, gentlemen! We must use what tools we have, and, for the moment, George McClellan *is* in command."

Welles and Stanton remained standing face-to-face for a moment longer until the tension in Stanton's features all suddenly went soft. He closed his eyes and quietly returned the document to the safety of his coat pocket.

"There will be another day, Gideon. And may God grant that it be soon."

George Brinton McClellan was miraculously cured of his chronic case of "the slows." The only thing that caused even the slightest delay was the time consumed in the ritual donning of the regalia of command. His staff, who had for the last several weeks been the only troops he actually commanded, witnessed and assisted in the ceremonial dressing of the general in his finest uniform, complete with the gold sash of command and the elegant dress sword which, in the manner of Emperor Napoleon's crown, he presumed to attach himself.

Once properly attired, he stood and admired himself in the full mirror, attending to the minutest of details, as any good soldier should.

"Very well, gentlemen," he said to his staff. "It is time for me to go out and pick up my army."

John Bell Hood was a Kentuckian for whom it was a personal affront that his home state remained tacitly within the Union of Invaders. Soon after hostilities had begun, Hood moved to Texas to raise a regiment, and proceeded to pound them into the toughest and most reckless sons-of-bitches in the whole damned Rebel army.

Hard-nosed, Texas-mean and Kentucky-stubborn, there was no way Hood was about to turn loose of the ambulances *his* men had captured at Chinn Ridge. Orders be damned. Chain-of-command be damned. Damn 'em all! They're mine and no lily-livered son-of-a-bitch on God's green earth will get 'em without a fight! A Matter of Honor.

"Release the equipment to General Evans as ordered, General Hood."

"I regret, General Longstreet, that as a matter of honor, I cannot and I shall not."

"He has issued you a direct order, General. Do you choose to disobey?"

"General Longstreet, my men took those wagons, died for those wagons. Hell! My men *need* those wagons! General Evans was nowhere in *sight* when we took those wagons and he has no right to them. Sir!"

"But General Evans is your superior officer, General Hood, and he has issued you an order!"

Hood snapped to attention, looked directly and defiantly straight ahead at nothing and refused to reply.

"Are you prepared to risk arrest and court-martial over such an issue?"

"I am, sir."

Longstreet bristled. Pride will be the death of this army. "Then proceed immediately to Culpeper and report yourself under arrest for insubordination." There was no anger in Longstreet's voice. Quiet exasperation. Stand the child in the corner until he agrees to behave.

This was absolutely the last thing Lee needed. Preparations were hastily being made for an invasion of the North. The war will be won here, or it will go on forever. And now he faced the prospect of entering Maryland short yet another of his finest generals. With so many good men down, Ewell, Taliaferro and more, he could not allow a petty "matter of honor" to cost him Hood as well.

Out of earshot of the combatants, Lee approached Old Pete to ask a personal favor.

"General Longstreet."

"Yes, sir."

"May I ask you please to reconsider the judgment against General Hood. I understand and agree that his disobedience cannot go unpunished, but sending him so far to the rear at such a time as he may be desperately needed is impractical. Remove him from command and send him to the rear of his column—but keep him close at hand. I fear he may soon be needed."

* * *

While Generals Pope and McDowell were universally despised, there was no one with a greater personal loathing of Pope than General John Hatch. He was a professional soldier and a cavalryman "by birth," but an earlier disagreement with Pope resulted in his "demotion" to an infantry command and the resentment he harbored toward his commanding officer would go with him to his grave.

Hatch rode alongside Pope and McDowell as they led the retreating forces back toward Washington, and it was he who first spotted the small band of mounted men approaching from the north.

Please, God, he thought, *let it be.*

He fought the urge to reach for his field glasses for confirmation, but he couldn't fight the smile that spread slowly across his face like a rising sun. By the time he was dead solid certain that his prayer had been answered, John Hatch beamed like a lighthouse. The riders were led by George McClellan. Now he only fought the urge to cheer like a schoolboy. He inched forward to hear what words would pass between the two competing generals.

"General Pope."

"How may I help you, General?"

"I have been ordered by the President of the United States to assume command of your armies as they return to Washington."

Pope was not surprised.

"Very well, sir. I request permission to proceed forward with them into the capital."

"Naturally, General." An uncomfortable moment passed while both men debated what to do or say next. The war provided the answer. "I hear cannon fire," McClellan said. "Is there an engagement?"

"Not that I am aware of. Our rear guard is being prodded but not so vigorously today."

"Proceed on into the capital then, General Pope." And with a smile perhaps a bit too broad McClellan added, "I shall ride to the sounds of battle."

A salute was mandatory by military courtesy, but both men sat defiantly watching each other, waiting for the other to demonstrate his submissiveness by being the first. McClellan sat straight in the saddle, looking directly into the eyes of his vanquished foe, while Pope, who naturally stood more than a foot taller than "Little Mac," somehow appeared to Hatch to be the smaller of the two.

Finally, the moment passed and Pope grudgingly offered his conniving "superior" a limp and resentful touch of the hat. McClellan, unable to resist adding a little flair for the benefit of all, tightened his knees into Dan Webster's ribs and bridled in the animal's snout so that he would drop slightly down into a well-rehearsed bow as his rider snapped off a salute that would make a cadet proud.

Hatch could no longer keep it in. He turned his horse so that he faced his own brigade, and with his back to Pope and McDowell, he shouted for all to hear, "Boys! McClellan is in command again! Three cheers!"

An artillery salute would not have been heard above the cheers that rolled like a wave southward into Virginia as word passed backward down the retreating lines. "Mac is back!" Hats sailed into the air. Flags came unfurled and the bands began to play martial tunes. "Mac! Mac! Mac!" The men shouted and rushed forward to touch his horse or his boot. McClellan beamed and stood high in the stirrups and removed his own hat and waved it over his head in salute to his army. The men were no longer hunched over. No longer tired. No longer beaten. Like Lazarus brought back from the dead, the entire Union army in a single, miraculous moment, returned to the land of the living, tall and proud and ready to turn and fight.

Corporal John Strickler got off the train at Washington's Union Station. He and his buddies knew nothing of the recent losses at Second Bull Run and were bursting with pride at their new blue uniforms and bright new flags and their visions of the growing capital. Strickler was especially proud. Two weeks in the army and he was a corporal already and having the time of his life.

Work on the Washington Monument had been halted and the huge base stood unfinished and ugly—but the dome of the Capitol Building was nearing completion and struck him as the most beautiful thing he had ever seen.

Most of the boys of the 130th had never been out of Pennsylvania before and rarely out of Harrisburg. But two weeks in the service had made them ready for a fight. Three weeks ago they had joined their brand-new regiment and had survived hours upon of hours of drilling and marching—every waking hour, it seemed, of every day for two whole weeks. Camp Curtin was behind them now and they were soldiers and ready "to see the elephant." Any day now, these former clerks and ware-housemen would get their guns and be taught how to use them. Any day now, they would be sent into battle against the goddamn Rebels and they were busting at their new brass buttons to get there.

As the 130th Pennsylvania climbed out of their freight cars in Washing-ton, the 6th Alabama jumped from theirs at Manassas Junction. Colonel John Brown Gordon watched as his men bounded from the train as anx-ious as boys to get out of school. They rushed into their lines, waiting for the fun to begin.

Unlike Strickler and his pals from Pennsylvania, these were battle-tested soldiers. Their officers weren't strangers anymore, but heroes. Gordon had escaped so many tight scrapes totally unscathed, but with his clothes torn and bullet-ripped, that his men thought him invinci-ble—bulletproof—and Gordon did nothing to disavow the reputation.

They belonged to Harvey Hill's division and had not been invited to the Second Manassas party. They had stayed behind to protect Rich-mond for as long as there was anything there to protect their capital from. Now that Virginia was Yankee-free, they could join the fun. The 6th Alabama ached for a fight, just like the boys from Harrisburg—and they already knew how to use their guns.

They and the other units up from Richmond barely replaced the dead and wounded from the recent hard work.

Stonewall Jackson again stayed up late, straining his eyes as he drafted the order of march for the morning. Copies were sent to his division commanders. There would be no misunderstandings this day, even if he had to violate his sacrament of secrecy.

Tired though he was, Jackson was certain that his internal organs had once again been bounced out of balance, so he walked around his tent for a while with his left arm held high over his head until he felt them return to their proper alignment. Then he prayed, and then he went to sleep.

CHAPTER 5

A MOST RAGGED, LEAN AND HUNGRY SET OF WOLVES

SEPTEMBER 3RD

W hy are your men not on the road, General Gregg?"
The proud South Carolinian bristled at Jackson's tone. He and his men had saved Jackson's ass only last week. They had suffered 613 casualties, including 41 officers, on the banks of the unfinished railroad, and those who had survived had been prepared to die. They had spent that night sleeping among the bodies of the men they had killed. Gregg had received not a single word of thanks or recognition from Jackson. In fact the first words that Stonewall had spoken to him since that day were, "Why are your men not on the road?"

Making no effort to disguise his disgust, Gregg sharply replied, "They are filling their canteens, sir. We shall be 'on the road' shortly."

Jackson nodded in spite of his irritation and continued to watch as the boys from South Carolina made their preparations. A moment later Hill rode up and positioned himself between the two men.

"Your units were to have been advancing by now, General Hill."

At this point Gregg was no more than fifteen minutes late in his departure, but Hill restrained himself from remarking upon it and said instead, "Yes, sir."

It was not until Jackson had seen the last of Gregg's heroes marching north that he turned south to check on the remainder of his command.

The long march continued late into the day and straggling became unbearable. The roads were still wet and the men slogged mile after mile on bloody, muddy, unshod feet. Jackson kept a close watch on Hill all morning long and was ready to pounce at the slightest provocation. The provocation, as it turned out, at least in Jackson's mind, was anything but slight.

The time came and went for a mandated rest, and still Hill's troops marched on, the lines stretching farther and farther apart. Hill and his staff rode at the head of the column with rarely a look back to check on their progress. Jackson could contain his fury no longer. He put his horse to a run and located Colonel Edward Thomas, commander of the leading brigade.

"Colonel—it is well past the time to halt your men in accordance with regulations. A fifteen-minute rest will commence immediately."

Colonel Thomas gave the order and the men gratefully fell out of ranks by the roadside. Up ahead, Hill rode on while Jackson moved off the road himself to witness developments.

The rest period expired and the men were back on their feet before Hill had noticed and returned.

"By whose orders was the column halted, Colonel?"

"By General Jackson's."

Hill felt the red hairs on the back of his neck bristle. His heart pounded and his muscles stiffened and the hot blood of anger rushed to his face. In an instant Jackson appeared in front of him, anxiously awaiting the climax of the confrontation that had begun on the banks of the Rapidan.

Little Powell removed his sword and handed it to his commander. "If you take command of my troops in my presence, take my sword also."

"Put up your sword and consider yourself under arrest for neglect of duty. General Branch—take command of the division."

"You're not fit to be a general!" Hill snapped. Without a salute he turned and rode to the rear to join John Bell Hood, another general under arrest, relieved of command and awaiting charges.

* * *

In pain and in sickness Lee's army marched on. It was a sight new to many Virginians this far north who were accustomed to the disciplined, well-dressed and well-equipped Union troops who had occupied their homeland for the better part of a year. It came as a shock for some to see their victorious army looking so sad.

One young man sat on a hill and watched all day as the noble Rebels passed below. He opened his diary and wrote ". . . They were the dirtiest, lousiest, filthiest, piratical-looking cut throat men I ever saw. A most ragged, lean and hungry set of wolves. Yet there was a dash about them that the Northern men lacked."

Lee's men would have laughed at the boy. It is somehow hard to feel "dashing" while your feet bleed and your stomach churns. But the green, lush fields of Maryland lay just ahead, and there, they were told, things would be better.

SEPTEMBER 4TH

There was not so much as a touch of fall in the air on this Thursday morning. It was a pleasant dawn, but not so cool as to offer any hope of relief from the relentless heat of midday. The wide, shallow waters of the Potomac River looked floated with a million copper pennies as a golden light skimmed over the high spots. The flora was still green with the growth of summer. It was so beautiful and peaceful a sight that even an army approached with quiet reverence. So quiet was this army that birds and crickets and even the morning breeze could be heard as it brushed past the trees.

Standing on the Virginia side of White's Ford, Robert E. Lee took a moment to himself to enjoy the scene and to think for just one more moment about the course he was taking. A half a mile away is Maryland—United States. Say what you will. Justify it however you will. In the North this army will be seen as invaders, though they didn't consider themselves as invaders when they came into Virginia. Words. Semantics. It has all gone on for so terribly long. Six weeks, people had thought it would last, and it has now been over a year and it must end. Those people have more than we do. More of everything. More guns, horses and millions more men. The longer it lasts, the less our chances of success. "Our last, best hope." Someone else's words, but this is ours. We must end it here. We must end it now. He felt the gaze of 40,000 men. They waited only for a sign from him.

He looked at Jackson and nodded. Stonewall smiled and rode his new cream-colored claybank well out into the Potomac. There he stopped, removed his hat and pointed with it toward the United States.

"Move out!"

A deafening cheer rose up from the churchlike stillness, the regimental band struck up "Maryland, My Maryland" as Lee had ordered, and the leading elements of the Confederate army splashed into the cool waters. The United States of America was under invasion and it was a grand and glorious sight.

No sooner had Stonewall set foot in Maryland than Lee's wishful prophecy began to fulfill itself. Jackson was greeted by Marylanders bearing gifts—the first was a wonderful fresh melon, and the second was a fine and beautiful silver mare.

Maryland and God, he thought, *may well be very kind to us.*

But not all Marylanders were so inclined. The sun wasn't high in the sky before a latter-day Paul Revere rode hellbent for leather down the muddy length of Pennsylvania Avenue yelling to all but the deaf and the dead, "Jackson's in Maryland—Jackson's in Maryland!"

He rode straight up to the portico of the Executive Mansion and raised such a ruckus that the President himself came out to hear what he had to say.

"There's Rebels by the thousands, sir—I mean President Lincoln, sir—I seen 'em myself! And it was Stonewall, too. I know it was!"

Lincoln thanked the man for the information, and asked him to keep it to himself, as though half of Washington didn't know by now. The President then called again on Halleck, and he and Halleck called again on McClellan.

The two men instructed McClellan to verify the man's story and if he found it true to prepare the army to move at once into Maryland. McClellan couldn't be faulted for assuming that he would move with it.

Once again the giant baboon and his pet monkey had presented themselves at George's door, hats in hand, to plead with him to rescue the Republic, and the once and future savior of the Union found himself in a mood to celebrate. The H Street home was lighted up like a cathedral on Christmas, and blue-clad officers of all grades were herded in to pay homage to the Young Napolean. All went well until late in the evening when a young captain decided to make himself stand out.

"Tom Smith, sir, West Point Class of '61, and proud to serve under the man who's going to whip Stonewall Jackson!"

McClellan went suddenly red in the face. The audacity of this young pup to imply that Jackson, of all people, was somehow worthy of McClellan's attention ignited the general's temper.

"George McClellan, young man, West Point Class of '46, and let me tell you a thing or two! That deplorable bumpkin you call 'Stonewall' was a classmate of mine and I have never in my entire life known anyone of less culture and intelligence! Less refined than a lump of coal! 'Stonewall' indeed! What the newspapers won't do to sell papers!"

Marcy heard the outburst, as did everyone else in the room, and saw it as his duty to rescue his son-in-law from any further embarrassment.

"All that said though, George, that was one hell of a class!"

McClellan recognized Marcy's good intentions and tried to pick up the conversation in a more normal tone.

"That it was, sir. I've counted six of my classmates as Union generals and four on the other side."

Anxious to show off their knowledge, several of those gathered began to list the more notorious names: John Gibbon, Jesse Reno and George Pickett. And then someone who didn't know any better blurted out, "A. P. Hill was in that class too, wasn't he?"

Marcy braced himself for another blast of George's temper, but McClellan was remarkably restrained.

"Ah, yes. My old roommate. Ambrose Powell Hill."

The youngster who had made the *faux pas* felt the stares from around the room and finally figured out that he had said something wrong. He went instantly pale.

"That's all right, son. I suppose not everyone knows."

Marcy sought to break the tension and relieve the lieutenant's embarrassment. "As a young cadet, Mr. Hill courted my daughter before she married George."

"And I'm afraid General Marcy was rather blunt in his rejection of Powell's proposal."

"You're being kind, George. I was *very* blunt. I'm afraid he's never forgiven either of us."

"He was a true gentleman, though, once the issue was decided. He even attended our wedding, but he could be very difficult." McClellan smiled broadly as he remembered, "Lo Armistead, another fine man over on the other side, was *discharged* from The Point for breaking a mess hall plate over Hill's head." He drew deeply on his cigar and smiled again. "My God, that was a thing of beauty."

SEPTEMBER 5TH

Kyd Douglas was tickled pink to be in Maryland for more reasons than one. This was his dad's old preaching circuit all around this neck of the woods. Hagerstown, Boonsboro, Sharpsburg. Boyish fantasies kept him awake, dreaming of riding into one of these towns where he knew almost everybody, side by side with General Jackson, all the girls out waving flags, cheering, reaching up just to touch him as he rode triumphantly by. Momma so proud. He was still awake and dreaming just before the sunrise, with a long day behind and a longer one ahead.

Douglas finally felt the army waking around him, but couldn't see much yet. Only shapes nearby, each going about his business, preparing for the march.

Well before the sunrise, Douglas and Westbrook watched as Stonewall mounted his new horse and they tried not to laugh when the creature obstinately refused to budge. An unbearable embarrassment for a Virginia man, an officer of any rank at all, and God help any man who laughed. A sharp and angry thrust of the spurs into the ribs of the animal brought her angrily up to her hind legs, and sent Stonewall suddenly and violently to the ground. He didn't fall. He was thrown to the ground in anger. Like Moses hurling the tablets. He landed hard, and square on the back of his head, bending and twisting his neck so violently that Douglas and every other man who saw knew immediately that Stonewall Jackson was dead. He lay on the ground as lifeless and limp as an empty glove. Dr. McGuire rushed to his side and found the general still breathing, but laboredly. For twenty minutes Jackson responded to nothing.

A hushed whisper passed down the lines. "Stonewall broke his neck."

Jackson was not a man who was loved by his army. He was cruel and stern and unforgiving. But he was also Stonewall Jackson. He was not the heart and soul of this army, but he was the pride, and 40,000 men quietly stood deathwatch over him and each and every one prayed, "Please, God. Don't take him away."

When Dr. McGuire finally brought him around, Jackson couldn't move his legs. He was loaded into an ambulance, and the march across Maryland continued, but the excitement that had thrilled all yesterday was gone and quickly replaced by foreboding. As the crossing of the Potomac continued today, the music was gone—not from the air, but from the hearts of the men. The "dash" of yesterday's march was gone, and the army moved quietly north.

The crossing of the river continued with Jackson in an ambulance—and with Lee in an ambulance, unable to grip the reins of his horse because of the splints and bandages on his wrists—and with Longstreet, who had worn a severe blister on his heel, in an ambulance as well—and with Generals Hood and Hill under arrest.

Lee lay in his ambulance, frustrated and angry. So very much needed doing, not the least of which was allowing himself to be seen by the men, to offer them some small inspiration to move on. Always important, but particularly now. So many good men lost at Manassas, the army already reduced by sickness. Bare feet that just could not walk another painful, bloody step. And now desertions by the thousands. Some felt that their work was done. They had enlisted to repel the invaders, and the Yankees were out of Virginia and it was time to go home and harvest the crops. And some, a few of course, were cowards.

Harvey Hill is up now, Lee remembered, searching his heart for some ray of hopeful news, but very little good news found Robert E. Lee's ears these days.

He lay in his ambulance, looking up at the canvas. Unable to sleep, he worried.

I am undertaking the campaign of the war with what is little more than a single corps. Invading the United States with only 40,000 men. Numbers. We cannot concern ourselves with numbers.

God be with us.

WASHINGTON

At a small table in a dark corner of Willard's Hotel several correspondents from Horace Greeley's *New York Tribune* sat and drank.

"The First Amendment has become a bad joke," Nathaniel Davidson said. "The army controls everything and we can't even send a telegram. The battle was over for three days before we could file our reports."

"You have to understand their situation." Smalley was almost patronizing.

The others were all angry and not in a mood to hear calm and rational observations from a Yale *and* Harvard graduate, especially since Bull Run had been Smalley's first real fight.

But Smalley didn't care what mood they were in. He had to get them out of the problem and into the solution. He continued as though *they* were the rookies. "The generals think we are all spies for the Rebels and, to an extent, they are right. We provide the enemy with information. It may be even more accurate information than they get from their professional spies. It favors the generals to have it published wrong, or late. At least too late to serve any purpose to the enemy."

It was four drinks past dark and the gathered newsmen were in no mood for compromise. It takes the fun and the fight out of a good argument. But Smalley continued. Clear and rational.

"And think about the chaos if each and every one of us, from all of the newspapers in the country, had access to the wires. There would be none left for the military."

Nat didn't want to hear about the army's problems. "Oh, come on, George. We have a right, granted to us by the Constitution, and they deliberately seek to deprive us of the right to do our job."

"Of course they do, Nathaniel. That's part of *their* job." Smalley tossed back another shot. The dust in the back of his throat was almost washed away, but not quite. "Pope can be blamed for a great many things, but depriving us of the use of his telegraph lines, with Jeb Stuart cutting them down every five minutes, is not a fault. We can sit here and cry about it till the war comes to an end, but it will never change. Not in this war or any other. What we must do is find a better way to file."

"The use of the telegraph is not their only tool, George. They also lie." Nat was getting continually drunker and angrier. "I've heard from twenty different people that the whole damned Rebel army is in *Maryland* for Christ's sake and the generals are telling us that it is a *foraging* expedition!"

"It may well be. But we have to learn not to rely only on our generals, but on our own wits. We must know the Rebel generals as well as we know our own." Smalley looked at his old friend Nat like he was a struggling student. "We are in the question-asking business, so let us ask ourselves a few. Why would they go into Maryland? A foraging expedition is a logical possibility, but, as you say, that is not likely. It may be another of Stuart's joyrides. It may be a feint to draw troops away from Washington and make the capital vulnerable, and it may be a total invasion aimed at Washington, Baltimore, Harrisburg or even Philadelphia."

"That would be madness for the Rebels to try to take Baltimore or Philly. Look at the lines of communications and supply that would have to be stretched clear around Washington."

"Not if Washington falls." Smalley waited long enough for that possibility to sink in before he continued. "This is what I mean about knowing their generals as well as our own. Lee is a master of maneuver. It might be madness for anyone *else* to attempt such an invasion, but for Lee it is brilliant."

"Damn it, George. We *have* to gain access to the army and find out what the hell's going on. Hell, I can't even get a pass."

By now Smalley was almost as drunk as Davidson, but George remained calm. "There are ways around that as well. I saw Coffin, my friend with the *Boston Journal in uniform* at Chantilly, and Crounse at the

Times paid a hundred dollars for a blank pass signed by Burnside. It may be a challenge, gentlemen, but it can be done."

Davidson was almost as angry at Smalley as he was at Pope. "And what, oh great one, is your plan?"

"While you are all running around pissing off the generals, I am making friends. I recommend that you all do likewise."

"That's easy to say."

"It's equally easy to do. All that is needed is for you to pack your pride in a haversack and perform some humble chores for them. They will become indebted and the meek shall inherit. Trust me. It works."

"Who are your special friends now?"

"I've ingratiated myself with General Sedgwick of late, but I need to befriend a corps commander, gentlemen, and, if you'll excuse me, I believe General Hooker has just entered the room. He will be given a corps and he looks as though he could use a drink." He stood to leave and patted Davidson on the shoulder. "Hooker could *always* use a drink."

Ambrose Burnside stood on Pennsylvania Avenue looking at Mr. Lincoln's big white house as though it were the gates of hell. He would rather do battle with Bobby Lee and the Devil side by side than face what he feared was coming. But into the gates he passed. Those were his orders and the President was waiting.

"General Burnside, welcome."

"Thank you, Mr. President, and how can I be of assistance?"

"General Burnside, as you know, the recent setbacks have caused the nation grave concern. We are more than a year into the war and we are back at the precise point from which we started. We must begin again. General Pope is defeated and I have sent him to the West to deal with the Indian problem, as he has lost the confidence of the army."

Burnside's knees weakened. He knew for certain what was coming now, and wanted no part of it. He had faced this problem before, and nothing had changed since then from his point of view. *There is a limit,* he thought, *to the number of times you can refuse the President of the United States.* He began to fumble nervously with his hat while he waited for Lincoln to continue.

"Our friend General McClellan is in command of the capital's defenses, and I understand the morale of the men is greatly restored."

Jump in now, Burnside thought. Make your pitch before he even starts his.

"Mr. President, it is the most amazing thing I have ever seen . . ." But Lincoln plowed right on, as though Burnside had never opened his mouth.

". . . but George is purely a defensive commander. He lacks the will to move on the offensive. We have very little time, General Burnside. We are informed that the enemy is on the move again, this time into Maryland, and I need—the *nation* needs—a commander to lead our armies against him." Even though he had been expecting it, the sound of the words made Burnside's heart sink.

"I fear that General McClellan is *not* that man. I hope, again, General Burnside, that you are. I have called you here today to offer you command of the Army of the Potomac and to ask you to move it at once against Lee in Maryland."

Burnside continued to twist his big floppy hat in his hands while he struggled to find his courage. Not battlefield courage. That came easy. The courage to refuse the President of the United States. In one short second all the negative thoughts, all the self-doubts, returned to the mind of Ambrose Burnside.

I am not that man either, he thought. A ticket seller for the railroad. A failed business. Then one quick and easy victory in the field and the President thinks I'm some kind of Caesar. Then he thought of McClellan. Strong. Straight. A friend who came to my rescue in the darkness. He has the skills. He has the swagger. If only he would use them.

"Mr. President, you and I have had this conversation before, and while I appreciate greatly your confidence in me, I must tell you again that I do not share it. You speak of the confidence of the army which Pope lacked and which George obviously has. That is the key, sir. McClellan is much inspired by the recent events and I think that the inspiration he has drawn from the men, and they from him, will push him forward. He deserves another opportunity, sir."

Lincoln's frustration boiled to the surface, and his tone was almost pleading. "General Burnside, we have reason to believe that the Rebels are in Maryland in force, while we are in total disarray. In *Maryland,* General. *Above* the capital. As far as we know, this city may be surrounded and isolated at this very moment. General Lee may choose to move on Harrisburg or Philadelphia. If any of these cities fall, the Union falls with it. The whole noble experiment of democracy, of majority rule, of laws over man—it can all be gone in a day."

As he spoke, Lincoln walked around behind his desk and opened a drawer. He removed from it a piece of paper and said, "I command your secrecy on this matter, General, but I must impress upon you the urgency of the moment."

He gently handed the document to Burnside. Now his tone was reverent. "I call this the Emancipation Proclamation. It frees the slaves in the South, General. It is a most serious matter above and beyond all others, for it precludes any chance of the European powers entering the war on the side of the enemy. It will reinspire hundreds of thousands of our countrymen to assist in the struggle. It is an excellent document, sir. It changes everything—it changes the very reasons we are fighting—it changes, well, it changes everything."

He paused briefly to let Burnside study the document, and consider what had already been said. But only briefly.

"This document can win us the war, but the nation isn't ready for it yet. Fresh on the heels of these defeats its effects will be minimized. I wait, General Burnside, only for a single victory, and that victory must come soon."

As the President spoke, Burnside glanced over the document. *All persons held as slaves . . . forever free.* The general's palms became wet and his hands began noticeably to shake and he didn't know why. He knew only that he wanted to drop it on the floor, to be rid of it like a hot rock. He had no feelings on the issue one way or the other. These matters were the concerns of statesmen and politicians. He knew the importance of it well enough. He knew it well enough to know that he wanted no part of it.

"Mr. President, McClellan is preparing the army to march even as we speak. The army is ready and anxious to march, to prove itself after its defeats. Another change of command at so critical a moment would assure nothing beyond certain defeat." Now it was Burnside's turn to plead. "Allow him to move with the army, sir, and to lead it one more time. If he fails—if we fail—come to me again and I shall not refuse you."

Lincoln took the Emancipation Proclamation from Burnside and said nothing for a long moment. He considered *ordering* Burnside to take command and finally being done with it, but perhaps the man was right. The command structure is in disarray now and the army is on the move. The timing may well be bad.

"General, if he fails—if *we* fail—there may be no next time."

Burnside wanted desperately to tell the President that the proclamation was a dangerous document, that it might well incite riots not only in the South but within the army. Desertions by the thousands or a rebellion within the officer corps. Again he heard that voice from the Peninsula that had haunted his memory for weeks. *"We'll march this army against Washington . . ."* But his opinion had not been sought and he was only a soldier. Burnside said nothing more. A very long, silent time passed. The dreadful silence of the dead that he thought would never end.

"Very well, General. But we *must* lick 'em this time." He placed the document back in the drawer. Forever Free. "We *must*."

Burnside saluted his Commander in Chief and left the Executive Mansion petrified of what McClellan might do if he knew about the document in Lincoln's desk. He couldn't wait to get out of the mansion and suck in some clean air. He leaned against a column for a moment to regain his balance.

At the Willard Hotel, "Fightin' Joe" Hooker leaned against the bar with another shot glass in his hand, courtesy of the *New York Tribune*. Smalley knew of Hooker's dislike of politicians in general, and of Old Abe in particular and sought to gain the favor of the general by instigating his wrath against the President. He pointed at a drawing of Lincoln behind the bar and said, "Some people blame everything on that man there."

"Do you know any history?"

"As much as most."

"You ever hear of the Battle of Angencourt?"

"Yes, sir. Hundred Years War."

"Right you are, young man." Smalley despised being patronized by generals, but he had a job to do, so he kept his mouth shut and wondered what in the hell Lincoln had to do with Angencourt.

"The British fought with longbows and the French with crossbows. The French were so damned sure their weapons and generals would carry the day that they let it be known that any English archer who was captured would have his middle finger cut off, so that he could never again pull a bowstring." Hooker was no longer talking to Smalley, but to the bar. And the bar listened.

"Well, the British won, and became very proud to display to the French that their middle fingers remained firmly intact." With this, he demonstrated to the likeness of Abraham Lincoln that he, too, still had a middle finger. And the bar laughed.

SEPTEMBER 6TH

Edwin Stanton was a man torn in two. Before him stood the greatest traitor in the history of the Republic, and Stanton wanted nothing more than to place him under arrest right here and right now. He wanted to see this man hanging by the neck in a public square, but right now the War Secretary had no cards left to play. Lee was in Maryland, the capital was still in panic and Lincoln had meekly surrendered to the course of least resistance. McClellan, hopefully only for the moment, was back in command and Stanton's hands were tied. He strained against binds but could not break free. Not yet. Not today.

McClellan oozed charm and pretended respect. The disingenuous little bastard made Stanton almost quiver in rage, disgust and frustration, but so it had to be, at least for now.

It was all the secretary could do to keep from exploding, especially when McClellan "requested" that Pope's unfounded charges against Generals Franklin and Fitz-John Porter be dropped and the two men be allowed to continue in command.

"General Porter is a military genius," McClellan said, "especially where it comes to organization and logistics—and at a time when the army is in such dire need of both, this man is absolutely indispensable to me."

Stanton was so angry by this time that it took every power in his being to refrain from launching into a tirade about malfeasance and cowardice and treason.

"If you say so, General, and with the approval of the President I'm certain that General Pope's charges can be set aside—at least for the moment." *Don't surrender your sword*, he thought. Keep it handy for future use.

"Of course I have no control over the future. That is entirely in the hands of General Pope, I'm afraid." The sword was safely in its scabbard. "But you may retain these men, at least for the moment."

By midmorning Lee's entire army was on the Maryland side of the Potomac and en route to Frederick. Jackson, thank God, was back on his feet, suffering from nothing more than a aching head and a bruised sense of pride.

As they rode into Poolesville, the townspeople lined the streets with tiny Stars and Bars, and the ladies of the community demanded to see General Lee. He graciously granted their request and what had been a warm welcome took on the air of a circus. A pair of young men enlisted on the spot in Jeb Stuart's cavalry, and a storekeeper opened up his shop, accepted Confederate scrip and sold his entire inventory in less than an hour. He then enlisted and headed off with the rest of the army, again on the road to Frederick.

The columns pulled up that evening three miles short of Frederick and, in a spot known as Best's Grove, Lee, Jackson, Longstreet and Stuart pitched their tents. For the army it was a routine day, but for the four Rebel leaders it was extraordinary. Word of their coming preceded them and the Southern sympathizers among the fine folks of Frederick would hear nothing of waiting another day to see the famous four. In carriages, on horseback and on foot they came to catch a glimpse. To Lee and Jackson the teenage girls stretched the limits of their gentility, and they strained to be polite until they, for the first time in the war, were forced to retreat into their tents. Longstreet and Stuart were a different story.

Old Pete accepted sympathy over his blistered heel as though it were the most gallant of wounds, and Stuart—well, Stuart was Stuart.

Kyd Douglas was both pleased and mortified when his mother and a small entourage of her friends rode down from Shepardstown to visit with him and join in the gawking. Her son was a celebrity all around Shepardstown and Sharpsburg for being the youngest member of Jackson's staff. Thanks to Mrs. Douglas all of western Maryland believed that the famous Stonewall had a twenty-two-year-old *Chief* of Staff. But today, Kyd Douglas was home, beaming like a lantern, and not a general in camp would insinuate that the young captain was anything less.

Introductions were easily made to Longstreet and Stuart as they were holding court. Douglas's intimacy with Jackson earned them easy passage into Stonewall's presence, where the general was typically gracious as always where women were concerned and complimentary of her son's talents. All that remained was to meet General Lee himself, and as they passed before his tent, Mrs. Douglas pleaded, "Oh, son—you're so well loved and influential here, surely you can arrange us an audience with General Lee."

"I'm sorry, Mother, but General Lee is injured and has terribly important matters to consider."

She was crushed. "I'm sorry for asking. Of course he is occupied."

"Douglas!" The voice from the tent was Lee's and the young captain snapped to attention, as proud as a peacock.

"Sir."

"I cannot believe that you would allow your own mother to come into my headquarters and deny me the honor of an introduction. I apologize, Mrs. Douglas, for your son's behavior. I fear the good manners he learned in your home have fallen off considerably since coming into the company of soldiers, but it is the only time I ever knew your son to fail in the performance of his duty, as General Jackson can testify."

"I appreciate the kind words, General, and we shall discuss his lack of manners when we get him back home."

While Lee practiced good manners, McClellan deliberately practiced bad. As the newly reorganized Army of the Potomac began its move northward, rather than marching down Pennsylvania Avenue in front of the Executive Mansion for the obligatory review by the President, they purposely detoured down Fifteenth Street and passed instead before the comparatively humble townhouse at the corner of Fifteenth and H, where they cheered lustily as McClellan stepped out onto his stoop and saluted them on.

Gideon Welles stood unnoticed in front of his own home directly across the street, smoking a cigar and drinking a brandy, and made note of the parade-route politics being played by Little Mac and his staff.

After his mother departed with her party to return to Shepardstown, Douglas returned to the mundane duties of his post. Lee sent him to fetch Jackson to his tent. Still aching from the fall, Jackson walked gingerly toward Lee's quarters and was suddenly assaulted by a pair of teenage girls from the town. They leaped from their carriage and began to prattle both at once and at such a pace that neither Jackson nor Douglas was able to understand a solitary word. They touched him, kissed him, hugged him and vanished back into the carriage so quickly that the mighty Stonewall was literally left stammering, hat in hand.

Left blinking his eyes and shaking his head in amusement, Douglas couldn't resist the obvious analogy. "Now you know how the Yankees felt back in the Valley. That was as grand a rapid flanking movement as you ever launched against Banks."

Jackson too shook his head and smiled and continued toward his appointment with Robert E. Lee.

September 7th
Sharpsburg, Maryland

Ada Mumma got up with the roosters. She then woke the whole house. No sleeping late on *this* day. *My* day. Her seventh birthday had finally come. It was her day to shine and stand out from all of the thousands of other little Mummas and Rohrbachs. *So* long between birthdays. Why does it have to take so long? And now, even on this beautiful, birthday Sunday morning, the grown-ups paid her too little attention. A pat on the head. A birthday wish. But then they'd go right back to getting ready for church and talking about the Rebels.

I *hate* the Rebels! I don't know what Rebels are, but they're bad and they're close to here and it's my birthday and it's all that Grandma 'n' Grandpa and all the grown-ups want to talk about.

She noticed that some of the grown-ups weren't behaving well and the slaves were nervous and all the talk for the last two days seemed to be about armies or politics or the impending arrival of her new brother or sister. Her mother was seven months along in her pregnancy and was now being cared for and attended to by family and servants alike. On this most important of all days, Mary, her slave nurse, seemed to be the only one who cared.

I *hate* the Rebels.

Today will be fun, though, after church. She hated church because it took her granddaddy away and he stayed up there in his regular seat in the "Amen Corner" for three hours every Sunday. She couldn't even sit with him because the women and children had to enter through the side door and sit in a section away from the men. But when church finally ended they would hitch up the wagons and drive over to Grandma Rohrbach's house. It was so pretty there. The wide creek ran nearby and they would picnic on the banks next to the beautiful Rohrbach Bridge and swim and skim rocks and float toy boats in the Antietam. Once church got out, Sundays were always fun.

Best's Grove

James Longstreet ventured out toward Lee's tent, but found the front flaps closed and tied. Kyd Douglas dozed under the sunflap, resting comfortably on a camp chair. Where Douglas was, Jackson wasn't far behind.

"Send for me, Douglas, when the general is free."

"General Longstreet! We need you." The flap opened and Lee came out. "I was just about to send for you—please come in."

Jackson was already inside, studying Lee's map. Lee pointed. "General Longstreet, those people are still holed up at Harper's Ferry. I had anticipated that they would have moved out by now, but Stuart's men report that the garrison still holds a full division of around twelve thousand. They threaten us, General." Lee looked into Longstreet's face and made a deliberate effort to soften his tone, like a man bearing sad tidings, for that was precisely what he was doing. "They threaten our supply lines and our lines of communication. It is unfortunately being reported that the deeper we drive into Maryland, the less hospitable the natives are becoming, so a constant and unmolested route must be maintained connecting us with the Shenandoah Valley. Before our march can continue, or even before a final objective can be determined, that garrison at Harper's Ferry must first be disposed of."

Longstreet recognized Lee's manner and tensed up. He knew what was coming.

"General Jackson and I have both been there. He has commanded the garrison there, and I was once called in to help put down that raid of John Brown's that has now become so famous. We are certain that it can be quickly and easily taken."

"I would rather take it a thousand times than defend it once," Jackson said. "It lies directly on the peninsula in the confluence of the Shenandoah and Potomac rivers. Mountainous heights lie here and here and here across the rivers from which artillery can fire down on the town unmolested. The entire garrison is at the bottom of a deep hole. A division posted on the peninsula can stay back and wait for them to come out—which they must."

Longstreet had to control himself to keep from shouting. "But sirs, this puts us on three different sides of two different rivers. None could reach the others under any circumstances."

"They won't have to, General," Jackson said. "It will be a cut-and-dried operation. My division here, Walker here, and McLaws with two divisions here, guarding the escape."

"And my corps, sir, where will it be?"

Lee took a breath and looked to Jackson for support. Longstreet was not going to like this. "We will wait here, near Boonsboro," Lee said. "The enemy surely knows that we are here and they must come out to protect Washington. With us so positioned, they cannot commit any significant portion of their army to the defense of Harper's Ferry. As soon as operations are complete there the army will be rejoined."

Longstreet once again could not believe what he heard. Lee was dividing the army again, and this time on enemy ground. Certainly the two wings would not be divided by as many miles as before Second Manassas, but Jackson's corps would be subdivided—three times. His frustration got the best of him and he responded more quickly and a bit more loudly than he intended.

"Generals, this is a venture not worth the game. I do not believe the enemy to be so disorganized and demoralized as seems to be the popular notion, and should he find us dispersed so . . ." Longstreet was tired of pleading the same case again and again to the same two men. He was tired of saying it and they were tired of hearing it, so he left his sentence hanging.

"Of course, General Longstreet, we have taken that all into account," Lee said. "We simply think that he will not have the time. If we do not tip our hand too soon and do not move until ready, the thing can be over and done with before he has a chance to counter. Plus, it is rumored in the northern press that McClellan is back in charge, and if that is the case, we needn't worry at all about a speedy reply."

"It is a twenty-mile march or more and our men have been marching or fighting every day for five weeks. We are much used up, sirs. If we are not pressed, I recommend rest."

"It will all be taken into account. I shall consider the matter further and watch to see what the enemy is up to. If they hug close to Washington our day is made and if they come out to meet us, well, that might be even better." Lee thoughtlessly tried to make a fist with his right hand and the pain that shot up from his injured wrist brought an aggravated grimace. "Give it more thought, gentlemen, and for now, I too could do with a little rest."

Longstreet had noticed Lee's pained expression. "How are the hands, General?"

"See for yourself. They are so heavily splinted I cannot mount a horse, grip my glasses, I am even having trouble feeding myself. It's a nuisance. I see your wound is not yet healed either."

Longstreet thought for a moment that Lee had made a joke about his blistered heel, but as neither Lee nor Jackson showed the slightest sign of amusement at the pun, Old Pete just smiled and said, "I just hope I don't have to go into battle wearing a bedroom slipper. Most undignified."

Private Barton Mitchell was on detail, assisting in the dismantling of the regimental kitchens of the 27th Indiana, when a great cheer rose up among the men in camp. He turned to see a mob of his fellow Indianans rush to the side of Ol' Dan Webster as McClellan rode through the ranks. "Don't leave us again, George," one man shouted as hundreds of hands reached out to touch the man and his horse. McClellan stood in the stirrups and waved his hat above his head in salute. Brave and veteran soldiers cried just at the nearness of the man. Mitchell joined in the cheering and thought, *Maybe this time, maybe with this man at our head we will finally be able to meet the enemy and win.* He went back to work loading cookstoves onto wagons. *Maybe this time.*

It was time now for McClellan to assume the lead, to leave Washington and take command in the field. He had no orders to do so and knew that it would be risky to seek permission, so he tore a page from Napoleon's book. He would simply *inform* his civilian "superiors" that he was gone. He took three of his calling cards and wrote on them the letters "P P C," *Pour Prendre Congé,* a French military idiom used by Napoleon to inform the government that he had departed on campaign. He had them delivered to the War Department, the Executive Mansion and the home of Secretary of State Seward. If his enemies wanted him to return to his thumb-sucking in Washington, they would have to come and get him, and not a man among them had the courage.

While elements of the Confederate army moved through Frederick, the command center remained at Best's Grove.

Jackson, still in pain from his fall and embarrassed by the attention paid him by the young ladies, chose to take refuge in his tent for most of the day. He found no excuse, however, to prevent him from attending services on this quiet Sunday evening.

"Douglas—you're from these parts. Find me a church to attend tonight. I prefer Presbyterian, but any Christian service will suffice, I suppose, in the eyes of God."

"Yes, sir. I'll inquire."

"And, Douglas—be sure to get us a pass."

"A pass, sir?"

"Of course a pass. No soldier can venture beyond the pickets without one, and I, you may not have noticed, am no less a soldier than any other. A pass is required and a pass shall be shown."

Douglas asked several of the townsfolk who were in and around the camp about Presbyterian services and found that the traveling minister was elsewhere this week and that no services were to be held in Frederick tonight. An old family friend, however, was holding services in the Reform Church, and he saw an opportunity to visit and attend services at the same time.

"I have located services, sir, and arranged for a pass approved by the Assistant Adjutant General and under the authorization of General Jackson himself."

Jackson was beginning to like the youngster so much that he acknowledged Douglas's joke with a smile and a nod. "Excellent, Captain. Let's go to church."

The Reverend Daniel Zacharias was many things. He was a close friend to the Douglas family and had shared the pulpit on many occasions with Kyd's father. He was, like Jackson, a pious and devout man. He was also strongly pro-Union.

As the half-dozen Rebel officers marched politely into the rearmost pew, Zacharias instantly broke into a cold sweat. He recognized Kyd Douglas and nodded in recognition. He knew by association that the infamous Stonewall Jackson was the man in the middle. He was a man of his convictions and knew that this would probably be the most important person who would ever hear him preach. He had to make his position known—it was an opportunity actually to preach to the sinner. The thought occurred to him to put aside his prepared text and attack the Rebel cause, but he had always tried to avoid the politics of the pulpit. He continued with his prepared text on the Sermon on the Mount.

It was not until the final prayer that he was able to screw up his courage and risk offending his guests.

". . . And lastly, our dear Lord in Heaven, cast down your blessings upon your beloved son, Abraham Lincoln. Guide him and protect him and give him strength and wisdom to overcome our enemies."

A heartfelt "Amen" filled the sanctuary, the organ struck up the introductory chords of "Through Christ Our Lord," the congregation sang so loudly that God could not fail to hear, and Stonewall Jackson woke up, picked up his hat from the floor and quickly departed.

On the ride back to Best's Grove, Douglas too had to screw up his courage to broach a subject with the general. It was Sunday after all and anyone discussing administrative issues with Jackson on the Sabbath risked an Old Testament wrath attack. But Kyd Douglas genuinely liked that A. P. Hill and Little Powell had sent for him and asked him to intervene with Jackson on his behalf. Douglas was well aware of Jackson's feelings about Hill as well, and was risking a double-charged blast.

"I spoke with General Hill this morning, sir, and he feels badly treated."

Jackson did not respond at all, so Douglas continued. "He asked that I submit to you this request for an official statement of charges against him."

Douglas handed Jackson a letter from Hill. Jackson took it without comment, placed it into his tunic without so much as a glance and rode on ahead of the churchgoers.

September 8th

Wilson!"

The voice was immediately recognizable. Custer. He had been a year behind James Wilson at The Point, and a mile ahead of him in demerits. The two friends embraced and Major Wilson was almost knocked over by the aroma. He coughed and stepped back, closed his eyes, scrunched up his face and waved his hand in front of his nose. "Cinnamon, you old cuss. I see you're still wearing that same dreadful hair jelly!"

"If it weren't for me this whole damned army would smell like horse dung. Let me look at you! Whoa—*Major* Wilson."

Ah. A wonderful moment not to be passed up. "That's absolutely correct, *Captain* Custer. And don't you forget it!"

"Well, I know you well enough to know that somebody gave you that oak leaf just to shut you up. What's your assignment?"

"I managed to beg a position on McClellan's staff, but it's only temporary until they find me a regiment."

It didn't take but a few minutes of storytelling before Wilson was deathly jealous of "Cinnamon." Custer had seen some serious fighting and had stories worth telling while Wilson had spent the war drawing pictures of anthills.

"Well, I think you're about to do some serious catching up here, Jimmy." Custer spotted a piece of lint on his uniform sleeve and carefully flicked it off. "There's about to be a serious brawl and before it's over you might even get that regiment of yours—right *after* I get mine!"

URBANA, MARYLAND

Stuart's cavalry rode out from Frederick in all directions to find out if the Federal army had responded to their presence in Maryland. In each and every town, ten different officers stopped to ask ten different people for directions to ten different Maryland locations, so as to confuse any Union intelligence-gatherers who might follow.

Stuart himself galloped through the streets of Urbana and took note of an extraordinary number of attractive young ladies. As he was an expert reconnoiterer, it didn't take him long to find out that Urbana was the location of one of Maryland's finest girls' schools. The sun was low, and it was near enough to time to call a halt anyway, so why not here?

"I find myself in the mood for dancing," he told his staff. "Call forward one of the regimental bands, decorate the great hall of the institution and issue invitations to the people of the town, regardless of politics. We shall educate the people of Urbana to the gentility of the South."

Lee knew the importance of being seen as liberators and not invaders and used this time to issue additional orders warning his men to be on their best behavior—or be shot. He called Colonel Taylor into his tent and dictated a letter to the people of Maryland. "No restraint upon your free will is intended. No intimidation will be allowed. This army will respect your choice whatever it may be; and while the Southern People will rejoice to welcome you to your natural position among them, they will only welcome you when you come of your own free will."

While the Confederate army took every precaution not to offend "the people of Maryland," this was still a military campaign, and precautions had to be taken to protect the army as well. Among these precautions was the interception of the mails and the censoring of private letters, one of which was a gem. The censors had so much fun with it they took turns reading it aloud to the amusement of company-sized gatherings . . .

"*I wish, my dearest Minnie, you could have witnessed the transit of the Rebel army through our streets. Three long dirty columns that kept on in an unceasing flow. I could scarcely believe my eyes. Was this body of men, moving along with no order, their guns carried in every fashion, no two dressed alike, their officers hardly distinguishable from the privates . . .*"

One man yelled out, "You can tell us apart, lady—the privates are the smart ones!"

"*. . . Were these, I asked myself in amazement, were these dirty, lank, ugly specimens of humanity . . .*"

"Ugly? She must'u've seen Harry!"

"*. . . with shocks of hair sticking through holes in their hats, and the dust thick on their dirty faces, the men that had coped and encountered successfully and driven back again and again our splendid legions?*"

"They don't look so splendid from the back, missy!"

"*I must confess, Minnie, that I felt humiliated at the thought that this horde of ragamuffins could set our grand army of the Union at defiance. Why, it seemed as if a single regiment of our gallant boys in blue could drive that dirty crew into the river without any trouble! Oh, they are so dirty! I don't think the Potomac River could wash them clean. And ragged! There is not a scarecrow in the cornfields that would not scorn to exchange clothes with them . . .*"

"Hey, I changed clothes with a scarecrow just yesterday, and he didn't even put up a fight. He did get the worst of the deal, though."

"*. . . I saw some strikingly handsome faces though . . .*"

"That was me!" about twenty men yelled at once.

"*. . . or rather they would have been so if they could have had a good scrubbing. They were very polite, I must confess . . .*"

"We have to be polite or get hanged."

"*Many of them were barefooted. Indeed, I felt sorry for the poor misguided wretches . . .*"

"We was misguided, all right. We was guided into Maryland!"

"*. . . for some of them limped along so painfully, trying to keep up with their comrades. But I must stop . . .*"

"Please do!"

There was a delay as George McClellan moved forward to establish his headquarters in Rockville, and the general rode ahead to see what the holdup might be. A company of troops was just standing by the roadside, clogging the movement. McClellan dismounted and walked forward into the group.

"What's the holdup here, men?"

No one spoke, but one man directed McClellan's attention off into the woods, where two Rebel soldiers, one blond and one redheaded, swayed under the limb of an oak tree with ropes around their necks.

It wasn't as though these men had never seen a dead man before, or even a hanging—but these corpses were different. They told a story beyond that of a pair of deserters or spies. There was more tragedy here than the early death of two young soldiers.

Neither could have weighed 120 pounds. The redhead was shoeless, and even in death blood continued to ooze from the soles of his feet and drip down onto the rocks beneath him. Attached to the shirt of the blond boy was a note that read, "*Hanged for Thievery.*"

"They stole a hog, General, sir," a soldier told McClellan. "At least that's what a farmer who lives around here told us."

McClellan examined them as they hung and had to notice the condition of their ragged clothes and emaciated bodies, but he said nothing. He searched through his saddlebag for his sharp knife, remounted Dan Webster and cut the men down.

"See to them, and clear this road."

* * *

Jeb Stuart could not have been happier. The room looked beautiful, dec-
orated with roses and regimental flags. The Great State of Mississippi
provided the music. The turnout was better than he could possibly have
hoped both in terms of quantity and quality. The ladies dressed in their
finest and most of the men had even made time to bathe. "This promises
to be an extraordinary evening," Stuart said over the music. He spotted a
young lady in blue and made his way through the crowd.

The ladies were lovely and the music was lively. The gray and gold of
the Rebel uniforms contrasted with the pastels of their partners' hoop-
skirts. Hundreds of candles lighted the hall and one of Urbana's loveliest
quickly became the center of every young Rebel's attention. She was
charming and beautiful. Red hair and eyes as blue as a Carolina sky. She
was free with a girlish laugh that would make the Devil smile. For all of
this, she might have been from Georgia. But this girl was unquestionably
not from Georgia.

For one thing, she painted her face. You had to look closely to tell, but
it was there sure enough. On her cheeks. Her dress was emerald green
and a full inch too short, so that when she would spin, it would follow,
offering the soldiers the promise of a glimpse of a foot or ankle. She
never missed an opportunity to spin. She was equally immodest up top.
Her freckled shoulders were all but bare, and the rise of her breasts on
the verge of escape. Of course, the men battled one another for position,
trying to gain an introduction, to view an elegant curtsey and a quick
peek down her cleavage. But they also wanted to listen to her talk. Most
had never heard a genuine Yankee girl speak before, and for many this
one might as well have been speaking Egyptian. She was obviously "not
from around here." Not a Maryland girl at all, but a genuine Yankee,
from way up north, and she talked so fast and said her words so funny the
men had to struggle to pick out words here and there. Hell. Who cares
what's she's saying anyway?

And as though all of this wasn't enough to assure her a place in Southern lore, to charm and beauty and exotic romance and a brazen display
of her body, she added mystery. She refused to share her name with anyone. With a dazzling smile and a practiced curtsey, she announced to
all: ". . . and you may call me 'the New York Rebel.'"

The music and the laughter drowned out the sounds of battle on the outskirts of town. The first Stuart heard of it was when artillery entered the fray. At precisely the same moment a harried young courier stormed into the hall and marched boldly up to the general.

"Yankees have assaulted our encampment, sir, and have pushed back the pickets."

The civilians had never been this close to the war before, and parents ran out onto the dance floor to claim their daughters and get them to safety. Stuart tried to calm them.

"Do not be concerned, ladies. This is a small matter. Please, you will be perfectly safe here and we shall all return to the festivities shortly. Gentlemen, to your horses."

Now safely away from Washington, McClellan decided to wire Halleck. Intelligence reports indicated that Jackson's force of about 7,000 had reached Frederick, but beyond that little was known. *"I think that we are now in position to prevent any attacks in force on Baltimore while we cover Washington on this side. They shall not take Baltimore without defeating this army—I am also in position to hasten to the assistance of Washington if necessary. As soon as I find out where to strike, I shall be after them without an hour's delay."*

Lincoln was sitting in his favorite chair in the War Office telegraph room when the message came down. He looked at it for a minute and handed it to Secretary Welles, "'... without an hour's delay,'" he said. "Now that would be a leopard changing his spots, but I hope to God that it's so."

SEPTEMBER 9TH

At 1:00 A.M. the dashing Rebel cavalry, having disposed of the Federal nuisance, returned to the dance hall. The Mississippi musicians had been given no orders to return to their unit and had prudently determined that it must have been Stuart's intention for them to wait there, with the ladies, for his return. Most, if not all, of the invited guests had remained as well, and the party resumed precisely where it had left off.

At 4:00 A.M. Amanda Leigh, beautiful, brunette and seventeen, excused herself to get some fresh air. Her scream cut through the hall as the sounds of distant artillery couldn't. An instant of silence was followed by a mad rush to the door.

For hours the elegant ladies of Urbana had been entertained by the storybook chivalry of Jeb Stuart's cavalry. Now it was time to come face-to-face with the realities of war.

A line of ambulances loaded with the bloody and mangled troopers was backed up in front of the dance hall. The girls of Urbana, those with the stomachs for it, soon became nurses. Still dressed in their best, the ladies—including "the New York Rebel"—went to work assisting the surgeons.

Thankfully for the novice nurses, most of the amputations had been done on the field. A single nurse witnessing her first limb removal was generally of no use at all, but twenty or more standing around watching a man's leg cut off would have been more harmful than helpful. The surgeries to be done here were bullet and shrapnel removals and arterial ligations and such—still unpleasant, but not so dramatic.

The New York Rebel continued to add to her reputation by rolling up her sleeves and diving right in. One soldier had a bullet wound above the knee. A brass screw-type tourniquet secured around the upper thigh cut the flow of blood.

"Just hold him down, ma'am, and distract his attention. Are you all right?"

She looked as though she had lost more blood than the patient as she fought to keep her composure.

The doctor cut off the trouser leg with a scalpel and threw the bloody scrap on the floor. He examined the wound for only a moment and then jammed his finger up into the man's leg. The man screamed in pain and passed out.

"That's okay, ma'am. They all do it, and it's best for everyone."

He continued to probe the wound with his finger as deeply as he could, but couldn't find the bullet.

"Damn! Sorry, ma'am." He withdrew his finger from the wound and wiped the blood on his already soaked apron. Someone handed her a dirty, wet cloth and she instinctively mopped the soldier's face with it. It was the first time she had looked at his face, and as the dirt and powder began to come off, she thought that he might be quite handsome.

She looked back at the doctor as he pulled from his bag a foot-long piece of hairpin-thin steel with an ebony handle. He ran the probe gently back up into the wound and wiggled it around until he found the bullet. Leaving the probe in place, he turned back to the bag and retrieved one of his forceps. Following the precise direction of the probe, he grabbed the bullet in the pincers. "Good. No bone. I don't think the bullet is deformed, either."

A moment later he pulled an ugly, bloody piece of lead from the hole in the man's leg and carefully placed it in the soldier's pocket.

He put the bullet probe and forceps carefully back into the proper slots in his surgeon's kit and took out an odd-looking pair of tweezers with holes in the separated ends. Once again he probed the wound and after several tries he managed to grab hold of the torn end of the artery and pull it out.

"I'm going to need your help now, young lady. Are you still with me?"

She nodded, not really sure what he had in mind, but at this point she had little choice in the matter. She, by God, would do whatever was necessary to help this man.

"Okay. You're going to have to hold these forceps precisely as I am holding them now. The artery is elastic and is going to try to retreat back inside the man's leg. Hold the forceps tightly closed with one hand and steady that with the other, as I am doing here. Do you understand?"

"Yes, sir."

"All right. Come on now."

The New York Rebel did as she was told, maybe pinching too tightly just to make sure. She turned her head away and took a deep breath to still a wave of nausea. Her knees shook, but her hands were steady.

The doctor now removed from his kit a bent sewing needle and a length of hair from a horse's tail that had been boiled to soften it and make it more like the silk thread he preferred. His hands moved so quickly that before she could build up the nerve to look back, he was done. He tossed the suture needle back into the box and took the forceps from her.

"Now, grab the thumbscrew on the tourniquet and slowly remove the tension."

It was difficult at first, but slowly it loosened. The doctor's attention was riveted on the freshly stitched end of the artery. "Good. No leakage. If there's no secondary hemorrhaging, young lady, you may have just saved this man's leg. We're not finished yet."

She watched in amazement as he stitched the wound shut. "Now, miss, we still have to dress the wound. That cloth you've been using there—is it still wet?"

She nodded.

"Hold it here while I secure it next to the wound."

The rag was soaked with the blood of a dozen men. What wasn't red with blood was black with powder, and she placed it directly on the fresh stitches while the doctor wrapped it with a bandage and tied it in place.

"Thank you, ma'am. You're a natural-born . . ."

The courageous New York Rebel's knees finally buckled and she fainted dead away.

It was Gideon Welles's habit to arrive at his office with the sunlight, and on this particular morning there was someone waiting when he arrived. Henry Wilson was chairman of the Senate Committee on Military Affairs. His appearance and aroma confirmed Welles's suspicion that the good senator had spent the night in Willard's lobby.

"I heard a disturbing rumor late last night, Gideon, and I think that you and the President should hear it as well. There may be no truth to it, but it comes from a source close to McClellan and—well, you should hear it."

"Go on."

"I had a late dinner last night at Willard's Hotel and remained afterwards to discuss matters of importance . . ."

Welles fought back a smile, trying to maintain a serious demeanor while he nodded the senator on.

"There were men there of McClellan's staff, Mr. Secretary, and they told me that there is a conspiracy afoot among certain generals for a *revolution . . .*" The good senator shouted the word so loudly that Welles was startled by it. " . . . and the establishment of a *provisional national government!*" Senator Wilson then nodded his head one emphatic time and folded his arms in an attitude that said: I told you so, now what are you going to do about it?

Wilson was a man who loved conspiracies and he was also a confidant of Stanton's. For all Welles knew, Stanton had sent him here. The man will not rest until McClellan is gone. Preferably *dead* and gone.

But the journalist in Welles knew "camp talk" when he heard it. "It does not surprise me, sir, that there may have been random talk and speculation among military men while idle in camp, but there is nothing serious or intentional in their loose remarks. They and the soldiers are citizens. The government and the country is theirs as well as ours. I shall, of course, pay close attention and be certain that the President is aware, but these speculations are nothing more than have appeared in the New York newspapers. Keep listening, Mr. Senator, and keep us informed, but at the moment General McClellan is occupied with more important matters." Welles placed his arm around the senator's shoulder and began ushering him slowly out of the room. Not an easy task considering the man hadn't bathed in a month, and reeked of stale bourbon as well.

Knowing the senator's love for secrets, he whispered to him, conspiratorially, "If he fails in the field he will no longer have the power to threaten the government—if he succeeds, he will no longer have the need."

Robert E. Lee called on his Assistant Adjutant General, R. H. Chilton, to take dictation. Normally Lee wrote the first copies of any General Orders himself, and it would fall upon Chilton to copy them for distribution, but with Lee unable to write, the process took some time.

This order would put into effect the operations against Harper's Ferry, which Lee determined would commence tomorrow. The army would be divided again, this time by twenty miles and three river crossings. While Longstreet's concerns had been dismissed, they had been heard, and Lee wanted to make absolutely certain that each commander knew his role and his precise timetable. This, more than anything else, was the purpose of General Order #191. It spelled out in detail each and every movement of each and every division. Every man knew where he should be and when he should be there. At least as far as that was concerned, nothing could possibly go wrong.

Jackson: through Martinsburg and Sharpsburg to Bolivar Heights overlooking Harper's Ferry.

Longstreet: to hold in reserve at Boonsboro.

McLaws: to Maryland Heights overlooking Harper's Ferry.

Walker: to Loudoun Heights overlooking Harper's Ferry.

D. H. Hill: to provide the rear guard at South Mountain.

All units to be in position by Friday morning.

Following accomplishment of the objective, all units were ordered to reunite at Boonsboro or Hagerstown.

Everything was neatly spelled out by 191. Nothing could possibly go wrong.

Chilton made copies for all interested parties and sent for six couriers to deliver them. One man folded his five times until it was small enough to fit in a hidden compartment on the inside of his belt. Another copy went into a hatband and another in a boot.

One of the couriers took three cigars from his vest pocket and carefully folded his copy around them so that it looked like nothing more than an innocent wrapper. He replaced the cigars in his pocket and rode off to deliver his copy of General Order #191 to General D. H. Hill.

Nothing could possibly go wrong.

Longstreet committed the order to memory, tore General Chilton's copy in as many pieces as possible and chewed it into pulp. Jackson realized that these orders detached Harvey Hill from his command and reassigned him to Longstreet. Stonewall had no way of knowing that his brother-in-law had already been copied, so, as a courtesy, he made an additional copy in his own hand so Harvey would know that he was aware of the transfer. He gave it to his most trusted courier.

Nothing could possibly go wrong.

CHAPTER 6

LET THE DAMNED
YANKEES COME TO US

SEPTEMBER IOTH

Stonewall Jackson had recovered enough from his fall to lead from the saddle again. In spite of the dawn movement, large numbers of townsfolk managed to drag themselves out of bed for one more glance at Stonewall and his army. It was an annoyance, but Jackson thought he would take advantage of one last opportunity to confuse the Yankees.

"Douglas."

"Sir?"

"Ride over to that group of citizens there and ask them the best route to Chambersburg. Listen carefully, take notes and when they're finished with their directions ask if any among them has access to a map."

"Chambersburg, sir?"

"Or anyplace north from here."

Douglas chuckled and smiled and did as he was told. Jackson shook his head and turned to Dr. McGuire and said, "That's a fine young boy right there, Doctor, but I think he would laugh at a funeral."

"Yup."

"*Always* grinnin' or laughin' 'bout something."

Now McGuire smiled. "Yes, sir. He does look like a schoolboy who's just stole his first kiss in the woods, don't he?"

"Well, he'll get serious soon enough."

His assignment complete, Douglas saluted the group of civilians and turned to ride away when a particularly lovely young lady grabbed his horse by the reins and offered him a handful of colorful feathers.

"Please accept these plumes, Colonel, from a Southern girl. They will make you look dashing in your hat."

Douglas considered thanking her for the considerable promotion, but thought better of it as any soldier would in such a situation. He secured the plumes in his band, saluted again and rejoined Jackson, smiling bigger than ever.

George McClellan was fuming mad. A one-sentence telegram from the President sat on his desk: *How does it look now? Lincoln.*

McClellan shouted at his father-in-law. "Let's tell the ignorant baboon how it looks now! Let's tell him that they outnumber us by twenty-five percent. Let's tell him that there are three corps of Union troops wasting their time in Virginia when they should be here—and let's tell him that if the Harper's Ferry garrison isn't sent here at once that they'll just be killed or captured by the Rebels!"

His fury exploded. He kicked over his desk, sending everything crashing to the floor. "Send him a message, General, and tell him all of that!"

WASHINGTON

Judas Priest! George is at it again! He wants me to abandon Washington to the enemy so that he can command every man east of the Mississippi!" Stanton never passed on an opportunity to ridicule McClellan. "As I told you before, Henry, if you sent him a million men he would claim the enemy had two million and would sit in the mud and cry for four."

Halleck shook his head and read McClellan's telegram to himself. "He is correct about one thing, though, Mr. Secretary. ' . . . If we defeat the army now arrayed before us, the Rebellion is crushed. . . . But if we should be so unfortunate as to meet with defeat, our country is at their mercy.' About *that*, Mr. Secretary, our reluctant commander may very well be correct."

"I received this morning a copy of Friday's *New York Tribune*. I have it here somewhere." Stanton rummaged through the overstuffed carpetbag that he always had with him, flowing over with documents and press clippings. "Ah, here. See what our friend Mr. Smalley estimates as the strength of the Rebels."

He tossed the paper on Halleck's desk. *"The strength of the Rebel army exaggerated,"* it said in ink too black and type too large for Halleck's liking.

"I wish to God I could find a way to jail this boy," Halleck said.

"He's not exactly a boy. And he is far from the worst of them. At least he appears to be a Republican."

"That does not concern me, sir. I am a soldier—and he is a spy."

"Be that as it may, General, read on."

" '*We have been whipped by an inferior force of inferior men, better handled than our own . . . with only sixty thousand . . .* ' Sixty? I don't believe McClellan, but I can't believe the Rebels licked us with only sixty thousand men."

"I believe it well enough, and have believed it all along. It is the thing that angers me most. In every major conflict, General Halleck, we have outnumbered the enemy, in my estimation, and the *Tribune* confirms my estimations, by a margin of two-or-more-to-one, and still we are whipped like sickly schoolboys. There is no reason for it, sir"—Stanton gave Halleck his best most serious look—"beyond treason."

NEAR FREDERICK, MARYLAND

What news today, Colonel Taylor?"

"Well, General Lee, sir, Stuart's spy network is furnishing fresh rumors from Pennsylvania."

"Let's hear them. Two weeks ago General Longstreet was only a rumor to General Pope."

It was as close to an attempt at humor as Taylor had ever heard come from the lips of Lee and he wanted to laugh out loud, but thought better of it and responded with only a smile. "Well, sir, rumor has it that Governor Curtin has raised a militia of eighty thousand recruits and is bringing them south from Harrisburg."

Lee took a deep breath and thought for a moment as he stared down at his map.

"I have heard that from another source as well. Curtin is their most active governor, and I am sure that he is concerned about our presence so close to his state. He has proved that he is capable of providing such numbers." He removed his spectacles and tried to rub his nose where they pinched too tightly, but his bandaged hands made even that a chore. He was about to tell Taylor to summon Longstreet when the general appeared at his tent.

"Ah, General Longstreet, new information has reached us that requires your divisions to continue the march as far north as Hagerstown. D. H. Hill will remain at Crampton's Gap through South Mountain to round up any refugees from Harper's Ferry, but you must move here to guard against an assault launched from Pennsylvania."

Longstreet saw red. Quickly in his mind he placed units on the map. An effective force of no more than 40,000 men was now to be spread all over western Maryland and Virginia. Ten thousand men here, 3,000 there, 8,000 across the river, some in Maryland, some in Virginia and some a stone's throw from Pennsylvania. He felt and heard his own heartbeat. The lines his imagination placed on the map were small and very far apart. Not a single unit could either save itself or rely upon swift assistance from another. Longstreet could hold his tongue no longer. He resisted the urge to shout.

"General Lee—I wish we could stand still and let the damned Yankees come to us."

"It is still McClellan, General," Lee said in an exasperatingly calm tone, "and he must be drawn to us. He will not come of his own free will. These additional threats must also be dealt with and I see no other way." Final. His tone said so. The order was issued. Longstreet was dismissed.

And so it was to be. One army was now five.

God help us, Longstreet thought as he saluted and left Lee's side.

"God help us," he said aloud after he was alone.

Only a cavalry detachment of about thirty men preceded Jackson on the long day's march to Boonsboro. Douglas was at his side the entire way because he had grown up in the area and was familiar with the terrain. As the day grew old it became obvious that the terrain was not the only local feature with which Douglas was familiar.

"Will we be stopping for the night at Boonsboro, sir?"

"Why do you ask, Captain?"

"I have, ah, friends there whom I might like to visit if the opportunity presents itself."

"Well, Boonsboro seems a convenient stopping place, but I don't recommend any side trips. We know that the Yankees are on the move, and you never know where their cavalry might show themselves."

"These friends might be helpful in telling us about the depth of the fords and the condition of the bridges. If there has been any cavalry about, they'll know that as well. It's official business, sir, and I'll be careful."

"See that you are."

The column came to a halt about a mile east of town and the camp was quickly constructed. It was almost dark by the time Kyd Douglas was able to ride into town on his "official business."

Douglas sought out his newfound friend, Joel Westbrook, to accompany him on his excursion. Westbrook was from Lumpkin, Georgia, and damned proud of it, but had never set foot outside of Stewart County before the war. He and Douglas, then, were two-of-a-kind. Both small-town Rebels out to set the world on fire. Both were teetotalers, as befitted members of Jackson's staff, but informed that Douglas's friend owned the local tobacco shop and stocked the finest cigars in Maryland, the temptation became too great for the scraggly bearded Georgia boy to pass up.

Douglas and Westbrook rode at a gallop into Boonsboro, looking forward to a memorable evening. They found one.

They approached the corner of Main Street and Sharpsburg Road and reached that major intersection just as a company of Union cavalry arrived from the opposite direction. Before they could say "hello," lead started to fly.

"Holy Jesus!" Douglas and Westbrook spurred their horses to perform four-legged pirouettes and bolted back for camp. "Shit! The general told me this would happen!"

Douglas returned fire, backward at a run—not an effective use of the government's bullets—and suddenly pulled his horse to a stop. "What the devil are you doing?" Westbrook shouted.

"They shot off my new hat!"

"And you're going back to *get* it?"

Another shot whistled past Douglas's nose, and he suddenly realized that retrieving the hat with the beautiful new plumage might well be an exhibition of poor judgment on the part of a Confederate officer. He spurred his horse back to a run and the chase resumed.

About a quarter of a mile down the road they saw a solitary soldier on foot and leading his horse, obviously enjoying the coolness of the night and reflecting on his loved ones back home.

"Yankees!" Westbrook shouted, and the soldier quickly mounted up. He pulled himself up into the saddle as the two adventurers passed him by. Douglas pulled his horse to a stop.

"Oh, God," Douglas said.

"What now?"

"That was General Jackson!"

At the top of his lungs he yelled, "Mount up men and charge! The Yankees are coming!"

Westbrook knew what Douglas had in mind, but he still couldn't believe it. The two men turned and ran back past General Jackson directly toward the Union cavalry, firing their pistols and yelling as loudly as they could.

It worked.

The Yankees, thinking they were being attacked by a Rebel company or worse, turned and ran. The chase continued as far as Douglas's hat but no farther. While Douglas would have preferred at that moment to face the Yankees rather than Stonewall Jackson, the better part of valor dictated a return to camp.

They halted at the picket line to find Stonewall himself, standing with his arms folded and wearing his most humorless expression.

"Congratulations, Captain Douglas." The young captain braced himself for the wrath of God. ". . . on your ability to select fast horses." There was a gleam in Jackson's eye. Douglas handed Jackson a pair of gloves he had found by the road. "Here, General," he said with a relieved smile, "I believe these are yours."

Without another word, Stonewall Jackson pulled on his gloves, mounted his horse and rode back to camp. Douglas and Westbrook followed—at a distance.

HEADQUARTERS,
ARMY OF THE POTOMAC

At long last Major James Wilson was getting to play with the big boys. Custer had shown him the ropes, introduced him around and found him a magnificent black stallion. He was large and nimble and his muscles so massive and well formed that he was as hard and as beautiful as a granite statue. This was an animal fully worthy of a portrait at The Point. Wilson may have had trouble getting along with people, but he had no trouble at all with horses. They shared the same spirit, these two. Arrogant and aggressive and uncomfortable at any gait slower than a flat-out run. Custer had given him the horse as a joke. Everybody else had wanted him, but nobody else could ride him. The major simply mounted up and began to put him through his paces, and before long he had attracted an audience that included most of McClellan's staff. He made sudden stops and turns. Finally, he pushed the animal to a run. Wilson remained bolt upright and glass-smooth in the saddle and then, to everybody's amazement, the rider leaned forward in the saddle and the horse understood and somehow found another level—another burst of speed that sent man and horse up and over a fully loaded caisson with feet to spare and without so much as a bump on the landing, and the spectators erupted into spontaneous applause.

"Suppose he'll do," Wilson told Custer with a smile the size of Texas. "He'll do just fine."

OUTSIDE BOONSBORO, MARYLAND

A courier rode forward to deliver a message to Kyd Douglas. "Please see me at your earliest convenience—Gen. A. P. Hill."

Douglas nodded and without explanation rode rearward.

"Captain, you have Jackson's ear. He will not hear me, but it is evident that a battle is at hand. I do not wish anyone else to command my division in an engagement. Tell General Jackson for me that I wish to rejoin my troops only until the present campaign is ended. I will then return to arrest and await the general's orders."

"Well, I wasn't of much help to you last time, General, but I shall try again. Good luck, sir."

"Thank you, Captain."

As Douglas argued Hill's case before Jackson, he felt as though he were pleading with a rancher on behalf of a horse thief. He feared a Jacksonian eruption every time he took a breath. "Very well," Jackson said when Douglas had finished. The astounded captain stopped his horse dead in his tracks and watched in amazement as Jackson rode calmly on.

Alone in his tent, George McClellan felt the very early beginnings of the "old sickness," as he called it. Nothing severe. Just the beginnings. A tightness in the neck. Nothing more than that. No idea as to Lee's intentions. Everybody else seemed to know for certain. Governor Curtin of Pennsylvania is on the verge of panic, absolutely doubtless that Lee is approaching Harrisburg with 150,000 men. Halleck cautioned him to watch for a feint. Protect Washington and Baltimore first. But the army had been seen approaching Hagerstown and Boonsboro. Several citizens of Frederick were adamant that Jackson was on his way to Chambersburg. The numbers had by now been blown so far out of proportion that even McClellan doubted the existence of an army a quarter of a million-strong. One thing and one thing only is absolutely verified—Lee has abandoned Frederick.

McClellan took out a fresh sheet of paper to write his nightly note to Mary Ellen, but the tightness in his neck was worse now and he couldn't think what to write. Where is Lee? What in God's creation is that man up to now? Maybe the numbers do add up. He must have 150,000 men at least or he wouldn't be spreading out like he is. Or like he seems to be. He wired Halleck once again: *Please send forward all the troops you can spare from Washington . . . If the enemy has left for Pennsylvania, I will follow him rapidly. I move my headquarters to Middlebrook immediately.*

The Confederate musicians again serenaded a Rebel crossing of the Potomac and the selected melodies again were appropriate. "Carry Me Back to Ole Virginny" was the tune selected for this day, but Jackson was in no mood for music. The march went well, but according to the latest reports the Yankees still had not vacated Martinsburg and taking care of that problem would add one full day and several long miles to his march. Martinsburg was an inconvenience, but what must be done, must be done.

Jackson's welcome into Frederick had been cordial—his welcome into Martinsburg was tumultuous. The "latest reports" had been wrong and the Union detachment there had evacuated to Harper's Ferry. The people of this loyal Virginia town were all that lay in wait to welcome the great Stonewall.

Flags flew and bands played and Stonewall sought refuge in the local hotel. He was allowed the use of the drawing room to file dispatches to keep Lee apprised of his progress. Schoolboys saw him through a break in the curtains and soon half of the town gathered outside the window.

"General, there are a great many people outside for whom it would be the greatest honor to speak with you," their host said.

"Very well, but we must soon be on our way."

Stonewall couldn't have been more surprised had McClellan's entire army burst through the doors as every female and schoolboy from four counties stormed the hotel lobby. Hundreds of screaming, giggling, jabbering youngsters mobbed around him, pushing books and scraps of paper under his nose for him to sign. He kept repeating, "Thank you. You're very kind," over and again. He felt a tug on his coat and heard a boy yell, "I got a button!" and in seconds his tunic had not a button left. Then came the *coup de grâce*. A woman in her thirties approached him with a pair of scissors that could cut a cable and pleaded for a lock of his hair.

Jackson scanned the room as though searching for a cavalry rescue and saw Douglas and Westbrook standing on the stairs—laughing. They didn't laugh for long. The look on their general's face told them in an instant that a stop must be put to this—now!

"No more, ladies! That's all for now. The general has an army to see to. Please, ladies. Thank you very kindly, but we must move out now."

It took a while, but at last the enemy battalions were pushed backward onto the porch and a squad of infantry brought in to protect the general's flanks against any future attacks.

On the ride out from town no one spoke to the general about the incident—no one dared.

Marcy's earlier suggestion that McClellan appeal directly to the President for reinforcements achieved its desired results. The response arrived at McClellan's headquarters dispatching Fitz-John Porter's corps of 13,000 additional troops from the capital to Maryland and assigning Colonel Miles's division at Harper's Ferry to McClellan as well.

SEPTEMBER 12TH

Please hear me, Miss Barton. On the last occasion the battle was fought near a railroad siding. Transportation for you and your supplies was a simple matter. The coming battle will be fought, frankly, God knows where and getting you there by train may well be impossible."

"Then give me wagons, sir."

"I beg your pardon."

"Wagons, sir. Five wagons, twenty horses and five teamsters to drive them. Then I can take these supplies wherever they are needed. I don't care if the battle is at Sharpsburg. If the army can go there, so can I. I need only the wagons and the men to drive them and I will leave tonight with General Porter."

Mitchell and Bloss marched side by side. The 27th Indiana was well back in the order of march.

"This is the slowest danged march we've been on yet."

"It's all those rookies up ahead. You remember what your first march was like. Soft feet make for hard marching."

"You heard any more about where we're headed?"

"Frederick, I think I heard Captain Kop say. He was sayin' we could have been there tonight with a good, hard march, but at this rate we'll be lucky to get there by supper time tomorrow."

There's nothing to do on a long foot march but complain and think. Complain about the officers and think about anything that will take your mind off your feet. Mitchell thought about Jemima back home. He finally had a letter. Almost a month old. Written before Cedar Mountain, but just now finding him. Good woman. Good family. Cedar Mountain came back to him. Seeing the Rebels from the back for a change. The feeling. The unbridled exhilaration of watching the damned Rebs run and then the horror, quick as a flash, as they turned, just all of a sudden like, and came back at us. Yelling. Making that awful noise. Chills. Froze. I just froze. Dead in my tracks. Still feel the tug of the bullet ripping through my coat. Lucky. Almost killed. Momma's letter ruined. Bloss pulling me away. Dragging me back. Running. Just turned our backs to the Rebels and ran.

Maybe "lucky's" not the right word.

A PIECE OF PAPER

SATURDAY MORNING

A t dawn 4,000 Rebels under Lafayette McLaws advanced slowly up the castle-steep cliffs of Maryland Heights, where 3,000 Yanks waited behind a line of felled trees. In Harper's Ferry the sounds of fighting from above almost brought a smile to the lips of Colonel Miles.

Caesar returning to Rome with Cleopatra on his arm might possibly claim a grander reception than McClellan received at Frederick. General Gibbon rode at his side and tried desperately to keep his horse from stepping on the men, women and children who mobbed the streets.

"Have you ever seen anything like this, John?" McClellan yelled. No, he had not—nor had anyone else. From the upper floors floated down torrents of flowers and streamers and flags. The very air turned red, white and blue. A thousand hands reached up to touch the Young Napoleon or to stroke Dan Webster. Women held up their babies for a kiss and grown men cried. Old Glory flew by the thousands, from three inches long to twelve feet. The sourest of veteran soldiers who no longer wept at the death of a friend wiped away tears of pride. Dan Webster looked as though he had just won a Derby as laden as he was with flowers and flags. For five days the Unionists of Frederick had suffered the disgrace of Rebel occupation and today they exploded from their oppression like uncorked champagne.

Young John Cook, the fifteen-year-old bugle boy from Battery "B" who only last week fought to conceal his tears of shame, made no effort to hide them this time. Any residue of disgrace that may have lingered on the Army of the Potomac was washed away by the outpouring of gratitude and patriotism rained down upon them by the good citizens of Frederick, Maryland.

Even George Smalley, who had been growing more cynical by the day, was genuinely moved by the moment. This was a great day in the life of America.

Mitchell and Bloss enjoyed their new roles as upper-classmen to the new recruits. The veterans of the 27th Indiana pitched their own tents on the outskirts of Frederick, precisely where the Rebels had been only two days before, and left the hard work of establishing a headquarters encampment to the rookies.

After a full morning of being adored by the young ladies and fed by the older ones, it was time for a rest. A little bragging and a lot of complaining went a long way on a slow day.

"General Williams ain't gonna get command of the corps I don't think." Bloss pulled a long sprig of grass and started chewing on it. It made him look more seasoned to the new men.

"How come?"

"He's only a brigadier and he ain't one of Mac's men. They'll bring in somebody new—bet the farm on it."

The two old buddies lay down in the grass and began to get comfortable when something white caught Mitchell's eye. He started to ignore it, but it was something to do on a slow day. He stood back up and walked into the deep grass to investigate.

"Blossie! Cigars!"

"Cigars? Where'd you get cigars?"

"They was lying right there in the grass. You got a match? Who am I asking? You ain't never got nothing. Anybody got a match? I got three cigars—one for me and one for Bloss and one for whoever can find a match."

"What's that?"

"What's what?"

"What's that writin' on the wrapper?"

"Damn, I don't know—I didn't read the damned wrapper." He bit the tip off of one of the cigars and spit it into the grass.

"Well, what's it say?"

The upper left corner read "Special Order No. 191." Across the page was "Hdqrs. Army of Northern Virginia."

Down the page were Roman numerals. By the number III, they saw the words "General Jackson's command . . ." By number IV, "General Longstreet's command." The list went on, General McLaws . . . General Walker . . . General Hill . . . and finally, "By command of General R. E. Lee."

Both men shouted at once—*"Captain Kop!"*

HARPER'S FERRY, VIRGINIA

Brigadier General Julius White had vacated Martinsburg in favor of Harper's Ferry in the path of Jackson's march. As Colonel Miles commanded the garrison there, White assumed the position of second-in-command. The two men stood side by side, each with his field glasses focused on Jackson's corps as the Rebels moved into position along Bolivar Heights.

"Well, Colonel. Our front door is closed and locked."

"To be expected, General, but this battle won't be won or lost on this line." He pointed high and to the left, to where the sounds of battle had been heard all morning long. "The key is Maryland Heights. If they can be halted there then maybe they'll call the whole thing off."

White looked up to the towering slopes and shook off a chill that struck him along with the thought of Confederate guns placed on those ridges.

"I have positioned almost half of my men along that ridge, and the Rebs'll have a hell of a time climbing that mountain."

"And what about Loudoun Heights?"

Miles shrugged his shoulders as though it were a matter of little concern. "We only have so many men, General."

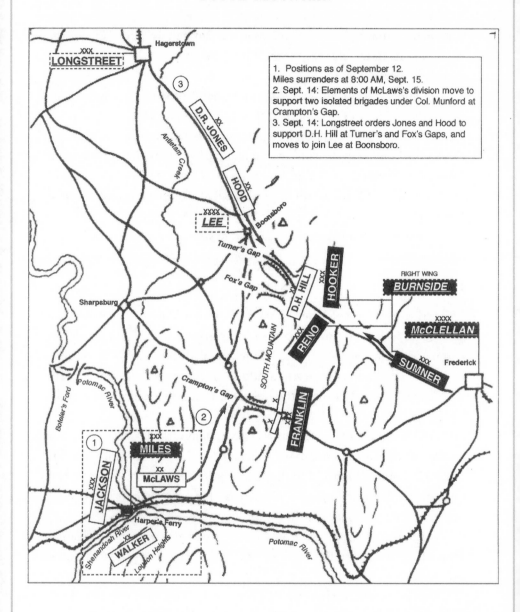

1. Positions as of September 12.
Miles surrenders at 8:00 AM, Sept. 15.
2. Sept. 14: Elements of McLaws's division move to
support two isolated brigades under Col. Munford at
Crampton's Gap.
3. Sept. 14: Longstreet orders Jones and Hood to
support D.H. Hill at Turner's and Fox's Gaps, and
moves to join Lee at Boonsboro.

"I have to tell you, Colonel Miles, that I see this as a totally untenable position." He nodded back toward Jackson's men. "Our only real avenue of escape is closed. Rebel guns on *either* heights will be able to destroy every building in this town if they have the time to do it."

Miles snapped back, "I know that. Jackson knows that and every man in either army knows that, General. But time is the question. It is the *only* question. McClellan is somewhere out there with a huge army. He *must* know that we're here. My orders are to hold this garrison, sir. I have sent couriers to McClellan to send help. I will do what I can."

Both men noticed at the same time that the distant sounds of battle had come to a halt.

"Well, Colonel. One way or another it sounds as though our fate may have already been decided."

On the other side of the hill, the new recruits of the 126th New York could not believe that war was this easy. First from behind their abitis of trees, and later from earthworks four hundred yards farther up the mountain, they had sat all morning long firing down into the Rebel advance until suddenly the Rebels broke and ran, hellbent back down the slopes. The grand legions of the South were not so grand at all. America's newest heroes stood to cheer their easily won victory and a hundred men died with their lungs full of "hoorahs." Before they had a chance to yell, a line of fire fell down on them from above and behind and the terrible, chilling sounds of the Rebel yell froze the survivors in mid-hoorah. They threw their rifles down on the ground and raised their hands high in the air.

Barksdale's brigade had spent the night scaling inclines to gain the Federal rear. A prearranged signal had warned the Confederates coming up the hill to move back and away so Rebels wouldn't fire on Rebels and in an instant Maryland Heights was clear. But the problem of pulling artillery up the towering inclines was only slightly less imposing a task for McLaws. A new road had to be cut up the side of the mountain. Another critical day would be lost.

Lafayette McLaws concentrated entirely on the issue at hand. He gave not a moment's thought to anything that might happen behind him. There was no need. After all, Stuart and Longstreet and Hill were all back there somewhere waiting to round up escapees from Harper's Ferry. If any trouble came his way from the east, they could take care of that.

OUTSIDE FREDERICK, MARYLAND

After the reception he and his army had received entering Frederick, McClellan had no concerns about the loyalty of the locals. That friendly feeling had to be maintained and nurtured, and to that end the general invited the town elders to his headquarters. The mayor was there along with leading merchants and religious leaders of the community. The purpose of the meeting was to assure the civic leaders that the army would condone no misbehavior on the part of its soldiers and that a provost marshal would be assigned to assist local authorities in maintaining the peace. Several of these same men had heard the same speech from General Lee less than a week before.

McClellan's adjutant, Colonel Pittman, burst in on the meeting without knocking. He was red-faced and breathing hard from the run up the hill. "General McClellan, sir?"

McClellan was irritated at the interruption, but tried not to let it show. "What can I do for you, Colonel?"

"Sir, I hate to interrupt your meeting, but some of the men have found what I think to be a rather important document and I thought that you would like to see it immediately."

McClellan glanced over a cover letter from General Williams explaining the circumstances of the find, and knowing that it must be critical to warrant such an interruption, he went quickly to the document itself. He read slowly, his face reflecting his increased excitement at every new paragraph.

"Are we certain as to the authenticity of these orders?"

Donald McGuire, Frederick's leading haberdasher and a member of the local commission, read what he could of the document over McClellan's shoulder and memorized what little he could see—"Special Order No. 191 . . . Jackson to Bolivar Heights . . . Longstreet to Boonsboro."

"Sir, I personally served along with General Chilton before the war," Pittman said. "He is now General Lee's assistant adjutant. We were quite close friends—close enough in fact that I can vouch that those orders are written in his hand."

McClellan's guests were astounded to see the little general raise his hands above his head and leap off the ground like a small boy after a high-hanging apple.

"Now I know what to do! Gentlemen, if you will please excuse us, this is a very pressing matter. Thank you for coming out. The provost marshal will present you his papers today, Mr. Mayor, but I now believe that our visit here will be a short one. Thank you again."

The visitors were out of the tent but could still hear the conversation behind them. "We must inform the President. Lee is ours, now. Lee *and* Jackson."

McGuire tried to behave exactly as the others did as they headed back to town to tell their stories, but he intended to tell his elsewhere. As soon as he could inconspicuously part company with the others, he rode off to Boonsboro to tell *his* story to Robert E. Lee.

McClellan couldn't wait to share the news. He bounded from his tent and was thrilled to see his old friend General John Gibbon, who had ridden with him into Frederick.

"John—come in here." McClellan closed his tent flaps. The gleam in his eye was that of a boy telling stories out of school. He took a deep breath to regain his composure and was suddenly again a general.

"Here is a piece of paper with which, if I cannot whip Bobby Lee, I will be willing to go home."

Gibbon instinctively reached out for the treasure and McClellan pulled it back.

"I will not show you the document now, but here is the signature, and it gives the movement of every division of Lee's army! This document is worth five corps to me, John. Tomorrow we will pitch into his center, and if your people will only do two good, hard days' marching I will put Lee in a position he will find it hard to get out of."

Few men were closer to McClellan than Gibbon. Porter perhaps, and Burnside. But since Second Bull Run, those two had been bickering and all three relationships seemed to suffer. Gibbon loved and respected Little Mac, but as he left the tent he couldn't help wondering, *Why tomorrow? If the lost dispatch is that damned revealing, why not today?* It wasn't yet noon and a "good, hard day's marching" could yet be done between now and darkness. McClellan commanded an army, and Gibbon only a brigade. It wasn't a brigadier's place to question the commanding general.

Gibbon returned to his own tent, and waited for orders to move— "tomorrow."

Saturday Afternoon

Lafayette McLaws wasn't the only Confederate general who ignored the passes through South Mountain. D. H. Hill, whose job it was to close those passes to escaping Yankees on the run from Harper's Ferry, also had his back to the Army of the Potomac. In three days on the outskirts of Boonsboro, Hill had not once ridden east to consider what his reactions might be to an attack against his rear.

Stuart's cavalry was stretched thin along the ranges of South Mountain and the parallel range known as the Catoctin Mountains, which were even farther to McLaws's rear. Stuart's attention too was directed westward toward Harper's Ferry, but early in the afternoon a unit of Pleasonton's cavalry happened upon a unit of Stuart's. So thinly were Jeb's troopers spread across two mountain ranges that any meeting of the two was improbable at best. Stuart's men were, after all, a third precautionary line designed to round up any escaping Yankees who were bold or clever enough to escape both McLaws and Hill.

Against this handful of Lee's legendary horsemen the maligned Union cavalry boasted a moral victory. *Any* victory at this stage of the conflict was a moral victory for the mounted men of the North. The Confederates abandoned their positions along the Catoctins and raced "forward" to report that Yankees approached from the rear.

To the President
September 13, 1862
I have the whole Rebel force in front of me and no time shall be lost . . . I think Lee has made a gross mistake and that he will be severely punished for it. The Army is in motion as rapidly as possible. I hope for great success

if the plans of the Rebels remain unchanged. I have all the plans of the Rebels and will catch them in their own trap if my men are equal to the emergency . . . All forces of Pennsylvania should be placed to cooperate at Chambersburg. My respects to Mrs. Lincoln. Received most enthusiastically by the ladies. Will send you trophies.

Geo. B. McClellan

"That damned Pinkerton is never around when you need him." McClellan looked at his watch. It was after 3:00 and getting late in the day. "I must know if these orders are authentic before I can move an inch. I would not put it past Lee and his conniving spies to have planted this thing here just for us to find—all nicely done in his adjutant's handwriting and all." He squinted his eyes tightly and bit his lower lip as a shooting pain raced from his shoulder to his brain. As soon as he was able to open his eyes again, he studied 191 for the thousandth time.

"According to the order Longstreet is ordered to Boonsboro, but too many good citizens report him in Hagerstown. I cannot dismiss those reports out of hand without knowing certainly one way or the other.

"Colonel Key."

"Sir."

McClellan scribbled a note: *Ascertain if the order of march contained herein has thus far been followed by the enemy.*

"Transcribe those supposed orders word for word and attach this note. Then send it to General Pleasonton with the cavalry." Then to Marcy, "Unlike our friend, Mr. Pope, I intend to *know* the whereabouts of Mr. Longstreet."

James Wilson mounted his new black stallion and headed for South Mountain in search of Alfred Pleasonton and George McClellan's cavalry. At 3:35, McClellan ordered Brigadier General Jacob D. Cox, commander of Ohio's Pride, the Kanawha Division, to move his 3,000 men to the base of South Mountain in support of Pleasonton. After taking care of that little detail, McClellan settled back and waited for confirmation that "the order of march" of the Confederate divisions had, indeed, been followed.

BOONSBORO, MARYLAND

Geneneral Hill."

"General Stuart. You were pushing Miss Skylark pretty hard up the hill there. You must have news for me."

Jeb Stuart and Harvey Hill were not the closest of friends. Hill thought that cavalry was a waste of good men and horses, especially under the leadership of a flamboyant cavalier more concerned with good press than the good cause, and Stuart, basically, thought Hill was a pompous ass.

"Nothing of great urgency, Harvey, but there seems to be some movement of the Yankees toward South Mountain."

Hill closed his eyes in concern. "In what numbers?"

"I am told a brigade or two. I suppose it could be as much as a division. There is some cavalry activity from that direction as well. Nothing major, but I thought you should be aware of it."

"Longstreet is still in Hagerstown, isn't he?"

"The last I heard. I will confirm that as soon as I know for certain myself."

"Damn. I only have five thousand men here. I do not possess the resources to . . ." He filled his lungs and discarded the thought. "Very well. I shall order Colquitt's brigade back into Turner's Gap as a precaution and put Garland on alert to join him should it become necessary. I truly cannot afford any additional expenditure of personnel."

Stuart tried not to show his contempt at Hill's expressions. Why use one syllable when four or five would do nicely?

SOUTH MOUNTAIN

Either too busy or having too much fun turning the tables on the world's most famous cavalryman, General Pleasonton was far too occupied to give thorough consideration to McClellan's dispatch. If all continued to go well, tomorrow *he* would be the world's most famous cavalryman and he didn't have time to concern himself with anything so mundane as intelligence-gathering operations. He scribbled a note, gave it to Wilson and put it out of his mind. "As near as I can judge, the order of march of the enemy that you sent me has been followed as closely as circumstances would permit."

Wilson was astounded. Only halfway up the hill Pleasonton could have no idea as to what might be waiting at the crest and yet the entire army was going to move, or not move, based on his word. He started to challenge Pleasonton, but thought better of it. Surely he knew more than he was telling. So Wilson fought the urge and headed back down the mountain.

He had been stewing on Pleasonton's incompetence for an hour or more on his way back to McClellan's headquarters and was glad to see Generals Reno and Cox headed for the mountain. He was not quite so glad when he realized that it wasn't Reno's entire corps, but only Cox's Kanawha Division making its way forward. He decided to check in with Reno and report on the front.

"General Pleasonton is lightly engaged with dismounted cavalry about halfway up the hill," Wilson reported, "but I have no idea what may lay farther up, sir."

Reno just nodded and Wilson couldn't hold back any longer.

"Sir, I'm not entirely certain that Pleasonton knows either."

Reno still said nothing and Wilson was getting angrier with every passing second.

"I'm supposed to report back to General McClellan, sir, and frankly I'm not confident . . . well, I just don't quite know what to tell him."

"You tell him that the Kanawha Division is on its way and that the mountain will be ours by morning." Reno gave his horse a quick spur and showed his back to the presumptuous young courier.

It was dusk before Wilson was able to deliver the messages from Pleasonton and Reno to General McClellan. He stood and watched as the commanding general read Pleasonton's note and when he was done Wilson told him about Reno's position that the Kanawha Division would be more than adequate to handle whatever may be waiting for them atop South Mountain. McClellan nodded and awaited the obligatory salute, but Wilson couldn't leave. "May I speak freely, sir?"

"Go on."

"Sir, I don't believe that either man has had an opportunity to adequately reconnoiter the top or the opposite side of the mountain. They may know what is there now, but I don't see how either can know what may be on the way."

"Is that all, Major?"

Not really, Wilson thought. He desperately wanted to tell the general to get off his butt and go there himself. He wanted to tell him to bring up the whole goddamned army and overwhelm whatever might be on top. He wanted to tell him that you can't win a war making timid little pissant probes. He wanted to tell him all of this—but he didn't.

It was almost dark when fifteen Rebel pickets jumped onto the road in front of a one-horse buggy. "What's your business, friend?"

"I am Donald McGuire, a citizen of Frederick and a friend of the South. I have vital information for General Lee."

WASHINGTON

Abraham Lincoln felt like he'd been running in waist-deep mud all day long. Constantly moving, struggling to free himself and get to where he needed to be, but going nowhere. Slowly. He met for most of the morning with influential Republicans who were scared to death that the November elections would sweep a new breed of Peace Democrats into the House of Representatives. Pennsylvania was probably gone, and New York was threatened. They told him nothing he didn't already know. They feared nothing he didn't already fear. Another item on an endless list of disastrous possibilities, any one of which would mean the death of the Republic. But he soothed their fears with the promise of major developments soon to come.

Office seekers badgered him and administrative details absorbed every daylight hour. He approved the release of five of the government's wagons for use by Clara Barton, and it was not until late when he was able to pull himself from the muck of this wasted day and make his way to the soldiers' home to visit with some of the wounded.

He returned to the Executive Mansion to be greeted by a delegation of ministers from Chicago who had come to the nation's capital to urge upon the President the emancipation of the slaves. To them he delivered his well-rehearsed private speech on the matter.

"What good would a proclamation of emancipation from me do, especially now? I do not want to issue a document that the whole world will see is inoperative, like the Pope's bull against the comet." Even as he spoke these words, he stood a scant five feet away from the Emancipation Proclamation. There it sat. Right there in that drawer. Ready to be pulled out and fired like a hidden pistol, but, also like a pistol, Lincoln knew it was best to pretend it wasn't there. And so he continued. "Would my word free the slaves when I cannot even enforce the Constitution in the Rebel states? Is there a single court or magistrate or individual that would be influenced by it there?" He asked these questions of the gathered ministers, but, at the same time, also of himself. "I will mention another thing, though it will meet only with your scorn and contempt. There are fifty thousand bayonets in the Union armies from the border slave states. It would be a *serious* matter if, in consequence of such a proclamation, they should go over to the Rebels." Keep the pistol in the drawer. "Do not misunderstand me because I have mentioned these objections. They indicate the difficulties that have thus far prevented action in some such way as you desire. I have not decided against a proclamation of liberty for the slaves but hold the matter under advisement. I can assure you that the subject is on my mind, by day and night, more than any other. Whatever shall appear to be God's will, I will do."

A bearded Baptist with hellfire and brimstone in his soul saw this as his opportunity to save the day for righteousness. He leaped from his chair and in a voice practiced at reaching beyond the rear pews and to the ears of the Almighty Himself he shouted at Lincoln, "It *is* a message to you from our Divine Master, *through me, commanding you, sir,* to open the doors of bondage that the slaves may go free!"

After the "Amens" subsided, the President, calmly and very quietly, almost in a whisper, said to the man, "The next time you speak with God please inform Him for me that I would very much like to speak with Him directly. That would seem to me to be more efficient."

SATURDAY NIGHT

G eneral Lee, sir."

"General Stuart. What news have you brought me?"

"Nothing good, I'm afraid."

"Go on."

"A gentleman from Frederick made his way to our lines today and he claims to have been in the presence of General McClellan when a copy of our Special Orders was delivered to him."

"To *McClellan*?"

"Yes, sir."

Lee felt his entire body tighten like a clenched fist. His stomach knotted and he couldn't take a breath. His knees felt weak as the full implication of what Stuart had said sank in. A vision of his map flashed through his mind with his army's position spread all across it. In an instant he knew precisely what he would do in McClellan's position and it would be devastating. The war, so winnable only a moment ago, might well be lost in forty-eight hours. The man from Frederick *must* be wrong.

"Do you believe him?"

"I'm afraid that I do, sir. He knew not only the number but some of the details. He said that a member of McClellan's staff even verified General Chilton's handwriting."

"Has McClellan responded in any way?"

"As you know, sir, his cavalry has approached South Mountain, probably to verify our positions, and a division or less seems to be on its way, but no major activity has been reported."

"Well, then, either the report is false and the man from Frederick is mistaken somehow, or McClellan . . . I don't know, General. If he has our plans, he will move. He must. Keep an eye to the east, General, but Harper's Ferry *must* fall."

Lee watched as Stuart went about his business. His wrists ached and his heart pounded. Please don't let it be true. His breathing became labored and Longstreet's words came to his mind. *It is a venture not worth the game*, he had said. *It can't be*, Lee thought. All of the copies are accounted for.

"Major Taylor."

"Sir?"

"Send for General Longstreet."

Nestled in the low point of South Mountain known as Turner's Gap, Colonel A. H. Colquitt looked down into the valley. It was dark by the time his brigade had reached a summit from which he could gain an eastward-looking view. Standing in a cleared field, he could see the lights of the hamlet of Bolivar below as well as the lights of campfires at the mountain's base—lots of campfires.

"Unless every man has built himself four fires, there's a hell of a lot more Yankees down there than Hill thinks there is. Courier!"

"Sir?"

"Get your butt back down the mountain and tell General Hill that two or maybe even three thousand Yankees are camped on the eastern slopes immediately below Turner's Gap. Ride!"

At 8:45 P.M. McClellan sent Halleck a brief wire that somehow neglected to mention 191:

"The whole force of the enemy is in front. They are not retreating into Virginia. Look well to Chambersburg. Shall lose no time. Will soon have decisive battle."

After sending this message, he met with his corps commanders to prepare tomorrow's action. He demonstrated for them the positions of Lee's army according to the found dispatch. On a map the size of a picnic table he brought everyone's attention to the two crossing points. On the north, Turner's Gap. On the south was Crampton's Gap. And near the top of the mountain, a smaller avenue cut off from Turner's Gap. Fox's Gap would be a good alternative for moving down the western banks, but offered no help on the way up.

"We have reason to believe that Harper's Ferry is still in Union hands. Sounds of battle from Maryland Heights indicate so and a cavalry officer arrived here this night requesting support for Colonel Miles.

"General Pleasonton has pushed the enemy cavalry back from this side of South Mountain and a brigade of General Burnside's wing is encamped below Turner's Gap in his support.

"General Franklin will move at first light with twenty thousand men on Crampton's Gap. If this position is heavily defended, General, make your dispositions for attack and commence it about a half an hour after you hear severe fighting at Turner's Gap to your north. If on your arrival you find it lightly guarded, your duty will be first to cut off, destroy or capture McLaws's command and relieve Colonel Miles. If you should find any bridges intact that would allow the remainder of the enemy to cross the Potomac, destroy them. At this point, if the primary assault of the army has not yet been successful, proceed to Boonsboro, gaining the enemy rear. If we have been successful you will be assigned a position near Sharpsburg to prevent Jackson from recrossing the river and coming to the aid of Longstreet and Hill.

"The First and Ninth Corps under General Burnside will march on Turner's Gap, to the north, followed by Sumner and Williams. This will bring an effective force of seventy thousand men against Turner's Gap. We shall breach that gap, sirs, and move against Hill and Longstreet before they can be reinforced by the Rebel armies at Harper's Ferry.

"My general idea is to cut the enemy in two and beat him in detail. Are there any questions?"

"What is the enemy's estimated strength?"

"Apparently Longstreet commands two corps. This would put their strength at Boonsboro at fifty to sixty thousand men. The units under Jackson and McLaws are reckoned at near that same strength. Walker probably does not command above a division—say ten to twelve thousand, but those units are all so badly divided that they can be dealt with singly after Longstreet has been disposed of."

The arithmetic bothered Ambrose Burnside and the math wasn't hard. Franklin with 20,000 against Crampton's Gap, and the rest of the whole damned army, 70,000 men, aimed at Turner's. Burnside had been McClellan's close friend for almost twenty years. If anyone was free to speak his mind, even at a council of war, it was Burn. "Do you not fear that you might be placing too heavy a burden on General Franklin?"

"There is no help for it. Every man under my command will be required for the fighting at Boonsboro or in Turner's Gap.

"General Franklin, I think the force you have is, with good management, sufficient for the end in view. If you differ widely from me and being on the spot you know better than I do the circumstances of the case, inform me at once and I will do my best to reinforce you. I ask of you at this important moment for all your intellect and the utmost activity a general can exercise. Knowing my views and intentions, you are fully authorized to change any of the details . . . provided the purpose is carried out—that purpose being to attack the enemy in detail and beat him!

"Gentlemen, you have your orders and you are dismissed."

McClellan's tent was on the highest point he could find and after his corps commanders left him, the Young Napoleon stood alone on the hillside and admired the spectacle below. Tens of thousands of campfires illuminated tents that glowed like lanterns for as far as he could see. The grounds were so quiet now, and the air so still that he could hear from a distance a single soldier with a mouth harp serenading the army with "Aura Lee."

God, that is a beautiful tune, he thought. God, how I love these men. Please, dear God . . . Please, dear God . . . what? Please, dear God, don't let them die? Don't let them suffer? Don't let them . . . lose. That's it. That's all I can pray for now. That's all that matters. Please, dear God, don't let me be beaten.

"General Lee—you sent for me?"

"Yes, General Longstreet, we've encountered some new problems, I'm afraid." No point in trying to soften the blow. May as well just get it out and over with. "Stuart believes that McClellan may have gotten his hands on a copy of our marching orders and is fully aware of the dispersal of our army."

Longstreet went pale. He thought for a moment that he might become ill.

"This is not known with any certitude, and as yet it doesn't seem as though he has reacted as he should to so vital a piece of intelligence. Harvey Hill has only recently informed me that two to three thousand of those people are camped on the eastern slopes of South Mountain at the mouth of Turner's Gap."

"More will be there soon, General, if Stuart is correct. Many more."

"I agree. Even our old friend George cannot pass on an opportunity of this magnitude. There is more disturbing news, I fear. The last we heard from General Jackson, McLaws had not yet secured Maryland Heights and it may take him some time to get his guns into place. It may be late in the day before operations can begin there."

Longstreet's tone became almost pleading. "Suspend those operations, sir. It will come as no news to you that I have feared this all along. If the Yankees come busting through that pass in the morning, sir"— Longstreet was an inch away from letting his "I told you so" cross the boundaries of propriety—"Well, I fear the worst, sir. I suggest, General Lee, that the entire army be ordered at once to suspend operations and unite together on some good ground of *our* choosing and, I say it again, sir—let the damned Yankees come to us!"

"There is no need just yet to be hasty, General. These gaps can be held. Surely not forever, but perhaps until Jackson can finish his business at Harper's Ferry tomorrow afternoon. I no longer believe us to be threatened from Pennsylvania and this frees your divisions to move to Hill's assistance."

Longstreet began to renew his assault on this incredibly dangerous delay, but before he could speak a word Lee put up his bandaged hand and said, "Begin your march at first light."

There was nothing for Pete Longstreet to do but salute and retire for the night.

An uphill avalanche of blue men tumble over a pitiful handful of grays. The blue men never fall but explode when hit into ten more and ten more and ten more until the green earth of the valley floor is flooded blue with soldiers. The blue ocean forms into a mighty river and continues its roaring flow—uphill.

Longstreet awoke with his heart pounding, his face hot and wet and with the rest of his body colder than the night after Christmas, but certain that he had never gone to sleep.

He put on his slippers and was reminded once again of the painful blister. Damned nuisance. He walked to the table where he wrote a note to General Lee. He pleaded his case one last time. "Our nation cannot withstand a single defeat of the magnitude facing us today. Should one infinitesimal portion of the plan go bad, one delay, one setback, one failure to hold, then all will be lost. Together at Sharpsburg we still risk defeat, but we risk defeat together."

He signed the note, sealed it and sent it to Lee's tent. Longstreet then lay back down and slept—without dreaming.

DESERTED BY
ALL THE WORLD

Sunday Morning

As though Harvey Hill wasn't nervous enough, at one in the morning a courier from General Lee arrived with his new instructions. "The gap must be held at all hazards until the operations at Harper's Ferry are finished. You must keep me informed of the strength of the enemy's forces. You will repair soonest to Turner's Gap to command the defenses there and to cooperate with General Stuart who will be responsible for the defense of Crampton's."

Then came the crusher. "General Longstreet will advance to your assistance first thing tomorrow."

Longstreet? he thought. *How many damned Yankees* are *there?*

Hill issued orders for Garland's Brigade to advance up the western slopes of South Mountain to join up with Colquitt at first light. There, he said, he would be waiting.

By the time Lincoln finished his meetings with politicians and preachers and wounded soldiers, it was 2:30 on Sunday morning. It was only then that he was able to read McClellan's fourteen-hour-old dispatch.

"The whole Rebel force in front of me . . .
"Lee has made a gross mistake . . .
"All of the plans of the Rebels . . ."

Lincoln went to sleep in the overstuffed chair with McClellan's wire in his lap.

Of the hundreds of Southern-born officers on active duty in the United States Army when the war began, few chose to retain their commissions, remain in blue and fight for the preservation of the Union. One of those men was Colonel Benjamin Franklin Davis, a son of Mississippi and the second-in-command of the cavalry detachment trapped at Harper's Ferry.

To Davis, above all others, the thought of surrender was abhorrent. The chagrin of being held prisoner by his neighbors, by his countrymen, by his own brothers would be intolerable, so Benjamin Franklin Davis devised a daring plan. Not a plan to save Harper's Ferry—it was far too late for that. Jackson's divisions were clearly visible beyond Bolivar Heights. Scouts reported artillery moving into place along Loudoun Heights, and yesterday's abortive battle on the Maryland side of the river made it all too clear that it was only a matter of time before exploding iron would fall into the deathpit that Harper's Ferry had become.

No, this was a plan to save the cavalry, and he took it to his commander, Colonel Arno Voss, who struggled, now as always, to understand Davis's thick Southern accent.

"We have done all that the cavalry can do here, sir. The horses are among the army's freshest and finest and are desperately low on forage. These animals cannot withstand a siege of forty-eight hours and even should they, it would only be to the benefit of the enemy when the creatures fall into enemy hands—and they will, sir, fall into enemy hands, as will we all."

"Sit down, Colonel. You're making me nervous." Davis unhooked his saber, placed it on a table and took a seat.

"I do not know whose decision it was to try to defend this place. It would be easier to defend the bottom of a dried-out well, but it is far too late to argue the point. The fact is that it is not defensible. Colonel Miles may be the only man on earth who fails to recognize that fact. Harper's Ferry will fall and it will fall soon. We can no longer contribute in any way to her defense and all that we are doing here is awaiting death or capture and I, sir, prefer the former."

"To the point, Colonel."

"If we are to fall into the hands of the Rebels, sir, what does it matter where?"

"To the *point*, Colonel."

"That *is* the point, sir. We can wait here to be surrendered by our moronic and drunken commanding officer . . ."

"Colonel Miles has not had a drop of whiskey since the incident at Bull Run—at First Bull Run."

"Be that as it may, sir, we can wait here until we are ordered to hand over untempered swords to Stonewall Jackson . . ." The chair couldn't hold him any longer. He stood and took a step closer to his commander. "Or we can make a run for it. If we are captured on the roads leading out of this Godforsaken hole in the earth, the results are the same except that at least we will have put up a fight. But there is a chance, sir, and I believe a fair one, that an escape *can* be made. The point is, sir, that nothing is lost by trying, and nothing is gained by waiting."

The sun brought no good news to D. H. Hill. This moment was the first time he laid eyes on Turner's Gap and it shook him greatly to see that the access to Harper's Ferry was wide and cut through by no fewer than five roads. Stuart had virtually abandoned Turner's Gap in favor of his primary position in Crampton's Gap, six miles to the south, generously contributing two hundred troopers and four pieces of horse artillery to Hill's defenses. Hill and one of his couriers found a high spot to get a better view of the valley as he gave the man his orders in the pompous tones that he believed so distinguished him from the other officers of either army. "Inform General Garland that his presence is required atop this knoll *posthaste*. Then continue on with a message for General Longstreet—Holy Mother of God!"

Not only had the campsites at the base of the mountain been abandoned, but across the valley, below the sunrise, rose a huge cloud of orange dust. Under this cloud, Hill instantly knew, an immense army marched.

"Tell him the enemy is being very heavily reinforced. Tell him we need him here *now*! Order Colonel Anderson up the hill immediately, only Ripley and Rodes are to remain where they are. Ride!"

As bad as it was, the full extent of his situation had not dawned on

Harvey Hill even yet. The units marching toward him out of the sun were the remainder of Burnside's corps, maybe 3,000 additional men under the command of Jesse Reno. Behind him was Joe Hooker, behind him was Edwin Sumner and behind him was Alpheus Williams. Together they commanded nearly 70,000 men. Hill commanded five.

As the Ohioans of Jacob Cox's Kanawha Division marched up the mountain, they happened upon a friendly officer on his way down.

"Colonel Moor, may I say that this is an odd place to find you?"

"I'm certain that it is, General. I was captured on Thursday and paroled last night. Naturally I am returning home to await an exchange so I can get back into the fight." It had been a long walk and a steep climb for Colonel Moor, and a convenient stump made a welcome chair. He began to remove his boots to give his weary feet a well-deserved rubbing. "What is your destination?"

"Turner's Gap, to join up with General Pleasonton's cavalry, and from there I believe into Boonsboro."

"Oh, my God."

"I beg your pardon, sir."

Augustus Moor immediately forgot his aching feet. For a man of honor, an officer and a gentleman, he faced the ultimate dilemma, but even duty to country could not justify the violation an oath sworn before God. The man's heart and soul struggled for a way to escape unbroken. God *or* country. Which will it be?

Cox waited patiently. He saw the distress in Moor's face and immediately recognized the scope of his dilemma. He saw the agony on his face and in his eyes. Every man in either army knew there was a chance this day would come. God *or* country.

"I can say no more, sir. By the terms of my release I am sworn to discuss with no one the positions of Rebel units." Another hesitation. "I can say only this, General. Please, be careful."

Cox needed to hear no more.

"All regiments forward at left oblique off the road. We'll move through the woods and off to the left. Courier! Ride to the rear and inform General Reno that we expect opposition at Turner's Gap.

Courier! Ride forward and tell General Pleasonton that the Rebels have forces at Turner's Gap. Left oblique now, men, and on up the hill."

HARPER'S FERRY

If Stonewall Jackson was impatient, General John Walker was toe-tapping. He had missed all the fun and glory of Second Manassas and was itching to kill some Yankees—especially at this range, with little or no danger to his guns or his men. The guns would soon be in place, but he was ordered by Jackson to wait for McLaws. Across the river at Maryland Heights, McLaws fought the war with axes as his men battled an obstinate army of trees to put a scar on the mountain wide enough and flat enough get his big guns to the top.

While McLaws concerned himself exclusively with the hacking down of timber, one of his subordinates finally focused on protecting his rear.

General Paul Semmes decided that a rearward glance might be in his best interest and his scouts found no one—no one—guarding Crampton's Gap. Jeb Stuart was not yet in place, so this approach to Hill's rear was as open as a church door on Easter Sunday. It was a door that must be shut, and Semmes consulted no one before ordering a regiment to close and lock it. Just one regiment and only as a precaution.

General Samuel Garland was a very happy man. The mail had finally caught up with him and his band of North Carolinians, and enclosed in a letter from his fiancée was a clipping from the *Richmond Dispatch* announcing their nuptials. Old Sam Garland, who had fought hard for acceptance in the highfalutin' world of Richmond's social scene, was the envy of every lad south of the Potomac. The prettiest girl in the fanciest family in all of Old Virginia had agreed to be his wife. Her mother's mother had been a Custis, so he would soon be related to Robert E. Lee, *and* to George Washington.

Garland's brigade made it up the mountain in record time and there he met with Hill and Colquitt at Turner's Gap.

"There's a road that cuts off the main pike and veers off toward our right flank toward that other little gap over there . . ."

"That's called Fox's Gap, sir," Colquitt said.

"Hold that road, General Garland. You're our right flank, and it may be so for a considerable time. Our orders are to hold 'at all hazards,' gentlemen. Post your men."

Too many roads. Too many Yankees. Hill knew this all too well. What he didn't know was that the very first Yankees coming up the mountain weren't using the roads. Thanks to Colonel Moor's thinly disguised warning, Ohio's Kanawha Division wasn't coming up the road, but through the woods, and at 9:00 A.M. 3,000 Yankees broke out of the *defilade* onto an open field and tumbled uphill directly at Garland's right flank, which lay in a farm road behind a stone wall. Garland had expected them to come up the main road, so he had placed his rookie regiments on the wings, the 13th North Carolina on the left, and the 19th on the right, and it was on the extreme right flank that the brunt of the Federal attack first fell. It seems to be a trick that Mars plays on armies, that no matter how the deck is stacked, the rookies draw the deuce. Garland chose to lead by example to head off a rout before it began. The "brave general at the front" technique worked well, and the North Carolinians, green and seasoned alike, lived up to their "tarheel" reputation. The Union troops pounded his lines, and while they bent for a moment here and there, Garland always managed to rally them back in line as the Yankees kept coming.

"Hold your lines, men! If they get past us they'll get General Lee! Hold your lines, men."

The fire came heavier and the roar of the musketry was constant now as more and more men of the Kanawha Division piled out of the woods and onto the field.

If things weren't bad enough for Sam Garland at this moment, he saw a team of Ohio gunners pushing and pulling their cannon into position. Their horses were already dead, so it was the men who dragged their 1,700-pound weapon up the hill and to within fifty yards of the Rebel lines. *Canister*, Garland thought. *Close enough for canister*. If this gun could not be taken out, it would soon become a gigantic shotgun, each shell scattering twenty-seven cast-iron balls square into the heart of his already faltering lines. Garland tried to remain calm, or at least to appear so to his men.

With his saber he pointed toward the gallant gunners. "Kill those men," he said almost casually.

In six minutes the Ohioans loaded and fired seven times square into the faces of the boys from North Carolina, and in seven minutes the entire nine-man crew lay dead on the field.

"General Garland, the men of the Thirteenth are taking some terrible fire, sir. Colonel Ruffin sends his regards, sir, and says he doesn't know how much longer he can hold."

Without a word Garland sprinted off to the left to try to work his rally magic there. He found Ruffin with his lines thinned and fifty yards from the Yankees.

"General, why do you stay here? You are in great danger," Ruffin screamed at his commander.

"I may as well be here as yourself."

"No. It is my duty to be here with my regiment, but you could better superintend your brigade from a safer position."

At that moment Ruffin's chest exploded, and Garland quickly dismounted and knelt at his side.

Softly through his pain, Ruffin whispered to Garland, "I am the only field officer left here, General. If I must go to the rear, you'll have to replace me." Garland called over a staff officer and started to speak when Ruffin's body went limp in his arms. Garland kissed the man's forehead and stood to resume his command when a bullet struck him square in the heart. At precisely that moment Colonel Scammon ordered his Ohioans to fix bayonets and charge.

Their general was dead, their colonel was dead and most of their comrades were dead or wounded as a thousand screaming Yankees came surging toward them now only thirty yards away, and the greenest of the tarheels, with only a captain to command them, turned at last and ran. The veteran troops made a valiant effort to fill in the hole. Some crashed into the Union attack prepared for a classic bayonet thrust, but most grabbed the hand-blistering hot barrels of their muskets and began swinging them like clubs and for a moment the hole filled back up with gray. Colonel Rutherford B. Hayes, a politically appointed officer, ordered his 23rd Ohio into the fray. "Give 'em hell! Give the sons-of-bitches hell!" he yelled as a ball tore into his arm, but he continued to stand and his men drove on. The Rebel lines broke for good and the rout that Garland had feared was on.

The roads between Hagerstown and South Mountain were clogged with Rebels. The remainder of Longstreet's corps, totaling only 6,600 men, had twelve hot miles to march, the last one being straight uphill. Nine hours would be making good time.

The march began as ordered at dawn. The men knew that this was an emergency movement, as it had not even been rumored before it was ordered. Lee had struggled to mount Traveller so that each and every man had to see him astride the great stallion as they left Hagerstown, another bellwether of impending battle. The implied importance of the day lent impetus to their steps and the march went well. Only John Bell Hood's division dreaded the action of the day. Their reckless but revered commander still rode at the rear, still under arrest for his argument over the ambulances after Second Manassas.

"HOOD, HOOD, HOOD," the Texans chanted as they paraded before Marse Robert. Lee raised his bandaged hand and all fell silent. "You shall have him, gentlemen," he said, and the chant began again, but this time it was "LEE, LEE, LEE."

"General Hood, come here," Lee said as the brash young general passed before him. "General, here I am just on the eve of entering into a battle, and with one of my best officers under arrest. If you will merely say that you regret this occurrence, I will release you and restore you to the command of your division."

Hood shook his head. "I regret, sir, that I cannot consistently do so."

"I am asking, General Hood, only that you express regret at the occurrence—not that you admit to insubordination."

"I regret, sir, that I cannot."

Lee hesitated an irritated instant. Pride. The real enemy. "Well, I will suspend your arrest till the impending battle is decided."

John Bell Hood saluted and, in a most dignified manner, said, "Thank you General Lee." Lee reluctantly returned the salute, and Hood spurred his horse to a run and "yahooed" his way to the front of his division.

Hood was back in command. A. P. Hill was back in command. Stonewall Jackson was back in the saddle. Of the infirmities and incarcerations that inflicted the Confederate commanders as they had crossed the Potomac ten days before, only two remained—Lee's bandaged wrists, and Longstreet's blistered heel.

SHARPSBURG, MARYLAND

Up the road apiece in Sharpsburg, this Sunday morning began like any other. James Kretzer's huge American flag stretched clear across Main Street. Ada Mumma played with her Rohrbach cousins and explained for the hundredth time that her name was pronounced "Moomaw," not Mumma, and David Miller strolled one more time into his beautiful cornfield. He pulled an ear from one of the six-foot-high stalks and peeled back the shucks. One more month was all he needed till he could harvest the beautiful field. The sounds of distant thunder troubled him. It was odd. The weather was clear in all directions, but he could swear that he heard thunder. The last thing he needed was a hailstorm. A little more rain wouldn't hurt, but a hailstorm was about the only thing left that could ruin his season.

Philip Pry lived high on a hill overlooking the pretty little town and the gentle hills and fertile valleys that surrounded it. He stood on the back side of his two-story brick plantation-style home and admired the view and thought how beautiful it would be in only a few weeks when autumn added her colors to the canvas.

HARPER'S FERRY

At Harper's Ferry, Benjamin Franklin Davis convinced Colonel Voss that his plan could work. Now only Colonel Miles stood in his way. The two cavalrymen decided to offer their plan first to General White and managed to enlist his support, and all three went to Miles to make the toughest sell of all.

"Colonel Davis," Miles said, "everybody wants to leave Harper's Ferry. Hell—*I* want to leave—but my orders from General in Chief Halleck are to hold to the last extremity. If I allow the cavalry to go, what do I tell the infantry and artillery?"

"That number of men cannot possibly sneak out of here, General.

And the artillery cannot easily be carried up those slopes." Miles struggled to understand both Davis's plan and his Mississippi accent. "Those men can help you defend your position and maybe hold out until help can arrive, if help is on the way. Cavalry can be of no help in a siege situation—it is, in fact sir, a hindrance."

"Colonel, this is totally against all regulations and contrary to sound military principles. It is wild, impractical and sure to invariably result in serious loss to the government. At this point, I do not believe that a mouse could escape from Harper's Ferry."

"Captain Russell made it out only last night."

"Captain Russell *may* have made it out, of that we cannot be certain. By God, we should all *hope* that he did because he carried with him our request for assistance to General McClellan. Communications have been down for so long I don't even know if the rest of the army even knows we're here. And—if Captain Russell *did* make it out, he did so with nine men, not twelve hundred!"

Davis stifled a profanity by slapping his thigh with the riding gloves he held in his right hand. "General, I *demand* the privilege of cutting my way out of here rather than waiting like a pig for the slaughter! You stand alone in opposition and I must now inform you, sir, that it is my intention to go with or *without* your consent!"

Miles looked around the room. "Is this correct, sirs? You are all in agreement with Colonel Davis?"

Each man nodded his assent.

"Obviously, then, there must be some merit to your proposal. I will offer you this, then. Return here to my office at seven o'clock tonight and bring your commanders with you. Discuss the particulars of the escape and if you can offer me an agreeable route of departure, I shall gladly wave you good-bye."

SOUTH MOUNTAIN

Looking down from South Mountain, Harvey Hill was moved by the sight. Out from under the morning sun marched an army so grand and beautiful that any soldier would be proud to be a part of it. The sight of Hannibal's approach to the Alps must have been much like

176 • RICHARD CROKER

it. Every man who saw it likened it to a snake that stretched for miles over and beyond the horizon to the other side of the earth. It was a snake with steely spines as 70,000 gun barrels caught the rays of the sun and relayed them forward to the pitiful band of exhausted Rebels waiting at the summit.

There is no shame in losing your life to an army so grand, thought Daniel Harvey Hill, as he was certain that he and all here were surely soon to die, no matter how many men arrived from the west. *And God looks with favor upon men who die on Sunday. Dear God, I have never felt such loneliness, I have never felt so deserted by all the world and the rest of mankind.*

Hill was shaken from his thoughts by a panicked messenger.

"General Hill—your right flank is turned." Winded from a run up the hill, he had to catch some air before he could deliver the truly bad news. "General Garland is dead."

"Run out two of the guns Stuart left us onto Colquitt's right."

"Sir, the gunners are dead, there's no one to man them!"

"There are men trained in artillery on my staff—find them and bring them any breathing body you can find. Cooks, teamsters, couriers, anybody! Those guns must be manned and Colquitt's right must be held. Anderson will be here shortly, God willing, and that army must *not be allowed* over this hill! And send a courier down to Boonsboro." Not until this moment had Hill considered totally abandoning his initial assignment. "Order Ripley and Rodes to join me here."

The Ohioans of the Kanawha Division weren't able to move another step. They had begun their ascent of South Mountain at dawn and made a tough climb and won a brutal fight.

General Cox personally interviewed captured North Carolinians who, to a man, bragged that the Yanks may have won for the moment, but there would be hell to pay for it when Longstreet arrived. Colonel Moor's exclamation echoed in Cox's mind . . . *"Oh, my God . . . Please be careful."* Cox was now certain that the Rebels to his right were massed in strength and that Longstreet was either present or near. It would be suicide for these tired and hungry men to attempt such an assault against such incredibly overpowering odds. There was, to his knowledge, no urgency, and plenty of reinforcements were close at hand. A wait of an hour or two would swell their numbers and improve their odds.

He ordered a halt. Cox would wait at least for the rest of Reno's corps and possibly even for Hooker's.

Six miles south, the 12,000 men of Franklin's corps advanced cautiously up the mountainside toward Crampton's Gap, where 300 of Stuart's troopers nervously waited.

Longstreet was still four hours away.

Sunday Afternoon

As services let out at the Dunker Church, no one in Sharpsburg continued to believe that the thunder they heard was coming from some distant or invisible clouds. The somber congregation looked up at their beautiful blue mountain to see columns of angry white smoke erupting from her peaks like a modern-day Mount Vesuvius.

The services were over, but the prayers continued.

To say that Ripley and Rodes "raced" up the western slopes of South Mountain would not be allegorical. They raced up the mountain. Ripley's Georgians took the early lead, but Rodes's men were led by the 6th Alabama, and the 6th Alabama was led by John Brown Gordon, and halfway up the grade the gasping Georgians pulled over to let Gordon's men through.

These were the men who believed their colonel to be bulletproof, and they'd be damned before they'd be second. Almost as much as they loved their colonel, they loved each other. These men were brothers, all figuratively and some literally. Some relations went further even than that.

On the run up the hill a young sergeant playfully nipped at the heels of a much older private. "Come on, old man," Sergeant Johnson prodded, "why're you breathing so hard?"

"If we ever get home, son, I'm gonna take you back out behind the woodshed and whup you like I used to when you was little—before you got to be a fancy-pants sergeant."

Sergeant Edward and Private Joseph Johnson tried to laugh, but it's hard to laugh and jog uphill at the same time.

"Quit your cuttin' up, boys," Gordon said. "We got a mountain to climb and some Yankees to kill when we get to the top."

By running the three miles up the mountain, Ripley and Rodes brought Harvey Hill both good news and bad. They scaled the mountain so quickly that they arrived on the scene only slightly behind Anderson, who had started hours earlier. While their arrival was timely, many were too exhausted to fight. Stragglers queued down the mountainside like an ant line.

HARPER'S FERRY

McLaws fought Federals and forests en route to his position atop Maryland Heights, but Walker faced neither on his climb to Loudoun's. By 1:00 P.M. he stood on the rim looking down into the bottom of the barrel, desperately aching to bomb Harper's Ferry to hell. Flag signals wagged to Jackson across the river, seeking instructions, but the reply was slow in coming. He pushed his guns out to the ledge, explaining that the order to fire might come at any moment, but secretly trying to draw the attention of the batteries below, giving him an excuse to "return fire" without orders. He stood on the ledge and looked down into the absolutely defenseless town. *It's like flying on the wings of a giant bird*, he thought, *able simply to drop cannonballs on it.*

His secret wishes came true. Union artillery lamely opened on Loudoun Heights, and Walker graciously returned the favor and the big gun duel over Harper's Ferry was finally under way.

SOUTH MOUNTAIN

It was not until noon that Franklin's corps finally reached the base of South Mountain on its assigned mission through Crampton's Gap and on to the rescue of Harper's Ferry. The detachment Jeb Stuart had left to guard the gap numbered three hundred men supported by one battery of four guns. These cavalrymen had no idea that General Paul

Semmes had been there earlier in the day and was on his way with help, but even that would bring their numbers only near the thousand mark.

Stuart's 300 posted themselves halfway up the mountain and watched as Franklin's 12,000 advanced. Uninhibited by the odds, the Rebels opened fire the moment the Yankees came within range. True to form, the Yankee army came to a halt while the generals decided what to do.

Semmes's Rebels heard the firing, and hastened their pace.

At Turner's Gap, Jacob Cox continued to rest his men and, under new orders from General Burnside, to await reinforcements. While Cox rested, the 3,000 men of Harvey Hill's three other brigades, Anderson's, Ripley's and Rodes's, moved into position and caught a few moments of badly needed rest themselves. At 2:00 P.M. the first of Longstreet's men crested the peak. Hill stood roadside and greeted them with hurried orders.

The leaders of Longstreet's march were commanded by D. R. Jones, a gracious man whom even General Lee called "Neighbor." "Send two brigades to the right, General, and have them report to General Ripley—he will command that flank. We lost valuable ground this morning, and I intend to take it back."

Exhausted from their thirteen-mile march and three-mile climb, the two thousand Southerners obediently moved to their assigned positions and arrived just in time to see Ripley's brigade marching off to war— down the wrong side of the mountain, with Ripley himself in the lead. At that precise moment, the Union assault finally began.

When General Cox saw the Rebel reinforcements coming onto line, he ordered his Ohioans to attack—to hell with Burnside's instructions to wait. They stumbled into the hole vacated by Ripley, and the club-swinging battle was rejoined almost precisely where it had left off. The numbers were, for the moment, closer than they had been all day, and the fighting so confused that lines became circles and soldiers firing at enemies missed and hit friends. For a solid hour they fought toe-to-toe, taking ground, giving ground and taking it back again.

Finally, Burnside's promised brigades arrived and the 6,000 additional Yankees were more than the Rebels could withstand. Overcome by the numbers, the Confederate right flank folded and grudgingly fought its way backward through the one-mile stretch of woods between Fox's Gap and Turner's. The two "fresh" Union brigades pushed the Rebels through the woods until the march became a trot, and the trot became a run. Boys from Virginia, North Carolina, Georgia and Alabama ran as fast as aching legs and bursting lungs would allow while boys from Michigan and Ohio chased them through the woods like dogs on the hunt until John Bell Hood ordered his men to stand and fire. Hidden in the *defilade*, 2,000 Texans rose from the brush and fired at once and hundreds of Union soldiers fell in a single ghastly roar of musket fire. Once again the Federal advance halted dead in its tracks. Longstreet had finally arrived, and now the Yankees had a fight on their hands.

At the southernmost gap, Crampton's, the Rebels didn't fare nearly so well. Semmes's men joined with Stuart's troopers, and they fought no less bravely than their friends six miles away, but no killer angels would rise up from hell and lay dead their pursuers. Once Franklin decided to move, he moved inexorably against the badly outnumbered but greatly determined Rebs. They gave ground slowly, but give it they did, and after two hours of "fire and fall back" the 800 remaining Rebels found themselves on the downhill side of the mountain and still with 12,000 Federal troops inching their way deliberately after them.

The order was given to retreat. No order was given to pursue.

When Franklin reached the mountaintop only the 800 retreating Rebels stood between himself and his objective—McLaws on Maryland Heights and Harper's Ferry beyond. And yet, on the crest of South Mountain, Major General William B. Franklin stopped and communicated with McClellan:

> *I report that I have been severely engaged with the enemy for the last hour . . . The force of the enemy is too great for us to take the pass to-night I am afraid. I shall await further orders here & shall attack again in the morning without further orders.*

Burnside had worried only yesterday that McClellan had given Franklin too much to do. Apparently Burnside had been right.

* * *

Approaching the other pass, Burnside's wing was in the lead. He focused on the enemy ahead of him without knowing that he had enemies of a different sort to his rear. McClellan rode with Hooker, back in the pack aways, giving "Fightin' Joe" an opportunity to lobby for independent command. He saw no reason why a corps commander should report to anyone commanding a "wing," whatever the hell that was—especially if that wing was commanded by Burnside.

Hooker wasn't the only Union general attacking Burnside's backside this day. Fitz-John Porter faulted Mac's old friend for the charges brought against him by Pope after Second Bull Run. The wires he had sent from Virginia had been routed through Burnside, and believing Burn to be a friend, Porter vented his spleen at Pope, complaining of his incompetent use of the army. He assumed all along that Burnside would edit the contents before forwarding them on to official Washington, but Burnside passed them along verbatim. The text of these telegrams had been the basis of Pope's charges against Porter, and Ambrose E. Burnside deserved to be punished.

The sounds of battle reached the advancing corps, but didn't particularly concern them. Some resistance was expected. Only when Burnside's courier arrived to urge Hooker on did anyone even comment upon it.

McClellan was with Hooker, which meant that the *New York Tribune* was along for the ride, because wherever Joe Hooker went, so did George Smalley.

Smalley took note of the fact that McClellan deferred to Hooker as the advance picked up tempo. *If McClellan is a god*, Smalley thought, he is a deistic one—one who sets things in motion and observes the results. The strategy was of his design—the tactics he left to others.

The reporter, forever seeking new ways to endear himself to people in power, noticed McClellan squinting as he looked to the sounds of battle. Smalley offered him his field glasses for a better look, and the commanding general shook his head. "No need," he said as he pulled off to the side of the column, allowing his army to pass him by. Cheers from the men of the First Corps drowned out the distant roar of battle as they marched past their Young Napoleon sitting astride the massive Ol' Dan Webster. McClellan waved his cap in his left hand and pointed to the smoke-capped mountain with his right. Even after the hot and dusty miles they had left behind them this day, a spring returned to the army's step. They had a mountain left to climb and a battle yet to fight, but for this man they would do it.

Hooker finally approached him with a plan. His First Corps should move to the extreme right flank. With Reno pressing from the left and Hooker from the right, the Rebels would be caught in the middle. Simple. Textbook. McClellan nodded and Hooker rode forward.

At 4:00 P.M. the First Corps finally began the long climb.

Infantry hates rivers and artillery hates mountains. That's just the way it is.

Johnny Cook hated seeing his buddies in Battery "B" struggle while he wasn't allowed to help. He was only the bugle boy and his assignment was to be constantly at the captain's side in the event of an emergency. As the six guns lumbered up the mountainside, he occasionally found an opportunity to edge up next to the wheel pair, the last two horses of six, to give them an extra nudge.

What Captain Campbell hated was letting the frail fifteen-year-old bugle boy out of his sight. Cook was a tiny thing with an angelic face and a head far too big for his body. Campbell had tried to send him home more than once, but the boy had been with him for almost a year now and the whole damned regiment looked out for him.

"Cook!"

"Sir."

"Get your rear end back over here."

"I was only trying to help, sir."

"Well, the next time you try to help I'm going to turn you over my knee. Here, Private! Now!"

Jesse Reno was a fine figure of a general. He was tall and thin. His hair was black and his beard was red and his features were those of a leader. He was another Southern-born man fighting for the North, and now he was on hand to assume command at Fox's Gap. The fight against Hood resumed immediately.

Forest fighting is the worst. It seems the enemy can always find a place to hide, while the good guys are left in the open. Hood made good use of the hills and valleys, the underbrush and stone walls that cut between the mountain farms, and Reno pushed forward a few hundred yards at a time, only to be fought to a halt, to regroup and move slowly forward again. The firing would subside for a while and then come up again from somewhere else. If ever a battle had an ebb and flow, this one did.

It had become so quiet that Reno believed the Rebs had pulled back again and the way ahead was clear. He rode out himself to give the orders to form up when Hood's men appeared again from nowhere and Jesse Reno was the first to die.

George Smalley was tired of riding in back with the generals. The sound of the guns pulled him too hard, and armed with a notepad and a pencil, he rode on ahead to watch the fight. He arrived just as one of Hooker's brigadiers, M. R. Patrick, called a halt to survey the heights.

"That's where they'll be waiting," he told his adjutant. "At least that's sure as hell where I'd be."

"How can you be sure, sir?"

Patrick pulled out his glasses for a closer look, but not a Reb was in sight. He sucked in his cheeks and bit down while he decided what he must do. "There's two ways to find out. I can send up pickets and waste a few dozen good men, or I can offer them a target they can't resist." He thought it over for a very few seconds and said, "Wait here. Not a man is to come forward. Do you understand, Major?"

"I suppose so, sir, but . . ."

The major felt a little faint when he realized what Patrick had in mind as the general spurred his horse and trotted forward until finally, as predicted, the Rebels could resist no longer and a hail of careless fire poured down the mountain at the selfless commander. This time the spurs dug deeper and horse and rider sped back downhill to safety.

"Did I tell you that's where they'd be?" He laughed. His face beamed red with excitement. The exhilaration of being shot at—and missed. "I told you that's where they'd be!"

Smalley grinned and wrote it all down.

SUNDAY NIGHT
HARPER'S FERRY

The appointed time arrived and Benjamin Franklin Davis conferred with his fellow officers about the route they should take in the cavalry's escape attempt from Harper's Ferry. Cannon fire continued to fall into the town from Loudoun Heights and the garrison might possibly last until morning, but might not last the night.

Three alternatives were discussed, all of them insane. They finally decided that they would cross the pontoon bridge over the Potomac and escape along a road at the base of Maryland Heights.

There is no other explanation for Davis's good fortune than that God was with him. The road selected was the very spot vacated by Semmes's men, who were now in retreat from Crampton's Gap. Another sign from heaven was the approach with darkness of a shield of clouds, covering the moon and turning the night as dark as pitch.

Colonel Miles feared a mutiny when the infantry and artillery heard of the plan. Several attempts were made to convince him that everyone should go, but on this point Miles stood firm. The cavalry would go, and no one else. Soldiers in bad times may envy the good fortunes of others, but never seek to deny it. As the 1,200 cavalrymen mounted up and prepared to leave, the infantrymen came forward and gave them tins of tobacco to help them through the night. Some gave the mounted men letters to mail "from the other side." No words were spoken. There was no need. Each man knew full well the emotions of the other.

At 8:00 P.M. the cavalry began their movement out from Harper's Ferry. No wagons, no ambulances. No tents or extra horses. They even left behind the regimental band.

The column rode first to General White's quarters, where Davis invited him to come along.

"It is a generous offer, Colonel, but I fear I may be needed here," he said with a nod over his shoulder and a roll of the eyes that said "this garrison is commanded by an idiot and a second-in-command might be valuable."

"Very well, sir. Thank you for your assistance."

White made eye contact with an old friend from Rhode Island, who said, "General White, sir, by morning we shall be in Pennsylvania, on the way to Richmond or in hell."

Both men smiled and Davis gave the signal to move out.

SOUTH MOUNTAIN

John Gibbon and his brigade of black-hatted veterans, the heroes of Brawner's Farm, attacked Turner's Gap directly up the middle, but he found himself pinned down by Rebel sharpshooters holed up in the upper rooms of a two-story farmhouse. He had been best man at Harvey Hill's wedding, and now their units stood face-to-face. Gibbon commanded infantry now, but his first love had always been the big guns. He called forward Battery "B" of the 4th U.S., which he had commanded out in Utah before the war. The designation "U.S." indicated that this unit was regular army—"old" army—and most of them were professional soldiers.

Young Johnny Cook, remembering the scolding he got from Captain Campbell on the way up the mountain, stood by as ordered and proudly watched as his batterymates went to work. Each of the nine-man crew had an assignment designated by a number.

For this job only one piece was brought forward, a twelve-pound Napoleon. Gunnery Sergeant Mitchell ordered, "Load," and the team moved crisply about their duties.

The muzzle was sponged. Number 2 took the exploding shell from the caisson and presented it to 5 for inspection. He then offered it to 6, who cut the fuse to the proper length for the estimated range before 5 placed it in the barrel. Number 1 then rammed the round "down the spout." Sergeant Mitchell moved around behind the piece, and by this time they were under fire by the Rebels in the house who knew they were soon to be in a world of fire themselves.

"Trail right. More. More. Halt. Screw down. More. Halt. Ready!"

The teamwork continued, seemingly oblivious to the small-arms fire digging up the dirt at their feet. Number 3 pricked the cartridge and 4 hooked the lanyard to the primer and jammed the primer in the vent.

Everyone covered their ears and stepped clear from the wheels that recoiled with every round.

"Fire!"

Not a man among them would admit that a first-round hit was a matter of sheer luck, especially one that got lobbed into a bedroom window from 1,500 yards.

Fire exploded from the windows and Rebels fled from the doors and Battery "B," of the 4th U.S. Artillery, went on about its business as though what they had just done was no more extraordinary than spitting in a cuspidor.

Darkness merely slowed the fighting on South Mountain. The 6th Alabama stood her ground behind a stone wall and turned back assault after assault from Hooker's corps. John Brown Gordon paced calmly along his lines, steadying his men, reassuring them, holding them firm.

This unit had been assembled in Montgomery in April of '61 and there wasn't a rookie among them. As cool as an April morning they held their ground. Gordon noticed Sergeant Johnson placing the stock of his musket on his father's shoulder while taking aim. "Where did you learn to shoot like that?"

"Something we picked up back home, sir," the sergeant shouted over the musket fire. "We took down a bunch of turkeys this way. It's a family joke back home, but it works good enough."

A family joke among the men of the 6th was to count the bullet holes in Gordon's uniform after every engagement. Tonight there were three and still not a drop of blood on him. His men didn't yield an inch.

At 10:00 P.M. the armies called it a day.

Lee was frantic for news. Still unable to ride because of his bandaged wrists, he spent the day at Boonsboro, listening to the battle and watching the stream of wounded men flow back down the mountain. When the shooting finally stopped he knew only one thing for certain—his army remained on the field. While this was very good news, it was the only news he had.

Lee couldn't go to the mountain, so Hill, Hood and Longstreet came to him.

As the senior man, Longstreet took the lead. "General Lee, the estimate of sixty thousand Federal troops is conservative. How we held the crest at all is a miracle, sir. Nothing short. But we have taken a terrible licking up there. The most we can send into battle tomorrow is nine thousand men and many of them are too weary to put up a good fight, and none will be able to fight like they did today.

"We hold only the crest above Turner's Gap. Fox's and Crampton's are both in the hands of the Federals."

Lee looked at Longstreet as though he were hearing last Sunday's sermon. Longstreet turned to Hill and Hood for support.

"I have one brigade that saw no action today, sir, and that is General Ripley's that spent the afternoon wandering around the wrong side of the mountain. He has just now returned and even *his* men are exhausted. Garland and Rodes's men are badly shot up. Colquitt held the pass alone this morning, and Rodes tonight. Beyond Ripley's brigade, I have not a man to offer you, sir."

"My Texans will answer the call," Hood said, "but in what numbers I cannot say."

"We lost nearly two thousand men today, General," Longstreet added. Lee's silence aggravated him and he pressed on, imploring Lee not to say what he knew the general was thinking. "We are badly used up. I left a single brigade in Hagerstown that can be called forward, but I can tell you only that it is my belief that it would be of no avail. Tomorrow morning McClellan will come pouring over that mountain in force, and there is little we can do to stop him. There are no defenses at all at Crampton's Gap and he now has an open road to McLaws . . ."

"And now is the time, General, for you to tell your old general that you were right all along."

"No, sir. It isn't that at all, but . . ."

"It *is* that, Pete. It's all right. The invasion has failed." Lee closed his eyes and looked almost to be sleeping. The other generals waited in silence and left Lee alone with his thoughts. When he spoke again, his attitude had completely changed. Suddenly he was rested, alert and ready to move on. "McClellan was informed of our plans and interrupted them, and now it's time to consider how we shall save this army from destruction. It is right to rejoin the wings as quickly as possible. I have, in fact, already sent off messages to McLaws and Jackson instructing them to cease operations at Harper's Ferry and to rendezvous with us near Sharpsburg. We shall see how the morning goes before deciding what next. We can retreat back over the river into Virginia, or we can make a stand there. It is good rolling ground where a small force can hide itself and defeat a much larger one. Perhaps we can hold there with what we have until Jackson arrives, between the town and this stream here." Lee looked down at the map and put on his spectacles. "Yes. Between Sharpsburg and Antietam Creek.

"Should that prove too dangerous, we can cross back over the river at this fording point. Without too much rain it should remain passable. But, who knows? I am informed that the ground is good, gentlemen. A good fight can be given there, and if Jackson arrives in time, maybe all is not yet lost."

A courier entered the tent and offered Lee a note. "Success tomorrow. Jackson." Lee folded it without comment and said, "Order your men off the mountain, Generals. They have done good work here today and saved us much needed time. Sharpsburg is the place, gentlemen. Sharpsburg and Antietam Creek."

CHAPTER 9

A LINE OF
BATTLE IS FORMED

The cavalry detachment from Harper's Ferry rode hard for nine hours, engaging Confederate pickets and sustaining light casualties throughout the night. Horses fell to exhaustion at the murderous pace and the men had to share mounts. Many slept as they rode, two to the saddle. Colonels Davis and Voss kept prodding the column forward, following the lead of their guide, a local man named Noakes. When scouts reported Rebel units to the front, Noakes directed them along back roads that were nothing more than seldom-used deer paths. With dawn still an hour away they heard an approaching wagon train.

"They're definitely Rebels, sir. About forty wagons guarded to the rear by a small cavalry detachment. Their lead wagon is about a mile ahead of us, sir, and coming directly our way."

"Noakes."

"Yes, sir."

"How do you read this?"

"My best guess is that they are headed for Boonsboro or Sharpsburg. There's an intersection only a few hundred yards ahead and if I am right they'll be turning off of this road and headed east. If we wait here, sir, I believe they'll go around us. It isn't likely that they will stay on this road, as you well know most of it isn't passable to wagons."

"What if they head west, where will that road take them?"

"It cuts only briefly to the west and swings back around to the north, towards Greencastle, Pennsylvania. It's the road we're headed for."

Davis smiled and said to Voss, "Interested in another little adventure, sir?"

Voss rolled his eyes. He'd had quite enough of the Mississippian's "little adventures."

The Yankee column rode up past the intersection and split in two, with six hundred troopers on one side of the road, and six hundred on the other, all off the roadway and well into the woods. Davis rode up and down both wings, repeating, "Now aw you funny tawkin' damned Yankees jes keep yo moufs shut and let me do aw the tawkin'."

The Rebel wagon train rode slowly through the darkness and into the trap, most of the teamsters asleep at the reins.

"Hold up there, cousin," Davis drawled in his finest Mississippi accent. "Which way you headin'?"

The lead wagoneer pulled to a halt and the entire train stopped behind him.

"Who's askin'?"

"A colonel in your cavalry," Davis replied, in all honesty from his point of view.

"Sharpsburg."

"Well, sir, I'm afraid there is to be a slight diversion. The woods around here are slap full of Yankees. Turn the train to the right here and we'll escort you between 'em." He smiled to himself, knowing that every word he had spoken was God's honest truth.

Without further explanation, the lead team turned to the right and headed for Pennsylvania. Twelve hundred Union cavalrymen rode out from the trees and formed lines on either side of the forty wagons, the total darkness making the color of their uniforms insignificant for the moment. Davis heard a horse approaching at a run and pulled up.

"By what authority have you turned this train?" the Rebel officer snapped. He immediately felt the cold, hard muzzle of a revolver pressed firmly against the back of his neck.

"By the authority of an officer of the United States Army," whispered

Captain Bill Frisbie. Davis finished the sentence. "... And it would behoove you, brother, to keep your silence about it." When it became apparent that the Rebel had no intentions of stirring up trouble, Davis poured the accent on even thicker. "Much obliged."

As the pitch-black night faded into the deep blues of predawn, a hellish fire fell from the heavens and into Harper's Ferry. At South Mountain Joe Hooker looked out over a battlefield on which he was opposed only by the dead, and on the Greencastle Pike, a Confederate wagoneer turned to his escort and asked, "What regiment are you from?"

"The Eighth New York."

"The hell you say!"

Lafayette McLaws was no longer under the false impression that "one or two brigades" threatened his rear, as Stuart had said. He knew now that a whole damned corps of McClellan's army approached from South Mountain and while his artillery poured fire into Harper's Ferry, McLaws dispatched his infantry to greet General Franklin should he come down the mountain with any bad intentions.

Reports flooded into McClellan's headquarters, each one more fantastic than the last. Lee wounded. Garland dead. The Rebels well on their way back into Virginia, in a panic and in a hurry. D. H. Hill killed. Southern casualties estimated at 15,000. By all reports, McClellan had won a magnificent victory, and his first instinct was to gloat to his enemies and share his glory with his wife.

To General Halleck he wired:

> *I have just learned from Genl. Hooker in the advance, who states that the information is perfectly reliable, that the enemy is making for Shepardstown in a perfect panic, & that Genl. Lee last night stated publicly that he must admit they had been shockingly whipped.*

For the pleasure of Mary Ellen, he held back nothing. "Glorious and complete victory ... 15,000 Rebels ... I thank God most humbly for His great mercy. R. E. Lee wounded," he wrote, "Hill reported killed."

As he read over the wire before sending it off, he remembered with a pang of jealousy that Mary Ellen had once been courted by a Rebel named Hill, and altered the copy to read "Hill (D. H.)."

HARPER'S FERRY

John Walker and Lafayette McLaws moved into position and A. P. Hill placed his guns on a point overlooking Bolivar Heights. The infantry prepared to launch or repel an attack, but Jackson was certain that no such wastefulness would be required. A good hour of bombardment should settle the question without a man being lost.

When the fire from all three heights opened at last, four days late, not an inch of ground was left uncovered. A Union man wrote that there was not a spot in all of Harper's Ferry on which a man could safely lay the palm of his hand without the risk of losing it. The town made famous by John Brown's raid became a cauldron of white-hot iron. Colonel Miles's determination to hold "to the last extremity" quickly faded, and Stonewall's estimate of "a good hour's" bombardment proved amazingly accurate.

At 7:30 A.M. a rider appeared from the wall of smoke carrying a flag, but no one was certain that it was a flag of surrender. When finally recognized as such, it took far too long to silence Stonewall's distant guns. It took so long that it cost Colonel Miles his life. A piece of shrapnel severed the artery of his right leg and he quickly bled to death.

When silence finally fell over the field, General White rode forward to be greeted by A. P. Hill and Kyd Douglas.

"I wish to discuss terms with General Jackson."

"Right this way, sir."

White wore his finest uniform, his best dress sword, highly polished boots and spotless white gloves. Stonewall was Stonewall; his now buttonless uniform badly disheveled and covered with a week's worth of bad roads.

Once White agreed to "unconditional surrender," Stonewall's terms were generous. All of White's men were to be paroled. They could keep their coats and blankets and two days of rations. The officers could keep their side arms and personal effects and the Confederacy would be happy to lend them sufficient wagons to transport them. The wagons, of course, to be returned as soon as convenient to a point behind Confederate lines. Jackson placed A. P. Hill in command at Harper's Ferry to enforce the terms and collect the spoils.

White agreed, and Harper's Ferry, what was left of it, fell once again under Confederate control.

Jackson left the details to Hill and informed Lee of the good news:

General; Through God's blessing, Harper's Ferry and its garrison are to be surrendered. Hill's troops will be left in command until the prisoners and public property shall have been disposed of. The other forces can move off this evening so soon as they get their rations. To what point shall they move?

Last night, in total blackness, Lee's men had moved in good order down the western banks of South Mountain. Today, in full daylight, the Union army couldn't get out of its own way. Fighting men approached intersections that were already jammed with miles of supply wagons. Burnside awaited orders and when he finally moved his path crossed that of Porter's newly arrived corps and both sat and waited for the other to get out of the way.

While they waited, the men did what most soldiers do best—they complained. The 51st New York, who referred to themselves as "The Shepard Rifles," had been with Burnside since the Battle of Roanoke Island back in January and were further battle-tested at Second Bull Run, Chantilly and yesterday at Turner's Gap. The 51st had a dual reputation—the men drank as hard as they fought, and today they made the acquaintance of their new commander, a former New York City dance instructor named Edward Ferrero. A wagon rolled forward loaded with their victor's share of rum rations, and as the men cheered the arrival, General Ferrero stepped forward.

"Men, first I want to thank you for your good work yesterday. New York is proud of you. It is my intention to keep it that way."

The men were paying little attention to the colonel as the kegs were being unloaded as he spoke.

"But no God-fearing Christian could ever take pride in any unit, no matter how successful it may be on the field, if it is known that they consume the Devil's brew." The Shepard Rifles were aghast as a staff officer stepped forward and offered Ferrero a heavy sledge. "This is an inappropriate award for true American heroes." The sledge dropped, the keg shattered and the golden liquid spilled out onto the ground. The men were too stunned to kill him or they very well might have.

"Now—let us pray."

Once begun, the march down the mountain was a gruesome one for John Strickler. Three weeks ago he was a clerk in a Harrisburg hat shop, and today he saw his first dead man. Southern soldiers lay stacked like cords of wood. He saw one soldier whose face had been covered with a foot-square piece of homespun broadcloth. Another had his eyes still open and others seemed to smile. Many looked as though their uniforms had been torn open by robbers of the dead. Strickler's stomach churned at the sight of men whose bowels spilled out from shirts callously ripped open.

"Who did that to those men, Sergeant?"

"Who did what to 'em?"

"Who pulled their shirts off of 'em like that?"

"They did it themselves, boy. They did it to see if they was gut-shot. If you get gut-shot you're dead. It might not even hurt very much, but soon enough you're a dead man. There ain't a sawbones in the army can save a man who's gut-shot, so they pull their shirts open to see."

Corporal Strickler fought back tears and swallowed his own bile so the men wouldn't see him throwing up, but he couldn't stop looking at the poor dead Rebels. The emaciated faces, the bare feet, the Bibles clutched to their hearts in death—these men weren't evil like the Rebels in the newspapers. Not a corpse among them could ever have dreamed of owning a slave. They were poor, hungry boys away from home for the very first time, just like him, and wanting nothing more than a good, hot meal or a pretty girl to talk to.

As he walked, he composed tonight's diary entry. "There was no secession in those rigid forms nor in those fixed eyes staring at the sky," he wrote in his mind. "Clearly this is not their war."

Burial details showed no such compassion. Farmer Wise caught blue-clad men throwing gray-clad corpses down into his spring-water well.

"I will bury them," he said, "for a dollar a corpse."

Ambrose Burnside agreed to the deal and left Wise to his own devices. His well was already ruined, so he filled it with corpses, sealed it closed and collected sixty dollars.

WASHINGTON

President Lincoln sent a wire to General McClellan: *God bless you and all with you. Destroy the Rebel army if possible.*

The President quickly returned to his office and took the Emancipation Proclamation from his desk drawer. He read it over again, made a change or two and then, after a second thought, he rolled it up and returned it to its place. As badly as he wanted to believe McClellan's claims, the victory would have to be verified before so drastic a step could be taken. He decided to wait in spite of the almost unbearable political pressure to free the slaves. Horace Greeley of the *New York Tribune* had published an open letter to the President which reported widespread rumors that emancipation was under consideration, but that a majority of the government could not be gotten. Lincoln considered for a moment what his response should be and, with election day coming, he determined that it was best, for the time, to stay the course. He wrote to Greeley, telling him that his entire purpose was to save the Union. "If I could preserve the Union without freeing any slave, I would do it, and if I could save it by freeing all the slaves I would do it; and if I could save it by freeing some and leaving others alone I would also do that. What I do about slavery and the colored race, I do because I believe it helps to save the Union."

The President sat alone in his office and rubbed his aching eyes so hard they appeared to bleed from within. He took a deep breath and laid his head briefly on his desk to try for just a moment's rest when Mary came in to complain of a headache. Even in these oppressive dog days of summer, she continued to dress in layer upon layer of mourning black. So thick were her veils that only in bright sunlight could she see clearly through them—through the veils and the tears that it seemed to Lincoln would never stop. Poor Mary. Poor Mother. He put his arm around her, kissed her lightly on the top of her head and guided her gently to the darkness of her room.

* * *

Gideon Welles walked with his son quickly down Fifteenth Street toward the telegraph room where he knew everyone would be gathering. "McClellan telegraphs a victory. He claims fifteen thousand Rebel casualties and says that General Lee admits they are badly whipped." His son raised his eyebrows—impressed at the news, but his enthusiasm was short lived as the Navy Secretary held up his hand and continued. "To whom Lee made this admission so that it should be brought straight to McClellan he does not say, and we are accustomed to hearing such tales from Pope. I am afraid it is not as decisive as McClellan would have us believe."

As he entered the office, Welles saw Edwin Stanton tugging at his gray chin whiskers so hard that Welles thought that today they would finally be pulled out entirely. A military victory of any proportion for McClellan was a personal defeat of gigantic proportions for Stanton. The dubious congratulations that passed around the room passed by Stanton entirely. He didn't want to hear of McClellan's success no matter how favorable it might be for the "cause." If McClellan had won the war it would be bad news for Stanton.

The flow of good news into McClellan's headquarters came suddenly to a stop with a morning dispatch from Franklin. "The Rebels are drawn up in force across Pleasant Valley. I am outnumbered two-to-one. If Harper's Ferry has fallen—and the cessation of firing makes me fear that it has—it is my opinion that I should be strongly reinforced."

That report was followed by another from one of Pleasonton's scouts: "A line of battle is formed on the other side of Antietam Creek and this side of Sharpsburg." No sooner had McClellan absorbed this than a golden-haired and garish young captain, wearing more braid than three brigadiers, rode up on a well-lathered horse with a message from General Sumner.

"They are in full view, General. Their line is a perfect one about a mile and a half long. We can have an equally good position as they now occupy. We can employ all the troops you can send us."

"Thank you, Captain Custer. Tell General Sumner to avoid a general engagement and that I am on my way to personally review the situation."

"Damn!" McClellan said to Marcy as Custer rode away. "Excuse my language, but that damned Bobby Lee just doesn't know when he's been licked! Wouldn't you have hightailed it back to Virginia by now if you'd taken the beating he took yesterday?"

"Probably, Mac, but I'm not Bobby Lee."

There was a touch of respect in Marcy's voice that McClellan didn't miss. Marcy hadn't intended it to sound quite so admiring as it did.

McClellan flushed with anger, at first at General Marcy, but he quickly redirected it at the man who was stealing his thunder.

"Well, if Bobby Lee wants another whipping, I shall give it to him!"

Marcy felt his son-in-law's anger and decided against reminding him that Harper's Ferry had fallen and, along with it, the 12,000 troops that McClellan had hoped to save. He thought to mention that Jackson would now be free to join Lee and that a failure to act quickly would mean a complete loss of the advantage gained by the finding of 191. He thought to mention it, but he did not.

As McClellan rode to Sharpsburg, Stonewall Jackson examined the ruins of Harper's Ferry. Eleven thousand Federal prisoners lined the road to watch him pass. Some saluted and those who did had their salutes returned. Most just stared, astounded at the sight of their mongrel conqueror. The men of Stonewall's staff knew it well by now, this baffled look of disappointment on the faces of the vanquished. "Oh, my God— Lay me down," Douglas said to Westbrook as they rode through the lines. Both men laughed at the proud old corps' unofficial new slogan.

"Boys, he isn't much for looks," one Yankee said, "but if we'd had him we wouldn't have been caught in this trap."

While the Union army bumbled down the mountain, Lee, Longstreet and Harvey Hill (considerably less dead than Mary Ellen McClellan had been told) reviewed their thin defensive lines on the outskirts of Sharpsburg.

"Spread your men thin, Generals, and push forward every gun you have—hold none in reserve—and show them plainly. General McClellan has acted boldly only once in his life and that was on good information. He will not act so boldly again today. No, sirs. Put forward a strong-looking front and there will be no battle today, of that I am certain—and probably none tomorrow."

Lee posted his right flank at the Rohrbach Bridge, and his left near the Dunker Church. The lines stretched along the edge of David Miller's cornfield and down a sunken farm road known to the locals as Hog Trough Road.

Lee glanced southward down the Hagerstown Pike, half praying, half actually expecting to see Jackson's men already parading to the rescue. No. Not yet. Not even soon. He had to smile at himself. Even Jackson's notorious "foot cavalry" can't scale those mountains in under a day. It's okay for generals to hope for miracles, just never to plan on 'em.

SEPTEMBER 16TH

Tiny Sharpsburg, Maryland, home to a thousand souls more or less, farmers, God-fearing folks, was about to become one of America's largest cities. By sunrise its new population numbered 80,000 thereabouts. And every road into town from South Mountain to Harper's Ferry was clogged with more on the way.

Shortly after midnight Jackson began the seventeen-mile march from Harper's Ferry to Sharpsburg. Longstreet's rear guard was on the march from Hagerstown, and sometime by late afternoon Lee expected his army to be wholly reunited save for Powell Hill's 2,500 troops still at Harper's Ferry. If straggling could be kept to a minimum, Lee hoped to have almost 40,000 men on the field, but as the sun rose Jackson, Walker and McLaws were still somewhere to Lee's rear. To his front were 60,000 Yankees, with 30,000 more on the way.

With a sharply executed maneuver yesterday, McClellan would have beaten half of Lee's army to the field, but the traffic jam on South Mountain precluded that. The Union legions arrived far too late to plan and execute an attack. The two armies spent the night counting the other's campfires, playing cards and swapping girlie pictures. Without looking very hard, an occasional game of craps or poker could be found on either side of the line. The camp followers pitched their own tents behind the Union First Corps since "Fightin' Joe" made no effort to discourage them. A girl couldn't make a living in Washington after the army left town, but the traveling troupe known as "Hooker's girls" did good business this night.

A swift movement at first light today could still cut through the tired and widespread Rebels, but a morning fog covered the low spots as well as the movements, positions and numbers of the Rebels across the creek.

McClellan found the best spot from which to view the coming show. The two-story, red-brick Pry house stood on the peak of Sharpsburg's tallest hill. Telescopes mounted on fence rails gave him a view of the field with the exception of his extreme left flank—the flank near the Rohrbach Bridge.

Randolph Marcy was in a difficult position. As chief of staff to his own son-in-law, diplomacy was his best tool. As the sun burned off the fog, Marcy saw the thinness of the Rebel lines. He had held his tongue too long. He had to say something.

"My God, this is a wonderful opportunity, Mac. Lee can't possibly have twenty thousand men down there. Jackson may be on his way from Harper's Ferry, but if we attack now . . ."

McClellan smiled at the naïveté of his well-meaning father-in-law.

"All of our best intelligence puts Lee's strength at a hundred and twenty thousand. Certainly it *appears* to be what you call a 'wonderful opportunity.' It is *designed* to appear so. What it is, is a trap."

As the morning progressed, his corps commanders gathered at the Pry house, and by noon all were present except for Franklin, who was still occupied with McLaws. Drawn to the commanding general like courtesans to the king, these men with their staffs formed quite a crowd on the hilltop until Hooker noted Rebel artillery turning their way and pointed it out to McClellan.

"We are becoming a target, gentlemen. Please repair to the house and wait for me there."

Every man had the same reaction—*surely he doesn't mean me*—so the group was slow to break up. Ambrose Burnside saw himself as second-in-command and deliberately sought to wait behind—but so did everybody else.

"Go! Before we're all dead men. All of you except Porter."

Porter?

Fitz-John Porter puffed up like a blowfish while the rest of the generals headed for the house. Burnside was astounded. His face burned with embarrassment, and only now did he begin to realize that his old friend Porter was conniving against him. This public chagrin indicated to all a changing of the guard within McClellan's inner circle. After all of their years together, starting with their youthful days at West Point, working together, living together, their wives best friends and Burnside turning down command of the army in favor of his friendship—after all of that—this.

Porter and McClellan mounted and rode along the slowly forming Union lines.

"Lee has selected some very good ground. There is no way of telling behind which hill how many men may be hiding. His lines appear so thin."

"He has the river to his back, John. I don't subscribe to all of the hero worship going on about Lee. He is an able general, but that is all. However, he is too good a general to fight a major battle with such thin lines and without a choice of escape routes. As best as we can tell, he has only one usable ford. No, these lines are disguised to *look* thin. It is a trap, just like at Bull Run."

McClellan winced at his own thoughtlessness when he remembered that it was Porter's men who had died in that trap, but Porter took no hurt in it. That had all been Pope's fault and Fitz-John felt neither shame nor remorse for the events of that day even though he might still face charges on his conduct.

"General Marcy encouraged me to attack just an hour or two ago, but I saw the folly of it. We won't attack until we're ready."

"It would be good to know certainly how strong he is, and where his guns are. That would at least tell us something."

McClellan smiled. "Guns are easily found."

He dug his spurs into Dan Webster's flanks and trotted to a hilltop. He pranced up and down along the ridge until Confederate gunners could resist no longer and fired from three different directions at the lone Union horseman. McClellan was safely back down in the ravine before any of the shells exploded, flushed with excitement and laughing like a fool. The men cheered and Porter shook his head.

"That was the most fun I've had in weeks!" McClellan shouted, and galloped off for more observations with Fitz-John Porter in tow.

Riding slowly now behind the ridges and very much alone, Porter seized the opportunity to speak his mind to his friend and commanding general.

"You have more problems, Mac, than only Bobby Lee. You have worse enemies, some of whom are wearing blue."

"Examples?"

"Burnside. I know he is your oldest friend, but ambition is poison. Your enemies in Washington favor him, Mac. By his own admission he has 'twice been offered the kingly crown.'"

"'And twice he has refused.'"

"To his credit. But should you perform magnificently here, and should there be any way for Stanton to place the credit for *your* success at Burnside's door, then surely a third offer will be made. Ultimately Caesar couldn't resist—Christ himself would be tempted."

"And what would you have me do, John?"

Porter's horse pranced around sideways and he had to get her under control before he answered. "Protect your flanks, Mac. Don't put Burn in a position where he could possibly come out of this the hero, even by mistake. Return your corps commanders to independent command. Dispense with the concept of 'wing' command. It served you well with the army on the move, but now it is time for battle. Reduce him to corps commander and move him to the flank—use him as a diversion—and let the fighting generals do the fighting."

"It is beneath you, John, to suggest that political interests should be placed ahead of tactics on the eve of battle."

"Perhaps it is, General, and I am not pleased with the prospect, but consider the larger picture. If you won't do this to protect yourself, do it to protect the nation."

McClellan didn't respond as he thought over what Porter had said and the junior general took advantage of the moment to drive the final nail. "Think of the consequences should Burnside be elevated to command of this army. The press is rife with rumors that Mr. Lincoln itches to make this a war of emancipation. He wouldn't dare do that with you in command, but he sure as *hell* will if Burn is in there. Hell, Mac—if he tells these men that they are fighting to free the niggers, half of them will pack up and go home. And think of Ambrose actually in command. The other half will die on some damned-fool charge somewhere. Lee will play him like a piano. This can easily be done without the politics being apparent, Mac. It can't hurt you, it can only save you—and the nation."

McClellan only nodded and asked, "You said 'enemies.' Who else?"

"Sumner."

"I am aware that he is not my most competent general, John. He cost me dearly at Gaines' Mill and probably even the entire Peninsula campaign, but I hardly consider him an enemy."

"You are correct, Mac. He means you no harm, but may do you harm nonetheless. Tomorrow will be the Devil's day and under no circumstances should you run the risk of Sumner ending up in command on the field. Most of his troops are green, and he is reckless. 'Tis a consummation *not* devoutly to be wished." Porter loved to butcher Shakespeare.

"Hold him in reserve, Mac."

"It is for those very reasons that I *cannot* hold him in reserve. Should the worse happen, and Lee break through with a hundred and twenty thousand troops, then the corps that I hold in reserve will be all that remains between the Rebels and Washington. The reserve corps must be among my best men, and the best generaled. The reserve corps will be yours."

Porter was disappointed, but he knew that McClellan was right. It was an important job, and could become a vital one.

"Yes, sir. But, please, keep my suggestions in mind. They are offered with the best interest of the army and the nation—and yourself—in mind."

"You are a good friend, John, and an equally good general. Your suggestions are well considered."

Six hours of daylight had passed before Jackson arrived and filed his men into line behind John Bell Hood at the Dunker Church.

Six hours.

Walker's men, who had farther to march than Jackson's, arrived even later, stretched out in a single-file line that ran God-only-knew how far back into Virginia. They were ushered, one man at a time, to the right, in support of Toombs above the Rohrbach Bridge. McLaws, concerned with Franklin's slow-moving Union corps, moved even slower yet, and was still nowhere to be seen.

From noon onward, tired and sleepless Rebels filed slowly into Sharpsburg. Many stopped by homes to beg for food. The smartest of the town's 1,300 residents abandoned their homes and took their families to Hagerstown, Boonsboro or Shepardstown. Some even took refuge in the caves they had known as children. Lee's "ragged, lean and hungry set of wolves" no longer feared the rope. Hanging is an easier death than starving, so many invited themselves into the unguarded homes to eat and drink their fill before they joined their units.

Porter and McClellan returned to the Pry house to meet with the bored and impatient generals.

"I have just returned from the field, gentlemen, and have devised our plan of attack for tomorrow. This battle will be won or lost on our right flank, on the ground next to that little schoolhouse."

"I believe that's a church, General."

"Whatever it is, that is the ground where the enemy appears most vulnerable. As a tactical necessity the First Corps under Hooker is to be separated from the Ninth. General Burnside will retain command of the Ninth and will move to the left, next to the lower bridge.

"General Hooker may advance against the church. General Mansfield, whom most of you know and who has just joined us on yesterday, will assume command of the Twelfth Corps. He will move in support of Hooker, and General Sumner, commanding the Second, will await orders to move in support of Mansfield if needed. On my orders, General Burnside will stage a diversionary attack against the bridge and against the Rebel right flank to prevent the enemy from reinforcing the troops at the church. Should this assault be successful he will move to cut off the enemy's escape route back into Virginia. General Porter will be held in reserve and General Franklin will be dispatched upon his arrival to wherever he may be needed.

"That is all, sirs. The nation is counting on you."

Without opportunity for discussion or objections, George McClellan turned and left the room.

In a matter of moments the Pry house was empty with one, very lonely exception. Ambrose Burnside remained seated. His normally soft and friendly eyes were hard and angry—his balding head wet and red. He couldn't comprehend the injustice of it all. Not only had Hooker been given independent command, he was to commence the battle and would retain overall command of the most vital part of the field. Burnside, however, was a "diversion." The humiliation was unbearable. The friendship was over. McClellan had not spoken to him. He had not even looked his way.

After all they had done together—this.

Never before in his life had he been so angry. *Someone will pay, by God, and the next time Abraham Lincoln calls, Ambrose Burnside will answer.*

"Sir, you know my Texans to be your bravest and best fighters," Hood said to General Lee. "They climbed that mountain and fought hard all day long on Sunday. But they have eaten nothing but green apples and hardtack for five days. Not a single cooked meal, General, in five days. I cannot ask them to bear the brunt of this coming battle on empty stomachs."

"And what do you suggest? Most of this army is hungry."

"Allow me to pull them back under darkness. Hold them in reserve tomorrow and allow them at least to breakfast. General Jackson is here now, and his men are well fed on the rations from Harper's Ferry. Pull him forward and me back. We will be ready when needed."

"I have no objection if General Jackson does not. He is in command on that part of the field, so you must discuss it with him."

John Bell Hood was in an awkward position. To have requested a pull-back on the eve of battle was against his nature. It had taken time to screw up his courage, even for this man whose courage in the face of the enemy was becoming notorious. And now he had to approach Jackson with the same proposal he had made to Lee.

"Your men will come forward immediately when called?"

"Of course they will, sir."

"Very well, then. Pull them back into the woods behind the church. Five hundred yards and no more."

"Thank you, sir."

"General Hood."

"Sir?"

"Immediately."

"General Burnside, sir."

"Yes?"

"I am Captain Duane of General McClellan's staff and the Army Engineers. The general has sent me here to position your divisions and to reconnoiter the most appropriate point for your crossing." It's hard to be pompous and swat bugs at the same time, but Captain Duane's horse had stirred up millions of the damned little things and they hovered around him like a cloud.

"Does General McClellan not consider me capable of making those decisions for myself?"

"I know nothing of that, sir. I only have my orders."

Another humiliation. This one blatant. "Very well, Captain Duane, make your survey and report back to me where General McClellan would have me cross."

"I shall require three members of your staff to accompany me and to report back to you. I'm afraid I have other pressing matters to consider beyond only this."

Captain Duane saluted and turned to go about his business. Burnside saluted his horse's ass and said, under his breath, "Report back to me where General McClellan would have me piss as well."

"Du müss gehen, Liebchen. Alles wir müssen gehen," Samuel Mumma told his granddaughter.

"Nein, Opa. I want to stay here." Ada was desperate. The tears were long since beyond her control. Her tiny body shook with fear. All the soldiers. She wrapped herself tightly around her grandfather's leg. *"Bitte, bitte, bitte, Opa!"*

"Mein kleines mädchen, du müss gehen. Is not safe here for little ones. Is not safe here for any ones. *Mit Ihnen gehen Mutter zum Rohrbach Haus! Ich liebe dich, Ada. Los."*

He picked up his favorite grandchild, placed her in the back of the

wagon and kissed her on the cheek. The wagon rolled off, headed for the
Rohrbach house across from the bridge. Ada rolled herself up tightly in a
ball and sobbed and trembled the whole way. Even at seven years old, she
understood that Opa was no safer here than she was.

This should have been Kyd Douglas's moment in the sun. The moment
of his dreams. His triumphal return. Riding side by side with Stonewall
Jackson into Sharpsburg. In his dreams there were flags and banners.
There were bands playing and pretty girls and dirty-faced little boys
cheering and tossing flowers. His people. But most of them were gone
now, the town almost empty of citizens and full of soldiers. The faces he
did see and recognize didn't recognize him. Didn't even look his way.
Loading wagons in a hurry. Some carried whatever they could on their
backs, their horses and wagons vanished overnight. No joy in the familiar faces, like in his dream. Only fear. Only panic.

They rode in past the Rohrbach house, the one in town. They had
another home up on the creek where Douglas had played as a child with
the Rohrbach and Mumma children after church when Dad preached
there. He caught a glimpse of Joseph Rohrbach up on the second-story
veranda looking down at Stonewall. Fear in his eyes and an old flintlock
musket in his hand. Douglas wanted to speak, just out of habit. Out of
courtesy. He wanted to save just one tiny moment of his lost dream. But
kind old Joseph Rohrbach looked for all the world like a madman. Like a
snarling she-wolf with her back to the mouth of the cave, protecting her
cubs. Vicious. Defiant. Wanting to kill and ready to die. Ready to take on
both armies with his pitiful little squirrel gun. Instead of speaking, Kyd
Douglas pulled his hat farther down over his face and looked the other
way, hoping to sneak by the Rohrbach house totally unnoticed. But it
was just now that Jeb Stuart came riding up from the rear, needing to
speak with Jackson, and the entire column came to a stop, directly under
the mad eyes of Joseph Rohrbach.

"There is high ground to your left, General. The natives call it
Nicodemus Hill. He who controls it, controls all approaches to the
church. I have stationed my artillery there, but without doubt it will
require infantry protection."

"It has already been arranged, General. General Early is assigned to protect you there and is on his way."

Douglas was relieved when they finally moved forward once again, out from under the Rohrbachs' front porch. Embarrassed or afraid or whatever it was he was feeling, it was not what he felt in his dreams. He felt sick.

Green corn, he thought.

John Strickler had just bought his first girlie cards the night before South Mountain. It didn't take him long to pick a favorite. She was a little heavy—soft around the hips—with large, beautiful breasts and a thick patch of black pubic hair. They were the first breasts he'd ever seen, but he could easily imagine how soft they would feel against his face and chest. He was doing just that when the sergeant saw what he was looking at.

"Put 'em away, Corporal, and give them to the rear guard tonight."

"Give 'em to the guards! Why?"

"'Cause if you take 'em into battle tomorrow and end up getting killed, they'll send 'em with the rest of your personal things back home to your momma."

Strickler flushed beet red at the thought of his mother looking at "Genevieve."

". . . and anything else you don't want your momma to see. Dice, cards, anything. Pass that along to your buddies. Don't worry. You'll get 'em back if you come out okay."

Strickler nodded in embarrassment and did as he was told.

John Brown Gordon moved his 6th Alabama down into the sunken road. It didn't take a Napoleon to figure out that this spot was dead in the middle of the long, thin Rebel line. The road wasn't only sunken by wear, but it lay between two hills. It wasn't exactly the always preferred "high ground," but a decent defensive position. They would be invisible to artillery down this low, but the enemy would be invisible to them as well until they crested the hill not sixty yards away.

The road was flanked on both sides by split-rail fences that General

Rodes had the men dismantle. They stacked the rails along the eastern edge for just a little more protection.

Sergeant Edward Johnson lay in the road next to his father and looked up the hill, and in his mind he could see the Yankees coming—rank after never-ending rank of them. He could see them coming. He could see them dying. In his dreams they dressed in black. Not in blue, but in black. Evil, sinister, black.

Gordon had a vision as well. *We're safe enough here for as long as they come at us over the hill, but God help us,* he prayed, *if they get alongside.*

He looked left and right, up and down the road, and it suddenly looked like a long, thin coffin. General Rodes stepped up beside him and said nothing for a while. Both men were having the same thought and knew it. No need to belabor the obvious.

"Gonna be hell to pay tomorrow, General."

"That doesn't even cover it, John. These men are going to need a ladder to get out of this ditch so they can *climb* into hell. And they'll be anxious to get there."

Musket fire opened to Gordon's left and every man on the field tensed up. The firing came from the tiny, white building up on the hill or from the cornfield across the street.

The pickets of Hooker's corps had pushed forward just a bit too far, to the point where they could shake hands with Jackson's men, and a ten-minute skirmish took fifteen lives.

The musket fire caught General Lee's attention as well, but it was obviously overanxious pickets mixing it up a bit. Lee finished reading his letter from home. Annie is not well. Down with a fever. Don't concern yourself, we're sure she'll be fine. *Please, God. Please look out for Annie.*

McClellan's 80,000 men hunkered in the darkness and ate dry coffee grounds mixed with sugar and complained about McClellan's "no fires" order. One hell of a way to spend your last night on earth.

There were 110,000 men on the field and not a man among them doubted that tomorrow would be the day—110,000 letters were written; 110,000 prayers were prayed.

George Smalley, now never more than a stone's throw from Hooker's side, heard the general complain as he bedded down, "If they had let us start earlier, we might have finished tonight."

"You were right about General Williams," Mitchell said to Bloss. "You said they would replace him with one of McClellan's men."

"Yup, I thought it would have been sooner."

"Mansfield is a fine-looking man. He *looks* like a general."

"I hear he's 'old' army, but hasn't seen a battle since Mexico."

"Well, he'll see one tomorrow."

"This is it, men," Captain Kop shouted. "We'll bed here for the night. Rest well. There'll be hell tomorrow."

Mitchell went down on one knee to remove the blanket from his pack and the aroma nearly knocked him over.

"Manure!"

"What did you say?"

"I said manure! The sons-of-bitches have us sleeping in a *shit* field!"

Almost immediately, it started to rain.

THE PRY HOUSE

George McClellan stood bolt upright on the highest point over-looking the valley, peering into the darkness, trying to make out the lines formed by the two great armies below.

He looked hard but saw little. His own orders. No fires. No point in telling General Lee our strength and position. The men hated it, and he hated doing it to them, but lives will be saved tomorrow by a little dis-comfort tonight. He couldn't help but think about his poor boys down there in the valley like every one was his own. It's a miserable way to spend your last night on earth. Cold. Wet. Miserable. That's what it is for thousands of those men down there. Their last night. Already at a huge disadvantage. Outnumbered by God-knows-what-to-one. Lincoln holding back tens of thousands of soldiers who could easily be here—should be here. Keeping them to himself like a miserly millionaire counting pennies.

The 12,000 men from Harper's Ferry are lost now as well. Surrendered almost without a fight. What a waste. Surrendered to Powell Hill, for crying out loud, and that bumpkin Jackson. A picture of Cadet Hill flashed through his mind from the days when they roomed together at The Point. Hill wasn't even a very good lieutenant in the old army and now a general, for the love of God, on the Rebel side. He thought about the days when Hill pined a year away planning to marry Mary Ellen. Thank God her father put a stop to that. *What would I do without Mary Ellen? What kind of life would she have now if she had married him instead of me?*

Nothing more to see here. Time to write her once more, before all hell breaks loose tomorrow. In the dryness of the Pry house, by the light of the fire, he wrote his third letter in two days. They must fill a steamer trunk by now, all the letters. He told her to keep them. Posterity. Memoirs. Maybe someday even presidential papers. Mostly tirades against the imbeciles back in Washington. Halleck, Stanton and Lincoln. Three monkeys in a tree. Not a whole brain between them.

The words flowed out of his pen as though they'd been memorized. Tomorrow the greatest battle of the century will be fought in this tiny little Northern town nobody has ever heard of. The future of the Republic hangs in the balance and still the three baboons hang from their tails and give me just enough to fail. Mary Ellen must be tired of hearing it by now, but he wrote on nonetheless. With enough men and enough horses Richmond would be ours by now. *They* lost the fight on the Peninsula, not me. One army. One week. One thrust and this whole damned war would have been over months ago. The South back in the Union, allowed to keep their precious slaves, and George McClellan sitting pretty for the presidency.

He stopped writing and just watched the fire burning warmly in the fireplace while he tried to figure them out—those fools in fancy suits and stovepipe hats. *It's not a difficult riddle,* he thought. A victory on the battlefield, an end to the war, and those three would have to fight for their very lives, voted out of office so quick . . . and Lincoln, the biggest baboon of them all, would be back in Bumpkinsville running his pitiful little one-horse law office again. So why *should* they give me the men I need? They *want* the war to go on. At the very least until after the

November elections. That's why Chase and Stanton want to free the niggers. Do that and the South will never come back. The war will have to go on till every last Rebel on earth is dead and gone. At least Lincoln understands that. At least he has the guts to stand up to the abolitionists.

But here we are again. With enough men, we could win this thing tomorrow. But they won't give me enough men. They wouldn't on the Peninsula, and they won't now. Lee may have 150,000 men sitting over there on the other side of the creek. He's a smart man. Not a god like everybody thinks, but smart. Thin-looking lines, trying to pull me in. Hannibal at Cannae. If they break out tomorrow and head for Washington, Lincoln's parade-ground soldiers certainly won't be able to stop them. And who will they blame when it's the *Rebel* army marching in front of the big white house? George McClellan. But the fault will be theirs. Napoleon himself couldn't overcome these odds. But Napoleon not only commanded, he ruled. When he needed men he didn't have to go begging to idiot bureaucrats. He got what he needed when he needed it.

Thoughts of how things should be continued to fill his mind. What the Union really needs is a general in the White House. If the people can only be made to see what we're up against, the incredible odds that face us every day, maybe they will rise up at last, throw the Republicans out of Congress and demand that the monkeys step aside and let the army run the war.

He felt the pain again. The neuralgia coming back. Anger triggered it. One of the things.

To the letter he added the usual reassurances. Your father is safe. Never in harm's way. No need to worry her with the Burnside story. Dearest friend for so many years, but not the man to command a corps on a day like this. Heartbreaking. She'll find out soon enough. It's all too hard. Too many men ruined by all this. Too many maimed. Too many killed.

"Dear God, please let it end."

Maybe tomorrow.

SHARPSBURG

I t seemed odd to Lee that the camp was so quiet. On this night of all
nights. He needed a quiet moment though. Everything happening so
quickly. The Peninsula. Manassas. Crossing into Maryland, so full of
hope. Flags flying. Music and cheering. And then the dispatch. How can
the fate of men and nations turn on something so stupid as a lost piece of
paper?

He looked out over the hopelessly thin lines. The rain and darkness
made him blind, but with his general's mind, he could see them clearly
enough. There was not a spot on the field where he could mass fire.
There was not a single line that could withstand a truly determined
assault. By first light tomorrow he could have 40,000 men up and in
place. With good luck and hard marching.

And now, news from home. Annie's sick. Please, dear God, not the
fever. Not Annie. She's so young yet. Just on the threshold of woman-
hood. He felt the tears begin. No time. Not now. Tomorrow. Think
about tomorrow. He tried to make a fist and the pain from his broken
wrist raced up his arm, bending him over and bringing a curse to his
mind, but not to his lips. Never to his lips. From one pain or the other
the tears fought harder, but Lee fought back.

Hoofbeats at a gallop. The quiet never lasts very long. Kyd Douglas.
Young, almost girlish and Rebel to the core. Kyd Douglas has never had
a bad day. He loves this war. Every minute of it. It's all a huge game to
him. An adventure. A chance to appear on stage with the likes of
Stonewall Jackson and Robert E. Lee. Kyd Douglas was having a grand
old time.

"General Lee. General Jackson sends his regards, sir, and begs to
inform you that his men from Bolivar Heights are moving into position."
He wiped the dirt and rainwater from his eyes. "General Powell Hill, sir,
remains at Harper's Ferry to parole the prisoners and claim the spoils.
McLaws and Anderson are being delayed, sir, but should be in line tonight or tomorrow."

Douglas smiled broadly, proud to bring good news to the great man.
The young officer looked down into the gray face and brown eyes of the

greatest man who ever lived and waited for Lee to speak. Tears? No. Of course not. Only rain.

"Tell General Jackson to move those men forward with all possible speed, Captain Douglas." Lee's voice was calm. Controlled. He spoke almost softly. "McLaws and Anderson in place as quickly as possible. There will be a fight here tomorrow and everything—everything, Captain—will be decided here. Do you understand?"

Douglas nodded and saluted and began to turn away, but Lee put up his bandaged hand to hold him in place for one more moment. If Lee had something more to add, he decided against it and only repeated himself one last time.

"Everything."

Douglas saluted and raced away through the rain at a full run. Douglas shouted a "yahoo" as he vanished and Lee shook his head in sad amazement.

Maybe not all is lost. Maybe not yet. It's still McClellan over there. Over on the other side of the creek. Jackson is up at last, but the men are tired. Seventeen miles today. And a tough seventeen miles. Big mountains. Bad roads. Bare feet. Stonewall will say that God gave us this day. Maybe so. "Providence" he will say. Providence and George McClellan. No other general in this world could have resisted such an opportunity. The lines are still thin tonight, but an attack today would have quickly and certainly resolved the issue. Probably 120,000 men against 20,000. McClellan had the largest army ever assembled and the most important piece of military intelligence ever handed to a commander, and still he waited. One more day. A day to rest. A day to dig in. One more day to bring up the troops and bring down the odds to a manageable three-to-one.

Lee shook his head. That's all past now. Give thanks and move on.

Movement caught his eye. A Negro. One of the slaves belonging to one of the officers playfully waving the flag. His flag. *Sic Semper Tyrannis.* Virginia. All for Virginia. God and country. And honor. For the flag. Not for the man. Not for the slaves one way or the other. In his mind he tried once again to solve the unsolvable question, as he had a thousand times before. Slaves will be the death of us. Deplorable institution. If the war comes down to that, we lose. We lose England and France. We lose the moral high ground that is now ours alone. We cannot win a war over slavery, but neither can we win without them and therein lies the great dilemma. It's the slaves who plant the crops and feed the army. They build the forts. Some even care for the wounded. Without the slaves we will lose a long, cruel and ugly war.

Last week we could have won it all. But the lost dispatch ended that. Tomorrow we shall either lose the war or save the army for another day.

With God's blessing we'll come back someday. Back through Maryland and into Pennsylvania. Someday.

But not tomorrow.

WASHINGTON

His hand shook as he returned the pen into its stand. Ugly hands. Long fingers. Swollen knuckles. Ancient calluses that would never go away. Ugly and black with ink. And now they ached. Cramped up from the writing.

By now the "old" Emancipation Proclamation was a rat's nest of notes, many written on the scraps of telegraph paper. Two months' worth of changes. But now it was new and clean and official and ready to announce to the world. Yes, it was all of that, but it was also something more. It was also a promise made to God. A promise now kept.

The armies will meet tomorrow. If everything goes well then the war may end, and there may be no need for it at all. The Union "as it was." If everything goes badly . . .

He tried to force the thought out of his mind, but it wouldn't leave. What happens if the Young Napoleon somehow bungles this one too, or finds another excuse not to fight at all? What if the capital falls? What then? Lee's army in Washington. Jefferson Davis in this house, behind this desk. What will the people do? What will England do? What will I do?

Tomorrow.

God, what I'd give for one good man. Just one!

His eyes always managed to find two words that were buried, deliberately hidden deep in the third paragraph of the new document. There were a thousand other words. Military jargon and legal mumbo-jumbo. But the thousand others didn't really matter. Only these two.

He made a fist to try to ease the pain in his right hand, but his heart remained focused on the words . . .

". . . forever free."

Tomorrow, Dear God, I will keep my promise. Give me a victory tomorrow and the slaves will be freed. Allow us only to push them back. Save Maryland. Save Pennsylvania. If we lose tomorrow, then all is lost. Heavenly Father.

Lincoln heard the door creak open only a crack. He didn't even look up.

"Come in, John." Who else would it be at this hour?

John Hay entered quietly. "I saw the light, sir. Is there anything I can do?"

Lincoln shook his head but honestly was glad to see his young secretary. He couldn't talk to Mary anymore. Not since Willie had died. The war was only a nuisance to her now. John was his only confidant. No one in the government. No one in the cabinet. Only this young man was left who had Lincoln's best interest at heart.

"Not unless you can kick the Rebels out of Maryland for me."

"If only I could, sir."

Silence as Lincoln looked back down at the Emancipation Proclamation. *What a wonderfully ugly man,* Hay thought. He resembles no one else in the world. Sometimes he stands like a giant or a god looking down on all the lesser men, the mortal men of the world. And other times, like now, he can make himself almost small. Stooped. Tired. Withered. Crushed by the weight.

"Well, sir. If there's nothing . . ."

"Seward was agitated today."

"Yes, sir. I noticed."

"He has got his hands on some horrifying rumors, John. From England." Hay stopped breathing. Short prayer. The only good news from England is no news.

"Lord Palmerston's carriage driver is a friend of ours," Lincoln said with only a slight smile. "He tells us that if we lose tomorrow, and the

Rebels are allowed to remain in Maryland to threaten Baltimore and Washington, that England, France and maybe even Russia will enter into conversations with the South, aimed at resuming commerce."

"It is something that could be overcome, Mr. President."

"No, John. I'm not sure that it could."

More silence. Only the rain. Lincoln's attention had been drawn to a map.

"It's a beautiful place, sir. I've been there, believe it or not."

"I beg your pardon."

"Sharpsburg. Nice farming land, down in a pretty little valley. Mostly Germans. It's got a nice, wide, beautiful little stream running through it."

"So I've heard. It's got an Indian name. I can't remember."

"Antietam, sir. Antietam Creek."

He glanced at the words one more time. These words will stop them. Not the army. Not the navy. No military force on earth could stop the British if they choose to challenge the blockade. But these words—these two words—they will stop them. Tomorrow, with a victory, the war will no longer be about politics, or states' rights, or cotton, or even wholly about the Union anymore. When the world hears these two words, nothing will be the same—ever again.

". . . forever free."

Tomorrow.

CHAPTER 10

THE CORNFIELD

SEPTEMBER 17TH

At 5:00 A.M. Joe Hooker summoned his division commanders to his headquarters for one final meeting. The yellow light from a single lantern cast sharp shadows as the men heard again what Fightin' Joe expected of them.

"It falls on us, gentlemen, to initiate this battle. Our orders are vague, but I believe we have General McClellan's permission to attack. And attack we must. We've already spent two days watching the enemy improve his positions and I'll be damned if I'll sit around and watch another. Thank God the rain has stopped." He took a breath and glanced slowly around at each of his division commanders—Ricketts, Doubleday and Meade—to see if any expression might give him a hint as to what to expect from them on this day. "As you know, there are three stands of woods that form a triangle around a cornfield. For our purposes we will call them the North Woods, at the apex where we are now, the East Woods on our left, where General Sumner is, and the West Woods on our right, which is held by the enemy. The white building on the hill on the edge of the West Woods is your goal, gentlemen. Aim all of your movements at this. General Ricketts will move through the cornfield. What is your order of march, General?"

"Duryea will lead, followed by Christian and Hartstuff."

"Excellent. General Doubleday will move down this road, here. The Hagerstown Pike." He looked up at the new division commander with a question on his face.

"Gibbon, Patrick and Phelps."

"Very good. I like what John has done with his brigade. He will do well. General Meade, you will be held primarily in reserve. At first light, however, I need to make certain that the low land to our left is clear. There will be fog in the low-lying places and it may be thick enough to conceal the enemy. Send down a single brigade and let me know if he is there in strength."

George Meade, known to his men as "the damned old goggle-eyed snappin' turtle," only nodded.

"When I hear back from General Meade I will order the attack. Any questions?"

No one spoke as they stood to leave. "Very well. To your posts then." As they left the tent the division commanders were astounded to see Hooker's huge white stallion groomed and saddled and ready for the day.

Ricketts turned to Hooker and said, "You're not going to ride that big white horse today, are you?"

"It gives the men courage to see us together. They can see me better, and he is a fine animal."

"That may be true, sir, but the Rebs will be able to see you better too."

Hooker only shrugged, and Ricketts, Doubleday and Meade saluted and rode off to join their divisions.

Hooker also mounted up and rode off to view the sunrise. Looking out over David Miller's cornfield on any other morning, Hooker would have seen only nature's glory, but on this morning he saw bayonets. First just a single glint of sunlight reflected off the steel tip of a single Rebel bayonet, held only slightly above the corn. Then ten—then twenty.

"I'm going to need artillery on that field before Ricketts can move."

Then musket fire exploded to his left and he listened closely. "That'll be Meade's men," he said and listened a moment longer. "That is light fighting. Commence artillery and order Ricketts and Doubleday forward. We will cease firing when Ricketts reaches the field."

THE CORNFIELD

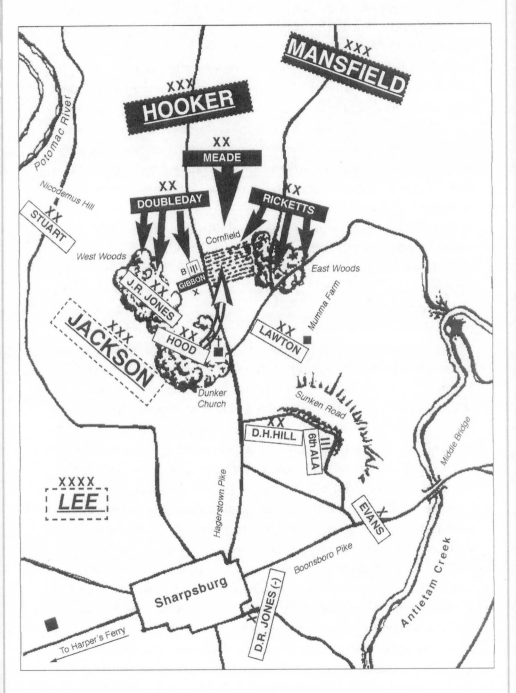

* * *

From his position on Nicodemus Hill, Jeb Stuart observed the first advances of the day. Gibbon's brigade moved out of the North Woods into the open, onto a plowed field between the woods and the cornfield. Stuart's artillery opened fire. Hooker's artillery returned it.

"Would you look at that!" Captain Blackford shouted and then laughed out loud. The men of his battery on Nicodemus Hill ceased firing to laugh along as a dozen women and children came tumbling out of the farmhouse immediately below them. The panicked civilians threw their arms helter-skelter over their heads and ran about in every possible direction, some completely around in circles. The Union gunners took note and held their fire as well.

Blackford rode down to the house and lifted the smaller children up onto his horse and herded the rest off the battlefield.

With the civilians ushered safely out of harm's way, Blackford rode forward, saluted the Union gunners and, by mutual consent, the business of killing resumed.

Hooker's big guns opened on the cornfield where he had seen the gleam of bayonets, and their fire was joined by the even bigger guns on the other side of the creek, up on the big hill by the Pry house. The biggest guns on the field, the twenty-pound Parrotts, joined in the fight with deadly accuracy from a distance of almost two miles, and in an instant the air above the corn filled with smoke, fire and iron and with the arms, legs and heads of Rebel pickets tossed thirty feet into the sky.

Now S. D. Lee's artillery, massed on the grounds around the Dunker Church, joined in and the land exploded and the sky above it burned.

"Today will be artillery hell," Lee yelled above the continual, ear-ringing thunder of his twenty-three guns firing, reloading and firing again as quickly as their crews could move.

Chris Yeager had been a policeman in New Jersey before the war, and now he was a private with the Union artillery. He offered a case round to his gunner for the cutting of the fuse as a Rebel shell exploded not ten yards away. He fell to his knees, but held on to the shell, his face and his hands burned and blistered. He wiped the blood from his eyes and looked to see that the fuse had *not* been cut, but it *had* been ignited by the

Rebel blast and was burning quickly to its charge. Wide-eyed and scared pissless, he grabbed the fuse to yank it out, but the damned thing wouldn't budge, so he clenched his fist and held it tightly, and watched as the powder sparked its way down into his fist. He fought the pain and the overpowering urge to release the fuse, toss the shell aside and run like hell. Sweat and blood filled his eyes. He screamed in pain and smelled his own burning flesh while his terrified batterymates scrambled for the nearest rocks, but he didn't turn loose and the flame died in his hand and he laughed. Still holding the shell nestled like a baby in the crook of his left arm and the remnants of the burned-out fuse in his right hand, he laughed. When his hand was finally pried loose from the fuse, his palm bled from where his fingernails had cut into his own cooked flesh.

Beyond the southern border of the cornfield Stonewall Jackson's divisions waited.

General Alexander Lawton shouted at his men over the roar of the cannon fire, "Pick a row of corn, men, and take aim, and when the Yankees step out, fire by files."

Duryea's brigade marched out of the cornfield and from a range of a hundred yards the Rebels rose up as a single, fire-breathing thing and hurled a thousand rounds of death into the front rank of Yankees, who fell like to a scythe from right to left. The second rank stepped over the bodies of their fallen friends and returned the Rebels' volley before they fell too, just one step closer to Jackson's line.

From the standing position the Rebels continued to send and receive volley after deadly volley, and the Yankees continued to march forward. Face-to-face they exchanged fire until they could stand no longer. The Rebels finally went prone and the Yankees followed suit—those who were left.

Colonel James Walker, whose Georgians anchored the Rebel right on this part of the field, saw his chance for glory. An attack launched right now might get around on Duryea's left and lay down an *enfilade* that could end this assault forever. At the top of his lungs, to be heard over the roar, Walker ordered, "Charge!" but not a Georgian moved. Not a single son-of-a-bitch among them stood. The only movement was that of half a dozen men who turned and stared at their commander in total disbelief.

"Charge!" he yelled again, and again the Rebels lay still in their ditch. Shaking with anger, Walker ran forward and kicked a man to get him to move. He was dead. So was the man next to him and the man next to him as well. Ten minutes before he'd commanded a hundred men, now sixty of them lay dead and most of the rest were wounded.

It was 6:30 A.M.

Duryea suffered and watched and waited.

"Where in the *hell* is Christian?"

In the East Woods, Bill Christian rode through the inner circle of artillery hell. Shells burst at his feet, limbs fell from the trees and men exploded before his very eyes in a scene too horrible for even Dante to imagine. He sat on his horse too completely transfixed to do or say anything. He watched the horrible show and moved as in a dream, wanting desperately to run, but he couldn't. Wanting desperately to be awake, but he couldn't. Wanting desperately to . . . Above the roar, through the smoke of his nightmare came a screaming, pleading human voice . . .

"For God's sake, Colonel—*do something!*"

Christian shook his head clear and it struck him like a round of solid shot. These poor dying men were *his* men. His responsibility. He and only he could save them.

"For God's sake, Colonel . . ."

"By the right flank—march!" Christian yelled without thinking, and the men obeyed. Fresh iron exploded over their heads and the panicked colonel ordered "Left oblique" and again the men obeyed and again more men died. "No! By the RIGHT flank . . ."

Another shell exploded directly under the nose of his mount and the animal smelled the fear and the blood and reared high. Christian tried to take another breath, desperately praying that he would get it right this time, but his throat was swollen shut with fear and no air could enter. The horse bolted and threw the colonel hard to the ground. He stood and chased after her, ducking and diving and covering his ears with his arms as if not hearing the battle would make it go away. His men watched in contempt as Bill Christian ran from the field in terror.

The next man in line, George Hartstuff, waited for Christian as well. He rode forward to investigate the delay and Jeb Stuart's artillery sighted on him. The superbly mounted Union officer, riding alone and slowly through the field, caught the attention of every gunner on Nicodemus Hill. Stuart saw him too, and recognized his old classmate simply by the way he rode. He watched intently through his glasses and heard a battery commander order "Fire." Stuart grimaced and looked away as the expertly timed shell exploded four feet over George's head. Horse and rider went quickly down, and Jeb stood motionless for a frightened moment until the dismounted Union general finally rose and hobbled painfully from the field.

Only then did Stuart breathe. "Take the rest of the day off, Cadet Hartstuff. And thanks for the whiskey at Cedar Mountain."

"Courier!" Jackson shouted.

"Sir."

"Compliments to General Hill. As there seems to be no assault against the center, inform him that we are suffering mightily here, and should we fail, his left will be exposed. Tell him we require assistance immediately."

Behind Stephen Lee's batteries at the Dunker Church, John Bell Hood's Texans built their fires and prepared to cook their long-awaited breakfast.

Behind the Rohrbach Bridge, in the cellar of the Rohrbach house, Ada Mumma was having great fun. All the beds had been moved down, and mattresses from Grandpa Mumma's house covered the floor. Uncountable little Mummas and Rohrbachs bounced around as though on a grand indoor family picnic.

The distant sounds of battle provided only a vague background to the racket of the children, but the hoofbeats of twenty horses in the yard attracted Ada's attention. She peeked out from the high, tiny basement window and saw mounted men in blue uniforms with brass buttons and gold braid and all of the armies of the world couldn't keep her in that shelter. She climbed the pulldown ladder and bolted onto the porch where one of the funniest-looking men she had ever seen was talking with Grandpa Rohrbach. He wore a big, silly hat that was round on the top, and his long, thick whiskers ran down the side of his round face and curved under his jawline and back upward to join with his mustache, while his cheeks and chin were shaved clean.

"How do you do, sir?" the general said as he dismounted. "I am General Ambrose Burnside."

"I know you, sir. I am Henry Rohrbach."

Ada ran directly up to Burnside and stared up at him like the man on the moon was on her front porch. He glanced at the beautiful, blond child and said, "Your family's not in this house?"

Burnside picked Ada up and placed her on his knee.

"Yes."

"Send them all away at once," Burnside said matter-of-factly. "Your buildings will all be destroyed as you are directly in the line of fire."

"All of the horses have been taken but one who is so lame the army wouldn't have him."

"Take him and risk getting beyond the lines. It is safer to go than to stay."

Ada's father, Henry Mumma, joined in the conversation and agreed to go. Mary, the Mumma house slave, ran onto the porch in a veritable dither and took Ada from the general with no ceremony at all.

"Missy, I been lookin' everywhere for you! Done thought the soldiers had carried you away. Your ma and grandma's been scared to death!"

The lame gelding was quickly hitched to the Rohrbachs' light carriage, which the family called "Rockaway." At 6:40 A.M. Ada, Mary and the rest of the ladies and children headed out to a neighbor's house at the base of South Mountain. Ada's father drove them, but the rest of the menfolk and the slaves remained behind.

Harvey Hill responded quickly to Jackson's request for reinforcements. Colquitt's and Ripley's and Garland's brigades (Garland's now under McRae), who had fought so long and hard on the roof of South Mountain, moved from Hill's left toward Miller's cornfield. Some of the forward-thinking Rebels took the time to touch the torch to the Mumma house and barn and all of its outbuildings so the Yankees wouldn't be able to use them should they take that ground.

Samuel Mumma, whose English got worse and worse the madder he got, rushed out of his home mixing German and English at such a rate that it might as well have been Greek to the boys from the Deep South. They were astounded to see him there and kept saying, "Sorry, sir, but you must leave."

"*Mein haus. Dieses mein haus.* It has in it *alles* of *mein* life," and one kind Rebel put his arm around the distressed old man and guided him from the field in tears.

The smoke from the house fire blended with the gunsmoke on the ground and the patches of ground fog that persisted, all adding to the confusion on the field. Union troops and artillery posted in the East Woods took Hill's brigades under fire and Jackson's reinforcements were forced to a halt on the Mumma farm.

Colonel Richard Coulter assumed command of Hartstuff's brigade, and they finally moved through the cornfield only to receive the same reception as Duryea. The battle resumed with the same deadly intensity over the same bloody ground.

Off to the Union right, John Gibbon led his brigade down the Hagerstown Pike, but only as far as David Miller's farmhouse in the northwest corner of the cornfield before he came under fire by a sparse but well-placed band of Rebel skirmishers. It took him half an hour to clear them out before the advance could continue. Once done, Gibbon, Patrick and Phelps continued the advance southward along both sides of the road with Gibbon's Black Hat Brigade in the lead.

Not to be flanked again, Gibbon sent out two companies of the 7th Wisconsin to protect his right. They made their way down into a gully filled with morning fog and gunsmoke so thick that if a man stopped for an instant he risked being run into by the man behind him. They veered left to gain some high ground above the smoke, and along the roadside their friends from home glanced down into the thick vale of fog and saw the soft silhouettes of approaching soldiers. They turned and opened fire. Boys from Baraboo died at the hands of their neighbors from Eau

Claire. The survivors on the low ground bolted, hellbent for the rear, and only a handful of yards farther down the road the Stonewall Brigade rose up from a clover patch and threw lead into Gibbon's newly exposed flank.

"Goddammit, bring up the goddamned GUNS!"

The fighting was hot only a few yards off to Gibbon's left and he couldn't move ten feet at a time. His blood was up and he wanted to be a part of the action. The *real* action, and this former artillery instructor knew just how to do it.

"Bring up the GUNS, goddammit. NOW!"

On the cornfield, more Rebel troops rushed through the smoke and into the fire and pushed Hartstuff's men backward over the same ground that Duryea had just abandoned. By now the going was harder because much of the corn was gone, cut sheer to the ground. Where the stalks had stood, bodies now lay, still precisely laid out in their ranks and files. Retreating Yankees and advancing Rebels had to climb over the corpses to get where they were going.

Colonel Peter Lyle assumed command and rallied Christian's abandoned brigade, and moved it forward, at last, out of the East Woods and into the cornfield and the men who had been led by a coward fought like heroes and the Rebel tide ebbed, and more bodies were added to the pile.

"General Hood, General Jackson sends his compliments and commands that you order your men forward—*immediately*."

Immediately.

Hood looked around at his bold but starving Texans and his heart broke. The bacon had just that instant hit the pans and the smell of cooking pork overpowered that of burning powder. Some had mixed bits of cornmeal in water and rolled the concoction into balls and slipped them over their ramrods to hold over the fire. Not a man had yet taken a bite when Hood yelled, "To arms!" Not a hero hesitated and John Bell Hood rushed 2,000 hungry, angry and screaming Texans headlong into the fight. Half went into the cornfield and half into the East Woods. Mounted officers guided their horses slowly and carefully so as to avoid trampling the helpless wounded who lay in their path. The Union lines stiffened against the fresh Rebel assault, and the front ranks of both armies stood toe-to-toe. Bayonets drew blood, rifle stocks shattered faces and weaponless men went at it with their fists and once again the tide of battle turned back in favor of the South.

One hour into the Battle of Antietam, 2,000 men lay dead and wounded on what had once been David Miller's cornfield.

7:00 A.M.

Hooker sat tall astride his giant white horse so near to the fighting that he heard the Rebel bullets whiz past him, but he paid them no heed. The breach in the Union lines created by Hood's attack had to be filled and a single regiment remained to the rear of Miller's farmhouse. Hooker looked to his right and saw a man in uniform, without insignia of rank.

"Who are you?"

"Special Correspondent of the *New York Tribune*, sir."

"Will you take an order for me? Tell the colonel of that regiment to take his men to the front and keep them there."

George Smalley rode rearward only a hundred yards before a shell exploded and his horse went down, but Smalley was unhurt and quickly found another horse and continued on his mission.

Gibbon's advance remained at a standstill. Two couriers approached him at once, one from either flank. They pulled up next to him at the same time and both started to speak at once.

"One disaster at a time! You first."

The man to his right said, "Our right flank skirmishers have been routed, sir, and the Rebels . . ."

Gibbon held up his hand and indicated to the other man that it was his turn to speak.

"A fresh division of Rebel troops has moved into the cornfield, sir, and General Ricketts urgently requests assistance."

To the man on his right Gibbon said, "Locate General Patrick and tell him to dispatch a brigade to the right and clear out that gully once and for all or we will be stuck here all day." To the man on his left he said, "Tell General Ricketts that help is on the way."

On his left flank, to the eastern side of the Pike, Gibbon sent the 2nd and 6th Wisconsin into the cornfield. Gibbon's Black Hats marched headlong into the hand-to-hand fight and knocked Hood's hungry and angry Texans backward—but only for an instant. They disengaged from the close-in fighting but then turned, reloaded their weapons and continued the fight at a more civilized range. The better riflemen could fire and load and fire again in "only" twenty seconds, but most dropped their own weapons to pick up the rifles of fallen comrades to fire them instead. Men from both sides, from Madison and Austin, stood and yelled and frantically fired. And they laughed, as odd as it may seem, in absolute uncontrolled hysteria, and amidst the laughter, back came Hood. The Wisconsin flag went down briefly only to be recovered by Major Dawes of the 6th. He stood on a wall and waved the blue banner to rally what remained of his state's men.

"Major!"

Dawes turned to see a filthy man with a blackened face and a single gold star on his shoulder.

"Here, Major. Move your men over," General Gibbon yelled, "we must save these guns!"

Gibbon's prized battery, the 4th U.S., had arrived in position with all hell breaking loose on both flanks, and they were in danger of losing their guns before they ever fired a shot.

George Smalley finally reached the lagging regiment Hooker had sent him to order forward.

"Colonel—you are ordered to move your men to the front and keep them there."

"Who are you?"

"The order is General Hooker's."

"It must come to me from a staff officer or from my brigade commander."

"Very good. I shall report to General Hooker that you refuse to obey."

"Oh, for God's sake, don't do that."

* * *

Ada Mumma cried hysterically as "Rockaway" bounced through an orchard on the "quiet" side of the field. She buried her face in Mary's breast as a minié ball ripped through the curtain on one side of the carriage and passed harmlessly out the other. Her mother, Jane, bent over double as best she could, and wrapped her arms around her belly in some desperate attempt to protect her unborn child. A shell exploded overhead and the lame old farm horse panicked and broke into a pathetic, three-legged run.

A thousand yards to the rear of the cornfield, Clara Barton pulled up to a field hospital with her five wagons of medical supplies and started directly to work.

Little Johnny Cook watched in amazement as General Gibbon returned to his guns with two hundred Wisconsiners in tow. Dead square in the middle of the road Captain Campbell spun his guns around, away from Stonewall's brigade to his right, and into Hood's Texans to his left.

"Our boys are pulling back, men, and the Rebels are right behind them. Load with double canister and fire on my command."

Twenty seconds later the first of the routed Yankees came running past his guns, followed almost immediately by Hood's screaming Rebels.

"FIRE!"

One after the other, four of the Napoleons fired. The canister shots exploded 10 yards beyond their muzzles and 215 half-pound balls spread across the advancing Rebel attackers, taking arms and legs and lives, and Hood's men were literally hurled backward into what little was left of the corn. The Texans regrouped again and the men of Campbell's battery began to fall as they attempted to reload. Sergeant West went down with a slug in the thigh and Private Ripley took one in the gut. His intestines spilled out of his shirt, and he calmly gathered them back in with his hands and walked slowly back to the Miller house to die. Sergeant Herzog was the next to fall, shot through the stomach as well. The pain was too excruciating for him to bare, just to hold on for an extra hour of agony. Crying and cursing, he put his revolver to his head, and an end to his pain.

"FIRE!" Campbell yelled again, and again the guns blasted double rounds of canister into the cornfield and the overloaded 2-gun recoiled so high and so far that the right wheel of the 2,300 pound cannon knocked down Gunnery Sergeant Mitchell and rolled backward over his chest. His anguished screams cut above the sounds of the battle, but only for a moment.

The loading process began again, but by now S. D. Lee's artillery at the Dunker Church and Stuart's on Nicodemus Hill had moved to take Campbell's Battery "B" under heavy gunfire of their own.

The captain dismounted and his tiny shadow, young John Cook, dismounted with him. Johnny's foot had no sooner touched the ground than an air burst showered jagged, hot iron over them, killing both horses—Pompeii, the captain's beautiful stallion, and Johnny's milk-white pony that the men pretended to hate so much. The bugle boy was knocked to the ground, but was only stunned by the burst. He stood as quickly as he could get his legs back under him and looked around to check on his captain and found him on the ground with his right arm gone and bleeding neck to hip, but he was still alive.

Cook, as tiny and as frail as he was, tried to pick him up to carry him to the Miller house.

"Find Lieutenant Stewart, Johnny, and tell him to assume command of the battery."

A grown-up finally ran up and took the captain away. Johnny watched and prayed that his friend would be all right, but the prayer had to be a short one. He still had work to do.

He turned back to the guns as four of the six were pulled away by the few remaining horses. The other two would have to be fought until taken, but they were critically undermanned. He saw the 2-gun manned by only three men where minutes ago she had been under the care of nine. She had continued to recoil farther and farther across the road and the elevation screw had turned itself so far down that when they *were* able to fire the canister, pellets passed harmlessly over the heads of the Rebels.

Battery "B," 4th U.S., was Gibbon's personal battery. It had been his when he was a captain in the "old" army back in some former life in some half-forgotten place called Utah. The general dismounted and ran forward and turned the screw himself to minimum elevation so that the barrel pointed down into the ground. The small crew feverishly worked to reload while Gibbon adjusted the screw and just as they finished the Rebs came again and this time it was Gibbon himself who ordered, "FIRE!" The muzzle blazed and the canister balls hit the ground and bounced up, taking with them dirt and rocks and huge splinters of wood from the fence rails into the faces of the oncoming Texans, and again Hood's men fell back.

It took a moment for the smoke to clear and when it did, Gibbon noticed little Johnny Cook, all ninety-two pounds of him, with that head too big for his body, standing stunned and black-faced at the front of the cannon. The fifteen-year-old bugle boy held a ramrod twice as tall as himself and his unblinking eyes were as big as a horse's.

The general smiled at the bugle boy and the loading process began again.

Two miles away and high atop a hill, George McClellan sat in Philip Pry's backyard. He struck a match and lighted his second cigar of the morning and watched the battle and spoke to no one.

"General Sumner is here to see you, sir."

"Sumner?"

"Yes, sir. He's in the house and he requests permission to move his corps forward."

"Tell him to stay where he is, and for God's sake don't bring him here. He'll receive his orders when it is time."

The crusty old gray-haired regular army general hated nothing more that watching others fight. There were three corps assigned to the Union right and why all three hadn't been ordered in at once was beyond him. A unified assault would have ended by now with the Rebel left easily turned. What in God's name was George McClellan waiting for?

Lee found Longstreet on the hill overlooking Antietam Creek, way around to the Confederate right and away from the battle. Longstreet too was observing a quiet moment as he looked with amazement at the Union position across the creek and wondered when they would come.

"Any activity, General?"

Longstreet was surprised to hear Lee's voice.

"You startled me, sir. I didn't hear you ride up."

"I'm afraid I am going nowhere quickly this day, General." He held up his hands to remind Longstreet of his bandaged wrists. "I have to be led around the field like a child on a pony."

"Perhaps you should have ridden Lucy today, sir."

"No. The men need to see me on Traveller, regardless of my condition. It appears quiet over there."

"Yes, sir, it is. You would think they would launch at least a diversionary assault. Something to hold us in place."

"Yes, you would think. But as they have not, we should take advantage of it. General Jackson is struggling over next to the church, General. We need reinforcements and Hood is already engaged."

"McLaws and Anderson have arrived from Harper's Ferry, sir, but are worn down from the night's march."

"Where is Walker?"

"Guarding the crossing, sir."

"Who is in command on the other side?"

"Burnside, we believe."

"Very well. Send Walker to Jackson's aid immediately."

"Understood, sir. You are aware that by sending Walker away you leave me with only Toombs guarding the bridge and he is not five-hundred-strong?"

"Their position is excellent and their opposition is reluctant. Inform me should they become hard-pressed. And, General . . ."

"Sir?"

"McLaws and Anderson will have very little time to rest."

Sitting astride his horse next to the Dunker Church, Stonewall Jackson could not afford a moment of reflection. To his left he saw fresh new columns of Yankee troops marching to Gibbon's rescue. Is there no end to them? No devils left in hell. He sent a courier to General Hood in the cornfield and found time to enjoy a peach while he awaited the response.

"Tell General Jackson unless I get reinforcements I must be forced back, but I am going on while I can."

The smoke had not yet cleared from Gibbon's and Cook's last round when a thousand of Meade's Pennsylvanians appeared, with American and state and regimental flags unfurled and muskets held at "charge bayonets." The units on the right saved Gibbon's guns, and the obstinate Texans moved slowly back. Colonel Work of the 1st Texas had brought 226 men into the cornfield, and watched only 60 withdraw against the onslaught. The 7th Wisconsin and 19th Indiana—the Black Hats—now turned east to follow up the assault that forced the 1st Texas back into the cornfield. The Texans, hugely outnumbered now, rallied around their colors and thirteen more died to keep the banner out of Union hands. They could have more easily stemmed the flow of the Potomac. The flag of the Lone Star State was finally pried from the hands of a dead man and carried to the rear as a trophy. Meade's Pennsylvanians smelled their very first victory and pursued the Texans directly into the waiting arms of Roswell Ripley's 1,300 Rebels, who greeted them at much the same spot and in much the same way as Lawton had greeted Duryea just over an hour ago. Harvey Hill himself led Ripley's men into the battle, and at a range of only thirty yards Rebels from Georgia and North Carolina welcomed Pennsylvania to the fight with another "stand and fire" surprise that sent the fresh Yanks reeling.

Even though the Union counterattack had halted for the moment, McIver Law of Hood's division felt the tide turning again against them.

"Courier! Back to the church as quickly as you can ride. Without reinforcements we will all die here! Ride!"

He didn't know that Harvey Hill had Colquitt on his way to the cornfield and McRae on his to the East Woods.

Colquitt's brigade advanced at the quick-step from the Mumma farm toward the cornfield, rushing to Ripley's aid, but came to a halt when startled by the thunder of hoofbeats from ahead.

"Cavalry!"

Men scattered and hit the ground in every direction, ready to fight off the advancing horsemen, when out from the woods six stampeding cows attacked at full tilt.

George Smalley rode back to Hooker's side and told him of the colonel's reluctance to obey his instructions.

"Yes, I see. But don't let the next man talk so much." The next unit Hooker ordered forward was Mansfield's Twelfth Corps.

7:30 A.M.

Meade's routed Pennsylvanians, many hellbent on running all the way back to Pittsburgh, came upon a lad, a teenage Yankee standing on a rock and waving his regimental colors. "Rally, boys, rally!" he screamed. His voice was high-pitched and sounded odd blending with the manly sounds of battle. "Die like men! Don't run like dogs!" At first one man came to his side and turned and loaded and fired back at the advancing Rebels—then another—then ten more and twenty more and in only a moment the boys from Philadelphia and Holidaysburg each one found his courage and turned and stood up to the damned Johnnys and again the Rebel tide came to a halt.

Kyd Douglas approached Jackson at a run.

"Sir, our officers are . . ." To hell with the formality. Almost in panic he continued. "Sir, Generals Lawton and Jones, John Jones, have been carried from the field, sir. I have no report as to their conditions. General Starke assumed command from Jones but he is dead." Douglas was violently ill. He fought back nausea and panic and tears. "The Stonewall Brigade is now commanded by a colonel and, General Jackson, sir, other brigades are being commanded by *captains*!"

Jackson finished his peach and said nothing.

Five hundred yards away Joe Hooker looked over what had been the cornfield and saw it covered corner to corner with dead and wounded men. The moaning and pleading of the wounded added a sustained bass note to the staccato rhythm of the battlefield, and Fightin' Joe remained precisely where he had started ninety gruesome minutes ago.

* * *

Clara Barton placed a chloroform-soaked rag over the soldier's face until she determined him to be "surgically asleep." A surgeon's assistant screwed the tourniquet tightly around the old sergeant's left thigh. The surgeon skillfully spun the flesh knife around his calf and with a scalpel he peeled back the skin to above the knee. He then used a larger amputation knife to cut through the muscle.

"Jesus God, this one's a mess. The bone is shattered and there are fragments all over the place. I can't get at this one with the Cap saw. Hand me the chain saw." Barton handed him an instrument that resembled a garrote. It had ivory handles on either end of a chain of tiny, sharp links. He wrapped it tightly around the man's leg and pulled the handles left then right over and over again as the wire slowly sawed through the flesh, then the muscle and then the bone. Finally, the leg fell loose and rolled off of the table and fell to the floor with a dull, wet thud. The shoe was still on the foot. The surgeon's assistant tossed the leg out of the window and into a ditch dug for the purpose. The pit already contained hundreds of arms, legs and hands. A mangy, yellow dog kept dragging off body parts until someone got sick of it and shot the poor mutt to death.

The doctor then smoothed down the rough edges of the exposed bone, stitched shut the main arteries and closed the skin back over the nub below the man's left knee. The procedure took more than fifteen minutes—entirely too long for one amputation.

Barton's neck and shoulders ached. She couldn't stand up straight and she realized that her dress weighed a ton. She reached down and picked up the hem and wrung the blood from it as a washerwoman might and then she wiped her hands on her hips. The wounded were stacking up in front of the house and each and every man begged for water. She took the time to go from one to another, dishing out the manna and receiving thanks.

She cradled a man's head in the crook of her left arm and gently placed a ladle to his lips. She felt a tug on the left sleeve of her dress and the man's head exploded in her arms.

Joseph K. F. Mansfield was of the West Point Class of 1822. This was his fortieth year in the army, and his first land battle of the war. He stood tall and straight and wore shoulder boards with gold tassels and was so vain about his long white hair and beard that he refused to wear a hat in battle. At age fifty-nine, he looked forward to his engagement with the anticipation of a freshly graduated cadet. Though he had been with them for only a matter of hours, his men loved him immediately. They had fought for "Commissary" Banks and Irwin McDowell, and were more than ready to prove themselves at last under the leadership of a real general, and Mansfield *looked* real enough.

The regimental bands played martial music and the flags came unfurled as he rode among them and they cheered him and waved their hats and chanted "Mans-field—Mans-field—Mans-field!"

Mitchell and Bloss shouted as loudly as the rest. They had had enough of losing and would take on the whole damned Rebel army alone if need be. They may have been even more enthusiastic than most, as it had been their finding of the lost dispatch that started the whole damned rigmarole in the first place.

"That's right, boys—cheer!" Mansfield cried back. "We're going to lick 'em today!"

Hooker rode back himself to urge the Twelfth Corps into battle. They made a magnificent picture as they exchanged salutes, Hooker astride the magnificent stallion, side by side with the white-haired father image of Mansfield. How could they lose with leaders such as these?

"The enemy are breaking through my lines!" Hooker yelled. "You must hold this wood!" Fightin' Joe waited for no response, no argument, no elaboration. He turned and pushed his stallion hard back to the front, leaving General Mansfield aghast. This wasn't part of the plan. Things were going well the last he heard, and his poor men were supposed to move in and clean up what little resistance was left. A desperate, major engagement had never entered his mind. This changed everything.

Mansfield turned to his left as his lead regiments spread out along a fence line on the eastern edge of the East Woods and fired on the men among the trees.

"*You must hold this wood,*" Hooker had said. *Hold it.* That meant that the East Wood was in the possession of *Union* troops who were dying at the hands of his own men.

"Cease firing!" he yelled. "You are firing at our own men!" He continued up the line, repeating the order. "Cease firing!"

He finally got his men under control and spurred his horse to a run. He made a gallant sight, tall in the saddle, white hair bare to the wind, as horse and rider smoothly leaped the three-rail fence.

"Those are Rebels, General!" one man yelled as the commander pranced bravely forward to see for himself.

"Yes—you're right," he said and an instant later twenty astounded Rebels confirmed his assessment with a volley that wounded both horse and rider. A squad of men went forward to assist Mansfield from his horse, and as he dismounted a gust of wind blew open his coat and the men saw the awful wound to his chest. Too old and fat and too badly wounded to run, but too proud to accept the help of his men, Mansfield calmly brushed the dirt from his uniform and marched slowly back toward the fence. His men resumed firing into the woods, but too late to save their new leader. He tried to climb the rails, but went down in the second volley of fire from the "Union" men behind the trees.

Ten minutes into his dream, Joseph Mansfield was carried from the field.

"General Sumner, sir."

Sumner rose from his seat on the front steps of the Pry house and noted that the staff officer who greeted him was only a major.

"Yes, Major?"

"General McClellan sends his regards and apologies, sir, but begs your forgiveness in the light of very pressing matters. He requests that you return to your corps and advance it forward in support of General Mansfield with General Hooker in command on the field. One division is to remain in the rear as a precaution until relieved by General Porter and shall be sent forward at that time."

"Thank you, Major. Tell General McClellan . . ." Sumner considered what he would *like* to tell General McClellan, but thought better of it. "Tell him I'm on my way."

Only after he thought Major Wilson was well out of earshot did Sumner whisper, ". . . and tell him that we should be fighting this damned battle to *win* and you're *never* going to win if you keep sending in your troops in driblets."

With the wounding of General Mansfield, Alpheus Williams resumed command of the Twelfth Corps, but had not been briefed as to its mission. Off he rode in search of General Hooker, while his men fought Indian-style in the East Woods. The remnants of Hood's division fought from behind the rocks and the trees and prayed to God and Robert E. Lee for help.

"General Hooker, General Mansfield is severely wounded, sir, and has been carried from the field. I am the ranking officer now in the Twelfth Corps. What are your orders, sir?"

Hooker dropped his head and shoulders in total dismay, not at the loss of General Mansfield, but at the loss of time. "General, we are on the verge of disaster, here. You must string your corps all along the line. Anchor your right flank in those woods, over there on the other side of the road, and curve your line backward, like a bow, back behind the cornfield, and anchor your left flank in the East Woods, where you are positioned now. As soon as we can withdraw the troops presently involved, you will move forward. Understood?"

"Understood, sir."

He understood all right, but accomplishing the complicated maneuver with primarily green troops could prove cumbersome. In fact, the effort to place the men into position, begun under Mansfield's instructions, was already chaotic.

The 128th Pennsylvania, like so many of the Keystone State's month-old units on the field this day, marched like cows to the slaughter. Some didn't know their left from their right, and it was this unit that led the Twelfth Corps into battle. They created a thousand-man Gordian knot at a critical point between the East Woods and the cornfield. At this crucial instant Colquitt's Rebels marched to Ripley's rescue and poured a heavy fire into the Union lines. Again, Mars played his humorless trick, and the rookies felt the heat first. The officers of the 128th seemed all to fall at once, and now not only were they green, but leaderless as well. Officers and sergeants from neighboring units rushed to the 128th.

Units beside them couldn't get by, and those behind couldn't get past. Mitchell and Bloss stood side by side, frustrated again. The Rebels stood in ranks in front of them, showering musket fire into the heart of their 27th Indiana, but the veterans couldn't return the fire because the rookies were in the way. The poor, inept boys from Pennsylvania had to be moved—one way or the other.

Colonel Joseph Knipe of the 46th Pennsylvania rode behind them like a cowboy herding cattle and forced them into some semblance of a line. He looked desperately around him to find someplace to put them where they would be out of the way, but only one avenue was available.

"Right *face*!

"Fix *bayonets*!

"Charge *bayonets*!

"*Charge!*"

What they lacked in skill, they made up for in courage. They yelled like Rebels and broke across the field alone and unsupported until they came face-to-face with Ripley's brigade. Many of them fell, but all of them were out of the way.

8:00 A.M.

Clear at last of the obstruction, Williams's men finally moved south across the cornfield. Mitchell and Bloss led the charge, as always, together. Fire and load and fire again, until Ripley's Rebels had finally had enough, but Colquitt's brigade was close at hand and coming to their aid. As the fresh Rebel brigade moved closer, its fire became more deadly. The Georgians marched up the hill into the face of the enemy with old-fashioned smoothbores that couldn't pierce a scarecrow at more than fifty yards. In close, however, they worked well enough. Equipped with "buck and ball" cartridges, each gun fired a regulation .69-caliber ball plus three pellets of buckshot. A well-placed round could kill one man, and wound a couple of more. The Yankees fought with rifled muskets, accurate and deadly at two hundred yards, and the Rebels took a terrible beating marching up the hill, but as one man fell, another took his place, and onward and upward Colquitt's men marched. The smoke of the battlefield took the side of the South for the moment, though it choked them and burned their eyes and made many of them sick. The Yankees stood on top of the hill and fired down into the haze at vague outlines of advancing men who just wouldn't stop coming. As the Rebels' weapons became effective, their numbers became few. Without reinforcements they would never make the hill. Colquitt ordered them prone.

"The smoke's so thick, sir, I can't see nothin' to shoot at."

"Then lie down and look for blue britches under the smoke and shoot right above 'em."

The young Rebel did as he was told and up on the hill Blossie fell to the ground, shot through the leg.

For two solid hours, S. D. Lee's "artillery hell" continued without pause. Stationed at the Dunker Church, his guns and gunners dwindled by opposing artillery fire. Horses lay whining and snorting in pain side by side with his men. Ammunition ran critically low.

Robert E. Lee, Jr., manned a gun in Poague's battery. Casualties forced him to the front of the gun, where his hands became blistered from ramming shells down a powder-clogged muzzle. Finally, the blisters burst and his palms bled. The tube became too white hot to touch and ignited the powder bag before he had a chance to stand clear and a twenty-foot stream of fire flashed past him and he survived even that. The hair and skin on the left side of his face were burned away in the blast, but he stood back up and resumed his position. Others with wounds so severe might have left the field to find an aid station, but Bobby Lee, Jr., didn't have that option. Marse Robert's son had to fight to the end or die.

Ambrose Burnside did nothing. He sat at his camp and listened to the battle and waited for his former friend, George McClellan, to tell him when to attack.

As Colquitt relieved Ripley in the cornfield, Garland's former command headed for the East Woods to reinforce the tattered remains of Hood's division. These boys, all from North Carolina, suffered a crisis of confidence. They had been outflanked at South Mountain and had narrowly saved their colors. Within a matter of seconds they had lost both their regimental and brigade commanders. They had seen them fall and die side by side only last Sunday. Sam Garland was their leader, their identity, and when he fell, they ran. They were what he was, and now he was no more. Almost timidly, the tarheels entered the thick stand of trees that Colonel Christian had fled in terror, the woods where General Mansfield had recently fallen and where blue and gray mixed in a battle that had no lines.

George Greene, the other brigade commander under Mansfield, had waited long enough for Williams to return from his meeting with General Hooker. A stream of blue-clad wounded flowed out from the woods and a courier arrived from Christian's devastated regiment pleading for help. Greene ordered the eight hundred men of the 28th Pennsylvania into the East Woods, and they marched square into the right flank of the nervously advancing North Carolinians.

Captain Thompson of the 5th North Carolina saw the Yankees coming, just as they had come at South Mountain just last Sunday.

"My God," he shouted, "we're being flanked again!"

Hood's men had fought in the woods for almost two solid hours, desperately holding on against assault after assault. Plea after plea went out for reinforcements starting over an hour ago, and just as their prayers were finally answered they could do nothing but watch in horror as their long-awaited rescuers bolted and ran without firing so much as a shot.

Instinctively, Hood's men took the Yankees under fire until one of their officers yelled, "Don't kill the Yankees—shoot at the goddamned yellow Rebels!" He then ran out from behind a tree and grabbed a fleeing officer and shook him by the lapels and screamed, "What is your regiment?"

"I'll be damned if I'll tell you!" the man screamed back as he broke and ran all the way to Sharpsburg. The East Woods again belonged to the Union.

Colquitt finally made it up the hill, much to the relief of Ripley's survivors. The Georgians and North Carolinians had fought the good fight, but they had no fight left. These tarheels, at least, had stuck. Of the 770

North Carolinians that Ripley had led into the cornfield, only 360 came back. The Georgians fared even worse. The 6th Georgia attacked with 250 men, and pulled back with 24. Ripley's brigade was finished, and Colquitt's wasn't much better off. They stood in lines of battle facing Williams's, 1,200 men from the 2nd Maine, the 3rd Wisconsin and the 27th Indiana. Mitchell had seen Bloss go down and helped him to the rear, but he knew his buddy would be fine and returned to his position.

The fire grew heavier now than ever. The file closers in the 27th had their work cut out for them. As one man fell, they pushed another forward into his place or forced men left or right over the dead or wounded to fill the gap. They fired so quickly at the Rebels that their rifle barrels became so hot that the powder charges exploded into their faces as they poured the black grains down the muzzle.

One Hoosier took a shot to the belly and fell back, but only a few steps. He pulled up his shirt and saw that he was a dead man. He picked up a fallen weapon and returned to the ranks.

"Where are you headed, soldier?"

"Well, I guess I'm hurt about as bad as I can be. I believe I'll go back and give 'em some more."

That bizarre, frantic, hysterical laughter spontaneously returned to the battle lines as men struggled to contain their emotions. The face-to-face firing grew too intense for either side to withstand. The Westerners went prone and Hooker went berserk.

His most reliable courier, that kid from the *Tribune*, was away on another errand and nowhere to be seen. Hooker conscripted a nearby cavalryman into the depleted courier corps.

"You, there . . . Corporal!"

"Sir!"

Hooker pointed at the 3rd Wisconsin and said, "Tell that regiment to fix bayonets and advance!"

The corporal did as he was told.

"Attack? That's insane! Tell that crazy son-of-a-bitch that we're almost out of ammunition down here and if he wants these boys to charge into that kind of fire to come down here and tell 'em himself!"

The general did as he was told.

"Why have my orders not been carried out?"

Colonel Ruger could no longer believe his eyes or his ears. He looked at Hooker with anger and dismay and shouted, "*Atten-tion*," and the 3rd Wisconsin rose to its feet and the 2nd Maine and the 27th Indiana stood with them.

"Fix bayonets! Charge bayonets! CHARGE!"

As Williams's troops lunged forward into Colquitt's, Greene pursued the retreat of the "flanked" North Carolinians out of the East Woods and onto the cornfield. They came out thirty yards from Colquitt's unprotected right flank. For the first time that day the Union forces launched a coordinated attack, first against the Confederate front, followed immediately by another against their flank. It hadn't been planned that way, it only happened.

Barton Mitchell led the 27th down the hill as cheers rose up and flags of all colors closed in on the Confederates from two sides, and in desperation the firing from the Rebel lines came in even heavier. No one bothered to reload anymore. They didn't have to. Too many loaded weapons lay on the field next to their fallen owners. Pick up a rifle and fire, throw it on the ground and pick up another, all the way down the hill.

Colquitt's Rebels pulled quickly backward toward and past the Dunker Church. Greene's Yankees poured onto the churchyard that thousands had died to reach, but they had outrun their artillery and run out of ammunition and the frustrated general reluctantly ordered a halt.

They stood on the hill and waved their flags and cheered and jeered at the retreating Rebels, who turned and fired one last parting shot and Barton W. Mitchell—the farm boy from Indiana who had found Lee's lost dispatch—spun to the ground with a minié ball in his chest.

The cornfield had changed again from gray to blue. The East Woods and the Dunker Church belonged to the Union. On the Confederate left flank, only portions of the West Woods remained in Rebel hands. Protected by Stuart's artillery now positioned on Hower's Ridge, the entire Confederate left was held by weary stragglers and the battered but proud remnants of Stonewall Jackson's corps.

Now in control of two-thirds of the field on the Confederate left, the Union army rested, and waited for fresh ammunition.

* * *

At 8:40 A.M. the trailing units of A. P. Hill's column marched out from Harper's Ferry on their way to Sharpsburg, seventeen mountainous miles away.

Ada Mumma curled up in a nice soft bed with a thick down mattress and slept with bad dreams while Mary sang and worried if the soldiers would come here too.

Ambrose Burnside continued to wait. If McClellan insisted on dictating what he was to do and where, he could damned well tell him *when* to do it as well.

"General Longstreet—Jackson is in desperate trouble. McLaws and Tige Anderson have rested enough. Order them to the church. And Hill has pulled men from his line in the road to Jackson's aid and they must be replaced. Send Dick Anderson to Hill." The commanding general saw the look of panic on Pete's face and said, "Powell Hill is on his way, General."

God willing, both men thought, but neither said.

Jackson called for Kyd Douglas. "Order the cavalry to round up whatever stragglers they can find—any man who can stand can fight—and bring them here."

"Yes, sir."

"And Douglas . . . Leave Hood's men be," he said in soft tones. "They've done enough today."

Douglas hesitated, simply out of shock. Never had he heard Stonewall Jackson tell anyone that they had "done enough." There was no such thing as "enough."

But Hood himself could not stand idly by.

"Colonel Lee. Ride back toward the town and find General Lee. Tell him that one more assault against us here will destroy the entire line. We are totally unprepared to receive it and if we are not reinforced immediately all will be lost."

Stephen Lee rode no more than a mile before he saw the general and Traveller, led by a staff officer. He delivered Hood's plea.

"Don't be excited about it, Colonel." The general certainly was not.

"Go tell General Hood to hold his ground. Reinforcements are now rapidly approaching between Sharpsburg and the ford. Tell him I am now coming to his support."

Colonel Lee saluted and started to turn away when General Lee saw the lead elements of McLaws's division approaching at the double-quick. "Colonel . . ."

"Sir?"

The general pointed with his bandaged right hand. The colonel nodded and smiled.

The brand-new, seven-hundred-man 125th Pennsylvania advanced down the Hagerstown Pike past the dead and dying, ignoring the cries for water and relief from the wounded who lay along the roadside. The 125th had been left behind by Williams's advance and had chased the battle for an hour without catching up, and now, by accident, they assumed the lead.

Fightin' Joe Hooker smelled his victory and urged his charger to a racetrack pace and sprinted to the front so he could see it, so he could be there to hear the cheers and wave the colors and claim the credit for defeating Stonewall at last. He leaned forward in the saddle, with his head down and the horse's mane streaming in the wind, until he came upon the cautiously advancing rookies of the 125th. With glory in his grasp Hooker wanted no one advancing cautiously.

"Colonel, what regiment is this?"

"The 125th Pennsylvania Volunteers, sir."

He pointed toward the West Woods next to the church and, red-faced with anger, he yelled at Jacob Higgins, "Advance and hold that woods!"

High in the saddle on his gigantic white horse, he looked as subtle as the sun, and the best damned sharpshooter in the whole damned Rebel army gauged the range and fired the shot that shattered Joe Hooker's foot.

"General McClellan, sir. A signal message from General Williams."

McClellan put his cigar in his mouth and read the dispatch to himself: *Genl Mansfield is dangerously wounded. Genl Hooker wounded severely in the foot. Genl Sumner I hear is advancing. We hold the field at present. Please give us all the aid you can.*

For the first time all morning a look of genuine concern appeared on George McClellan's face. He handed the message to Fitz-John Porter.

"Our worst fears come true, Fitz. Sumner commands in the field."

"MY GOD, WE MUST GET OUT OF THIS"

9:00 A.M.

Edwin Sumner's corps advanced toward the Dunker Church under the flags of two divisions. John Sedgwick led the march with William French twenty minutes behind. In accordance with orders, Israel Richardson's division remained two miles to the rear, waiting for a division of Fitz-John Porter's men to replace them on the field. These men forded the creek and marched due west through the now quiet East Woods, over the bodies that covered the cornfield and on toward the Dunker Church, now against only occasional pockets of resistance.

Sumner recognized a classic bad omen of the battlefield. The flow of wounded rearward is always something to be expected, but when each wounded soldier is assisted to the rear by a healthy one, it is a certain indication that things are going badly ahead.

Sumner himself rode at the head of his corps and behind him marched the 5,500 soldiers of Sedgwick's division in three long, tightly formed rectangles of men. Somewhere back down the hill General French followed with three more boxes of men, and two miles behind them, Israel Richardson finally moved his boxes forward as well. The flags waved and the bands played and it made a beautiful blue parade.

As they approached the cornfield the sixty-five-year-old lifelong cavalry officer, known to his men as "Bull" Sumner, spotted a dirty but familiar face.

"General Ricketts, where is the First Corps formed?"

"Formed, sir? The First Corps is formed nowhere. Hooker himself is down, I understand, and I doubt that three hundred men are available to answer the call."

"Very well," Sumner said, and rode along. Ricketts stood amazed and watched the parade march grandly by.

Duryea could tell that his commander was angry.

"What was that all about?"

"He asked me nothing! That old man is marching onto the field blind—onto a field where you and I have just been engaged, a field that he has *never* seen—and he asked me nothing of it!"

"Maybe he was briefed by McClellan."

"I pray so, Abram, but I fear not. And where, for that matter, is *he*? Have you seen McClellan today? Nor have I. For God's sake, Abram, I've seen General *Lee* today—I know it was Lee on that ridge watching every move this morning, and he would vanish and reappear somewhere else like some kind of damned magician's rabbit, but the Young Napoleon is nowhere to be seen. Between the two of us, sir, this battle should have easily been won by now, and *would* have been had Hooker been in charge!"

"General Ricketts—I fear your disappointment is speaking for you."

Ricketts's disappointment exploded into uncontrolled anger.

"General Duryea—today's fight is being conducted almost as a *defensive* battle on our part. The enemy has the river to his back and we hold entire corps in reserve—*against what?*—and are being fed piecemeal to a hungry enemy! First us, then Mansfield and now that old fool Sumner! You know it, sir, and I dare say there is not a man on this field who does not—Robert E. Lee included!"

He sat astride his horse and watched as Sedgwick's division marched by in grand style.

"I can't allow this to happen, Abram." He galloped off in pursuit of Bull Sumner, but had not gone a hundred yards before a shell exploded over his head and General John Ricketts, the first man into the cornfield, was carried unconscious from the field.

Bull Sumner marched on.

Rebel stragglers from the long march from Harper's Ferry continued to limp into Sharpsburg only to be pushed directly into the West Woods and into the line of battle. Many were so lame that had they been horses they would have been shot. Stuart sacrificed the infantry shield protecting the guns on the hill and sent Jubal Early's brigade of 1,200 men down the hill and into the woods. Every Rebel general knew that every man who could pull a trigger had to go to the West Woods.

From the East Woods Sumner paraded his men forward. From the opposite outskirts of Sharpsburg, McLaws and Walker ran theirs.

The 125th Pennsylvania, separated from Williams's brigade of Mansfield's corps and spurred forward by Hooker's final rebuke, inched its way forward and by its very presence pushed Jackson's battered Rebels backward, deeper into the West Woods until the men in the new, blue uniforms came, at last, uncontested onto the grounds behind the Dunker Church. For the first time in three hours, the battlefield fell ominously quiet.

George McClellan dictated an order for Burnside to initiate his assault. The order was dated "Sept. 17, 9:10 A.M.," over three hours into the fight. Three miles away the 12,500 men of Burnside's Ninth Corps looked down into the valley at Joseph Rohrbach's beautiful stone bridge and patiently waited. So uninvolved in the fight were Burnside's charges, that they had time for mail call. Rebel artillery hummed harmlessly overhead as the Confederates fired blindly over the hills onto points where they thought the Yankees might be waiting. Some dozed in the morning sun while the men of the 21st Massachusetts gathered round a newly received local newspaper to gather the latest from home. A stray round fell directly to their right, exploding dirt and rocks and shell fragments all around them. They all hit the ground and came up dirty, but no one was hurt. The regimental colors took a beating and one man attempted to repair the staff while the others returned to their paper. Commissary

Sergeant William McKinley passed among the men pouring fresh, hot coffee.

Sumner saw General Hooker's ambulance en route to the rear and ordered it to a halt so that he could confer with a corps commander, but found Fightin' Joe semiconscious from lack of blood. General Williams came forward as the senior commander on the field, but a single star on the shoulder of a young man meant nothing to Sumner, who had fought the Indians before Williams was born.

"General Sumner, sir."

"How may I assist you, General?"

Williams was taken aback by Sumner's arrogant attitude. He didn't even pull his horse to a stop to hear what the senior commander on the field had to say.

"I think that I might be of assistance to *you*, sir. I have been engaged on this field for over an hour and know something of the land and the situation."

"The land and the situation are plainly seen to me, General."

"Sir, my *corps* is available and is lacking only in ammunition." Williams emphasized the word "corps" to let Sumner know that in spite of the single star, he commanded more than only a brigade.

"General, your little corps is fought out and badly scattered. I haven't the time to wait for you to reorganize. I haven't the time, for that matter, even for this conversation. Now if you'll excuse me, General."

Sumner put the spurs to his horse and pulled quickly away.

Still in parade-ground formation, the great, long, parallel lines of brigades marched across the cornfield, across the carnage of three hours of fighting where thousands of men, blue and gray, covered the ground, cried for help and pleaded for water. John Sedgwick led his men across this field and pictured in his mind the macabre road to hell's gates. Fleetingly he remembered Dante's dire inscription, "All hope abandon, ye who enter here."

Jeb Stuart saw their line of march, anticipated where they were going and shifted his artillery accordingly.

From the Pry house hill on the other side of the field, George Smalley sideled up next to Porter and McClellan to watch the spectacle below. As Sumner's corps marched across the cornfield under their unfurled flags, not a word was spoken between the commanders looking down. Not a person who viewed it from high atop this hill was unmoved by the sight of this gallant army marching proudly to the fight. Smalley looked into the face of George McClellan as he watched the movement and jotted down only a couple of words. "Awe," he wrote, and "reverence."

The green troops of the 125th Pennsylvania continued to wait precisely where Hooker had placed them. "Tige" Anderson's five hundred Confederates came up over a ridge and found themselves face-to-face and evenly matched with the 125th. Jubal Early's brigade, down from Nicodemus Hill, joined in the killing from the flank and the Pennsylvania rookies began to fall.

Colonel Higgins, commanding the 125th, was in far too deep. Without help all were soon to die. He had to send a courier out of this trap to look for help and he logically selected his younger brother for the chore.

"Joseph. Take my horse and ride to the rear. Find General Crawford and tell him that we hold these woods, but are completely outflanked and unsupported."

Lieutenant Higgins mounted without hesitation and asked, "Where may I find the general?"

"The last I saw of him, he was on the cornfield!" The colonel slapped the horse's flanks and sent his seventeen-year-old brother safely to the rear.

The renewed sounds of battle drew Sumner personally forward, and he rode at a gallop directly to the 125th.

"Who commands here?"

"I do, sir, Colonel Jacob Higgins, and we are flanked. We have turned back three minor assaults, sir, but I fear we cannot hold for much longer."

"You *must* hold, sir, but reinforcements are only minutes away. Hold firm, Colonel."

Sumner hightailed it back to his advancing columns and ordered a regiment to wheel to the left and double-quick to Higgins's rescue. The

34th New York moved toward the Dunker Church and into the West Woods.

The rest of Sumner's men continued their slow, precise and majestic march toward the woods that held the church.

McLaws and Walker continued their quick and disordered run toward the very same spot. Without knowing it, the Rebel units were aimed at Sumner like an arrow toward a bird in flight.

As the two small armies continued on their collision course toward the Dunker Church, a courier left the Pry house with a written dispatch addressed to General Sumner: "General McClellan desires you to be very careful how you advance, as he fears our right is suffering."

As Sumner led Sedgwick's division onto the Hagerstown Pike, his second division, French's, exited the East Woods, now half an hour to the rear. The ground here swells and dips like the waters of an angry ocean, and while Sedgwick marched directly to his front, he was out of French's line of sight. To the left French *did* see enormous numbers of men in blue, mostly Greene's troops, still waiting for artillery, ammunition and orders to attack. French assumed them to be Sedgwick's men and ordered a left-flank maneuver that headed his men south, toward the sunken road.

Sumner and Sedgwick were now on their own as their 5,500 men climbed the remains of the split-rail fence that continued to stand along the western edge of the Hagerstown Pike. Jeb Stuart privately congratulated himself on his own foresight and ordered, "FIRE!" His batteries lobbed shot and shell deep into the Union lines, but Sumner's men continued the advance in their tightly packed formations.

Sumner breathed a sigh of relief once his men cleared the pike. Marching recklessly in formations, without flankers to either side or skirmishers to the front, they survived the trek across open ground almost without loss. All that remained now was a left-flank swing that would bring the division fully across the Rebel left for a forward thrust south. *The hard part*, he thought, *is over*. He filled his lungs to order the turn when out from the woods rose a thousand whooping, yipping Rebels, firing headlong into his exposed left flank. The divisions of Lafayette McLaws and John Walker, still breathing hard from their long run through town, fired down the ranks at an angle that made the Yankees almost impossible to miss. Sumner didn't have the time to consider his response before Jubal Early joined in the fight and Stuart's artillery opened again from the opposite flank. Like two trains on one track, the Rebel units came together head-on, with Edwin Sumner caught helplessly in between. Sumner, outnumbered and outflanked, took fire from three separate sides, and worse yet, the initial assault came against his trailing brigade so that the men in the lead had to run the gantlet rearward in order to escape. So close were his men packed together in formation that maneuver was impossible. Return fire was out of the question. Edwin Sumner had marched his men grandly into a three-sided trap that hadn't existed two minutes before. Lafayette McLaws shook his head in wonder and thanked God for his good fortune.

Sedgwick looked to his corps commander for help, but all Bull Sumner could say was, "My God. We must get out of this."

The old man remained calm in the eye of the storm and ordered the rear ranks to "about face" in an effort to march them back out the way they had come in. In the first seconds of the engagement, the 2,100 men of the Philadelphia Brigade had already suffered 500 wounded and 100 more dead. The rest ran for their lives.

Napoleon Jackson Tecumseh Dana's brigade stood in the middle and knew only that the fight was on. They had no idea where it came from or where it was headed. Bull Sumner rode into their ranks amid the chaos and noise and bellowed at the top of his lungs. It was his cannon of a voice that had given him his nickname and not his courage in the ring, but even at that the men could not hear a word. They added to the thunder of battle their cheers for the gray-haired old general, who they thought appeared among them to rally them on. They waved their hats and screamed in salute and continued blindly forward in total ignorance as Sumner continued to yell, "Back, boys! For God's sake, move BACK!"

The Tammany regiment from New York City took the greatest heat, but Dana held them in line in spite of his own wound. The smoke became so thick that "front" and "rear" lost their meaning, and again

Yankees killed Yankees. The 15th Massachusetts took Rebel fire from the front and Union fire from the rear. They suffered 344 casualties, more than 50 percent of their original numbers. Most were shot in the back by the men of the 59th New York.

The 125th Pennsylvania, which had held so bravely while they awaited relief from Sumner's corps, bolted at the first sight of McLaws's division and ran straight into the welcoming arms of Greene's idle men, still awaiting artillery support on the rise just to the east of the church. Greene had long since tired of waiting, and as the 125th moved back, Greene came forward at a run with Captain John Tompkins's six-gun battery in tow. The 7th South Carolina had drawn the short straw of pursuit and followed the Pennsylvanians directly into the barrels of Tompkins's guns. So closely did Aiken's South Carolinians pursue the 125th that the cannoneers could not afford to wait for all of the Pennsylvania boys to get clear before they blasted double-loaded canister directly into their faces. Colonel Aiken fell dead along with half of the 270 Rebels who followed him in.

A few moments later a single Union soldier walked calmly over the quiet field and retrieved the Rebels' regimental flag by simply picking it up off the ground. He handed the colors to his captain and asked, "Will I get the medal for this, sir?"

"Of course you will, Corporal Orth. Everybody else does."

In the West Woods the true Union heroes continued to die before the gray wave of McLaws's advance. Sedgwick carried three bullets in his body. God only knew if they came from Confederate guns or Union.

Captain Oliver Wendell Holmes, Jr., a brilliant young lawyer from Boston, was horrified to find one of his own men facing the wrong way and firing into Union lines.

"Cease that fire, Private!"

The man looked panicked and ignored the order. Holmes became enraged and drew his sword and pushed the man over with it. The private stood and screamed into Holmes's face, "Those are Rebels, sir!" Holmes finally realized the private was right and he turned to order "about face" when a minié ball tore through his neck. His world turned dark, and the splendid young lawyer fell face first onto the ground.

Sumner managed through sheer determination to hold at least some of the division together long enough to make an ordered retreat out of the West Woods and past the Nicodemus house. A pursuing Rebel soldier peeked inside to see what he could see and heard a chorus of pleas from the blue-clad wounded for just a sip of water. The Rebel tossed in his canteen and continued his attack.

Sedgwick's retreat took the remains of his division back across the Hagerstown Pike, back onto the cornfield and back toward the East Woods. The Rebels pursued by as few as fifteen yards, constantly loading, yelling and firing into the fleeing Yankees. They crossed the Pike and the Rebels followed and as the gray troops came upon the fence line all hell exploded before them. The barrels of the guns pointed directly into the ground sent fire and dirt and rocks and splinters of fencing directly into their ranks and the Confederate pursuit came to a quick and deadly halt.

John Gibbon looked again at Johnny Cook and the general and the bugle boy smiled once again.

A retreating Rebel soldier stuck his head into the Nicodemus house and said, "Can I have my canteen back?" A wounded Union soldier tossed it to him and he continued back to the West Woods to regroup with the rest of the Rebs.

In only fifteen minutes of fighting, Sumner lost nearly 2,000 men. He fell exhausted from his horse, dazed by the disaster and heartsick for his men. He still hadn't heard from General French. *Where in the hell is French?* Men spoke to him, but he didn't hear. Someone placed a piece of paper in his hand and said something else he didn't understand. The oldest, most experienced man on the field leaned against a tree and struggled to breathe as he wiped the sweat and tears and powder from his face. *My God, what a disaster.*

Finally, he opened the folded document he held in his hand. He didn't know what it was or where it had come from.

"General McClellan desires you to be very careful how you advance, as he fears our right is suffering."

* * *

The battlefield fell quiet once again. Hood and McLaws rode forward to report to Jackson, and the three men sat for a while in silence looking out over the grounds of the church and onto the cornfield. Standing on any corner of the thirty acres, a man could walk to the corner opposite without touching the earth for stepping on the bodies of the dead and the wounded. So thick was the carnage that the field itself seemed to move, and groan, and plead for help.

Jackson looked over this field and he took a bite from his peach and to Lafayette McLaws, he said, "God has been very kind to us this day."

THE SUNKEN ROAD

10:00 A.M.

On the western outskirts of town, James Longstreet sat side by side with "Neighbor" Jones, and both generals looked over the valley and the creek that ran through it. As usual, Longstreet was worried.

"Now you fully understand the meaning of robbing 'Pete' to pay Paul," Jones said.

Longstreet smiled for the first time in hours.

"I don't fault General Lee. He has done what he had to do . . . what the Yankees allowed him to do. But Walker, McLaws and *both* Andersons are no longer available to me here. I am left with only your men in the town and Toombs's brigade down by the bridge. Toombs has four hundred men down there and Burnside has twelve thousand or more." He peered through his field glasses for the hundredth time, looking for any sign of movement on the part of the Yankees. "They are *going* to cross that creek, Neighbor, and soon, and there's going to be hell to pay when they do."

Still looking through his glasses he shifted his focus to the near banks of Antietam Creek to where Toombs's four hundred Georgians waited.

All 400.

*   *   *

On the opposite side of the creek, Major James Wilson handed Ambrose Burnside the orders for which he had waited for over four hours, the wording of which confirmed Burnside's fears.

"General Franklin's command is within one mile and a half of here. General McClellan desires you to open your attack."

"This is what we've been waiting all morning for? For yet another corps to come forward to be held in reserve? We are not fighting this battle to *win*, my friends. It appears we fight it not to lose."

Wilson took careful note of Burnside's response, but since he agreed with the general's assessment, he kept it to himself rather than repeating it to McClellan.

And so, the assault on the bridge finally began as Colonel George Crook's brigade marched behind the ridge line, so as to come over the hill to attack the bridge head-on. General Isaac Rodman marched his division downstream toward the ford, selected last night by McClellan's personal engineer, to assault the Rebels from their flank. It would take some time for them to get into position. Lee's right, for the moment, remained safe.

Returning from an inspection of his left flank, Harvey Hill saw at a distance Generals Lee and Longstreet conducting an impromptu meeting with his regimental commanders.

"You and your men now hold the key to our entire position, gentlemen," Lee said to the somber officers. "You are the center, and a wedge driven through here will divide our entire force. Understood?"

John Brown Gordon spoke for them all, and loudly enough for the troops to hear. "These men are going to stay here, General, till the sun goes down or victory is won!" With a bandaged hand, Lee saluted the men as a cheer rose up from the heart of the 6th Alabama and spread its way outward to the flanks. The troops then returned their attention to the hill that crested sixty yards above them, and waited for the first signs of the Union attack.

Lee and Longstreet then climbed, on foot, to the top of a hill a hundred yards to the rear of the road, and there Harvey Hill, still mounted, caught up with them. Horse and rider were wet with sweat, and it was a fight for Hill to take a breath.

"We make an irresistible target situated here, General Hill," Long-street pointed out. "I would personally prefer it were you to dismount."

"I'm afraid that fatigue has set in, General Longstreet, and I prefer to remain mounted."

"Very well, but if you insist on riding up there and drawing the fire, give us a little interval."

From another hilltop half a mile away, Captain Weed agreed with Longstreet—the target was indeed irresistible.

"See that horseman on that hill there?"

His gunners had long since ceased to be amazed at the outrageous things that Weed would suggest—and then do. Behind his back and without a word being spoken, bets were offered and taken, even though it had become difficult to find a man willing to wager against their sure-fire captain. He personally sighted his twenty-pound Parrott on General Hill's horse and backed ever so slowly away, as though a light touch or a slight breeze might alter his masterful trajectory. He almost whispered the command "Fire."

Longstreet saw the white smoke of the discharge and said to Lee, "There is a shot for General Hill."

The round exploded directly at the horse's front feet, severing the bay's forelegs at the knees. The poor animal went down nose first and remained in that position with his rear flanks still elevated, and Harvey Hill still fully mounted with his feet almost touching the ground. His two distinguished observers both fought back laughter at the sight of the pompous Hill standing in the stirrups, with the carcass of a wounded horse between his legs and totally unable to disengage himself.

Cheers went up from behind Weed's smoking gun, and greenbacks changed hands. Captain Weed raised his eyebrows, smiled and lighted a cigar.

Harvey Hill was as helpless as an infant. A normal dismount proved impossible to accomplish, but entertaining to watch—so amusing that Longstreet turned his back and covered his mouth with a gloved hand so as not to offend the general with his laughter. Hill tried to lift his right leg backward over the animal's rump just as he normally would, but it was elevated far too high and Hill very nearly injured himself trying not to fall.

"Bring your leg forward, Harvey, over the pommel." Hill did as Longstreet suggested and almost fell again when his left foot stuck in the stirrup.

He drew his pistol and let the discharge cover his expletive as he put the anguished animal away.

"Pardon me, sirs, but that's the third damned horse that's been shot out from under me today!"

"God have pity on the next poor beast."

"Back to work, gentlemen," Lee said. "Here they come."

Beyond the sunken road, and beyond the hill facing it, stood William Roulette's farmhouse and barn. There the Rebel skirmishers waited to alert their comrades to any Union advance, and there William French's division blindly marched, still more or less lost and thinking they followed Sumner and Sedgwick.

There is no need to describe General William French. His men called him "Old Blinky."

"Look at all them flags," a young Rebel said. "Damn, there's a mess of 'em."

"Yeah, but look closer."

"What?"

"Most of them flags is brand spanking new. They're clean and nice and ain't got no holes in 'em or nothing. Most of them boys is rookies, cousin, and they've done seen their mommas for the very last time. Let's spoil some of them flags and get the hell outta here."

The lead brigade under General Max Weber had been in the service for a while but had served only on garrison duty and had never fired their weapons in anger. Many of the men of the second brigade, under Colonel Dwight Morris, had never fired theirs at all.

The skirmish at the Roulette farm was barely even that. The Rebel pickets fired and fled, and the Yankees marched on. As the Confederate advance guard rushed back into the road, Colonel Parker calmed and readied his men.

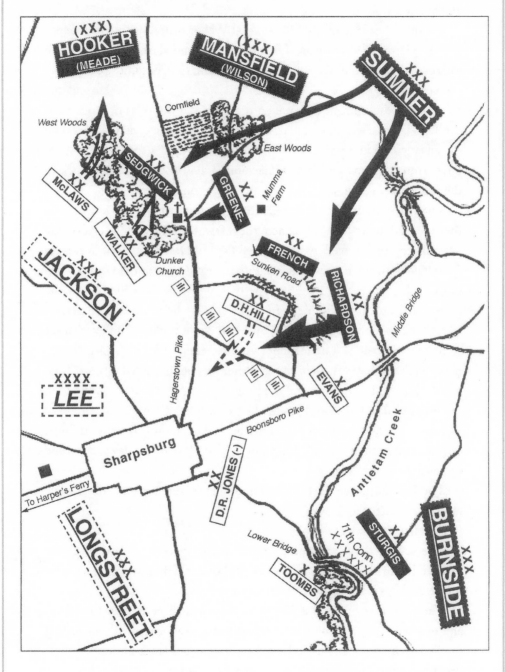

(XXX)
HOOKER
(MEADE)

(XXX)
MANSFIELD
(WILSON)

SUMNER
xxx

Cornfield

West Woods

East Woods

SEDGWICK
XX

GREENE-
XX

Mumma
Farm

McLAWS
XX

WALKER
XX

Dunker
Church

JACKSON
xxx

FRENCH
XX

Sunken Road

RICHARDSON
XX

Middle Bridge

D.H.HILL
XX

LEE
XXXX

EVANS
X

Boonsboro Pike

Sharpsburg

Antietam Creek

To Harper's Ferry

D.R. JONES (-)
XX

STURGIS
XX

BURNSIDE
xxx

LONGSTREET
xxx

Lower Bridge

71th Conn.
XXXXX

TOOMBS
X

Hagerstown Pike

"Wait to fire until you see their belt buckles and cartridge boxes, men, and aim at these."

On the other side of the hill General Weber ordered, "Fix bayonets," and the clatter of steel on steel further alerted and alarmed the Rebels in the road. They could hear the Yankees coming but could not see them— not yet.

Between the hills, in the sunken road, behind the piles of fence rails, the Rebels watched and waited. Seemingly all at once, as the orders of the advancing Union officers came, clearly heard over the hill, the 2,500 boys from Alabama and North Carolina pulled their hammers back to the full cock position and steadied their rifles on the fence rails.

Their first view was of the golden eagles that topped the flagstaffs as they peaked over the hill. Then they saw the flags themselves—the national colors followed by the spotless flags of Delaware, New York, and Maryland with the names of the regiments stitched into the fabric. Then the Rebels saw the bayonets and the hats and then they clearly saw the faces of the oncoming soldiers. In perfect order they marched, in perfect step to the cadence of the drums, over and down the hill, and ever closer to the enemy below. The leading rank held their rifles at "charge bayo- nets," with the butts at their hips and their bayonets angled upward. The second rank and those beyond held theirs at "right shoulder shift," with the muzzles pointed directly at the heavens.

John Brown Gordon stood calmly behind his men and, more to him- self than to them, he said, "What a pity to spoil with bullets such a scene of martial beauty."

The Rebels viewed the procession in silent reverence until the Yankee boys were thirty yards away, then fired.

The front rank went instantly down.

The second rank shouldered their weapons to return the fire, but most fell with their rifles still loaded and over the hill marched another file of Yankees—and another—and another.

The 900 men of the 1st Delaware marched directly into the storm and in a sudden, ghastly instant, 450 fell in agony or in death, including the lieutenant colonel who led them and the sergeant who bore their col- ors. One after another, each member of the color guard laid down his rifle to pick up the flag, and one after another they died.

Weber's 2,000-man assault continued for five minutes only, and when it ended 800 men lay on the little hill in front of the sunken road, including the wounded general himself. The remainder of the brigade withdrew back over the crest of the hill to safety where they nursed their wounds and waited for the next in line, Colonel Morris, to march his men forward into hell. The Rebels took a breath and reloaded their weapons and watched and waited again.

In the road Colonel Gordon noticed a tear in his right sleeve, but no blood, and he smiled. Beyond the rise "Old Blinky" pushed two more brigades forward up the hill—Morris followed by Kimball. Again the new recruits led the veterans.

The firing ahead subsided, and Morris's color bearers picked up the pace. Rebel artillery sought the range and the earth exploded around them as they came up through Roulette's farm, pushing down fences and trampling over their own fallen men as they marched. Each man fixed his attention firmly on the flag and on the job that lay ahead.

They urged the remnants of Weber's exhausted brigade back into line, some at the point of a bayonet, to join with them in the second assault.

The 1st Delaware needed no urging—their regimental colors remained on the field, unguarded. Rebel after Rebel bolted forward from the safety of the road and up the hill in the face of fire to try to capture the pennant and each of them failed. Squad-sized units then made the attempt, but the muskets of the 5th Maryland joined the Delawarians and the fight for the flag drew to another stalemate.

"I need volunteers!" Captain Rickards shouted. "Our colors lie in that field and they *must* be retrieved. I don't know why you men volunteered to fight this war, for Union—against slavery—I myself own slaves—but none of that matters now. All that matters is that our colors are our honor, and they lie abandoned on that hillside. I shall lead the attack to retrieve our honor. Who will go with me?"

Thirty men answered the call, men who had only moments before fled that very field in the face of terrible battle, and over the hill they went, again, to recover their honor. Captain Rickards was the first to fall, dead on the field. They made it to within ten yards of their goal, and no closer.

Colonel Morris's 2,000 men approached the opposite base of Roulette's swale, and again the Rebel hammers clicked back to full cock as they anxiously watched for the telltale flags to appear again over the near horizon.

Six weeks ago Corporal John Strickler was selling hats to ladies in Harrisburg. Now he looked proudly up at the beautiful blue flag emblazoned with the seal of the State of Pennsylvania and the words embroidered in gold across it, "The 130th Pennsylvania Regiment." His socks were still wet from crossing the creek and he had a rock in his shoe, but all of Lee's legions wouldn't chase him away now. His new uniform at last was dirty and the bands played and "the elephant" waited just over the next hill. His rifle had come right out of the box only a week ago and, though it had not yet been fired, he had cleaned it twenty times. Someone else loaded it for him and Strickler could not wait to kill a Rebel.

From his side of the hill, it appeared to be only a pleasant rise—a beautiful hilltop on which to picnic with your best girl on a Sunday afternoon—but the white smoke that rose beyond it made it ugly, and the bleeding and armless men who crawled back over it made it terrifying. Strickler watched the files to his front climb the swale and disappear down the other side. His hands suddenly began to shake and even over the sounds of the guns and the drums and a thousand screaming men John Strickler thought he could hear the pounding of his own heart.

Again the Rebels saw the golden eagles—then the flags—and then the bayonets, the hats and the faces of the soldiers. As he watched the Yankees come, Sergeant Edward Johnson put his left hand on his father's right shoulder and remembered his premonition from yesterday. The Yankee uniforms were still so new they appeared black instead of blue. Evil, sinister black.

John Brown Gordon shook his head in disbelief and admiration for the men coming forward over the hill, and again at the top of his lungs he ordered, "FIRE!" and again hundreds of young men died without firing a shot and on came more. Just like before.

The third rank was the first to return a volley, but most had never fired their rifles before this very moment and didn't know what to expect or how to take aim or how to reload on the march. Many closed their eyes and aimed for the heavens, but down the hill they marched and the Rebels furiously fired and loaded and yelled, "Go back, you black devils!"

"First rank—charge bayonets!"

Strickler, now ten yards from the top of the hill, spun his weapon around with the butt at his hip, his right hand on the trigger and his left arm extended. Finally, he was there, on top of Roulette's swale, looking down onto the angry, wounded, fire-breathing "elephant" with hundreds— maybe thousands—of dead or crying men stacked deep on the ridge fifty yards down and a thousand yards across and he didn't want to see the elephant anymore.

The Rebels, too, were stacked deep, but living. Those in the rear loaded and passed weapons forward for those in the front to shoot.

"CHARGE!" Morris yelled, and Strickler broke into a run and fired his rifle for the very first time as he tried not to fall down or trip over a dead man.

Down in the road Edward Johnson rested his rifle on his father's right shoulder and laughed at the ease with which he took down three Yankees within a single minute. He had fought for hours on days before this one, expending his entire allocation of forty rounds without being able to swear that a single Yankee had taken one of *his* bullets. Today the "black devils" came on so thick and close that taking aim was a waste of valuable time. He only pointed—and fired.

Strickler screamed as the bullet tore through his shoulder. He pulled himself up in some misguided effort to stand and another minié ball caught him in the leg. For some strange reason he thought about the girlie pictures that he had left with the rear guard. *"Thank God I don't have 'Genevive' with me for Momma to see."*

Some of the veteran Rebels could not contain themselves any longer, and groups of George Anderson's North Carolinians, holding the road to Gordon's right, spontaneously sprang forward over the fence rails, up the hill and headlong into the confused Union lines. Longstreet saw the results of the ragged little charge and ordered a unified attack from the left.

Like their neighbors who had fallen in the cornfield, the Pennsylvania rookies were green, but they were also brave. Their march down the hill halted, but didn't retreat, and as the Confederates left their lines to spring forward, the young Yankees suddenly had real targets to shoot at and they learned very quickly how to point, if not aim, their rifles. Reloading was no longer a problem as hundreds of perfectly good, pre-loaded weapons littered the ground before them.

Only three hundred yards to the north, John Tompkins saw the Rebels bolt out of the road and only a slight turn of his guns offered a beautiful line of fire at the sunken road. He took the advancing Rebels under an *enfilade* fire, and the abortive counterattack retreated back to the relative safety of their road and returned to the routine of killing advancing Yankees. On the other side of the hill another brigade—2,000 *more* Union troops—marched across Roulette's fields toward the hill and toward the Rebels' safe little haven.

As his men advanced through Roulette's farm, General Kimball noticed that his leading ranks, suddenly and for no apparent reason, began to break and scatter. Occasional artillery bursts exploded around them, but that had been happening for the past half mile. More and more men bolted and dived for the ground, and Kimball couldn't figure for the life of him what the hell was going on until he felt a pinprick on the right side of his face and a painful shock down the entire right side of his body. Then came another to the back of his left hand and he instinctively ducked and weaved in the saddle. His horse began to buck and whinny as he fought off the attack of ten, then twenty, then a hundred angry honeybees. Roulette's hives lay on their sides ahead, upended by Rebel guns, and the mad-as-hornets honeybees took their anger out on the wrong army. Even through this chaos, Kimball's brigade marched on through the seemingly endless lines of wounded men who stumbled toward them, pointing the way to the sunken road.

Kimball's men were a mixture of veterans and rookies. Three of his four regiments had endured the Shenandoah campaign and had actually performed well there while few others had. Only the 132nd Pennsylvania, another of Governor Curtin's nine-month militias, had to be rallied back into the line following the bee assault, and only they hesitated at the sight of the retreating wounded.

"Now, boys, we are going," General Kimball calmly told them, "and we'll stay with them all day if they want us to. Fix bayonets! Double quick—March!"

Again the golden eagles and the flags and soldiers crested the hill and again the Rebels waited. Kimball watched as the ranks before him climbed the eastern slope and descended over it out of his view. He was stunned by the sound of a thousand Rebel muskets that all fired at once and tore through the sons of Ohio and Indiana and "West" Virginia and yet another rookie regiment just up from Pennsylvania. The men marched forward, heads bent down with their arms over their faces as though walking against a winter wind, and the boys from Alabama and North Carolina cheered them for their bravery as they shot them down.

Against the never-ending flow of wounded and demoralized soldiers hobbling back over the hill, General Kimball rode cautiously to the top of the ridge and looked down. For fifty yards in front of him and five hundred yards to either side, the hillside was blue. In half an hour, General French had marched 6,000 men over the grassy hill where nearly 2,000 of them remained.

"God save my poor boys," Kimball said as just to his right three enlisted men assisted a twice-wounded corporal from the field. As they reached the crest, one final Rebel bullet struck Corporal Strickler in the heel.

"My God," he cried, "my dear God in heaven. My God, must I be killed by inches?"

Kimball heard the boy's plea and said aloud, "You are not alone, young man. One corps, one brigade, one soldier at a time, this whole damned army is being killed by inches."

John Brown Gordon picked up his cap off the ground and stuck his finger through the twin bullet holes in the crown. He ran his fingers through his hair and looked at his hand.

No blood.

Next in this deadly line for the Yanks was Israel Richardson's division. As they finally crossed the Antietam they took a moment to squeeze their socks dry, and shake the rocks from their shoes before moving on toward the sunken road.

* * *

Ten miles away on the road from Harper's Ferry, A. P. Hill's face glowed red with heat and anxiety. His men had made good time so far, but the pace had already slowed, and the weaker of his charges fell by the way.

"Lee is waiting for us, men! Move on. Move on. Lee needs us, boys. Keep moving."

Seven miles in three hours, the redheaded general thought. *I wonder what Thomas "Stonewall" will say about that.*

Vindicating his marching skills for the benefit of a madman was not Hill's singular motivation. At the end of the march, he knew, waited George McClellan and Randolph Marcy, Mary Ellen's husband and father. Sometimes at night he could still picture her face or hear her voice and always he carried with him the heartless rejection of his proposal of marriage. *"A life of exile, deprivation and poverty."* It had all been for the best, after all. Had it worked out with Mary Ellen he would never have met Dolly, the love of his life, second only to their two-year-old daughter, Netty. And yet the heartless rejection still stung, and left Hill with much to prove. *Deprivation and poverty.* The test of who was truly the better man for Mary Ellen Marcy waited at the end of this march.

"Move on now, men. Close it up. Lee needs us. Keep moving."

WASHINGTON

While the fate of the Republic hung in the balance along the banks of Antietam Creek, the President of the United States knew absolutely nothing about it. There were rumors, yes, but there were always rumors. Lincoln had heard not a word from his commanding general. Is there a fight? Is Lee beaten or is he on his way to Washington with a conquering horde a quarter-of-a-million-strong? Which one of these? Abraham Lincoln spent September 17th in frustrated agony. He had not a hint.

THE ROHRBACH BRIDGE

The 11th Connecticut was commanded by Colonel Henry Kingsbury, who, at twenty-nine years old, was young to be a colonel. He was the son of one of Ambrose Burnside's dearest friends and the brother-in-law of Confederate General D. R. Jones, the man everyone knew as "Neighbor." While the rest of his brigade hid behind a ridge and felt their way through the woods toward the point where they thought the Rohrbach Bridge might be, Kingsbury was sent out onto the flanks, into the open, to find the bridge—and the Rebels. Burnside watched Kingsbury's approach from a hill to the east of the bridge—Jones watched from a hill to the west. Through his glasses, the Rebel general recognized the flag of the 11th Connecticut, and easily spotted his brother-in-law at its head. Neighbor Jones clutched his chest for the first time today.

"Are you okay, sir?"

"Yes. Yes." The staff officer continued to look at his commander with concern, and after a while Jones said, "I think that's my sister's husband leading that darned fool charge down there."

Both men understood just how foolish the charge was. "I pray not, sir." Neighbor Jones only nodded. The pain in his chest gone for the moment.

Captain Griswold took his Connecticut company directly to the bank of the Antietam, too far downstream from Farmer Rohrbach's bridge, and the men of the 2nd Georgia, high on the hill opposite, fired down on them from their battleworks. The Connecticut boys found themselves caught in a storm of lead and hesitated, but Griswold held them in line and pushed them toward the creek for a wet crossing. He decided to lead from ahead instead of from behind and dashed his horse into the creek and was killed before his stirrups got wet. Colonel Kingsbury himself then assumed the lead, drew his saber and paraded his horse forward into the waist-deep waters. The first bullet shattered his shoulder and the saber fell into the flowing stream. The second lodged in his left hip and the third in his left knee. The young colonel fell into the water, but somehow managed to push his way up to show his men that he was still alive, and they rushed to the rescue as the Georgians continued a constant fire from the absolute safety of their hillside entrenchments. Thirty men died trying to save their colonel, and their bodies floated slowly downstream. Kingsbury was finally pulled ashore more dead than alive, but alive nonetheless, and resting in friendly hands. His men lifted him up to carry him to the Rohrbach house, and as they started up the hill a fourth Rebel bullet struck the brave young colonel and lodged in his abdomen. Two men prayed as Kingsbury was carried from the field—Neighbor Jones on one side of the creek, and Ambrose Burnside on the other.

"Damn that little son-of-a-bitch! General McClellan sent us his hand-picked engineer to select a crossing point for us and *this* is what he picked?" Issaac Rodman was shaking mad, and the sounds of musket fire from upstream added to the urgency of the matter. "A single man couldn't climb that hill over there. Half of my damned men would drown here if we tried to cross! Damn."

He thought about the situation for a minute and finally he shook his head and said, "Let's keep moving downstream. There's got to be something better than this."

Hearing the musketry from Colonel Kingsbury's assault on the other side of the hill, Colonel Crooke ordered his attack. They should have come out directly opposite the bridge to storm across it in coordination, with Rodman fording upstream, but Rodman wasn't there—and neither was the bridge.

More than two hundred yards downstream from Joseph Rohrbach's bridge, Crook's brigade crested the ridge line and immediately hit the dirt under the deadly accurate fire of Confederate artillery. There they lay, and there they stayed.

"Things are not going well, Mac," Porter said. "Damn Sumner! His men are scattered all over the goddamned field!"

"And the rest of the Rebel army is waiting out there somewhere, John, just itching to attack. What's with Burnside? Why don't we hear from him? He must take that bridge and threaten Sharpsburg or Lee will spring his trap against us there in the center. Send a messenger to Burnside. Tell him if it costs him ten thousand men, he must go now! And position every piece of artillery you can find to your own support in the rear, John. Lee's going to attack, and he's going to try to burst through right there."

George McClellan pointed down the hill at the long, thin line of Rebel troops that stretched along the nine-hundred-yard front in the sunken road. Colonel John Brown Gordon paced again behind his men as they looked up at the hilltop, and waited for the flags to come again. *Until the sun goes down*, he had promised General Lee. Gordon looked up to check on old Sol's progress and filled his lungs with air that tasted like sulfur and wished the old boy to hurry. Next he checked his pocket watch. It wasn't yet 10:30.

If the sun wouldn't help Colonel Gordon, Dick Anderson might. From the heights above the bridge, Lee sent Anderson to replace Hill's men lost in the cornfield, but to get to the sunken road, the 3,400 men had to march through the fields and orchards of Henry Piper. The Piper farm had some fields already plowed under and awaiting fall planting as well as his orchard of apple trees, and yet another field of Maryland corn standing pristine and beautiful and six feet tall. These fields were clearly open to the view of McClellan's twenty-pound Parrotts in Philip Pry's backyard. At a range of almost two miles, the big guns opened on Piper's fields. They were joined closer in by French's Napoleons, and into this new ring of artillery hell Anderson's men marched.

Solid shot is just what it says—generally twelve pounds of solid iron without explosives of any sort. Like a huge rock thrown at incredible velocity, a round of solid shot would often hit the ground and roll and appear to be harmless until it took a man's leg. Anderson watched as one such ball struck an infantryman square in the face, and the headless body took three more steps before it fell to the ground. General Wright's horse took another round and the unharmed brigadier stood and led his men on foot. Then came Anderson's turn. An exploding shell took the general from his men before they even reached the farmhouse. With Anderson severely wounded, the rescue attempt fell under the command of Brigadier General Roger Pryor, a former congressman from Virginia who wanted to win battles as a step toward the governorship of the Old Dominion. Dick Anderson was immediately and sorely missed as his men came to a halt.

While Anderson's confused brigade moved slowly northwest toward the sunken road, Israel Richardson's veteran Yankees resumed their march southeast. They were supposed to have been Sumner's reserves, but instead of following Sumner into the East Woods, they followed French to the sunken road.

"I have told you before, men," Richardson told his brigade and regimental commanders, "and you know it to be true from our time together on the Peninsula, that I will never order you or your men anywhere that I would not myself go.

"The Rebels hold a strong position at the bottom of that hill. We must go there. Prepare your regiments to move forward lightly. Blanket rolls, canteens and haversacks are to be left here. Address your men, sirs, and prepare to follow me."

Brigadier General Thomas F. Meagher commanded the Irish Brigade, composed almost entirely of immigrants to New York. They thought of themselves, and perhaps justifiably so, as the fightingest sons-of-bitches in the whole damned Yankee army.

After Richardson turned his back to lead the attack, Meagher reached inside his tunic and retrieved his flask. He made no effort to conceal it from his men as he tossed back his head and pulled heartily on the smooth, hot Irish whiskey. He wiped his mouth on his sleeve and turned to address his men.

"All right, laddies, 'tis time again to go forward." He grabbed the elegant regimental colors from the hand of the bearer and held the sacred flag high above his head. " 'Tis time again to follow the green into glorious battle. But we are going to try it a wee bit different from our friends up ahead. The moment you top that rise and take in a clear view of our Southern cousins, you will halt right then and there and fire down into 'em. Don't be waitin' for them to fire first at you. You will offer them two volleys, and two volleys only, and then we shall rush down the slopes like bats out of hell and offer them the cold steel of our bayonets.

" 'Tis an important job that you have this day, boys. Fix bayonets, and don't let down the green!"

The cheers from the Irishmen covered the somewhat less inspiring speech that Colonel Cross offered his New Hampshire troops farther down the line.

"Men, you are about to engage in battle," he said. "You have never disgraced your state. I hope you won't this time. If any man runs, I want the file closers to shoot him. If they don't, I shall myself. That's all I have to say. Fix bayonets."

In the road the Confederates waited again, but this time when the golden eagles appeared over the hilltop, they were followed by flags of green—emerald green satin, with golden harps and shamrocks and words the Rebels couldn't read elegantly embroidered around them.

"It's those danged green-flag boys again, fellas."

Colonels Gordon and Tew continued to stand tall at the rear of the Rebel lines—lines that had grown steadily thinner with each renewed assault. The 6th Alabama was positioned at a turn in the road where it bent sharply backward and to their right, and around the turn was Tew's 2nd North Carolina.

The Rebels cocked their rifles as the Irish Brigade pulled to a halt at the top of the ridge and lowered their smoothbores to unleash their first volley of buck-and-ball and Colonel Tew, in midconversation with John Brown Gordon, took a bullet to the brain and fell instantly dead at Gordon's feet. The invincible colonel filled his lungs to command "Fire" and felt hot lead tear through the muscles of his right calf. He himself had begun to believe in his charmed existence, and the thought that a Yankee bullet had actually drawn blood surprised him at first, and then it made him angry. He limped forward to join his men who stood to welcome the Irishmen into the fight, but the "green-flag boys" came head-on toward George Anderson's North Carolina brigade, which enabled them to fire down the line at Gordon's 6th at an *enfilade* angle that meant if a ball missed its intended target, it would strike the man behind. Within a minute another Yankee bullet exploded through Gordon's right thigh, but neither shell struck bone, and he disparately held his 6th Alabama in line, painfully walking behind them. The boot on his right foot quickly filled with blood.

On the Rebel right George Anderson also paced bravely behind his North Carolinians, and also paid for his courage when a shell took his foot. He too tried to remain in command, but he lost too much blood too quickly and was carried from the field.

The first of Dick Anderson's brigades finally made it through Piper's fields and into line alongside of George Anderson's tarheels. The fall of Richard and the subsequent lack of leadership on the part of General Pryor left the remaining brigades floundering in the fields.

The Irish Brigade stood its ground valiantly, but the bayonet charge never materialized. The fire from the road was too thick.

"Did you hear that, Captain McGee?"

"Hear what, General Meagher? I can't even hear myself prayin'."

"I swear to you by all the Saints in Heaven that the shootin's so thick here I heard two bullets hit each other in midair right next to me left ear." Even over this mighty roar of battle, Meagher thought he heard something else as well. Not clearly. He couldn't tell if it was the voice of a priest, blessing the men somewhere near, or the voice of his own mind, or maybe it was even the tiny, whispering voice of God Himself. *"Dóminus vobiscum."* He made the sign of the cross and responded as he had since childhood, *"Et cum spíritu,"* and the voice answered back, *"Benedicat vus omnipotens Deus, Pater, et Filius et Spritus Sanctus."* But then, suddenly, he had no more time for God. "Holy Mother of Jesus, the green's gone down! Boys, raise the colors and follow me!" McGee relieved the wounded bearer of his responsibility and waved the flag defiantly at the Rebels in the road. The Irishmen regrouped and the Rebels focused their fire on the heroic captain. The flag staff snapped in half and he lifted her from the ground as another round relieved him of his hat. McGee raised the brigade's green flag again for all to see before he fell dead at the same moment that Meagher fell from his horse and was carried from the field. The Irish assault halted on the hillside but didn't fall back and didn't stop firing. Almost like a terrible period at the end of the ten-minute charge, another Yankee bullet found John Brown Gordon, this one passing through the ligaments of his left arm just as the war between Ireland and North Carolina briefly subsided.

Dizzy from the lack of blood, Gordon continued to walk along his lines during the lull using an expended musket as a crutch, and his shocked men couldn't help but notice his wounds. Gordon was alive, but the legend of the bulletproof colonel finally died in Sharpsburg's sunken road.

"Gordon to the rear—Gordon to the rear," they began to chant, but he silenced them with the wave of his hand and continued to inspect his lines and a new and better legend of John Brown Gordon was born.

He looked down at his feet and saw the grizzled old private Joseph Johnson cradling the body of Edward, his son. His filthy, powder-blackened face streaked with tears, he looked at Gordon and forced himself to speak. "Here we are. My son is dead and I shall go soon. But it is all right." He stroked Edward's lifeless face and kissed him good-bye and struggled to say something more but could not. He lay the boy's head back down in the road and only then did Gordon see the ugly wound in the old man's chest. Joseph Johnson placed his head on Edward's shoulder and closed his eyes and died.

The shouted commands of Union officers came clearly heard again from the other side of the hill, and one more time Gordon checked the progress of the sun. *"Till the sun goes down or victory is won."* He removed Edward Johnson's haversack and tied the strap around his leg as a tourniquet and struggled to stop the world from spinning out of control.

The sun hadn't moved.

The eagles—the flags—the bayonets and the soldiers marched again over Roulette's swale. Again the Rebels cocked their pieces.

At the Rohrbach Bridge, the disgruntled General Burnside knew that Crook was pinned down and pinned down to stay. Those men, he knew, served some useful purpose there. They encouraged the Rebels to expend their ammunition to little or no avail and could provide cover for a proper assault. The "wing commander" had deeded his staff over to the new corps commander, and now acted as his own courier. Burnside left his headquarters and sought out General Sturgis and ordered him to launch that "proper" assault.

Rodman still held the bulk of his division at Captain Duane's ford while search parties moved farther downstream in hope of finding a more appropriate crossing point. His men sat on the hillside waiting for orders.

"What's that down there in the creek?"

Private Squashic glanced down the hill into the Antietam's flowing waters.

"Oh, my God." He tried to hold down his breakfast, but couldn't. First one, then five, then fifteen bodies of dead Union soldiers floated facedown in the Antietam. These were the men who had gone to the rescue of Colonel Kingsbury thirty minutes before.

As Rodman's men tried to fish Connecticut's heroes from the creek, the 2nd Maryland and the 6th New Hampshire prepared to launch Burnside's second desperate assault across farmer Rohrbach's bridge.

Toombs's 400 Georgians on the other side of the stream fell under severe artillery fire and the hills opposite them came alive with muskets as 300 Union soldiers made a mad dash along the banks of the Antietam over 250 yards of unprotected ground. The instant they broke into the open, the Rebels fired by files and a small handful of Burnside's boys actually made it as far as the bridge.

Israel Richardson had been angry all morning long. Angry at McClellan for his failure to launch a coordinated, three-corps attack first thing after dawn—angry for being held in reserve while the rest of Sumner's corps moved forward, further delaying his participation—and angry now that his prized Irish Brigade was dying on the hillside and no help was coming.

In the happiest of times Richardson showed the sternest of facades. He wore a mustache only. His cheeks were hollow and his eyes perpetually angry. He suffered fools harshly. These were *not* the happiest of times, and John Caldwell, in Richardson's eyes, at the moment, was a fool. Israel Richardson was furious. He unsheathed his saber, dismounted and ran into the center of Caldwell's brigade, which seemed to be marching off aimlessly around the Confederate right.

"Where is General Caldwell?"

"To the rear, sir. Over there—behind that haystack!"

"Goddamn the field officers! I am assuming personal command of this brigade!"

He raised his saber above his head, and over the deafening sounds of the battle but loudly enough for all to hear he commanded, "By the right flank—MARCH!"

The maneuver brought the brigade back on line to attack the Rebels head-on and relieve the Irishmen dying on the hill.

Colonel Joseph Barnes, commanding the Irish Brigade's 29th Massachusetts, could withstand the agony of watching his men die not a moment longer, but the thought of backing up over the hill to safety never entered his mind.

"Men of the fighting Twenty-ninth—ATTENTION!"

Without exception, in the face of horrendous fire, the only regiment of the Irish Brigade that was *not* Irish rose as if for the benediction.

"*CHARGE!*"

John Brown Gordon took another bullet in the arm, and, as he looked down to examine his fourth and newest wound, a fifth minié ball took most of his face. His last conscious thought before the world turned black was to pull his bullet-riddled cap over the wound.

Richardson approached the crest of Roulette's swale, and heard the rising sounds of battle. "On the double-quick, MARCH!" and Caldwell's brigade finally stormed over the hill.

Desperate for Rebel reinforcements, Rodes moved to the rear and found one of Dick Anderson's lost brigades hiding in Piper's orchard and eating green apples. He rallied the Mississippians and finally brought them forward, but the sunken road was full of Rebels, living and dead, and the new troops had no place to go. So they simply continued forward, through the road, up the hill and directly into the midst of Richardson's oncoming Yankees. The entire valley was now filled with white smoke and the constant roaring of a thousand guns and the horrifying screams and shouts of a thousand desperate men. Chaos. Shocked by the bold and sudden turn of events, confused by the stream of retreating Rebels and advancing Yankees coming toward them, many of the grays could not withstand anymore. After three hours of turning back assault after brutal assault, the road filled with dead and dying men. Those left to fight could no longer get a firm footing for standing on corpses or in a gruesome, slimy, ankle-deep mud concocted of dirt and blood. Enough was enough, and North Carolina began one man at a time to give up the fight and flee to the rear.

Tompkins's Rhode Island battery high on a hill three hundred yards away moved their guns only slightly to gain an *enfilade* and their fire was devastating.

J. D. Wells of Company "F" of the 4th North Carolina faced the same dilemma as every other man in the road. To run—or to die. He chose to die and he stood and fired his very last cartridge into the face of an Irishman not ten feet away before taking four bullets all at once. He died before he hit the ground.

The remainder of Pryor's division, still huddled down in Piper's fields and orchards, fell back before the retreating heroes, some with a rifle in one hand and an apple in the other. The demoralized Yankees from French's initial charges felt the turning of the tide and rallied behind Richardson and suddenly thousands came pouring over the deadly rise directly at the leaderless 6th Alabama, which held its ground at the bend in the road and well out in front of its brothers to either side.

The noise became unbearable. The musket fire was a constant roaring and every cannon within a thousand yards was fired, reloaded and fired again as quickly as their panicked gunners could move. Unwounded soldiers bled from the ears and orders loudly shouted went unheard by the very closest men. In the midst of this Lieutenant Colonel Lightfoot, now in command of Gordon's 6th, saw plainly that his position could hold no longer. French's men assaulted him head-on, while the Irish Brigade and Caldwell's fresh reinforcements firmly established an *enfilade* fire from the right, while artillery shot and shell poured in from the left. The safe haven of their little sunken road suddenly became a deathtrap.

Face-to-face and not inches apart, Lightfoot yelled at General Rodes, "We are under heavy *enfilade*, sir, and our salient point is under heavy attack. We cannot hold in our present condition, sir."

Rodes screamed back at him, but the battle was so intense that Lightfoot heard only bits of the orders.

"Move back . . . new position . . . extricate . . . *enfilade*."

Lightfoot did not have time to ask the general to repeat himself, but he had heard enough to confirm that he and Rodes agreed on their only course of action.

"Sixth Alabama—about FACE—forward MARCH!"

Major Hobson, commanding the 5th Alabama to Lightfoot's left, saw the men of the 6th turn to abandon the road.

"Where the hell are you going?"

"We are ordered to move back."

"Are those orders intended for the entire brigade?"

"Of course—they must be."

Old Pete, sitting astride his favorite battle horse, Hero, heard the increased sounds of battle and while he could not see his own lines from where he sat next to the Piper farm, he could easily see the new Federal assault aimed at them.

"Courier— We must relieve the pressure on our center. General Jackson must commence a counterattack against their positions at the church. Tell him—hell, never mind. I'll do it myself."

Rodes became dizzy at the sight as his entire brigade turned to leave the line they had fought so hard for three hours to hold. He saw Colonel Lightfoot trying to hold together what remained of the 6th Alabama as they headed for the relative safety of Sharpsburg.

"What in the name of God are you doing?"

"You ordered us back, sir."

"I ordered you back down the road to new positions, to extricate yourself from the *enfilade—I didn't* order you to *retreat!*"

The road emptied of all but the dead and dying. The exuberant Yankees bounded down the hill, screaming like Indians, and poured a ceaseless fire on the beaten Rebels.

From his box seat at the Pry house, George McClellan jumped up and laughed. He slapped strangers on the back and said, "It is the most beautiful field I ever saw—and the grandest battle! If we whip them today, it will wipe out Bull Run forever!"

Longstreet personally rode from regiment to regiment, scraping together all of the idle men he could find. He soon came across General Hood observing the action in the center.

"General Hood, where is your division, sir?"

Hood looked at James Longstreet, amazed at the question. He shook his head and tried desperately to decide what to say. He took a deep breath and his voice quivered as he answered.

"Dead on the field, sir."

Longstreet continued his search for a regiment or two—just enough to restart the fighting on the left and ease the pressure in the middle. He came across Jeb Stuart's brother-in-law, John R. Cooke.

"What units are these, John, and at what strength?"

"The Twenty-seventh North Carolina and the Third Arkansas, sir, and we have a thousand men."

Longstreet rose up in his saddle and pointed to Tompkins's Rhode Island battery. "There is an enemy battery just on that hill there. It must be taken."

Until this moment the 27th North Carolina and the 3rd Arkansas of Walker's division had been tucked safely away between the two battles—between the cornfield and the sunken road. For two weeks Lieutenant Colonel Singleterry, who commanded the 27th, had kept a close watch over his charges. Most had been reluctant to cross the Potomac and many let their concerns be known. These men had no quarrel with Maryland. Almost all of them had opposed secession and had answered the call to arms solely to repel an invading army, a task they felt they had accomplished at Second Manassas. They had no interest in becoming invaders themselves and Singleterry feared mutiny.

Posted in such a way as to act as Jackson's extreme right or Hill's extreme left, these thousand men had watched the war move around them for five hours, but now, after noon, came their turn, and Singleterry secretly worried about how his men would perform.

Cooke ordered them to prepare for the attack when an officer so drunk he could barely remain in the saddle rode out from the West Woods, determined to assume command. He waved his hat over his head and shouted, "Come on, boys! I'm leading the charge!"

Captain Graham heard the drunken command and couldn't believe his ears. Singleterry nodded to his old friend, and Graham handled the situation as best he knew how.

"You are a liar, sir!" he yelled loudly enough for the entire regiment to hear. "We are the Twenty-seventh North Carolina—and we lead our own charges!"

With that, he yanked the reins from the drunkard's hands, turned the mount back around, facing the rear, and slapped the animal on the flanks, sending the whole package reeling back to the woods, and for the first time since they set foot on Maryland soil, the 27th North Carolina rose and cheered and marched into battle.

* * *

For almost two hours George Greene had maintained his weak hold on the West Woods while waiting for help from Sumner, and only now did an unfortunate messenger tell him that Sedgwick's division was decimated, and that French and Richardson were occupied elsewhere. No help was coming.

He spewed forth a string of profanities that would have made Hooker blush.

"Do you realize what this *does* to me? Not only can I *not* advance, but I am stuck out here in the middle of goddamned nowhere with not a single damned platoon to guard my flanks—it's a bloody miracle they haven't kicked my ass out of here hours ago!"

Farther around the Confederate left, Jackson looked out onto the grounds of the Dunker Church, and the sight of it still in Union hands very nearly made him swear.

"Colonel Ransom."

"Sir."

"It appears to me that the church is very lightly defended. Move on it and let us see their response."

Only moments before Colonel Singleterry had worried about the morale and fighting spirit of the 27th North Carolina, but now he saw the color bearer way too far out in front. Singleterry rode forward to slow him down. "Colonel, I can't let that Arkansas feller get ahead of me!"

Richard Singleterry marched into battle with one less problem.

In another coincidence of war, Cooke moved north toward the Dunker Church at precisely the same moment that Ransom moved east, headed for the same target. George Greene found himself caught in the middle, and in a matter of minutes the Dunker Church belonged to Jackson again.

"General Jackson sends his compliments, General Longstreet, and begs to inform the general that the church is once again in Confederate hands."

Longstreet's reaction dumbfounded the courier.

"Damn!"

"I beg your pardon, sir?"

"I didn't want the damned Yankees to *retreat!* I wanted 'em to put up a fight. I wanted 'em to call for reinforcements. I wanted . . . Damn."

He looked back down the hill at the center of the Rebel lines, if they could be called "lines." They stood wide open and inviting. Jackson's beleaguered troops tended their wounds in the West Woods and around the grounds of the newly regained church. D. H. Hill's brigades were in panicked flight to Sharpsburg, and only 3,000 Rebels remained who had not yet seen battle. Richardson and French had 7,000 Union troops *left*, and only half a mile from town—half a mile from cutting the Army of Northern Virginia in half and trapping Stonewall Jackson with the river at his back.

Harvey Hill saw the danger, as did Longstreet, and each man took it upon himself to "join the army" and take up arms alongside his men.

Hill stood on the Hagerstown Pike with a bayoneted musket in his hands and personally rallied every man of courage he could muster into one last effort to establish a desperate final line of defense.

Longstreet found a serviceable but unmanned cannon and ordered his staff to dismount and prepare the gun for firing. Pete painfully climbed down off Hero and assumed the dual roles of horse tender and gunner. The unpracticed officers took considerable time in loading, and Longstreet, still distracted by his blistered heel and trying to move about the uneven field in his carpet slippers, sighted the weapon himself on Richardson's advancing troops.

Hill accumulated only two hundred men to launch a counterattack against the oncoming thousands.

"Are you men prepared to attack?"

Attack? They had thought their purpose would be to stand and hold, but *Attack?* The men stood in astonished silence until Robert Linwood, a scrawny Georgia sergeant with an ugly scar that parted his beard from the top of his right ear all the way down his neck and into his collar, finally stepped forward and spoke up.

"You lead, Gen'l, and I'll foller."

Harvey Hill came to attention, brought his own weapon to his hip and ordered, "Charge bayonets—CHARGE!"

* * *

General Lee saw the danger as well, but he also knew that precious little infantry was available, and two-hundred-man charges, no matter how gallant, were doomed to fail. No—artillery, and only artillery, would save this day, and he set about finding it himself.

To the rear of Jackson's old lines a staff officer led Traveller on the search, with the general privately cursing his bandaged wrists that slowed him so. Bits and pieces of artillery batteries were scattered about—some without horses, some without tenders and ammunition, and some, of course, without crews.

"Colonel!"

"Sir."

"Mix whatever batteries together you can. Pay no attention to whose command they belong. We need artillery badly, and we need it now all along that road there. Every gun, every man, every shell or rock you can find must move now!"

"Yes, sir."

Lee watched as Stephen Lee threw together twenty guns from what was nothing more than a large pile of artillery trash. One gun at a time rolled out to the Hagerstown Pike and atop any high ground they could find around Mr. Piper's farm. The men were haggard and fought out. Some limping or bleeding as the artillery commander prodded them forward with the flat of his sword.

"General Lee?"

The commanding general looked down from his horse at a filthy young artilleryman. Half of his face was black with powder and the rest was blistered raw where the flesh was burned away and blood oozed out from the wound.

"General, are you going to send us in again?"

Only then did Bobby Lee recognize his own youngest son.

The general hesitated as he choked back his own emotions. His poor, sick wife leaped for an instant into the general's heart, pleading with him to excuse the boy and send him back to safety. And Annie. *Please, God. Not the fever.*

"Yes, son. You all must do what you can to help drive these people back."

They looked into each other's eyes for just long enough to say good-bye without saying good-bye.

The younger Lee turned slowly to join his new battery. The older whispered a prayer and watched him go.

The thrown-together line of guns accumulated by General Lee threw up one hell of a wall of fire as Richardson's men stormed across Piper's fields, and, for the second time that day a determined Union assault fell short because it outran its own artillery.

"We need guns here!" Richardson shouted at McClellan's courier, James Wilson. "Where the hell is our artillery?"

"There is none available, sir." Wilson was embarrassed and angered by the message he had to deliver. He knew full well there was more than enough of both.

"None? That's impossible! There are four damned corps active on this very field, and you tell me there is no artillery available?"

"I'm afraid so, sir. It has all been ordered to the rear to defend against a possible Rebel counterattack."

"A *counterattack?* With what will Mr. Lee attack? He has nothing left to attack *with!* I am inches away from splitting his whole damned army in half and pushing every son-of-a-bitch with him into the goddamned Potomac! If he were going to counterattack, he would have done it long before now! I need *guns,* and I will end this thing right now! Who in the hell *issued* those orders?"

"General Porter, sir, under instructions from General McClellan."

Richardson felt the hairs on the back of his neck rise. He looked out over the field, where thousands of brave and anxious soldiers waited only for twenty Rebel guns to be silenced. He threw down his unlighted cigar and kicked it away.

"Well, Generals Porter and McClellan are *fools* then, sir, and nothing less!"

For the second time in less than three hours Wilson heard the Union's commanding general ridiculed by a man with stars on his shoulders; first Burnside and now Richardson. Both times he agreed, and both times he kept his mouth shut.

Richardson bellowed over the thunder, maybe in hope that God would hear, "Bring up the goddamned artillery and bring it up NOW!"

General Hill's two-hundred-man charge met with the expected results. It lasted only minutes before Hill acknowledged the folly of it, but an entire Union regiment turned to face it, further slowing Richardson's advance.

"I found you some guns, sir."

Richardson thanked God for answering his prayers before looking at the weapons. Had he looked first, he might not have been so quick to offer thanks.

With hundreds of pieces of Federal artillery parked hub-to-hub a half a mile away, Richardson fought the war with four 6-pound smoothbores. In the entire Army of the Potomac this was all of the artillery available for the forwardmost units. Glorified, oversized muskets was all they were, but they were all he had, and with them he tried to take Lee's makeshift line under fire.

On this field, at this time, not only one but two general officers manned artillery pieces. As Israel Richardson took personal command of his newfound battery of tiny guns, James Longstreet continued command of his solitary cannon. The arrival of Richardson's "big" guns to their front attracted the attention of every gunner in gray, and almost at once they took the pitiful battery under fire. For yards around Richardson's position the air burned and pieces of hot iron the size of a large man's fist bolted down from the sky, and Israel Richardson, the man who had broken the Rebel center, went down to his knees as shrapnel tore through his ribs and missed his heart by the width of a hair.

John Brown Gordon, the hero of the 6th Alabama, lay face down on a stretcher with his hat still clutched to his face. "Good thing that cap had a hole in it, Colonel," the surgeon told him. "Hadn't been for that you might have drowned in your own danged blood."

BURNSIDE'S BRIDGE

NOON

James Longstreet found General Lee so close to the action that Pete worried for his safety. If anything happened to Lee, Longstreet would have to assume command and that was a promotion Old Pete did not seek.

Normally it was Longstreet who saw the worst, but now even Lee, though he put his best face forward, struggled to find hope.

"Our boys must rally and hold one more time, General, or this could be the end of it all."

"We've held well so far, General, but our center no longer exists. A single enemy division can walk through that hole and straight into the town. We must either reinforce General Hill or create a diversion to pull them away from there. Those guns can't hold forever."

"But we have nothing left, General. In our entire army there are not three thousand men who have not yet been fought out, and that is all that remains on our right flank." Lee shut his eyes tightly. Longstreet couldn't tell if he grimaced from the pain in his wrists or the pain in his heart. "If Burnside crosses that creek every man will be needed there to keep the fords open to our rear—every man and more. If we fail there . . ."

Lee couldn't contemplate what the "if" might be. He rubbed his aching wrists and tried to devise one more miracle.

"A diversion it is then—by Jackson on the left. He must scrape together an adequate force to move around behind them. That will force them to respond."

Winfield Scott Hancock had been a wasted man. A professional soldier and West Point graduate, he had proven himself a courageous and impetuous battlefield commander in Mexico. He studied and considered himself an expert on the tactics of Caesar, Napoleon and Peter the Great among others, but he also had skill as an administrator and for virtually the entire thirteen years of his military career he commanded only documents in a Godforsaken California outpost called Los Angeles. Even the name was a joke.

When the war began, Hancock pulled every string he could grab to gain a combat commission. He wrote to his namesake, General Winfield Scott and to Postmaster General Montgomery Blair, an old friend of his father's. He became bitter and drank perhaps a little too much as, one by one, his closest friends packed their bags and headed off to war—most of them bound south. The war was four months old—almost over—by the time he received his transfer from Los Angeles to Washington, where he was ordered to report (God forbid) to the Quartermaster Corps. It was only by the purest coincidence that he ran into George McClellan in the lobby of the Willard Hotel. The general remembered him from Mexico and told him to delay reporting for as long as he could while a brigade was found for him to command.

Brigadier General Winfield Scott Hancock was forever indebted to George B. McClellan.

As Franklin's corps finally arrived on the field from its unpleasant duty in Pleasant Valley, Hancock was dispatched into the East Woods to clean out pockets of Hood's stubborn Texans, who refused to run and who would occasionally spring from nowhere just to cause trouble. Shortly after noon, also out from nowhere, burst the 27th North Carolina and the 3rd Arkansas, no longer the reluctant invaders, causing something more than only trouble. The Rebels had pushed the Yankees back so easily from the grounds of the Dunker Church that they continued across the cornfield and into the East Woods.

Hancock was already in a bad frame of mind as he came upon an isolated and apparently leaderless unit pinned down in the middle of the woods by Hood's remnants. They were well out in front and totally unprotected.

"Men, who put you here?"

"Our major!"

"And where *is* your major?"

"Over there behind that large white oak tree to our rear."

Hancock was a sitting duck atop his horse, but rose up even higher in the saddle to see if he could find the hidden major.

"Tell him to come here instantly!"

The young private had no interest in standing up, but he also had no option. Bent over at the waist and diving left to right and back again, he hurried to the hiding major with Hancock's orders.

Major Thomas Huling huddled behind the tree, his face white and wet. It had been ten minutes since he had even ventured to take a peek around the protective timber, but now he, too, had no option but to go forward and do his job. He would rather face the Rebels than Hancock. Just as Hancock began his well-deserved chewing out, a member of his staff interrupted.

"The enemy is coming straight toward us!"

"Damn them! Let them come! That's what we're here for! Step back, men, step back."

Hancock pulled his revolver and fired over the heads of his men as they pulled back slowly in the face of Singleterry's boys from the 27th North Carolina. Hancock masterfully directed his troops back to within the range of an artillery battery waiting behind some bushes and totally invisible to the approaching Rebs.

"Now, Captain," Hancock calmly said when his troops were safely behind the guns, "let 'em have it."

The guns spewed fire and canister into the advancing Rebels, and Longstreet's desperate assault finally came to a halt.

"A message from General McClellan, sir."

Hancock read the note with mixed emotions. "General Richardson severely wounded. Proceed immediately to assume command of his division."

His *division*. Israel Richardson was a fine man, a good friend and a great general. It was a terrible loss. But now all the wasted years of waiting mattered very little. A division command, and perhaps a major generalcy, waited for him now, just over the next hill, and "Winnie" Hancock couldn't wait.

"This position must be held at all hazards, Major." He pulled his silver flask from his tunic pocket and offered himself a congratulatory toast before spurring his horse to his new command.

"What is your name, Private?"

The astounded young man from Charlotte looked up at his questioner to see Stonewall Jackson.

"Private Hood, sir. William Hood."

"Do you know your numbers, Private?"

"Good as many an' better'n most, sir."

"Good. I want you to climb up in that tree there—way up to the very top. Can you do that?"

"Like a squirrel, General, sir."

"And when you get to the top, I want you to count the flags that you'll see over on the other side of that hill. There might be a mess of 'em. Can you do that, too?"

"You betcha, General, sir."

As barefooted as the day he was born, the seventeen-year-old veteran shimmied up the hickory tree and climbed it like a ladder. This was obviously not the first tree he had ever climbed.

"What do you see, Private."

"Holy Jesus, General," the boy said and immediately knew that if Jackson had heard him blaspheme so shamelessly that he would be in big trouble.

"What was that, Private?"

"There's oceans of 'em, General." About that time a Federal sharpshooter spotted the young Rebel in the treetop and began to take his aim.

"Count the flags, Private. I need to know the number."

Private Hood began to count and before he got to "three" a bullet clipped the tree and Hood tasted bark. He counted faster, but now the whole Yankee army knew he was there, and it became a matter of pride to see who could bring him down.

"Eighteen, nineteen, twenty . . ." The hickory tree took a terrible beating. Limbs as thick as a small man's arm fell to the ground, sheared off by musket fire, and still Private Hood counted.

"Thirty-two, thirty-three, thirty-four . . ." A minié ball nicked his thumb, but he never blinked, for fear he would lose count and have to start again.

"Thirty-seven, thirty-eight, thirty-nine . . ."

"That will do. Come down, sir."

As promised, like a squirrel, he touched only three limbs on his way down and landed, flat-footed and safe, at General Jackson's feet.

"Nice job, Private . . . ?"

"Hood. Private Hood, sir."

"Nice job, Private Hood. Stay with me, now. I may require your services again. Courier!"

"Sir."

"Go to General Lee and tell him that a flanking movement against the enemy on this side of the field could result only in disaster. Ride."

THE ROHRBACH BRIDGE

Edward Ferrero, the teetotaling dance instructor–turned-colonel who attempted to enforce temperance on his hard-drinking brigade, addressed the 51st New York and 51st Pennsylvania, which stood massed behind a hill three hundred yards downstream from the Rohrbach Bridge.

"It is General Burnside's especial request that the two Fifty-firsts take that bridge! Will you do it?"

Ferrero expected the obligatory cheer from the ranks, but was embarrassed when answered only by an awkward moment of total silence.

Finally, one of the heroes of New York's Shepard Rifles summoned up more courage than would be needed to assault the bridge and shouted, "Will you give us our whiskey, General, if we make it?"

"Yes, by God!" he said, and *now*, by God, the men cheered.

"General Burnside. General McClellan orders that you carry that bridge, immediately and at all costs!"

"General McClellan appears to think I am not trying my best to carry this bridge; you are the third or fourth one who has been to me this morning with similar orders."

Colonel Sackett stepped backward at Burnside's angry response and reached into his pocket for the written orders, signed by McClellan, relieving Burnside of his command, but he was interrupted by the sounds of battle as the two 51st's broke out of the woods and over the hill on their hundred-yard dash to the mouth of the bridge. Far to their left, Rodman at last had found a crossing point acceptable only because it was so far downstream that it could be made unopposed, and as the two 51st's began their attack, Rodman began, one man at time, to send his 3,000 troops across the Antietam.

General Edwin Sumner was at least physically recovered from his debacle in the West Woods and had moved to the vicinity of the sunken road to assume command of the lost two-thirds of his corps. General Franklin's corps arrived fresh and new and ready to fight at just the same time.

"General Sumner?"

"General Franklin. We are very pleased to see you, sir. You and your men are badly needed here."

"So I see, General. It appears that you have done good work here. The enemy lines seem broken, and my men are fully prepared to continue your assault."

"Assault?" Bull Sumner went suddenly pale and his stomach churned at the very thought of it. "No, sir. There will be no further assaults. You have not been in there, sir, and I have, and I can tell you that enough men have died this day, and the enemy lines are far from broken. Those woods there are *full* of Rebels and they are ready even at this moment to launch their *own* assault against *us*. No, sir. I am the general commanding on this field and you are ordered to place your divisions into *defensive* positions and prepare to repel an attack."

William Franklin, who was so cautious he had allowed his entire corps to be held at bay by 1,300 Rebels at Crampton's Gap, saw the fear in Sumner's eyes and heard it in the old man's normally powerful voice. He saw for himself that the Rebels were beaten and needed just one more push to fold.

"General Sumner. Look there. A handful of guns stand guard over that road. There are no pickets. There is no infantry guarding its flanks. Some of those guns are manned by only two or three men. I promise you, sir, there is *no one there*!"

"And I promise *you*, sir, that if there is no one there *now*, there soon will be. If we attack and fail, our entire right flank will be routed. Your divisions are the only men left on this portion of the field with any fight left in them and a successful Rebel assault would find itself in General McClellan's rear. And I promise you further, sir, that there will be no further assaults on this day."

"This attack will not fail, General. There is no one there to stop it!"

Again James Wilson found himself witness to a discussion of strategy, this time with two generals in heated argument on the field of battle. The whole damned thing was falling apart before his eyes. Thousands of men lay dead and wounded all around him wherever he rode, the Rebel defenses were thinner than paper and all the while the Union's corps commanders fought among themselves.

"General McClellan's instructions, sirs," the young major forced himself to say, "are for General Sumner to get up his men and hold his position at all hazards."

Sumner and Franklin exchanged glances. Franklin pleaded with his eyes for Sumner to turn him loose, but the old veteran had seen more carnage today than in all of the battles of his entire career combined.

Franklin saw a hint of hesitation in Sumner's manner, and he pulled him aside and spoke to him quietly.

"George issued those orders before my corps came up. The situation is entirely different now." Franklin was pleased that Sumner hesitated and allowed him to continue. "Edwin—think what will become of your reputation if I am right, and you refuse to attack. At the very least send to McClellan and seek further instructions."

Franklin hit on the right word. Sumner's reputation had suffered too greatly in this fight and another wound could prove fatal.

"Go back, young man, and ask General McClellan if I shall make a simultaneous advance with my whole line at the risk of not being able to rally a man on this side of the creek if I am driven back."

"General McClellan's instructions say nothing about any advance, sir. You are instructed to hold your position at all hazards, sir. That is all."

"I *heard* what you said, Major! Now hear *me*! Go back, young man, and bring me an answer to my question!"

A. P. Hill approached Sharpsburg so closely now that the sounds of artillery rumbled ahead. Little Powell could smell the sulfur in the air from four miles away and the battle pulled him passionately to it. In his mind he saw Lee and Jackson and thousands of desperate men waiting only for him. He saw never-ending waves of blue soldiers and he saw his old roommate, George McClellan, and his wife, Mary Ellen.

"Move on, men. We're almost there now. Hear the battle? Move on now, men. Lee needs us. Close it up. Keep moving."

With thirteen agonizing miles behind him, one exhausted Rebel couldn't take another step and had the misfortune of stumbling to his hands and knees directly in front of Powell Hill's horse. The general leaned over and slapped the poor Virginian on the backside with the flat of his sword. Private Cline's feet bled and the slap to his rear brought tears to his eyes. He wanted nothing more than to be back home in Winchester, where he knew his brothers were all complaining about the hard work of the harvest in the daytime but singing along with Daddy's fiddle at night. He stood slowly and continued the march while singing a mountain song as he ran, to distract himself from the pain.

"Keep moving, men. Close it up now. Lee needs us. Keep moving."

The two 51st's came over the hill against a terrible fire from the bluffs beyond the bridge. They halted in the middle of the open field for only a moment to return the Rebels' fire and the hesitation cost them dearly.

"At the double-quick—CHARGE!" Ferrero yelled and the Shepard Rifles from New York and the other 51st from Pennsylvania rushed farmer Rohrbach's bridge against a storm of minié balls and artillery fire and somehow managed to spread out along the creek bank. Some moved forward to pull down the rails of a fence to provide at least some protection. The lucky ones took cover behind the wing walls that split off from either side of the stone structure while others, for sheer lack of cover, had no option but to continue across the twelve-foot-wide span, where they quickly drew all of the Rebels' fire and went down in a pile.

Then, without apparent reason, the killing musket fire slowed. The artillery continued, but the muskets slowed almost to a halt. One Union man heard an odd sound to his rear and turned to see a two-foot-long section of railroad iron hit the ground and bounce.

"Look at that! The damned Rebels are shooting train tracks at us."

"Yeah, and that's about all they're shooting. The sons-of-bitches are out of ammunition, looks like to me."

"CHARGE!"

The two 51st's stood and ran along their respective banks. The color bearers from both regiments met in the middle and turned to cross, funneling their regiments onto the bridge against renewed Confederate musket fire. With each passing moment the crossing became more and more difficult as the bridge became flooded with blood and filled with Union casualties.

"RENO—RENO," the men shouted, remembering their brave and beloved commander who had fallen on South Mountain. They pushed themselves finally across and the Pennsylvanians turned right and the New Yorkers left, spreading out along the other side of the creek bank, leaving room in the middle for whoever might follow. No one did.

Colonel Crooke, pinned down upstream since his first abortive attempt two hours before, saw the opportunity and forded the stream farther to the south; while two miles downstream, General Rodman's division finally completed its crossing of Antietam Creek at the difficult Snavely's Ford. Burnside was at last across the bridge.

Colonel Benning, commanding the 245 remaining Georgians on the hill over the bridge, ordered his men back. Out of ammunition after facing three assaults, the defiant Rebels had no choice.

"General Franklin is on the scene, sir, and believes that another assault against the center could be successful. General Sumner is not in agreement." Wilson took a breath to continue, but McClellan interrupted.

"Franklin believes that he can launch a successful assault?"

"That is correct, sir, and General Sumner wants to know if he should make a simultaneous advance with his entire line at the risk of not being able to rally a man on his side of the creek should he fail. Their argument is quite heated, sir."

"Major, return to General Sumner and tell him to bring every man and gun into ranks and, if practicable, to push forward with General Franklin's divisions and to hold the line with his own command in concert with General Mansfield's and Hooker's."

No sooner had Wilson left than Colonel Thomas Key arrived with a message from the left.

"General Burnside sends his compliments, sir, and reports that he is across the creek in strength. He says to tell you, sir, that he should now be able to hold that position."

"*Hold* it? He should be able to do *that* with five thousand men. Tell General Burnside that our entire day rests on his continuing his attack *immediately*. And Colonel Key—Colonel Sackett has a document with him that he should feel free to deliver to General Burnside should he fail to move with dispatch."

Fitz-John Porter turned his back to McClellan as though he were viewing the situation on the sunken road and under his breath he said, "So much for Ambrose Burnside," and he tried not to smile.

Burnside ordered the regiments that had carried the bridge to continue their movement against Sharpsburg.

"Our men have no ammunition, sir. They must either be replaced or resupplied before renewing the attack or they will be needlessly slaughtered."

"Call forward General Willcox's division."

* * *

"Go back, young man," Sumner spoke to McClellan's courier as though he were an errant son, "and tell General McClellan I *have* no command. Tell him my command . . . and Hooker's command are all cut up and demoralized. Tell him General Franklin has the only organized command on this part of the field!"

Wilson was exhausted. His horse was tired and frothing, but he turned and rode one more time up the mountain to the Pry house. He continued to hear the words in his mind—the words of Generals Burnside and Richardson and Franklin. The farther he rode, the angrier his thoughts became. *Sumner has lost his nerve and McClellan has lost control—if he had ever had it. The whole goddamned thing is slipping away. All of these brave men are dying for absolutely nothing. After seven hours of fighting and tens of thousands of casualties, all that we have gained is that stinking little road, and without another attack even that is worthless.* His anger was on the verge of exploding into rage. *All for want of a general—just one goddamned general with the guts and the talent to finish this thing. Sumner has neither at this point. Franklin may have the guts but not the talent. Hooker. Hooker. If only Joe Hooker could ride back onto the field astride that giant white stallion just one more time, to lead one more charge, then Lee and the whole damned Rebel army will be totally destroyed. We are one general and one hour away from winning this whole damned war, and the only son-of-a-bitch who can win it is lying on a cot in the Pry house with a scratch on his goddamned foot.*

Maybe Franklin will prevail, Wilson thought, as he galloped back up the hill. *Maybe McClellan will at last show some gumption and finish what he began.*

Maybe hell will freeze.

Nudged by Fitz-John Porter to communicate with "our friends in Washington," McClellan prepared his first wire of the day to the government. He scribbled on the telegraph form:

To Henry Halleck: *Outside Sharpsburg*
                                                      1:45 P.M.
We are in the midst of the most terrible battle of the war, perhaps of history—thus far it looks well, but I have great odds against me. Hurry up

all the troops possible. Our loss has been terrific, but we have gained much ground. I have thrown the mass of the Army on their left flank. Burnside is now attacking their right & I hold my small reserve consisting of Porter's (5th Corps) ready to attack the center as soon as the flank movements are developed. It will either be a great defeat or a most glorious victory. I think & hope that God will give us the latter.

G. B. McClellan

He read back over it before handing it to the dispatcher. He struck out the final two sentences and added, *I hope that God will give us a glorious victory.*

The dispatcher saluted and turned to go, but McClellan stopped him. "One more moment, Corporal." He took another sheet and to Mary Ellen he wrote:

We are in the midst of the most terrible battle of the age. So far God had given us success, but with many variations during the day. The battle is not yet over & I write this in the midst of it. I trust that God will smile upon our cause. I am well. None of your immediate friends killed that I hear of. Your father with me quite safe.

G. B. McClellan

"General McClellan, sir."

"Go ahead, Major."

Wilson panted for a moment before he could get his breath. "General Sumner says to inform you, sir, that he has no command. That his and Hooker's are badly cut up and demoralized and that General Franklin has the only organized command on that part of the field."

"Does General Franklin agree?"

"General Franklin was not present, sir, but, if I may, the situation has not changed. I do not believe anything has happened that would alter General Franklin's position."

McClellan tossed aside his cigar and stood up from his lawn chair. "General Porter—I believe that this crisis will not be resolved without us. Let us 'ride into the valley' and see for ourselves."

Fitz-John Porter hesitated for a moment and looked down onto the sunken road. The view was totally obstructed by a blanket of smoke that covered the field like a shroud. Wilson heard him mutter, "Into the valley of the shadow of death," before he ran to catch up with his leader. The young major ran for a fresh horse to accompany the generals to Sumner's headquarters. He had read most of the book and was not about to be deprived of the final chapters.

The McClellan entourage came down off the mountaintop and weaved its way down from the Pry house toward the sunken road through lines of Union troops. Some were wounded, some were fought out, and some were fresh, but Major Wilson noticed one disturbing thing about them all. The cheers that had greeted the Young Napoleon at every sighting for the past two weeks were totally silenced. Not a single man opened his mouth to "hoorah" as their commanding general rode by. They looked up at him, but it was as though he wasn't there. What was it that Wilson saw in each and every face? Defeat? Exhaustion? Fear? Disillusionment? Disgust.

These men knew what Wilson knew. They had seen it all before. They were being wasted again. They fought and died bravely, but again, it would be all for nothing. That is what Wilson saw.

McClellan saw nothing.

CHAPTER 14

MY REGARDS
TO MARY ELLEN

2:00 P.M.

Robert E. Lee's frustration at being led around the battlefield was compounded by his inability even to grasp his own field glasses. It was more of a habit than a necessity, but it was a good habit, and Lee missed the comforting feel of the glasses in his hands. Even now he squinted to see Franklin's corps as it moved forward to occupy the sunken road behind Hancock's stagnant division. He shook his head in wonder at the miracle of their timidity. The Yankees had paid so dearly for what they had gained, but showed little inclination to finish the job. If they were coming on as they should, they would have done so by now. He decided that he had little to fear from the fresh Union troops.

"Amazing," Lee said to himself as Longstreet approached.

"What's the situation on the right, General?"

"Sir, the Yankees are preparing for an assault. They seem to be bringing across a full division, but every man, gun and wagon is using the bridge. There are three fords available to them now, but they seem intent on staying dry. At the rate they are funneling their men and equipment across that skinny little bridge—well, sir, it could take two hours to get 'em across the way they're coming. And it doesn't appear that one man is going to come forward till all are across. I could be wrong, sir, but that is how it seems."

"That is how it is, General. Ever since their first attack this morning, everyone has moved with caution. Jackson reports forty Federal regiments to our left, beyond the church, playing cards and cooking rations. You yourself saw a full division fought to a halt by a dozen guns and a handful of infantry. Our cavalry reports Porter's corps remains encamped to the rear. I only wonder how Burnside managed to hold his men back this morning." He shook his head in amazement. "One brave man, Pete, is all they need today, on any part of the field."

"I pray they don't find him, sir."

"They won't. My greatest fear now is that the soldiers will begin leading the generals. Only then will we be beaten."

Winfield Scott Hancock saw immediately the glorious opportunity that Israel Richardson had left him. His men were well forward and ready to the man to break through Lee's shattered ranks. His blood was up, he felt his own heart pounding furiously in his chest and he could not wait to finish the job Richardson had begun. He needed only two things: three batteries of artillery, just eighteen or twenty guns; and orders to proceed. His men cheered him as he rode past them at a run, leaping fences on his way to find Sumner. He pulled to a dusty stop and dismounted in a single motion, anxious to get what he required and return to his division. He arrived to find Sumner, Franklin, Porter and the Young Napoleon himself in the midst of a council of war, right there on the battlefield.

Franklin was angry.

"The men are *not* demoralized, sirs. Hooker's men by now are well rested. I am told that Meade's division remains virtually intact. Mansfield's corps fought only briefly on the cornfield. Generals Greene and Williams need only to rally their men—"

Bull Sumner interrupted with his cannonlike voice. "General Greene has recently been pushed back away from the church and is in total disarray. My own corps is demolished."

Hancock was dazed. *Demolished?* He had only just left Richardson's division. The gallant green flags of the Irish Brigade were soiled, but the division had just got its dander up and was anxious to attack an obviously inferior foe. He started to speak, but discretion overrode the urge. It would not be a great start for his first moments of division command to be spent contradicting his immediate superior officer. He literally bit his tongue and prayed for Franklin to prevail.

The entourage walked a hundred yards to the front so George McClellan could view the situation for himself. They stood atop Roulette's swale and looked down into the sunken road. Three thousand blue-clad bodies cluttered the downslope. Along the bottom of the hill ran the road, filled in places six deep with Confederate dead and wounded. The whole line writhed like a giant, dying snake as the wounded tried to crawl out from under the dead. Out from the middle of one pile of dead Rebels, a single arm extended, waving piteously for help from underneath the bodies of his fallen comrades. McClellan focused on the hand moving slowly from side to side as though beckoning him and his army on across the road. He remembered the story from Melville's book about the great white whale and the ship's captain, dead and lashed to the evil creature's back, summoning his whalers to follow and join him in hell.

Tears rose up in the great general's eyes. The men on the hillside were the same men who had cheered him so gallantly for so long. Litter bearers passed directly in front of him carrying a young sergeant who bled from the stump where his right leg had been. The veteran soldier cried like a child. McClellan couldn't look any longer and turned his back to the carnage, trying not to let his fellow warriors see how deeply moved he was. He looked to Fitz-John Porter for help.

"Mac—I have two divisions and General Franklin has three. They may number twenty thousand or fewer, and they are all of your army that remains between this point and Washington. Remember, General, I command the last reserve of the last army of the Republic."

Franklin was desperate to reiterate his notion that Hooker and Mansfield also had 10,000 to 15,000 left on the field with a great deal of fight left in them, but he saw by McClellan's face that this battle was lost—both of them.

"Generals," McClellan said, "General Burnside at this moment, at long last, is busy on our left. I have great expectations on that part of the field. I do not believe that an assault here at this moment would be prudent. Hold your positions, gentlemen, at all hazards."

He struck out to find Ol' Dan so he could mount and ride and get the hell out of this place.

Neighbor Jones watched from the outskirts of Sharpsburg as the 13,000 men of Burnside's Ninth Corps gathered on the near bank of the Antietam. Burnside himself stood at the western mouth, directing traffic as men and supply wagons and artillery waited their turns to cross.

Farther north was yet another bridge, the "middle bridge," and beyond that waited even more fresh Union divisions. Jones's orders from Longstreet were to hold the town of Sharpsburg and to protect at all costs the roads leading north to Boteler's Ford—the Army of Northern Virginia's only escape route back into Virginia.

Burnside was coming, there was no doubt of that, but who else might join him and when? Lee and Longstreet seemed to believe that no one would—ever—but Jones had to make his dispositions in such a way as to defend against any eventuality. He had over a mile of front to defend and only 2,800 men with which to do it. He felt suddenly dizzy, something that had happened to him more and more frequently of late. His heart pounded and he pretended to be casual as he grabbed his chest and struggled to suck in a deep breath of air. A pain shot through his right arm, worse this time than last, but he had to go on. He knew the chest pains would quickly pass—they always did.

James Wilson could no longer contain his fury. McClellan and his cowardly generals were fully prepared to let this magnificent opportunity pass. The Confederacy was on its knees only hundreds of yards away. One more push and the rebellion would be put down—the war would be over. Again his thoughts went to Joe Hooker. He glanced over at the Pry house where he knew Fightin' Joe lay, and he saw a familiar face in unfamiliar attire. Wearing a uniform without any insignia or designation of rank, the man looked out over the field and scribbled notes on a pad. He was the correspondent from the *Tribune*—the one who had been with Hooker ever since Bull Run.

Suddenly Wilson knew what he must do. This damned reporter was the key, the only hope. But what was his name? Little? Small? Smalley.

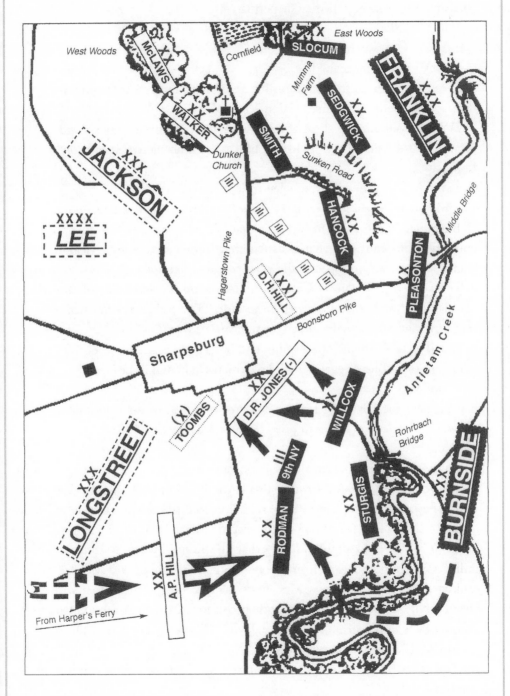

George Smalley. The major took a moment to organize his thoughts before he approached the newspaperman.

"Mr. Smalley?"

"Yes."

"May I have a moment?"

Smalley resented the intrusion for a moment, but it wasn't often he was approached. "Of course, Major."

Wilson took him by the elbow and directed him to the opposite side of the house where they could not be seen, which increased Smalley's curiosity.

"Are you fully aware, sir, of what is happening here?"

"Major, I am a reporter. It is my job to know what is happening. Unfortunately there are a great many people who see it as *their* jobs to *keep* me from knowing what is happening. I don't have a great deal of time, so please tell me specifically what you are talking about."

"Very well." Wilson took a breath. He was on the verge of violating his oath and he hesitated for just an instant. "The Rebels are finished. I am sure that even a civilian like yourself can see that."

Smalley took offense at the comment, but a good reporter never shuts the door on a source regardless of how offensive he might be.

"Go on."

"Against the advice of a great many of his staff, of his *commanders*, General McClellan refuses to press the attack against either the right or the center."

Wilson hesitated and Smalley said nothing.

"Several of us believe, sir, that this battle is being badly fought. We have the opportunity to crush the rebellion, right here and right now. But McClellan is . . . afraid, sir. He is scared to death that *Lee* is going to attack *him*! He is so afraid of losing that he will not give us a chance to win." Wilson looked away from the newspaperman and over at McClellan and Porter lounging on Mrs. Pry's living room furniture that had been carelessly dragged outside for their comfort. "Most of us think that this battle is only half finished and half won. There is still time to finish it, but McClellan will do no more."

"Why are you telling me this, Major? Frankly, it sounds to me like mutiny."

Wilson's frayed nerves snapped. "I know that as well as you do! We all know it! But we also know it is the only way to crush Lee and end the rebellion and save the country." He took a breath to calm himself and pressed his point a little more quietly. "I am a soldier, sir. These other members of the staff who agree with me are general officers and even corps commanders. Any effort on any of our parts to encourage, or even insinuate, that General McClellan should be relieved of his command would be regarded, as you say, as mutiny. Even discussing it with you could result in my court-martial—possibly even a firing squad. But you, sir, are a civilian, and safe from military justice. And"—Wilson paused for effect and continued—"you are a friend of General Hooker's."

The impact of what he was being asked to do hit Smalley so hard it almost knocked him backward. He was a reporter—an observer of events. But at the earliest blush of dawn he had crossed the line from observer to participant when he agreed to act as Hooker's courier. He had donned the uniform and risked his life. But this? This was mutiny in the face of the enemy. But he also knew that every word the young major had spoken was absolutely true.

"What is it, Major, that you are asking me to do?"

"Go to General Hooker. Explain the situation on the field and urge him to take command of this army and drive Lee into the Potomac!"

"You forget, Major, that General Hooker is a soldier as well. Even should he be physically able I am certain that he will no more consider such a thing than any of your other . . ." Smalley had to search for the proper word, ". . . conspirators."

Wilson knew that Smalley was right, and an uncomfortable silence followed until the major found an alternative solution. "Ask General Hooker if he is able, then, to resume command of his own corps. If his men see him return to the fight, carrying the flag and on his great white horse, I am certain that they would pick up the battle. It is all that would be needed, sir. Mr. Smalley—it could end the war."

Nothing more could be said. Smalley thought for a long moment and watched McClellan sitting in his comfortable chair, smoking his cigar and looking out over the field as though he were front-row center at a concert or a play. After the hours of deafening cannon fire, the near silence spoke loudly enough to underscore Wilson's point.

"I promise you nothing, Major, but it is past time that I should pay General Hooker a visit. I should inquire about his health."

It was a pitiful line of heroes that continued the long march from Harper's Ferry. Young Private Cline was neither the first nor the last to feel the flat of A. P. Hill's sword, but the red-haired general noticed that the pace of the march had recently picked up. The sounds of battle had diminished and the men, those who remained on their feet, feared that they had missed it.

Riding back to push forward the trailing columns, Hill saw a lieutenant scurry off behind a tree.

"Come here, you cowardly little son-of-a-bitch!"

"Sir, I can't take another . . ."

"Give me your sword!"

Hill dismounted as the youngster did as he was told. The red-shirted general received the weapon and broke it over the former lieutenant's shoulder. He remounted and returned to his mission.

"Close it up. Lee needs us."

Lee made it clear to Neighbor Jones that he had all of the infantry that he would have. No more was available. The ailing South Carolinian stood on a hill with Sharpsburg at his back and looked through his glasses at the oncoming thousands. He had placed his troops sparingly but well. Line after line of skirmishers hid in the cornfields and along the roads and ditches that cut through the farmland. The crews manning his twenty-eight guns had a wonderful view of the field, but four hours of daylight remained, and the Yankees had only 1,500 yards to cover. He saw no chance to defeat the advancing corps, but prayed that he could delay them until nightfall.

Every time the Union soldiers attempted an advance, they were met by small but well-concealed units of Rebels, protected by artillery from Sharpsburg posted on a hill directly adjacent to the town limits. The infantry would stand and fire and hold their lines as long as practical and then withdraw, leading the pursuing Yankees only to the next line of waiting Rebels. The going was slow until the Union artillery found the range to the hill and the Confederate guns and caissons began exploding on the ridge. The town itself, spared significant bombardment until now, caught much of the Union cannon fire that overshot the Rebel positions.

Robert E. Lee sat astride Traveller and calmly watched Ambrose Burnside's slow, bloody advance. From the top of a hill, on the very edge of town, he had a clear view down into the valley as the huge blue army forced its way forward. He saw General Jones move two regiments up and along a stone wall that stood only fifty yards outside of town. *We will allow those people that far*, Lee thought, *but not a single step farther*. He tried to get Jones's attention for a moment, just to register his approval, and he saw the young general grasp his chest and bend slightly forward in the saddle. He thought that Jones might be wounded until he sat back upright as though nothing had happened.

"Well, my brave young courier. I am happy to see you. What better a person to report to me than a reporter. How goes it on the field?"

Smalley couldn't help stealing a glance at the wounded general's foot, but it was covered. A bloody, empty boot, cut open with a knife, lay ominously beside the bed.

"Frankly, General, it could be going better. Your corps has advanced no farther than when you left it. Mansfield's managed to take the church and Sumner's men are in that farm road on the left but . . ."

"But what, boy?"

"But they halted as well."

"Damn! What the hell is the matter?"

"General McClellan seems—reluctant, sir, to press his gains. Apparently he fears a Rebel counterattack."

"Goddammit!" Then, mostly to himself rather than to Smalley, he whispered, "We are led by a bunch of damned old women! Lee has nothing to counterattack *with*!"

"How are you, sir?"

"I'm shot in the goddamned foot! How in the hell do you *think* I am?"

"I am asking, sir, if you will be able to mount your horse again today."

"No. It is impossible."

"Or to take command of your corps again in any way—in a carriage if one can be found. The men would take heart, sir, to see you again on the field."

"No. I cannot move. I am perfectly helpless." Finally, it dawned on the wounded general the full import of what was being said. "Why do you ask? What do you mean? Who sent you here?"

A nearby surgeon caught Smalley's eye and emphatically shook his head.

"Friends of the general, sir. That is all. I shall come back, to check on you again."

The *Tribune* correspondent turned to leave.

"Smalley . . ." It was the first time the general had called him by name.

"Sir?"

"You did good and brave work today." Before the reporter could respond, Fightin' Joe Hooker returned to drugged sleep.

As Smalley left the Pry house, Wilson was standing in the yard, waiting very anxiously. Smalley only shook his head and walked on by.

3:30 P.M.

Like a man climbing a cliff, Rodman's division had to pull itself up one single step at a time, gain a foothold and pull itself up again, one small step higher. As the Rebel skirmishers deliberately withdrew, the Confederate lines grew fuller and stiffer until not a hundred yards from the town limits the Yankees came upon Jones's stone wall. The remaining Rebel artillery positioned itself in *defilade*, down in a shallow hollow with their muzzles directly at ground level so that the rounds of double canister scraped the earth en route to their targets. The Federal pressure mounted as Willcox's 3,500-man division caught up, doubling the Union's numbers, and the fighting became furious with the lines not fifty yards apart. The artillery of both sides fell quiet as the men moved too close to each other, and shot or shell stood just as much chance of killing their own men as those of the enemy. They fought at this range for ten minutes before the 9th New York Zouaves stood and charged the Rebel lines and the Virginians stood to greet them. Again rifles became clubs and the Confederate dam was pierced and blue poured through it like water. Hundreds of Confederate soldiers ran backward into the streets of Sharpsburg—backward to avoid the humiliation of a back wound. The gaily clad Zouaves, bright blue coats and crimson red fezs, stopped their assault to stand on the wall and shout. Their regiment had begun the march up from the bridge with nine hundred men, only half of whom reached the wall. Neighbor Jones could believe neither his good fortune nor his bad. His lines were wounded, but the bleeding, for the moment, had stopped.

"You would think that they had just won a game of baseball," he said.

Finally, Union artillery felt safe in opening fire on the retreating Rebels, and the few citizens who remained in Sharpsburg were thrown into a panic as shells exploded and windows shattered in the streets of the town. In the cellar of the Kretzer home, women screamed and babies cried. Dogs barked and old men prayed.

Lee made himself visible to the men in the hope that he might be able to rally them, and for a moment the break mended itself. No man could bring himself to retreat behind Robert E. Lee and Traveller, but every man knew that so few could never hold for long against so many. Even Lee lost hope at the sight of two more blue divisions coming to the aid of Rodman and Willcox. One approached from the creek and another up the road from the right. He had not a notion as to who these new armies might be, so he rode to the side of an artillery spotter.

"Lieutenant."

"Sir."

Lee nodded to his front, toward the bridge. "What troops are those?"

Lieutenant Ramsey offered the general his telescope, but Lee held up his bandaged hands and said, "Can't use it."

Ramsey raised the glass and took a moment to focus. By his reaction Lee knew the answer before the cannoneer spoke.

"They are flying the United States flag."

"And that army, coming there," Lee said, indicating the columns to his right, "what flag do they march under?"

Again Ramsey lifted his telescope, and again he focused, and again Lee knew the answer before it was spoken.

"They are flying the Virginia and Confederate flags, sir!"

Robert E. Lee smiled. "It is A. P. Hill from Harper's Ferry."

Part of the spoils of victory at the Federal supply garrison were fresh new uniforms—all of them blue.

The parade of Federal brigades marched calmly toward the town and suddenly found themselves, they thought, reinforced—until the 2,500 "reinforcements" poured a deadly fire into their exposed left flank. General Rodman himself was among the first to fall as Hill's exhausted and footsore Rebels broke into a double-quick and tore into the confused Union ranks.

Leading the Rebel advance was the scimitar-carrying South Carolinian Maxcy Gregg, one of the heroes of Second Manassas. Only minutes into the fight a tremendous pain shot through his right hip. Tears filled his eyes and he became instantly too dizzy to remain mounted. He leaned into the pain and as he fell from his horse his personal aide, Alexander Haskell, caught him and lowered him softly to the ground. Stretcher bearers came forward as Gregg said, "Captain Haskell. Notify and put the next officer in command."

The stretcher bearers examined the fallen general and one of them said, "General, you aren't wounded—you're only bruised!"

Gregg shook off the pain and the astonishment and reached down to touch his "wound." He looked at his hand and saw no blood and laughed. With effort he stood and looked around for his horse, which had taken the ball that had grazed Gregg's hip.

"Unharness this animal," Gregg ordered, and the stretcher bearers unhitched a scrawny mare from their ambulance as he removed his saddle. Gregg climbed aboard and resumed the fight from the back of the nastiest-looking nag on the field.

The Federal brigades that had breached the wall stood unprotected and fell back. Jones's silent artillery roared back to life against the retreating Yankees. Lee and Longstreet, together with Jones and Toombs, rallied the men from the town and the wound in Jones's line miraculously healed. The Yankee assault, just inches from success, just yards from town, found itself suddenly exposed and vulnerable and Ambrose Burnside ordered it abandoned.

Ambrose Powell Hill had marched his "Light Division" seventeen miles in seven hours. They broke onto the field without breaking stride and sent five times their number running for cover, hightailing it back to Antietam Creek and the protection of massed artillery. Burnside pleaded to McClellan for reinforcements. He knew better than anyone, with the possible exception of Robert E. Lee, how close he had come to closing the trap on the Army of Northern Virginia—literally inches. Another charge, properly supported by reinforcements (as promised last night), would capture or destroy the whole damned lot of them.

George Smalley nudged his way next to McClellan and Fitz-John Porter as reports from their left flank poured in. He saw the questioning look that passed between the two generals when Burnside's first plea for help arrived. Porter shook his head and Smalley took it to mean that no more infantry could be risked. A moment later and wholly out of character, he saw Fitz-John Porter smile. *You would almost think he was happy about Burnside's failure*, Smalley wrote in his book. He thought better of it, though, and struck it out.

Powell Hill reported to Lee, and the stone-faced commanding general greeted him with a hug. No words passed between them until Hill inquired, "Where do you suspect General McClellan might be at this moment, sir?"

"On that hill there is my best guess. As far as I know he's been there all day."

Hill turned, looked and saluted. "General McClellan—General Marcy—my regards to Mary Ellen."

"General McClellan, sir. General Burnside sends his compliments and reports that without additional men and guns he will not be able to hold his position for another half an hour."

It was Burnside's second request for assistance in fifteen minutes.

"Tell General Burnside that this is the battle of the war. He must hold his ground till dark at any cost. I will send him Miller's battery. I can do nothing more. I have no infantry. Tell him if he cannot hold his ground, then the bridge—to the last man! Always the bridge. If the bridge is lost, all is lost!"

•

George Smalley took down every word. *I have no infantry.* Smalley remembered the tens of thousands of men held in the rear. He remembered the lines of cold, fully equipped and unused guns parked wheel-to-wheel on the other side of the creek. He remembered Major Wilson's words . . . *This battle is only half finished . . . but McClellan will do no more.*

Clara Barton left the farmhouse where she had been assisting the surgeons since slightly after dawn. The firing, mercifully, had finally come to a halt and the sun was low in the sky. She had to escape the "hospital" in the hopes of getting only one breath of fresh air, but the air was anything but fresh. It smelled of sulfur and blood and there was no escaping it. The wounded men, waiting in agony for their turns on the surgeon's table, filled the field in front of the house. There was no end in sight to her gruesome work.

She felt a tug on the blood-soaked hem of her dress. "Lady . . ."

Barton looked down at the soldier who was shot in the face. He touched his left cheek and said, "Can you tell me what this is that burns so?"

"It must be a ball."

"It is terribly painful. Won't you please take it out?"

"I'll call for a surgeon."

"No! They cannot come to me. I must wait my turn, and this is such a little wound. You can get the ball. Please take the ball out for me. You cannot hurt me, dear lady."

She continued to look at him, not knowing what to do. She had witnessed thousands of surgeries but had never performed one. The soldier's pleading face pulled at her heart and then she felt another tug on her dress. A sergeant with a thigh wound crawled to her side and offered her a knife. She tested the blade and found it sharp enough, and the ball protruded outwardly, wedged between his cheekbone and the skin. One small incision and it fell easily into her hand. She handed it to her first surgical patient and returned to the house to assist the real surgeons.

Surgeon Dunn, soaked with blood, exhausted and frustrated to tears, dreaded the approaching darkness. He had no light to work by, and thousands of surgeries yet to perform. If anyone ever actually saw an angel, he saw one now—a tiny angel, dressed in black and carrying a lantern.

"Clara—where did you find that?"

"I brought it. I have twenty more."

"I wonder why the army didn't think of that."

"The army didn't think of this either," she said as she pulled open one of her twelve cases of wine. Dr. Dunn laughed, opened the first bottle and took the first sip for himself. Barton noticed the packing stuff that clung to the glass and she laughed too. She turned back to the opened case and took out a handful. "And even I didn't think of this."

"What?"

"Look here at what some kind soul has done. These cases aren't packed with sawdust—this is cornmeal!"

Ada Mumma and her family had escaped the gunfire but not the battle. Their friend's home at the base of South Mountain was filled with Union wounded and the seven-year-old was banished to the cellar, where she waited, scared and hungry, for the day to end.

A day alone is an eternity for a frightened child, and when Mary the house slave finally came to pick her up, Ada ran crying into her arms, but startled back when she felt the wetness on her apron. Mary was covered in blood and Ada screamed and frantically tried to wipe her face clean with her hands. She ran back into the corner where she had spent most of the day and cried hysterically until Mary took off the apron and held her close and said, "It's all right, chile. Come on now. We's goin' to Boonsboro. It'll be better there."

James Longstreet rode through the streets of Sharpsburg and past the Reform Church on Main Street. The pews had been ripped out to make room for the wounded, and private soldiers hacked at the lumber to make coffins for the officers. Martha Kretzer, whose father's gigantic American flag had been tactfully hidden, ran out of her house and grabbed hold of Hero's reins.

"Captain, my house is on fire! Please help."

Longstreet dismounted and rounded up twenty healthy men who

were scrounging for food and helped the lady douse the flames. Lee, along with all of his other surviving generals, waited in another home two blocks north and worried about Old Pete.

When Longstreet bolted through the door the look of relief was clearly visible on Lee's face. "Ah, here he is," Lee said. "Here's my old war-horse."

George McClellan was jubilant. At long last September 17, 1862, surrendered to the darkness. The long-awaited enemy attack amazingly never came. Surely it would come tomorrow, but for the moment, and against tremendous odds, he had averted the defeat that would have lost the war.

That very same darkness brought Robert E. Lee the very same good news.

In the homes and the churches; in the barns and on the field lay 23,111 men—dead, dying or wounded.

23,111.

CHAPTER 15

THE REST IS SILENCE

8:00 P.M.

After fourteen hours of both observing and participating in the battle (and dabbling briefly in mutiny), it came time for George Smalley to go to work. Day one of "the battle of the war" faded to a quiet halt and Smalley gathered together his fellow *Tribune* correspondents to write and file their report.

They had selected a meeting point yesterday, and as they arrived tonight they found it full to overflowing with dying and wounded men—as was every four-walled structure within ten miles. Huddled in a corner, and by the light of a single candle, the four men planned their scoop.

"The first priority is to get this story filed," Smalley announced, "and there is absolutely no way in hell that it will be filed from here tonight. I want you all to give me your notes, and one of you to give me your horse, and I'll leave here immediately for Frederick and send the wire from there."

"But the battle is surely not over. Don't you think we should wait for the conclusion so that we can write the entire story?"

Smalley was not the senior man present, but he had become the most respected. There was no chain of command that put him in charge of the meeting—he simply *took* charge. His *forte* was his knowledge of the commanders and his ability to anticipate how they would react and respond. This was why he attached himself to Hooker, and this was why he knew that the battle was finished.

"The story is written, gentlemen. This battle shall never be resumed. General Lee *cannot*—and General McClellan *will* not. I am prepared to risk my career on it."

"You'd damned well *better* be prepared to risk your career on it, because that may be exactly what you are doing."

"It's a safe wager. If there is an engagement tomorrow I am certain that it will be minor—it will be, in fact, a *dis*engagement. And even if I am wrong, and our friend McClellan grows some guts overnight, the three of you will remain here to carry on. Your notes, please, gentlemen."

"Be careful, George. The roads are still full of Rebels and God only knows where Stuart may be. And allow me to go on record as disagreeing with you on tomorrow's probabilities. I see no way General McClellan cannot press his advantage in the morning. If you write otherwise and the battle—and the war—is won tomorrow, we all, and our paper as well, will be made to look like idiots."

"You're quite correct, Nathaniel, of course. I give my word that I shall not commit one way or the other, only to say that the opportunity exists. Should the fight begin again in earnest in the morning, one of you must get word immediately to Mr. Greeley in New York. Now, please, gentlemen—your notes."

Frederick was thirty miles away, and Smalley had slept for only two hours the night before. He pointed his equally exhausted, borrowed horse in the general direction of Frederick, Maryland, and tried to sleep in the saddle en route.

With the arrival of Lee's "old war-horse," the Confederate council of war moved back outdoors, to the spot on the north end of town where Lee had observed the action around the Dunker Church. They stood with their backs to a campfire and looked out over the field. The fires built by McClellan's army stretched so far off into the distance that it became difficult to tell where the fires ended and the stars began. Lee began to take his gruesome roll.

"General Longstreet," he asked gently, "how is it on your part of the line?"

"It is as bad as it can be. There is little better than a skirmish line left on my front."

"General Jackson?"

Jackson could always be relied upon to be Longstreet's opposite. With total confidence in his own ability and in the bravery of his men, he normally put the best possible face on even the most desperate situations—but not tonight. "These are the greatest odds, General, we have ever faced. And I have no generals remaining to me, sir. I have *captains*, men whose names I don't even know, commanding brigades!"

"General Hood, how is it with your division?"

Until now the conversation had been quiet and civil, but John Bell Hood, by his nature, was neither, and at the moment he could not comprehend even why this conversation was taking place.

This loud, bold, brash young general opened his mouth to speak, but the words caught in his throat and came out almost in a whisper. "I have no division, General Lee." He had meant to sound angry, but instead he sounded pitiful. "They are lying on the field where you sent them!" Hood reined in his emotions, looked down at his own boots and respectfully reported, "My division has been almost wiped out."

Lee stood straight and proud and looked back again toward the field. The crackling of the fire was the only sound until Longstreet realized that Lee was thinking the unthinkable. The defensive general decided to take to the offense and put an end to the madness before Lee spoke.

"General—there is not a man in your army who did not fight this day. It is my opinion, sir, that we have lost ten thousand men—one full quarter of those available, and add to that two thousand more casualties lost at South Mountain. Our artillery is a shambles and low on ammunition. Some damned Yankee cavalry regiment captured a third of my reserve artillery ammunition before it ever got here." He was out of breath by now, but couldn't afford to pause—to give Lee an opportunity to jump in and issue an order that could not be rescinded. He gulped a breath almost like a drowning man would and continued hurriedly. "Reliable informants and Stuart's scouts report five full divisions of *unused* Federal troops on the other side of the creek. They have almost as many men in reserve, General, as we have total!" Good. Now it was all said, but Lee still did not speak.

"We have fought well, today, sir, but we are fought out. Ammunition is low—particularly for the artillery. The ford, thanks be to God, is still open. It is my recommendation, sir, that we use it, and save this army to fight another day." Silence. The gray generals, all but Longstreet and Lee, stood with their heads down and waited. The issue was now solely in the hands of God and Robert E. Lee.

Finally, without taking his eyes off the field, Lee spoke: "Gentlemen, we will not cross the Potomac tonight. You will go to your respective commands, strengthen your lines. Send two officers from each brigade toward the ford to collect your stragglers and get them up. If McClellan wants to fight in the morning, I will give him battle again. Go."

And go they did—all except Longstreet. Lee continued to gaze out over the campfires of the Union army, but he felt Old Pete's presence.

"Do not be worried, General. Unless we find it feasible to turn their right flank, there will be no fight tomorrow. McClellan will not come after us, and we need the time. The ordnance at Harper's Ferry needs another day to be salvaged. Our men are too weary to march any distance and we must care for the wounded and prepare them for transport. Most importantly, James"—now Lee turned and looked Longstreet in the eyes—"I will not be driven from the field by George McClellan. We cannot allow him to claim a total victory over us. Too much could turn on it—militarily and politically. We will return to Virginia, as you say, but it will be a *voluntary* withdrawal, at a time of our own choosing."

McClellan rode with his entourage back to his new headquarters in Keedysville.

"You fought a masterful battle today, George," Porter told him. "You held off almost twice your numbers and may well have saved the Republic. They will study this fight at The Point for years to come, and I want to be the first to salute you for it."

Little Mac sat just a bit taller in his saddle and returned Porter's salute with a smile. "I appreciate your kind words, John, but I still fear that all is not yet finished. Lee was attempting to soften us up this day, and tomorrow he will attack."

The staff dismounted at headquarters, where a fine and well-prepared meal awaited their arrival. They laughed and bragged and drank wine and gathered around the fire to hear the Young Napoleon's victory address.

"Two weeks ago," McClellan told them, "this army was a beaten and demoralized mob. The enemy was invested with the prestige of former successes and inflated with a recent triumph. In that short period of time, we have not only made our depressed soldiers an army again, but have given the nation its greatest victory to date. Our men will spend this night as conquerors on a field won by their valor and covered with the dead and wounded of the enemy. I congratulate you, gentlemen, on a job well done."

Many of them slept that night in beds.

On the straw-covered floor of Roulette's barn rested sixty wounded men, brought there from all parts of the field. They also discussed the day's events—those, at least, who were able.

Corporal Strickler, who had suffered three wounds on Roulette's swale, listened as the more experienced men talked.

"We hit them today like a hammer. First one blow, then another," Sergeant Bloss said. "If we had gone in all at once, like the Rebs did at Bull Run, we would have licked 'em easy."

"We took the damned church and then gave it back. You know what? McClellan ain't no better'n the others. Ol' Abe still better find us some more generals."

"He's gonna *have* to after today. Lots of 'em went down."

"Yeah, my damned *corps* commander got shot ten minutes into the fight. He just got here yesterday and now he's already wounded."

"Dead."

"What?"

"You're talking about Mansfield, right?"

"Yeah."

"I heard he's dead. And Hooker's got his foot blowed off and Sedgwick and Richardson and Rodman and Ricketts all went down. General Meagher and General Hartstuff got shot too."

"General Meagher didn't get shot." The voice had a brogue so thick you could smell it.

"I heard he got shot leading a charge down that hill."

"Aye, he led the charge all right, laddie, but he no more got shot than Old Abe Lincoln. He was so drunk he fell off of his horse and couldn't get back on. That, by God's, what happened to my fine general. Now don't get me wrong—a fine and brave man he is. Some of that bravery, though, just happens to come from a lovely silver flask of fine Irish whiskey."

That was the picture Barton Mitchell had in his mind as he rolled over next to a man with a candle and wrote a letter home to Indiana.

Dear Momma,

I'm hurt pretty bad, but alive and that's more than I can say for many. We had a awful fight today and expect another tomorrow.

I think I had a big part in it, and not just on the field. Me and Blossie was lying in the grass the other day and I found this letter that was signed by General Lee. I gave it to my captain and he told me it went all the way up to General McClellan and the very next day we were on the move. He got killed today. Not McClellan but the captain. Lots of men got killed today . . .

The famous Kyd Douglas smile was gone. Still sick and grieving for a dozen lost friends, he thought about home. A half-hour ride up the hill. His family. His bed. Away from the blood and the death. He nearly fell from his horse as Jackson and the rest of his staff set up camp on the northern end of town. It wasn't even really a camp. No tents were pitched, no cots brought out. A single fire glowed from a hole dug in the ground and the general lay down in the grass and went quickly to sleep. It was almost midnight when Jeb Stuart rode up.

"Hello, Thomas."

"How is it with you, Jeb?"

"Well, you know that hill I was on today?"

"Yes. The one on the left. You did grand work there today, General. You kept most of those Yankees away all morning long. I don't know for the life of me why they didn't try to take it from you."

"Well, God smiled on us today, sir, but I am not so certain about tomorrow. You know we had to come down off of it today, before McLaws came up, and now you've got my artillery scattered all over the place, and, well, General, that hill must look mighty inviting to the Yankees, or it will in the morning. If they get up there and put some guns on that hill they'll play hell with us all along your left flank."

"There's no one up there now?"

"I left the better part of a squad up there, and only two guns. I haven't heard from 'em in a while. We need to get some people up there, General—tonight."

"Douglas."

"Sir."

"What's that hill called up there?"

"That's on the Nicodemus farm, sir, so they call it Nicodemus Hill."

"General Stuart believes, and I agree, that we need to get some men up there tonight. I want you to ride out and locate General Early. He's camped near the church. Tell him to move fifty men up there to hold that hill."

Douglas and his friend from Georgia, Westbrook, mounted up and moved slowly toward the Dunker Church. It was a short but emotional ride for young Captain Douglas. All of his life he'd had friends in Sharpsburg. His father preached here, he played here as a child and later he courted young ladies who lived here. To see it now, and remember it then, was too much for Douglas to handle. Dead and wounded men still covered the fields around the church. The cries and curses and pleadings for water were enough to bring a tear to the eye of the Devil himself. Douglas's horse, Ashby, had survived the battle without so much as a flinch, but now he could feel the animal quiver in fear as he smelled the blood and tried to avoid stepping on human bodies in the darkness. As he looked around him, Douglas saw the ghostly outlines of soldiers. Blue or gray? He couldn't tell in the dark and it mattered very little now anyway. Some tried one last time to stand, only to fall back down onto the body of a dead or wounded friend or foe. The fortunate dead lay in grotesque poses, some with arms held stiffly up to heaven as they had died pleading to God for just one more drop of water or one last breath of air. Douglas grimaced in disgust and chills ran down his spine. He had been ill for a day or two anyway, and now he was sure that he was about to lose whatever little his stomach held. His ever-present smile was gone. The fun was gone. The adventure. Ashby stumbled into a hole that was filled with blood and splattered it up on Douglas's leg, and both horse and rider had had enough. Douglas calmed Ashby, dismounted and begged Westbrook to lead the animal on while he walked. It would be easier on both of them.

More by instinct than design, Captain Oliver Wendell Holmes, Jr., white and dizzy from the loss of blood, managed to stumble back to the Union lines. By some stroke of fate he made it back to his very own unit, the 20th Massachusetts. A friend, Captain LaDuc, cleaned and bandaged his neck wound.

"It's a good thing, LaDuc, that I required no amputation. I have little confidence in your surgery."

After Holmes had been bandaged and sent off to the rear, Captain LaDuc penned a telegram to the wounded captain's family: *Capt. Holmes wounded shot through the neck though not mortal at Keedysville.* He addressed it to "The Autocrat of the Breakfast Table—Boston Massachusetts."

SEPTEMBER 18TH

At 3:00 A.M., six hours after he had left Antietam Creek behind him, George Smalley arrived in Frederick and located the telegraph office. Naturally he found it closed and he sat on the step and slept until the operator arrived at 7:00 A.M.

"I have an urgent wire that must be sent to the *New York Tribune* immediately."

"Good luck, mister. The wires have been taken over by the army. I'll be happy to send it when there's time, but there ain't no guarantees as to when or even if it'll get there. And keep it short. If it ain't short I can't send it."

It was the best Smalley could do at the moment. He jotted down a brief personal message, alerting the editors that a battle had been fought and a story was coming. He had that sent off first.

Then, back on the front step of the telegraph office, he began to write what would have to be an abbreviated, early-edition version of his report. Through the fitful sleep on horseback and stairstep he had given the writing of the story very little thought. He was just too tired. But now, he had to write, and he had to write quickly.

The greatest battle of the war was fought to-day, lasting from daylight till dark, and closing without decisive result. The whole forces of McClellan and Lee were engaged for fourteen hours. Two hundred thousand men have fought with the utmost determination on both sides. Neither can claim a complete victory . . .

For over an hour he wrote his "abbreviated" story that, if it reached New York at all, would fill two entire broadsheet pages. He handed the sheets to the telegrapher, who continued to *dit* and *daw* with his right hand as he accepted the document with the left.

"I told you to keep it short!"

"That *is* short." He slipped ten dollars into the irate operator's coat pocket and said, "Do what you can." He had no time to wait to find its fate. He had a train to catch.

"They are to hold the ground they occupy, but are not to attack without further orders." Those were the early-morning instructions issued to McClellan's commanders in the field. Hold the ground.

For the first time in nineteen hours, the telegraph lines at the war office began to click through a message from George McClellan to his "superiors" in Washington:

The battle of yesterday continued for fourteen hours, and until after dark. We held all we gained except a portion of the extreme left that was obliged to abandon a part of what it had gained. Our losses very heavy, especially in General officers. The battle will probably be renewed today. Send all the troops you can by the most expeditious route.

G. B. McClellan
Maj. Genl. Comdg.

To Mary Ellen he wrote, "Those in whose judgment I rely tell me that I fought the battle splendidly & that it was a masterpiece of art."

No sounds of battle urged him back toward Sharpsburg. Not until after 9:00 A.M. did he mount and ride to the scene of yesterday's engagement. Not until ten did General Franklin renew his urgings for a fresh attack.

"That hill up there appears to be ours for the taking, General. A single division will have it in our hands in a moment, and guns placed along that rise will *enfilade* their entire left flank."

"General Franklin," Sumner boomed again, "I must repeat that you have no concept of what lies beyond that hill. I do. I was there before you ever arrived on the field. General McClellan, too much blood was spilled on that field yesterday. It's another of Bobby Lee's traps, sir. No one knows that better than I."

McClellan had slept not at all last night. Visions of mutilated men reappeared every time he closed his eyes. The piteous sounds they made followed him from the battlefield and spent the night in his mind. If he closed his eyes now, he knew he would see that arm again—that Rebel arm, Ahab's arm, extended up through a pile of dead men to beckon him forward. He looked now at the living. Thousands of his boys lay on the ground, weapons in their hands, ready and anxious, incredibly, to go forward again at just one word from him.

"General Franklin—I appreciate your opinion, but I must look to the larger picture. I do not see that we are absolutely assured of success in such a venture, and a defeat here would permit Lee's army to march as it pleases against Washington, Baltimore, Philadelphia or New York. One loss here, sirs, and all is lost. Hold your positions, gentlemen."

As he watched the general and his escort ride away from the battlefield and back toward their comfortable headquarters, Major James Wilson recalled a line from somewhere in the works of Shakespeare. It was odd, because it wasn't one of the most quoted, and he surely wasn't a scholar, but the line came into his mind nonetheless and he spoke it aloud.

" 'And the rest,' " he said, " 'is silence.' "

Not more than two hundred yards separated the Union troops in the sunken road from the shadow of a line thrown up by the Rebels. The forward pickets were face-to-face and in easy shouting range of each other.

"There's a lot of hurt men out there, Yank, from both sides. S'pose we could come over and get some of ours?"

"We got orders to shoot anybody that tries. Until the generals get together and start a truce we can't do nothing."

"Damn the generals, Billy. There's men not twenty yards in front of us—yours and ours. Let's just go out 'n' grab a few 'n' bring 'em back. I'm sick to death of hearing 'em cry and you are too."

Almost a full minute passed before he answered, "Okay, Johnny, I'm coming over. If anybody shoots there'll be hell to pay."

"Ain't nobody gonna shoot you, Billy. I'm coming out too."

And so it began, with only two men at first, walking timidly out onto the field to pick up one wounded soldier. Five minutes later there were ten men from each side on the field, lifting or dragging anguished but grateful men from the spots where some had laid for twenty hours.

Winfield Hancock sat on his horse and looked over the list of wounded officers. Since he had never ridden with Richardson's division before, he recognized none of the names.

"What's the situation with General Meagher?"

"That's pronounced 'Mar,' sir."

"No. General Meagher—M-E-A-G-H-E-R."

"That's right, sir, but it's pronounced Mar."

"All of *that* is pronounced Mar?"

"Your command includes the Irish Brigade now, sir. You are going to have to accustom yourself to some fairly exotic peculiarities. In answer to your question, though, General Meagher was knocked from his horse by enemy artillery and was dazed somewhat by the fall. He is quite well today. In fact, that's him coming this way."

"General Hancock," the Irishman brogued as he pulled to a halt. "I am General Meagher, sir, commanding the Irish Brigade—apparently a truce has been agreed to and collection of the wounded has begun."

"I know of no truce, General Meagher. Ride forward and report back to me as to under whose orders those men are on the field."

It took Meagher only five minutes to figure out what was going on.

"There is no official truce, General. The forward pickets 'reached an agreement,' sir, if you get my meaning."

"No agreements may be reached between privates, General."

"But General—'tis a job that needs doing."

"I am aware of that, General, but I am also ordered to shoot those men, and I do not have the authority to offer a truce."

"You may have the authority to *accept* one, though, sir, were it offered by them."

Hancock got his "meaning."

"Send a messenger across to General Pryor and inform him that any communication having for its object the collection of the wounded must proceed from them, expressing a desire, however, that they might be removed."

Meagher smiled and snapped off a salute. "Yes, sir."

"And General Meagher—have the courier inquire as to the health and condition of General Lewis Armistead. I will be grateful to know of him."

"Yes, sir."

While waiting on their arms for the battle to resume, most of the survivors took advantage of the time to write letters home, or to jot an entry or two in their journals. General John Gibbon took advantage of the time to do some writing as well: "Recommended for the Medal of Honor—Private John Cook, bugle boy, Battery B, 4th U.S. Artillery."

While the soldiers wrote home from Sharpsburg, a telegraph operator in Frederick whittled his way down through the pile of boring but important official documents until, well after noon, he reached George Smalley's ream. He rolled his eyes and started to set it aside, but then he read the opening sentence. *The greatest battle of the war was fought to-day, lasting from daylight till dark, and closing without a decisive result.* He remembered the ten-dollar bill in his pocket and struggled to find a justification for using the government's valuable time for personal profit. He placed it on top of his pile and coded out "To the War Department, Washington, D.C., from George W. Smalley, special correspondent to the *New York Daily Tribune* . . . *The greatest battle of the war was fought to-day* . . ."

* * *

"General Pryor sends his compliments, sir, and begs to inform the general that he too has no authorization to offer any truce for any purpose."

The disappointment registered on Hancock's face. He believed in military protocol—without it all would be senseless chaos. But here, today, because of it, hundreds of men who could have been comforted or even saved would die agonizing deaths while waiting for help from only twenty yards away.

"So be it, then. Order our men to cease the recovery operations in the field. Tell them to fire upon any Rebels attempting to advance beyond their current positions, and tell them also that I personally will shoot any of our men who make any excursions forward for the purpose of pilfering from the dead."

"Yes, sir . . . and General . . ."

"Yes?"

"General Pryor also says to inform you that General Armistead was wounded slightly in yesterday's battle. It is not thought serious."

"Thank God for that."

Abraham Lincoln knew only what McClellan chose to tell him, and since the beginning of the battle thirty-two hours ago, that had amounted to two wires, the most recent of which was six hours old and said only that *"the battle will probably be renewed today. Send all the troops you can by the most expeditious route."*

But now the lines at the War Department came alive once again. Lincoln, Edwin Stanton and Henry Halleck hovered over the shoulder of the transcriber as he wrote, *"The greatest battle of the war was fought today, lasting from daylight till dark . . ."*

The words came too quickly for anyone to speak or react.

". . . McClellan has partially carried the Rebel position . . ."

". . . Hooker, Sumner and Franklin . . . driven the enemy from the ground . . . On the Rebel right they have lost the bridge . . . The Rebels have everywhere lost ground . . . their rear and only line of retreat seriously threatened."

"Trapped," Halleck said. "It looks like we've got the whole damned lot of 'em trapped!"

Lincoln was pleased as well, but knew better than to celebrate too early. "The hen, General Halleck, is the wisest of all of God's creatures, for she never cackles until *after* the egg is laid."

It was not until fourteen paragraphs into Smalley's "short" story that the true scope of the battle began to come through.

"*Meade thrown back . . . Ricketts hard pressed . . . Mansfield mortally wounded . . . Hartstuff severely wounded . . . Hooker was wounded in the left foot . . . Sedgwick in the shoulder, leg and wrist . . . Gen. Dana, Gen. Richardson . . .*"

The list was staggering. "My, God," Halleck said. "We've lost some of our finest officers."

Stanton had taken a disliking to Halleck—in fact he had taken a disliking to anyone in the army over the rank of corporal. "We are not aware of the extent of any of their wounds other than Joe Mansfield's, may he rest in peace. I am certain that he died gallantly, as he would have wanted. I pray that all the rest survive, but, if this report is to be believed, and your Young Napoleon finishes the job today, their services may no longer be required."

Neither Lincoln nor Halleck reacted to Stanton's callous remarks as all three continued to read.

For "Neighbor" Jones the chest pains had finally become unbearable. He lay in bed lightly sedated and spoke to no one until James Longstreet came for a visit.

"Pete—what do you hear from the other side?"

"We have good information. What do you want to know?"

"The Eleventh Connecticut—I saw their colors yesterday at the bridge."

"They were engaged, Neighbor."

"Colonel Kingsbury—he commands the Eleventh. He's my sister's husband, Pete. If my men killed him . . ."

"We have reports that he was carried from the field following the first assault against the bridge, but I don't know the extent of his wounds. Shoot, Neighbor—we don't have any way of knowing for certain that it was him."

"God, Pete. Who would have thought that this damned thing would have gone on so long? Who would have thought that he and I would come face-to-face on the very same battlefield?"

Jones grabbed his chest and a doctor came over and placed a wet cloth on his face.

"Please, God . . . don't let him have died at the hands of my men. Oh, please God . . ."

Jones wept himself to sleep and Longstreet left the room.

Across the creek at the Rohrbach house, Ambrose Burnside also wept as the body of Henry Kingsbury was placed in a box for shipment home.

At 2:00 P.M. George Smalley boarded a military train bound for Baltimore. The stack of notes, his and those of the other *Tribune* correspondents, remained stuffed helter-skelter in his satchel. Since Hooker had launched his sunrise assault thirty-two hours ago, Smalley had had time only to wash his face. His plan was to organize the notes and write his story on the train, but the fitful sleep he had managed was not nearly enough, and he fell instantly asleep the moment he took his seat on the train and did not awake until the whistle blew in Baltimore. As soon as his feet hit the platform, he began to make his inquiries.

"Where is the telegraph office?"

"Just around on the other side of the building."

"When is the next train to New York?"

"Ten minutes off of track two."

"Damn."

Now he faced yet another dilemma. To get on the train, and write on his way to New York; or to sit on the platform to write, and risk another delay in transmitting what had to be a great many words.

"Is the telegraph office under military control?"

"You're in Baltimore, mister. *Everything* is under military control."

He bought a ticket and wrote on the train.

"Mein Gott." Samuel Mumma said, seeing his beautiful home in ashes. The corner posts and door frames only remained upright, and on one of them he found his pocket watch hanging from a nail. He wiped the soot

off on his shirt, and looked lovingly for a moment at his last remaining possession. His grandfather had brought it with him from Germany, and now all that the family had started with was all the family had left. *"Mein Gott,"* he whispered again and put the watch in his pocket and left behind the ashes of his home.

Every other structure in and around Sharpsburg remained intact—damaged, perhaps, but intact.

Even Ada Mumma returned to Grandpa Rohrbach's house next to Burnside's Bridge. The beautiful home, the one the general himself had warned would surely be demolished, remained standing on the hill overlooking the creek. But it was only the walls and the roof that appeared anything like what she had left behind. The grand old trees that stood behind the house were scarred and broken. The livestock that had run freely around the buildings for all of Ada's life was gone. But it would be a long time before she would notice any of these minor changes, for the yard and the house were filled with wounded soldiers. Ada had not had a happy moment since long before the battle began, but on seeing Grandma Rohrbach through the kitchen window, she broke into a run, almost tripping over the bodies that lay on her yard like leaves. She leaped over a pile of severed arms and legs as though it were a muddy puddle left by a summer rain. She wanted a hug. She couldn't see the exhaustion on Martha Rohrbach's face. She couldn't tell that her grandmother struggled only to remain standing, but she could tell that Grandma Rohrbach was not happy to see her in the middle of all of this.

"Oh, no, child," Grandma said when Ada was still half a room away. "You've got no business being here."

The seven-year-old stopped in her tracks, crushed to tears. All she wanted was a hug.

"Come here, baby. Grandma needs a hug."

Ada's pregnant mother lumbered through the house and was welcomed with a stern look as Martha still held Ada closely. "It's no better anyplace else, Momma. Daddy Mumma's farm is burned to the ground, and every house from here to Boonsboro is a hospital—or a morgue." She looked around her at all the wounded men lying on the floor of the house she grew up in and began to cry. "We had no place else to go, Momma."

Martha Rohrbach had one arm left free, and time enough for just one more hug.

James Wilson had awakened that morning hoping against hope that McClellan would prove him wrong and renew the assault. All that miserable day long he had ridden among the men, living, dead and wounded, and his anger dissolved into despondency. Thousands of brave and gallant men dead and thousands more maimed for life. And all for what?

Like the rest of the Army of the Potomac he sat under a tree, surrounded by tens of thousands of men and still alone with his thoughts. *Ten days ago I couldn't wait to get here, and now I can't wait to get away.*

"You Major Wilson?"

He looked up and saw a grizzled old sergeant standing over him.

"I am."

The man gave him one of those sloppy, reluctant salutes that old veterans tend to offer shave-tail young officers and said, "Sergeant Silbersack, sir, and I've spent most of the afternoon lookin' for you."

"Well, you've found me now." The salute was returned in the manner it was offered. "What can I do for you?"

"You got orders, sir." He handed the major a wire. "Seems I ain't the only one's been lookin' for you. General Halleck damn near reported you AWOL till some major reminded him you'd been sent up here."

"AWOL!"

"Not to worry, sir. It's all been taken care of. Anyways you're to report to Washington and from there to General Grant out West."

Wilson grinned. *Be careful what you wish for,* he thought.

"All right, Sergeant. Thank you."

Salutes were exchanged again and the sergeant was gone.

Grant, huh? He stood up and wiped the dirt off his butt. *Very well. Better a drunk than a coward.*

When the darkness finally fell on September 18th, Jeb Stuart's cavalry fired their torches and rode out into the Potomac, lighting the limits of the ford like a grand Parisian boulevard so that Lee's "lean and hungry set of wolves" could safely return to the welcoming arms of Old Virginia.

Illuminated by the torchlight, Lee sat astride Traveller, stirrup-deep in the waters of the river, and watched each and every man cross until, at last, in the early hours of Friday morning, General Walker rode up next to him.

"What remains behind?"

"Only a few ambulances and a battery of artillery, and they are close."

Only then did Lee relax. "Thank God," he said.

CHAPTER 16

A MATTER
OF INDIFFERENCE

SEPTEMBER 19TH

The Rebels have fled, sir—back to Virginia!"

The roar in McClellan's camp rivaled the sounds of the battle itself. Brave soldiers hugged and yelled and celebrated their hard-won victory. McClellan's eyes teared with pride and joy and relief. In his mind all of his critics had been silenced at last—once and for all time. *Maryland is saved—Pennsylvania is saved—the Union—the Republic—all saved and all saved by me! Lee is gone and Stanton, by God, soon will be. Who could now deny that I am the greatest general this nation has known since Washington himself?*

"General Porter!"

"Sir."

"Bring forward your corps, General, and make certain that every mother's son of them no longer soils the hallowed ground of these United States! I don't want a single Rebel left in Maryland!"

"Yes, sir!"

Porter was thrilled by the opportunity to grab some little part of the glory. His men moved out toward Boteler's Ford, where the Rebel rear guard allowed them to get waist-deep in the waters of the Potomac before they opened fire. It was a feisty action for a nip at the heels of a retreating army. Porter lost 250 men, but Lee, who had left behind forty-four guns, lost them all. Jackson ordered A. P. Hill to return to the ford, stop the pursuit and retrieve whatever guns he could.

In Washington the War Department filled with anxious officials hoping for news from the front. While the President of the United States waited, George McClellan wired his wife: *Our victory complete. Enemy has left his dead & wounded on the field. Our people now in pursuit. Your father and I are well.*

A cup of coffee and a cigar later, McClellan informed the civilian authorities in the nation's capital of all he felt they needed to know:

Henry Halleck
Headquarters, Army of the Potomac
   Near Sharpsburg, Sept. 19, 8:30 am. But little occurred yesterday except skirmishing, we being fully occupied in replenishing ammunition, taking care of wounded, etc. Last night the enemy abandoned his position leaving his dead & wounded on the field. We are again in pursuit. I do not yet know whether he is falling back to an interior position or crossing the river. We may safely claim a complete victory.

                                                                    G. B. McClellan
                                                                    Maj Gen

" 'In pursuit' my monkey's uncle. Mr. President, that son-of-a-bitch let all of yesterday go by without action. According to that newspaperman, Lee was trapped with the river to his back and was there for the killing, and I will wager a dollar to a dime that he is no more 'in pursuit' than a sheep pursues a wolf."

"And since when, Mr. Stanton, do you put so much faith in the reports of the *Tribune?*"

"Other than this flimsy excuse for a report, it is the only information that we have, Mr. President, and I assure you that it is more reliable than Mr. McClellan's."

"I pray to God that you are wrong, sir, and believe that you are." Lincoln lowered his tone to speak with Stanton alone. "Mr. Secretary—the nation needs a victory, and while an opportunity may have been missed, as far as the nation is concerned, a victory has been won." It was almost as if he were teaching a serious lesson to a small child. "I, for one, have no intention of stating otherwise. Gentlemen, please keep me informed of any fresh developments. I shall be in my office."

The President strolled happily across the lawn and bounded up the stairs three at a time. He spoke to the never-ending line of office seekers who perpetually snaked through the corridors of the Executive Mansion. John Hay went slack-jawed at the "Tycoon's" newfound exuberance. The President entered his office and went directly to his desk, where he removed a document from a drawer. His eyes went immediately to those all-important two words—"forever free"—the most important words he would ever write.

George Smalley sat under the light of the single candle and contemplated the most important words *he* would ever write. The farther he got away from the battle, and the more he delved into the notes of his colleagues, the more significant the events became. His previous effort had been hastily written, and lacked the appropriate drama. He had witnessed the most momentous event in the history of the nation and it was his duty to report it as such. His new story would have a new lead, written in the Smalley style, and reflecting the enormity of the day—the bloodiest single day in American history.

"Fierce and desperate battle between 200,000 men has raged since daylight, yet night closes on an uncertain field. The greatest fight since Waterloo— all over the field contested with an obstinacy equal even to Waterloo. If not wholly a victory tonight, I believe it is a prelude to victory tomorrow . . ." Smalley smiled to himself as he served the ball neatly into McClellan's court. *If he attacks and wins today, then I am a genius,* he thought. If he fails to attack, or if he attacks and loses, then he is a fool. And I have now kept my word to poor, old, overcautious Nathaniel. Damn, I'm good.

The story (and the hedging) continued: *"But what can be foretold of the future of a fight in which from 5 in the morning till 7 at night the best troops of the continent have fought without decisive result?*

"I have no time for speculation—no time even to gather the details of the battle—only time to state its broadest features—then mount and spur for New York."

He got off the train in Hoboken, New Jersey, and ferried over from the Manhattan Transfer. Once on the island he hired a carriage to the *Tribune*. He was surprised to find the offices and the presses quiet, but the silence erupted into cheers as every copy boy, writer and pressman stood and applauded Smalley's entrance. So shocked was he by the reception that he glanced briefly behind him to see who had followed him in, but the applause was for him. Not another paper in the city, and, as far as anyone knew, not another paper in the country had yet printed a word about the Battle of Antietam. Smalley, and Greeley, and the *New York Daily Tribune* had scooped the nation on the most important story of the century, and George Smalley was the hero of the war of the words.

Greeley had received both Smalley's note and the wire from the War Department. He noted that the original wire had been sent from Frederick and was certain from that that Smalley was on his way home with more copy on the battle. Based on his instincts, and his knowledge of his star reporter, he ordered the second edition of Saturday held for Smalley's arrival. The welcoming celebration was cut short by the deadline—everyone had work to do. Smalley pulled from his valise the worst assortment of scribbled notes ever seen by anyone there, and went straight to work, side by side with the typesetters.

John Hay noticed that the President was back in his office, a rarity with the eastern armies so close together. He entered unannounced and found Lincoln with his head down on his desk. Hay started to pull the drapes to allow the "Tycoon" his rest when Lincoln said, "No, John. Leave them be."

"I thought you were sleeping, sir."

"Would that I were, John."

The President leaned back in his chair and rubbed his eyes and breathed deeply. The silence was awkward.

"It looks like McClellan has finally brought you a victory."

"Has he? I wish I could be more certain. I wish I could be more certain of a great many things where the Young Napoleon is concerned."

Hay gave him a questioning look.

"He tells us that he is in pursuit of the Rebels. Secretary Stanton thinks not, and I tend to agree. McClellan's historical timidity tells me otherwise. For weeks he has been under orders to destroy the enemy. I do not know if it is tenacity, ability or desire that he lacks. It is the third of those that concerns me most."

"The desire, sir?"

"Too many rumors reach this desk of officers who fight battles with no desire whatsoever to win them. Their hope is to fight both armies to exhaustion and force us politicians into a negotiation that would result in a return to the Union as it was. At first, John, I ruled these rumors out. No soldier can . . ." The President closed his eyes tightly and rubbed his neck. A deep breath. "Maybe I simply chose not to believe them, but too many times I've heard it. Regardless, the Union 'as it was' will soon be gone forever. Tomorrow or Monday. Very soon."

Lincoln put his head back down on the desk and Hay drew the drapes.

George McClellan was truly not a well man. His recurring bouts of neuralgia attacked his entire face from the muscles around his forehead and his eyes, all the way down his neck and deeply into his right shoulder. During the worst attacks he ached so badly that he could do nothing but lie for hours in the dark with his eyes tightly closed against the pain. The disease struck him, it seemed, always at the worst of times, and this was one of those times. He rode in an ambulance from Keedysville to Sharpsburg, where the gruesome work of clearing the battlefield was under way. On the outskirts of town bodies were piled so deep that an unmounted man could not see over them. Ambulance trains that appeared miles long carted mutilated men off to points unknown. The carcasses of the fallen horses—hundreds of them—had to wait for the burial of the human carnage. Confederate dead were piled onto buckboards for transport to Frederick and disposal in mass, unmarked graves, far from the field of honor. Blood drained off the backs and through the planks of the wagons like crimson water off a washboard. After watching for only a minute, McClellan felt the return of the dreaded illness. He ordered Sumner to occupy Harper's Ferry and retired to the sterile environs of his Keedysville headquarters to recover.

SEPTEMBER 20TH

At dawn on Saturday Porter's troops were roused from their sleep by the rude awakening of the Rebel yell. A.P. Hill's troops stormed at them from three directions, and the Yankees, who slept on their arms, rose to defend themselves.

"Who the hell *is* this guy?" a young New Yorker asked.

"It's that damned Powell Hill again. I recognize those flags from Virginia."

"Ain't he the one who wanted to marry Mac's wife?"

"That's the one!"

"Damn it, Ellie—why didn't you marry *him*?"

The soldiers from the Empire State fought with brand-new Enfield rifles. The springs in the hammers were so lame that they did not strike the caps with enough force to ignite the charge, but the men couldn't tell in the noise and excitement of the moment that their weapons were not firing. Soldiers rammed round after round down the muzzles until many were six deep without a single shot being fired It was a rout, and the Yankees were in the river in fifteen minutes. Many died there from wounds or from drowning. Hill retrieved Lee's guns, and the Rebel withdrawal continued without interruption.

My dearest wife;

Am glad to say that I am much better today, for to tell you the truth I have been under the weather since the battle . . . Our victory was complete & the disorganized Rebel army has rapidly returned to Virginia—its dreams of "invading Penna" dissipated forever. I feel some little pride in having, with a beaten and demoralized army, defeated Lee so utterly, & saved the North so completely. Well—one of these days history will, I trust, do me justice in deciding that it was not my fault that the campaign of the Peninsula was not successful.

An opportunity has presented itself through the Governors of some of the states to enable me to take my stand. I have insisted that Stanton shall be removed & that Halleck shall give way to me as Comndr in Chief. I will not serve under him, for he is an incompetent fool, in no way fit for

*the important position he holds . . . The only safety for the country & for
me is to get rid of them—no success is possible with them. I am tired of
fighting against such disadvantages & feel it is now time for the country to
come to my help & remove these difficulties from my path. If my countrymen will not open their eyes & assert themselves they must pardon me if I
decline longer to pursue the thankless avocation of serving them.*

*I have shown that I can fight battles and win them! I think that my
enemies are pretty effectively killed by this time! May they remain so!!*

Tempers flared at the War Office. Stanton snapped at Halleck,
"Where in the *hell* is he? What in the *hell* is he doing? You are his commanding officer! *Find out!*"

Halleck angrily scribbled a dispatch for McClellan and threw it down
on the table in front of the telegraph operator. *"We are still left entirely in
the dark in regard to your own movements and those of the enemy. This should
not be so! You should keep me advised of both so far as you know them."*

Marcy was afraid that this was the time. McClellan looked about to
explode with anger.

"I told them absolutely everything I knew yesterday! Every communication I receive from these morons is couched in a spirit of fault-finding.
They have not found the time to say one word in commendation of this
army and the work that they did here. They have not even so much as
alluded to it!"

He looked around his tent, which was stacked high with the trappings
of conquest. Dozens of captured Confederate battle flags lay on the
ground on one side, and in another corner were piled the surrendered
swords of Rebel officers, maybe a hundred of them.

"Look at all of this, Marcy." He grabbed up a handful of sabers and
shook them in his father-in-law's face. "Abraham Lincoln should present
himself here and kiss these very boots. I have delivered him and the
nation from disaster and all I receive in return is chastisement for not
doing more!" He threw the sabers back down onto the pile with a terrible racket. "My future will be determined *this week*, General. A delegation of governors was through here yesterday and I took the stand with

them that Stanton must leave, and I be restored to my rightful position as General in Chief. They assured me that they would take this ultimatum to the President. Unless these two conditions are fulfilled, I will leave the service. I have done all that can be asked in *twice* saving the country! It is a matter of indifference to me whether they come to terms or not. Total indifference."

TO MAKE MEN FREE

Sunday is the Lord's Day, and this particular Sunday was allowed to pass in peace. Prayers went up from both sides of the Potomac, each certain that the Holy Father shared their particular view of the world and of the struggle.

Not so certain was Abraham Lincoln. Not a regular churchgoer, he attended early services on this particular Sabbath and returned to his desk to polish his proclamation, but the magnitude of it continued to frighten him. Once opened, this Pandora's box could never again be closed. All that would be closed was any possibility of a return to the Union as it was. He faced a decision that could never be rescinded. It was a decision the repercussions of which could not be anticipated. It was the most important decision he, or possibly any other president, would ever make. It had to be right.

It was his habit, when studying vital questions, to set down his thoughts on paper. He had no particular reason for doing so. These papers were not intended for publication, nor for inclusion as a part or parcel of any speech, but he loved the language and prided himself in his command of it. He viewed these essays as mental exercises and as a method of debating an issue with himself. Not a day had passed since

July 22nd, when he first proposed the proclamation to his cabinet, that the President had not thought about it. Hardly a day had passed since that time that he had not taken it from his desk and read it or changed it; admired it or prayed about it. Whenever he held it, for some reason he could not explain, he handled it gingerly—as though it were a fragile or hallowed thing. Tomorrow the journey toward freedom would take its final turn, God willing. Lincoln's only remaining question was if God, in fact, *was* willing. He set the Emancipation Proclamation aside for a moment, placed a clean sheet of paper on the desktop, dipped his pen into the well and wrote . . .

> *The will of God prevails. In great contests each party claims to act in accordance with the will of God. Both may be, and one must be, wrong. God cannot be for and against the same thing at the same time. In the present civil war it is quite possible that God's purpose is something different from the purpose of either party; and yet the human instrumentalities, working just as they do, are of the best adaptation to effect his purpose. I am almost ready to say that this is probably true; that God wills this contest, and wills that it shall not end yet. By his mere great power on the minds of the now contestants, he could have either saved or destroyed the Union without a human contest. Yet the contest began. And, having begun, he could give the final victory to either side any day. Yet the contest proceeds.*

He stopped and read back over what he had just put down. He read it again and stood and walked a few steps to look out of the window. Fall was now in her full splendor. Washington and Virginia across the river had donned God's coat of many colors in preparation for the coming winter. The weather was fine, the day was clear and the roads were firm; and yet McClellan sat frittering away these few, precious good days that remained before the army would no longer be able to move.

"There must be something more," he said, aloud to himself. "In God's eye, there must be something more—a higher issue than Union alone."

John Hay entered to find the "Tycoon" with his head bowed and his eyes closed, but Hay couldn't tell if he was praying or simply resting his eyes. Lincoln looked up and nodded to his young secretary before tossing one paper away and placing another in his desk drawer. Hay reminded him of an appointment for which he was late and Lincoln thanked him and left the room. Hay retrieved and read the President's discarded essay. He then returned to his private quarters and placed it into the pages of his diary, for posterity.

SEPTEMBER 22ND

Gideon Welles came to the Executive Mansion early on Monday for a special meeting called by the President. He was early, but not first. He approached the cabinet room anticipating a serious meeting, for the President had long since stopped holding such gatherings without purpose. He was surprised, then, to hear the sounds of laughter (mostly that of the President himself) coming from the hallowed halls. *It has been a very long time*, Welles thought, *since I have heard that laugh*.

"Father Neptune," Lincoln said as the Navy Secretary entered, "you are just in time for a slight bit of entertainment before we set about the business of the day. Mr. Ward has sent me a copy of his most recent work and it has in it a chapter that I found most amusing. It is called 'High-Handed Outrage in Utica.' You all know the style in which Artemus Ward writes, so I shall attempt to emulate his patterns of speech as written."

Around the room there was subtle eye-rolling as the President began.

" 'In the fall of 1856,' " Lincoln read, " 'I showed my show in Utiky, a trooly grate sitty in the State of New York. One day what was my skorn & disgust t' see a big burly feller walk to the cage containin' my wax figgers of the Lord's Last Supper, and cease Judas Iscarrot by the feet and drag him out on the ground. He then commenced to pound him as hard as he cood. "What under the son are you abowt?" cried I.*

" 'Sez he, "What did you bring this pussylanermus cuss here for?" ' "

Here Lincoln began to bounce around in his chair like a tall, thin, ugly puppet.

" 'Sez I, "You egrejus ass, that air's a wax figger." '

" 'Sez he, "That's all well fer you t' say, but I tell you, old man, that Judas Iscarrot can't show hisself in Uticky with impunerty by a darn site!" with which observasun he kaved in Judassis hed.' "

Whether it was the story, or the language, or the sight of the President of the United States bouncing around in a chair making faces, no one could tell, but the entire cabinet (with the exception of Stanton, who had not so much as smiled since the cradle) broke into laughter. Lincoln continued to laugh as he held up his hand to regain their attention.

"*'The young man belonged to 1 of the first famerlies of Uticky. I sood him and the joory brawt in a verdick of Arson in the 3rd degree.'*"

No one enjoyed the "entertainment" more than Abe himself. He often thought of himself as an undiscovered actor. Even in the old days back in Springfield the part of lawyering he enjoyed most was being the center of attention in the courtroom, where he could put on a bit of a show for the "joory." Lincoln laughed so hard he couldn't talk—God, it had been months since he had laughed so hard.

Seward was the last to arrive. Lincoln stood up and greeted the Secretary of State by putting his arm around his shoulder, which added to the lightness of the moment as the President stood a full foot or more taller.

"Well, well. The State Department has finally arrived—punctual to a fault and thereby missing the festivities. Or, should I say, the frivolities?"

The other members welcomed Seward and soon all were seated. In that moment, Lincoln's mood shifted 180 degrees.

"If we could all gather round now, I have some urgent business. Gentlemen: I have, as you are aware, thought a great deal about the relation of the war to slavery; and you all remember that, several weeks ago, I read to you an order I had prepared on this subject, which, on account of objections made by some of you, was not issued. Ever since then, my mind has been much occupied with this subject and I have thought all along that the time for acting on it might very probably come. I think the time has come now."

Lincoln saw the look of incredulity on several faces. The agreement had been to wait for a victory, and these expressions told Lincoln quickly and in no uncertain terms that a great many of these men felt strongly that the wait was not yet over. He held up his hand and looked sternly at Seward.

"I wish it were a better time. I wish we were in a better condition. The action of the army against the Rebels has not been quite what I should have best liked. But they have been driven out of Maryland, and Pennsylvania is no longer in danger of invasion. When the Rebel army was at Frederick, I determined, as soon as it should be driven out of Maryland, to issue a proclamation of emancipation such as I thought most likely to be useful. I said nothing to anyone; but I made the promise to myself— and to my Maker. The Rebel army is now driven out, and I am going to fulfill that promise. God has decided this question in favor of the slaves.

"This I say without intending anything but respect for any one of you, but I already know the views of each on this question. They have been hitherto expressed, and I have considered them as thoroughly and carefully as I can. What I have written is that which my reflections have determined me to say. If there is anything in the expressions I use, or in any other minor matter, which any one of you thinks had best be changed I shall be glad to receive the suggestions. One other observation I will make. I know very well that many others might, in this matter, as in others, do better than I can; and if I were satisfied that the public confidence was more fully possessed by any one of them than by me, and knew of any constitutional way in which he could be put in my place, he should have it. I would gladly yield it to him. But though I believe that I have not so much confidence of the people as I had some time since, I do not know that, all things considered, any other person has more; and, however this may be, there is no way in which I can have any other man put where I am. I am here. I must do the best I can, and bear the responsibility of taking the course which I feel I ought to take."

Not a man spoke or moved or even cleared his throat as Lincoln read slowly through the document. It offered "pecuniary aid" to the loyal slave states should they voluntarily adopt measures that would now or in the future abolish slavery within their particular borders. It promised to continue efforts to colonize "persons of African descent" upon this continent or elsewhere. Even the concept of compensation had found its way back into the document. Loyal slave owners would be paid for their slaves upon the restoration of constitutional relations. When he had finished, the room remained quiet for some time before the discussion began.

In the end it was Seward who cracked open the door and began the debate. "The general question having been decided," the Secretary of State recommended changes in the wording so as to perpetuate the document beyond the term of the incumbent. The question was seconded by Chase and approved by the President.

Montgomery Blair held his tongue for as long as he could. "My position on the issue is well known, sir, and I modestly request permission to offer up a memorandum expressing my opposition."

"That is your right and your prerogative, General Blair, but your views are welcome here as well."

"First, every man in this room is aware of the fact that with conditions I do not oppose the abolition of slavery. It is the timing and the method to which I object. Beyond the fact that it is obviously unconstitutional, I believe that the lives lost in the defense of Maryland will have gone for naught because the release of this policy, even though Maryland is exempted by it, will push her and the other Border States into the rebellion, regardless of your efforts to accommodate them. The fall of Washington will then quickly follow. This will then have a demoralizing effect upon the entire nation in general and upon the members of the army in particular. The army will respond badly at any rate. We are all aware that the bulk of the officer corps opposes such an uncompromising position, but the rank and file, sirs, could well revolt. There exists yet another concern that I have, though it pertains again primarily to the timing of the matter. We will be placing into the hands of the Democrats, I fear, a club with which to beat us in the coming elections."

"You understand, General Blair, that I have given all of these matters close consideration. As to the Border States, perhaps they will attempt to leave us, and perhaps not. Regardless, we must make the forward movement. They will acquiesce—if not immediately, soon; for they must be satisfied that slavery has received its death blow *from the slave owners*. It cannot survive the rebellion. As to the officer corps—they are my responsibility to control, and the rank and file, theirs. As to the Democrats, their clubs will be used against us whatever course we take."

Another silence followed, this time interrupted by Secretary Stanton. "It is a momentous document, sirs, and there are three men here who have not yet taken a favorable stand. A united front is urgent in this matter—Mr. Chase?"

The Treasury Secretary couldn't resist taking one last try at his favorite lost cause.

"I must state, once again, that we should take advantage of this opportunity to begin the enlistment of colored troops into . . ."

The cabinet didn't let him finish. They filled the room with groans of total exasperation. Blair was the one who spoke. "If you arm the slaves, I will join the rebellion!"

"Gentlemen—move on," Lincoln said.

"Mr. Chase—are you for or against?"

"For."

"Mr. Welles?"

The Navy Secretary said it was a military necessity and he would see to it that the Navy would comply with and enforce the order.

"That leaves only Mr. Blair in opposition."

The Postmaster General thought in silence for a moment and said, "As it is the timing and the method of the executive action to which I object, and a written objection might well be misconstrued, and as I agree with the major purpose of the document, in the interest of unanimity, I shall withdraw my objection."

Silence. Every man in the room sat alone with his thoughts and fears. Every man in the room prayed. Thy will be done.

"Very well then. So it shall be done. Mr. Seward . . ." Lincoln gingerly handed him the precious paper, ". . . add to it what you must to make it legal and we shall announce it tomorrow."

On the field at Sharpsburg, the burial details continued. Carcasses of dead horses were piled and burned, making the air black and rancid. The men on their morbid mission covered their faces to protect themselves from the stench. Most of the corpses of both sides had been stripped of anything of value before the Rebels had fled on Friday. Hardly a body wore a decent pair of shoes—the Rebels never had any, and many of the Yankees had been robbed of theirs by the Southerners either during the battle on Wednesday or the cease-fire on Thursday and good shoes, even in the Union army, were far too valuable to bury.

The digging of individual graves even for the victors became pure folly as the black and bloated bodies cooked in the near ninety-degree heat. Union soldiers laid out their own comrades forty to a grave in long, shallow trenches.

McClellan was nowhere to be seen.

The amputations were done. The wounded who could travel were slowly being shipped to Hagerstown, or Frederick, or back to Washington. Those more seriously wounded—those who were not expected to survive—remained in Sharpsburg. Joe Hooker returned to the capital. Israel Richardson remained at the Pry house.

Clara Barton, who could not have claimed eight hours' sleep in the last seventy-two, climbed up into one of her wagons. Her supplies were gone, and so were the army's, and she could offer no further help here. She slept in the back of a buckboard as it bounced and creaked its way back to Washington.

By now family members from Alabama to Massachusetts moved on Maryland in numbers almost as great as the armies themselves. Oliver Wendell Holmes, Sr., stumbled around the battlefield grimly looking into the face of each and every cadaver he saw. He prayed a thousand times, "Please don't let it be him," and a thousand times he gave his thanks. He finally located Captain LaDuc, the sender of the bad news, who informed him that the younger Holmes was well, and on his way to Hagerstown.

Across the river in a home commandeered for use as a Rebel hospital, a doctor warned the five-times-wounded Colonel John Brown Gordon that the missus had come all the way up from Georgia. She waited in the next room, insisting that she would be delayed not a moment longer. Gordon rose from the bed, his leg splinted, his arm slung and his face covered with a blood-soaked bandage that left all but the eyes to the horrors of the imagination.

"Well, my dear," he said, "you've found him. You've found your handsome husband at last."

Lincoln read McClellan's most recent dispatch, and the very familiarity of it almost brought tears to his eyes:

> *When I was assigned to the command of this army in Washington, it was suffering under the disheartening influence of defeat. It had been greatly reduced by casualties in Gen. Pope's campaign, and its efficiency had been much impaired. The sanguinary battles fought by these troops at South Mountain and Antietam Creek have resulted in a loss to us of 10 general officers and many regimental and company officers, besides a large num-*

ber of enlisted men. The army corps have been badly cut up and scattered by the overwhelming numbers brought against them in the battle of the 17th instant, and the entire army has been greatly exhausted by unavoidable overwork, hunger, and want of sleep and rest. When the enemy recrossed the Potomac the means of transportation at my disposal was inadequate to furnish a single day's supply of subsistence in advance. Under these circumstances, I did not feel authorized to cross the river in pursuit of the retreating enemy, and thereby place that stream—which is liable at any time to rise above a fording stage—between this army and its base of supply.

Since his heroics at Sharpsburg, Powell Hill had glowed in the light of his success, but the glow was dimmed by the recollection of his humiliation at the hands of Stonewall at Chantilly. Nothing more had been said in the meantime, and Hill retained his command without comment, but this was not good enough for a gentleman of his stature. Dishonor and injustice had been done him and he had no intentions of allowing the matter to die a graceful death. The words "neglect of duty" stung in his memory. "Neglect of *duty!*" It was the same to him as neglect of God, or of country. No man of conscience could allow that blot to remain even tacitly on his name, and A. P. Hill was a man of conscience. He put his complaints in writing.

As he read Hill's document, a curse word actually passed through Jackson's mind that would never pass his lips. "I respectfully represent," Hill wrote, "that I deem myself to have been treated with injustice and censured and punished at the head of my command, and request that a Court of Inquiry be granted me."

Jackson's anger at his least-favorite general flared again as strong and hateful as on the day that Hill had disobeyed the mandated rest period. He immediately sat at his desk, referred to his diary of Hill's transgressions, and composed a lengthy and bitter statement of charges and forwarded the whole package to General Lee for action.

It was just the sort of thing Lee hated most.

Seward returned to the Executive Mansion with the legal language appropriately inserted into the Emancipation Proclamation. The entire cabinet, including Blair, returned without being summoned to witness the event. The Secretary of State placed the document on the President's desk and stood aside to watch with the others.

Lincoln had been in office now almost exactly a year and a half, and throughout that time his official signature had been "A. Lincoln." Whether signing a letter or a law, it was always "A. Lincoln." Strong. Confident. Familiar. Now he took his pen and dipped it into the well. He dabbed it onto a blotter to be certain that it would not drip. He hesitated a moment as his hand shook briefly. He steadied himself, said a brief, private prayer and, with his hand still shaking, he signed the Emancipation Proclamation—"Abraham Lincoln."

CHAPTER 18

SUCH AN ACCURSED DOCTRINE

The war in the East was not the only war. Robert E. Lee's incursion into Maryland was not the Confederacy's only encroachment into the loyal Border States, and neither was George McClellan's procrastination unique in the Union army.

"Out West," Confederate Generals Braxton Bragg and Kirby Smith had marched in timely concert with Lee into Kentucky. Their successes brought them so close to Cincinnati that a panic gripped Ohio. The Rebel army had moved so far north that it had outstripped its supply lines and was compelled to halt. Smith held Lexington, Bragg was fifty miles away in Bardstown and Union General Don Carlos Buell waited in Louisville for the Rebels to resume the initiative.

As he wrote out the orders, Halleck had to wonder. Maybe it was because Kentucky was the state of his birth that made Lincoln decide to act there and not in Maryland. Maybe it was the incessant reports of discontent within the Army of the Ohio that made him believe that Buell was vulnerable while the well-loved McClellan was protected. Maybe it was an opportunity to send a powerful message to the Young Napoleon without the risk of political disaster. That was one thing Halleck had learned well in his two months in the capital; the war outside of this city is between the North and the South, but inside of Washington it's between Democrats and Republicans, and, in its own way, the political war is no less bloody. Whatever the reason, Lincoln could tolerate no more. With instructions to refrain from delivering any message if he found Buell engaged in battle, or preparing to do battle, a courier left from Washington on this day with Halleck's orders relieving General Buell and placing George Thomas in command.

That night, the President sat in the drawing room of the Executive Mansion and spoke softly with Mary, trying to calm her from her most recent tirade. Her expenses were again being ridiculed by the Democrats on Capitol Hill, and Mary railed at the President that he surely had the power to put a halt to their incessant meddling in her personal affairs. Mrs. Lincoln placed Mr. Lincoln in an impossible situation because the Congress was right and the President knew it. Their family conversation halted when he heard a commotion on the lawn below his window. The day had gone quietly with still no news from McClellan, no news of servile uprisings resulting from the release of the proclamation and no rebellion (as yet) by the enlisted men in the army. Now the sounds of hundreds of people milling around the lawn reached his ears and he feared for a moment that it might well be a lynch mob. Mary was offended by the intrusion.

"Now darn it, Father! You would think that those people had more of a right to your attention than even I do!"

"Rest your soul, Mother. No one has more of a right to me than you do. But this must be seen to, and I promise that I shall return. You be thinking of what we have said here, and I will be back in only a moment."

The President opened the French windows and heard the cheers of a thousand or more abolitionists gathered below. Lighted by a hundred torches and a thousand candles, they began to chant "Speech—speech—speech." He didn't know what to say. He didn't know who they were or why they were here. Taken totally and pleasantly by surprise, he did the best he could.

"I appear before you to do little more than acknowledge the courtesy you pay me and to thank you for it. I have not been distinctly informed why it is that on this occasion you appear to do me this honor, though I suppose it is because of the proclamation. What I did, I did after a very full deliberation, and under a very heavy and solemn sense of responsibility. I can only trust in God I have made no mistake. I shall make no attempt on this occasion to sustain what I have done or said by any comment. It is now for the country and the world to pass judgment, and maybe take action upon it."

Mary joined him at the window and listened as the deeply moved crowd sang the anthem of their movement. In the light of the torches they could see that grown men cried as they sang, "As He died to make men holy / Let us die to make men free / As God goes marching on."

"This is an abomination! The man has no legal or moral right to enforce his radical views on the nation by some kind of executive *fiat!*" McClellan yelled so loudly at his father-in-law and Fitz-John Porter that it brought tears to his own eyes from the pain of his neuralgia.

"Once the Rebels are gone from this place, my friends, so shall I be. It is very doubtful that I shall be able to remain in the service."

"Mac. Think about what you are saying," Marcy said. "You have twice saved the Union. The nation needs you. And think—with whom will the government replace you? Burnside? Sumner?"

"The nation may well need me, sir, but those of us in this tent seem to be the only people on the face of this earth who understand that. But this proclamation and the continuation of Stanton and Halleck in office make it almost impossible for me to retain my commission and self-respect at the same time. I cannot make up my mind to fight for such an accursed doctrine as that of a servile insurrection—it is too infamous. Stanton is as great a villain as ever and Halleck as great a fool—he has no brains whatever!"

"There is not a man in this army who will argue with anything you've said, Mac." If anything, Porter was angrier even than McClellan. "These are the absurd proclamations of a political coward."

Marcy continued to dwell on his son-in-law's threatened resignation. "I must caution you though, George, not to react too hastily." He had selected the word deliberately as he knew McClellan could not tolerate the thought of being considered "hasty." "There are a great many options to be considered, and resignation at this moment may be tantamount to surrender. Perhaps by one method or another, this 'accursed doctrine,' as you call it, may be reversed."

"By what methods?"

"You have political friends from Maine to Kentucky who will gladly follow your lead." He hesitated for a moment before he continued, knowing full well the significance of what he was about to say. "And, for at least as long as you hold your command, this army will do whatever you say."

The three men sat in silence for a long moment while they considered the implications of what had just been said. Then a wave of fear ran through Marcy's spine and he decided to back off a step before this went too far.

"Again, George—just mind your options and, at least for the moment, retain your commission. Without it, you have no options at all."

SEPTEMBER 25TH

We have heard nothing to date regarding blood being spilled anywhere in response to the proclamation, Mr. President." As a part of John Hay's secretarial responsibilities it was his job to keep Lincoln apprised of the public mood.

"The loyal governors have adjourned their meeting in Altoona and issued a statement promising continued support for the war effort and there is some tacit support for the proclamation as well. Only the Border States and New Jersey refused to sign. The governor of New Jersey, as you know, is a Democrat and a friend of McClellan's."

"Any mention of McClellan in the document?"

"No, sir."

"That is, to me, a very good sign, John. Do you agree?"

"Of course it is, sir. There are no signs yet of any uprisings anywhere—even in Maryland or Kentucky. The opposition is coming primarily from the Democratic politicians."

"Ah. The 'club' the Postmaster General warned us of has been quickly unsheathed."

"Yes, sir. The party platform in New York calls the proclamation, ah, let's see . . ." He pulled out an article from the *New York Times* "Yes—'a proposal for the butchery of women and children . . . ' "

"Oh, my. They do strike early and low, don't they?"

"It goes on, sir. ' . . . For scenes of lust and rapine and of arson and murder.' And Mr. Seymour . . ."

"He's their candidate for governor?"

"Yes, sir. He says, 'If it be true that slavery must be abolished to save this Union, then the people of the South should be allowed to withdraw.' "

Lincoln leaned forward in his chair and groaned.

"In Ohio, I have a quote here, but don't know who it's from, someone in the party said, 'In the name of God, no more bloodshed to gratify a religious fanaticism,' and the party slogan has been unofficially altered. What was 'The Constitution as it is—The Union as it was,' now reads, 'The Constitution as it is—The Union as it was—and the niggers where they are.' "

"These people are fools, John. The whole grand experiment of democracy is at stake here. Majority rule is out the window. If *we* fail then *democracy* fails, here and everywhere. Do they not . . ." Lincoln stopped in midsentence, realizing that he was preaching to the choir. " 'The Union as it was.' You know, John, that that is no longer possible. Once the news of our little piece of paper reaches the ears of the colored people down South, slavery will be dead forever."

Hay only nodded. He knew the "Tycoon" as well as anyone, but even he had trouble figuring out where the sermon began and where it ended. Besides, he loved listening to the man talk, so he made it a point never to rush in before he was certain that the President had completed his thought.

"And speaking of 'the Union as it was,' John, have we heard any additional rumors from our friends in the military regarding organized efforts to fight this war to a draw?"

"As a matter of fact, sir, we have. It seems that a young major with connections to McClellan's staff stated the principle as though it were gospel for all to hear at Willard's very shortly after Antietam. I have the man's name, sir, and the name of the man with whom he was speaking."

"And they are . . . ?"

"Let me see, here. Major John Key is the culprit, sir, and he was speaking with Major Levi Turner."

"Key?"

"Yes, sir. His brother is Colonel Thomas Key, who serves in some capacity on General McClellan's staff."

"And he said in public that the army followed a deliberate pattern of failure in an attempt to force a return to the prewar status quo?"

"So it has been reported, sir."

"Let's locate those two young men, John, and bring them here. A stop must be put to this, my friend, and this little incident may provide us with an opportunity to demonstrate that it will not be tolerated."

"Yes, sir."

"And, John . . ."

"Sir?"

"There is a new development that I hope you will be able to gauge the public response to. I have expanded the suspension of *habeas corpus* where it applies to persons discouraging enlistments or encouraging or aiding in the rebellion anywhere in the nation. There may be some adverse reaction and I should be interested to know of it."

A messenger from the War Office knocked and entered. He gave the President a note from Edwin Stanton attached to a dispatch from McClellan. The note read, "We now base our military strategies on the opinions of Rebel officers' wives." The dispatch read:

> *The wife of a Confederate officer, who arrived in Sharpsburg today from Virginia, told her father—a Union man—that the entire Rebel army which was left from the battle of the 17th instant was still opposite us, awaiting reenforcements from Gordonsville; that the Rebels expected to give us another battle between here and Winchester, and were anxious for us to cross the river.*

SEPTEMBER 26TH

While the politicians concerned themselves with military matters, the generals concerned *themselves* with politics. McClellan followed his father-in-law's advice and studied his options in the light of the political developments. He began a letter-writing campaign to see what support might be his should he decide to act—one way or the other. To William Aspinwall, an old friend from the railroad days and an influential New York Democrat, he wrote:

> *I am very anxious to know how you and men like you regard the recent Proclamations of the President inaugurating servile war, emancipating the slaves, & at one stroke of the pen changing our free institutions into a despotism—for such I regard as the natural effect of the last Proclamation suspending Habeas Corpus throughout the land.*
>
> *I shall probably be in the vicinity for some days, & if you regard the matter as gravely as I do, would be glad to communicate with you.*

Fitz-John Porter enlisted in McClellan's army of letter writers with all the enthusiasm of a new recruit, and was not nearly so cautious as his commander. To the Democratically inclined *New York World* he wrote that ". . . the proclamation was ridiculed in the army—caused disgust, discontent and expressions of disloyalty to the views of the administration and amount, I have heard, to insubordination . . . All such bulletins tend to prolong the war by rousing the bitter feelings of the South . . . (It) will go far towards producing an expression on the part of the Army that will startle the country and give us a Military Dictator."

Not all of the letters postmarked at Sharpsburg that night advocated so drastic a solution to the question. Barton Mitchell penned another letter home as well:

> *Momma;*
>
> *The doctors tell me that they're gonna have to leave the bullet in me. It's too close to my heart to try to take out, but I can't even feel it in there. They say I'll probly be all right but they're gonna keep me here for a while til I can move around better. I may even be able to come home for a spell. I don't know how much help I'll be, but I sure would love to see home again.*
>
> *All the army is talking about Uncle Abe's new proclamation about the niggers. Some say it's long overdue and now they have somthin to fight for and some say they'd rather pack their bags and take their chances with the law rather than die for the darkies. I don't know. If I ever get well I'll go*

back to fightin to save the Union for as long as they need me I suppose. Nothin should stand in the way of the Union—niggers nor anything else, but seems to me we should win the war first and worry bout the slaves later. Most of the smart ones think slavery is gonna be gone one way or the other, but if that's true then what's all the fuss about?

I'm having some little trouble with Blossie. Lots of people are making a big thing out of that piece of paper I found back before the battle, talking about how important it was and all, and now, all of the sudden Blossie's tellin everybody that he found it. He was there when I found it, but I was the one who saw it lying there and picked it up and all. He just took it out of my hands and read some of the words and it was him that gave it to the captain, but I found it and now he's tellin everybody that he did. We've been friends for a long time and it hurts seeing him try to take the credit for somethin good I did. I don't know if he's tellin everybody back home that it was him or not, but please tell Jemima that it was me that found it and not John. I want her to know at least.

SEPTEMBER 27TH

Again the amateurs in the government pressed McClellan to move, to make battle and to make headlines before the army was ready, and again he had to take time away from his busy schedule to lecture baboons in the fundamentals of elementary logistics. To Halleck he wired: "... *This Army is not now in condition to undertake another campaign ... the old regiments are reduced to mere skeletons ... retain in Washington merely the force necessary to garrison it and to send everything else available to reinforce this Army.*"

"Gentlemen, please come in and be seated."

The President indicated two ladder-back chairs that had been placed opposite his desk, and Majors Turner and Key took their seats.

"It is my understanding that the two of you were overheard at the Willard last week discussing military strategy, and that you, Major Key, expressed the opinion that certain of our generals were fighting this war with something other than a complete military victory as the goal." Both men were astounded that the President of the United States even knew

about the barroom conversation, much less that he would attach any significance to it. Neither could conceal his amazement. The President
continued. "I am very anxious to hear the totality of that conversation.
Major Turner, please begin." Lincoln placed a sheet of clean white paper
on his desk, dipped his pen into the well, looked up at the startled youngster and awaited his reply.

"As I remember it, the conversation was, I asked the question why we
did not bag them after the battle of Sharpsburg. Major Key's reply was,
'That is not the game; the object is that neither army shall get much
advantage of the other; that both shall be kept in the field till they are
exhausted when we shall make a compromise and save slavery.' He said
that was 'the only way the Union could be preserved, if we come
together fraternally and slavery be saved.'"

"Is that, in fact, Major Key, what was said?"

"It is, sir."

Rather than prompt additional information, Lincoln simply looked at
the young major and raised his eyebrows and waited for one or the other
of them to continue.

Key hated Lincoln. Almost everybody did. His anger welled up, and
he took the offensive. "The point of the conflict as we understand it, sir,"
he said, more as though he were speaking to a child rather than the President of the United States, "is to preserve the Union. For that noble purpose I believe all of us are prepared to die. The Union *without* slavery can
never exist without the killing of every man, woman and child of the
South. A return to the Union as it was is the only possible solution.
There is nothing treasonous in what I said, or in what I believe, Mr.
President, and if it be, then there are thousands of traitors fighting and
dying for the Union every day."

"Mr. President. I have conversed with Major Key on many occasions
regarding the current difficulties, and never once have I heard him utter
a word that could be construed as treason or even disloyalty. I have not
heard a single sentiment unfavorable to the maintenance of the Union.
Our conversation at Willard's, sir, was a private one."

Again Lincoln waited for either party to continue. This time neither
did.

"Major Key—if there *is* a game, even among Union men, to have our army *not* take every advantage of the enemy whenever it can, then it is my object to break up that game. Thank you for your time, gentlemen."

Lincoln watched as the two officers stood, saluted and left the room. At the bottom of the papers where he had taken his notes, the President wrote, "In my view, it is wholly inadmissible for any gentleman holding a military commission from the United States to utter such sentiments as Major Key is within proved to have done. Therefore, let Major John J. Key be forthwith dismissed from the military service of the United States."

He handed the document to John Hay, who read it and allowed the surprise to register on his face.

"Do you think it drastic, John?"

"It seems a harsh treatment, sir, for an after-dinner conversation."

"I am dismissing Major Key because I think his silly, treasonable expressions are 'staff talk.' I wish to make an example. No, John—of course it is not fair. But the talk must stop before it becomes policy"— he glanced down at McClellan's most recent set of excuses which remained on his desktop—"if it has not already—and this action, I hope, will stop it."

That evening there was "staff talk" of a more serious nature. The mails were slow and responses to his political inquiries would take time in arriving, so McClellan decided that it was time for the military minds to be consulted. A dinner was prepared and Generals Burnside, Cox and John Cochrane were invited to attend. These were military men, general officers, whom McClellan knew to have the confidence of the administration and he needed to know their reaction to the proclamations. He also needed to know on which side they would fall should a drastic decision have to be made.

Burnside thought he put up a good front, but throughout the meal McClellan's former closest friend contributed little to the conversation.

After the meal, enlisted men cleared the table and provided cigars for all of the guests. McClellan then turned the conversation to politics.

"Gentlemen—I should like to seek your advice on a matter of grave concern to me, and, I believe, to the nation. The President's recent dictates regarding emancipation and the further suspension of *habeas corpus* seem to me to be, to say the very least, drastic. First, and do not misunderstand me on this matter, I must say that I do not oppose emancipation. Slavery as an institution, I feel certain, is quite dead. It is *not*, however, the issue of this war." He looked to his guests to see what their reactions might be, but there were none. "The abolition of slavery should be carried out gradually over a period of time which will allow for the economic ramifications of the matter to settle themselves. It should *not*, in my estimation, be allowed to interfere with the proper conduct of the war. The Rebels, who might be convinced to reenter the Union as it was, will never consent to terms that must deprive them of their livelihoods, and the war, therefore, will be further drawn out and made more difficult, if not impossible, to win. It is a matter of high principle to me that the issue of this conflict is that of Union—nothing more, and nothing less!" He realized that he had begun to shout, so he readjusted his volume and his posture. "It is further a matter of high principle to me that I cannot participate further if it is to become a servile insurrection—which the recent proclamation seeks to make it."

A sip of wine and a brief glance around the table and McClellan then plunged into the heart of the matter. "I have recently been approached by respected and influential citizens and by officers of highest rank in the army, and urged by them to take a public position against it."

Then, quietly and almost in passing, he sent his guests into shock.

"There is little doubt that I have the total support of this army . . ."

Burnside went pale and very nearly dropped his cigar. He remembered instantly the officers back on the Peninsula who threatened to "move this army *against* Washington, remove those old women in the government and run this war as it should be run!" He could still see the man's face lighted by the campfire and hear his angry and frustrated words just as they had been spoken. He remembered his own reaction as he shouted at the men that this was "flat treason, by God," and he wanted to say the same words now, but the words wouldn't come. Surely Mac couldn't be considering such a thing, but what else could he mean? "Total support of the army." What else could he mean? Burnside said a brief prayer and listened more intently, desperately hoping he was wrong.

". . . They will as one man enforce any decision I should make . . ."

McClellan saw very quickly that he had broached the subject too quickly and raised his hand to stop any interruption.

". . . the nature of which has not yet been determined. It is, in fact, that determination—the nature of my response—that I seek your advice on."

Cox and Cochrane began to speak at once. Burnside remained seated in shocked silence. It occurred to him that if McClellan responded in any way other than total compliance that he would be relieved of duty, and that if McClellan should exit the picture then he—Burnside—would once again be offered command of the army, an offer that he had already accepted in advance. The room began to spin around him and he blamed the cigar and put it out, half smoked.

Cochrane yielded to his superior officer and Jacob Cox spoke first.

"As you have brought us here to seek our advice, I assume that we are free to speak frankly."

"Of course."

"I speak only for myself when I say that I believe the Emancipation Proclamation to be both a political *and* a military matter. It is clear that the slave labor in the South sustains their troops in the field. Anything that might reduce that support equally reduces their strength. This is the stated purpose of the document. It is issued by the Commander in Chief and therefore may be construed as a direct order."

Here Cox glanced around the room to see if he had support on his flanks or if he proceeded at his own risk. Burnside nodded, Cochrane smiled and Cox continued.

"General McClellan, it is my firm belief, as a military man, and the politics of the matter aside, that anything short of at least tacit compliance could well be seen as insubordination or worse. It might well be viewed as usurpation." His throat went suddenly dry and he desperately wanted to sip his wine, but first he had to finish what he had begun. "I recommend, sir, that your only possible reaction is no reaction at all."

McClellan looked to Cochrane, who only nodded and said, "Agreed."

Then he went to Burnside and looked in his direction a long while before Burn spoke without so much as a glance McClellan's way.

"Mac—for as long as you hold your commission, any effort on your part to oppose this doctrine will be a fatal error. Your military career will be over and your political career threatened. There is no doctrine more sacred in our land than that of civilian authority over the military. In our line of work we sometimes find that doctrine regrettable, but it forms the very heart of all of our most cherished institutions. Forget that, George, for one single instant, and this army, which we all agree will follow you gladly to the grave, as we all just saw—they will abandon you, George. If you should choose to disobey *your* orders, how can you expect them to follow theirs? You will lead the charge and turn to find not a man behind you. They will all be gone . . ." He looked up for the first time at his old best friend and felt sorry for him. For the first time in twenty years of friendship, Ambrose Burnside looked into the face of George McClellan and saw a defeated man. He remembered the feeling of being abandoned before and during the battle, and he remembered the threatening orders he had received while attempting to cross the bridge and he didn't feel sorry for his old friend anymore. He finished his thought. ". . . Myself included."

After all of this had time to sink in, McClellan finally spoke. "Yes, General. Of course you're right. But I must return to that which I alluded to earlier. I cannot command an army of servile insurrection. Resignation from public service is another possibility if it can be done honorably."

Cochrane saw an opportunity to repair what damage may have been done to his career by siding with Burnside and Cox against McClellan's scheme, and he came to the general's aid.

"You have proven yourself to be this nation's greatest commander. I have grave questions as to what could be done without you."

"Your kind words are appreciated, John, and you may rest assured that I do not intend to do anything rash." Every man in the room save McClellan saw the irony of that statement after what had gone before, but no one reacted.

"I do not enjoy such confidence from the government, nor from our newly appointed General in Chief, whom we all know to be an incompetent fool. If I am to remain in the service, Stanton and Halleck—or at least Halleck—must go. Somehow—they must go."

And suddenly the meeting was over. "Gentlemen, I appreciate you coming here tonight and offering me your candid opinions and you may rest assured that I shall take them all into account."

The three men retired to their various units, taking with them their individual thoughts and fears. Most fearful of all was Ambrose Burnside, who now felt certain that, come what may, the command of the Army of the Potomac would soon be his—and he wanted nothing of it.

CHAPTER 19

THE VISIT

SEPTEMBER 28TH

Sunday would not be a day of rest for George McClellan. He was greeted at dawn with a logistical nightmare. Trainloads of equipment had stopped not on sidings, but on tracks, blocking traffic throughout Maryland and refusing to move until given absolute final destinations. Horses intended for units in Sharpsburg and Harper's Ferry instead went to garrison troops on the outskirts of Washington. Quartermaster officers at every level neglected to order vital supplies until such time as the need had already become critical. The finger-pointing started early.

In Louisville, Kentucky, Don Carlos Buell's day got off to an even worse start. He slept on the softest bed in the largest room at the finest hotel in Louisville until gunshots exploded him out of his sleep and onto his feet. These were not the big guns firing off in the distance somewhere, but pistol shots in the hallway directly outside of his room! His first thought was of Rebel raiders and he reached for his revolver. There was a commotion in the hall, but no attempt to enter his room. He caught sight of himself in the glass, still clad in his nightshirt and cap, and prayed he would not be taken prisoner in such undignified attire. He began to dress and a heavy knock was followed by a frantic voice.

"General Buell, sir."

"Just one moment." The general made himself presentable and opened the door. The hall was full of uniformed men (all, to his relief, wearing blue). "What in the hell is going on out here?"

"Sir, General Davis has just shot General Nelson!"

"*Our* General Davis just shot *our* General Nelson?"

"Yes, sir. They argued down in the lobby and General Nelson ordered General Davis out of his command. General Davis took offense, sir, and borrowed a gun and followed General Nelson up the stairs and—and— well, he just shot him, sir. We have moved him into a room across the hall and called for a surgeon, but to my eyes it does not look good. General Nelson has requested a preacher to come and baptize him."

"Judas Priest. As if I don't have *enough* problems without my own generals shooting each other!"

"There's is one more thing, sir."

"And what on God's green earth might that be?"

"There's a courier here to see you with a message from General Halleck."

From the back of the crowded hallway stepped a dust-covered colonel who handed Buell an official, handwritten dispatch.

"This news, at least, is better," Buell said. "I have been relieved of command."

"I would really prefer fighting three battles than writing the report of one," McClellan told General Marcy at breakfast. Today was the deadline he had set for himself in gathering all of the necessary information for the filing of his initial report. "You are necessarily combating the *amour propre*, the vanity, of every officer concerned when you say one word in commendation of anybody else. Each one is firmly convinced of the fact that no one but he had anything to do with the result. Every commander of a brigade becomes firmly convinced that he fought the whole battle and that he arranged the general plan of which he knew absolutely nothing!"

"A man's vanity must be appealed to from time to time, George. Any man who does not consider himself worthy probably is not."

"And then friendships enter the question. That is the toughest part of all. I ought to rap Burnside very severely, and probably will—yet I hate to do it. He is very slow and is not fit to command more than a regiment. If I rap him as he deserves he will be my mortal enemy hereafter—if I do not praise him as he thinks he deserves and as I know he does not, he will at least be a very lukewarm friend. It is too difficult."

McClellan looked at his reflection in the glass as he made certain that the part in his hair was perfectly straight before going out for the day. His personal valet entered with an envelope.

"A letter, sir, from the Postmaster General. I thought you should have it before you left."

McClellan pretended not to be surprised and told the man to put it on the map table. As soon as he left the general opened it quickly. Montgomery Blair was perhaps his only remaining friend on the cabinet. His opinion on the proclamation had not been sought, but was apparently being offered nonetheless. God, how good it would be to hear just one sane voice coming out of the capital. How good it would be to receive encouragement to protest this evil document in some grand style from the very heart of the administration.

He read over the letter briefly, wadded it into a ball and threw it violently across the tent.

"Not good news, I take it," Marcy said.

"Our President has made himself king! Now he has cashiered a major—John Key—Tom's brother—for comments he made in a *dinner* conversation. It's not enough for him to suspend *habeas corpus*—now he rescinds freedom of speech as well!"

"May I ask what the young man said?"

"Some nonsense about the Rebels getting away from here because we *allowed* them to. Because we don't want to beat them because we don't want to free the niggers! Damn this whole slavery question anyway. It just muddies the water. Why can't we be allowed to fight just one war at a time?"

Marcy knew his son-in-law well enough to know that there was more to the letter than that. It took a great deal to make George swear.

"What did the Postmaster General suggest you do?"

"Comply."

"I beg your pardon?"

"He says I should comply with the President's proclamation. He says I must disassociate myself from any such talk as this. He says that if I have presidential aspirations, I cannot be seen as supporting slavery even as a price of peace. Not only should I comply with the proclamation, but I should *support* it. That city would corrupt Saint Peter and Paul too."

SEPTEMBER 29TH

Again President Lincoln sat alone in his office. Again he placed a paper on his desk and again he began to compose an essay. For twenty minutes he wrote, trying to arrange in his own mind his thoughts and options regarding his reluctant subordinate in Maryland. Was McClellan participating in some deluded and tacit plot to aid the rebellion? Lincoln thought not, but the general's actions implied otherwise. Was the Rebel army so superior in size and ability to his own as to enable them to perform feats of which Union troops were not capable? No. Of course not. Yet why are they capable of moving along the arc of the circle faster than we can move down the chord? Would the dismissal of McClellan result in a mutiny by the army that loved him so dearly? Probably not. Would the dismissal of McClellan result in political disaster? Yes.

Ultimately, Lincoln knew, it would have to be a military decision and nothing more. If McClellan permits Lee to cross the Blue Ridge and place himself between Richmond and the Army of the Potomac, Lincoln decided, then the Young Napoleon would be gone. Damn the political consequences. But, for the moment, until the fall elections were over, the President had no options. The decision would be military, but the timing had to be based on practical politics. Until the elections were over, he knew, he had to retain McClellan in command and do his best to pry the army away from Sharpsburg using other means. He would appeal to McClellan's vanity, threaten, plead or order him to move. Lincoln rubbed his eyes and said aloud, "We must use what tools we have."

He held his essay over the open flame of his desk lamp and watched as it turned from flame to ash. "Mr. Hay!" he called.

John entered quickly.

"I shall be going to Sharpsburg tomorrow. No. I'll go on Wednesday. That will be two weeks precisely after the battle. Perhaps some significance will be read into that."

"Should I notify Secretary Stanton and General Halleck?"

"No! God, no, don't do that. My good friend from Illinois, Mr. Hatch, is in town. He will accompany me, and every Democrat I can lay my hands on. Send for General McClernand. He is an old friend, a fine general and an ardent Democrat. And John Garrett over at the B & O. Maybe a railroad man should be in the entourage as well. But none of McClellan's enemies. I do not wish to attack the man—I hope to appeal to him."

"And speaking of General Halleck, sir, he has just this moment arrived and is waiting to see you."

"Henry," the President shouted, hoping that Halleck had not overheard the previous conversation, ". . . come in here."

Halleck walked slowly into the room with a paper in his hand. "I have a dispatch from General Thomas, Mr. President."

Lincoln read the document. "General Buell's preparations have been completed to move against the enemy, and I therefore respectfully ask that he may be retained in command. My position is very embarrassing."

"And your recommendation, General?"

"Suspend the order, sir, and give General Buell one final chance to move."

Lincoln was reluctant to reverse the order. It would lessen the message being sent to McClellan. But if Buell was in fact prepared to move, then the timing was obviously bad. "So be it, General, but see to it that he moves and moves quickly. I hope to have God on my side, but I *must* have Kentucky! I think to lose Kentucky is nearly the same as to lose the whole game."

Over the next few days the results of McClellan's inquiries poured in from all quarters. The revered Francis Blair, Montgomery's father and a Washington fixture for decades, wrote a letter seconding that of his son. William Aspinwall appeared unannounced at army headquarters to tell him that the Democratic Party discouraged the general from taking any public stand whatsoever. Comply, comply, comply. It seemed to McClellan to be a never-ending parade of naysayers, each one in line behind the other, all carrying the same timid advice: comply—or, at the very least, do not resist. Then McClellan received word that the ultimate naysayer of them all was on his way to Harper's Ferry. On Wednesday, October 1st, McClellan waited at the Harper's Ferry station to greet the President when he arrived. No business was conducted beyond a brief review of the troops. They stayed the night there and on Thursday they rode to Sharpsburg.

OCTOBER 2ND

Where is Mr. Lincoln?"

"He has left the city, Mr. Stanton."

The War Secretary immediately began to tug on his beard as the anger built. He looked at the porter and was suddenly angry at *him*. "Where in the hell did he go?"

"He didn't tell me, Mr. Stanton. He just left yesterday with General McClernand and some other gentlemen I don't know."

"Well, when in God's name will he be back?"

Now the porter, a black man who was accustomed to outrageous behavior by powerful persons, fought to control his own temper. He had learned from his father, who had been a slave, the fine art of humble but sarcastic responses in such situations. "He doesn't always confide in me his plans, sir, but he took a trunk."

The general and his Commander in Chief rode together from Harper's Ferry to Sharpsburg.

What a pair these two made—the President and his general.

McClellan, regally attired in his finest dress blues, rode ramrod-straight in the saddle, the golden sash of command showing above his brightly polished gunbelt. The leather and steel of the saddle were so highly polished that they caught and reflected the sun in tiny, brilliant bursts of light. The blanket was of blue and gold embroidered with stars and golden eagles, making the powerful and beautiful Ol' Dan Webster appear proud to be bearing his master. Lincoln rode a small, sad and swaybacked mare. The President's feet seemed almost to touch the ground and the legs of his trousers rode up almost to his knees. He continued to wear his favorite stovepipe hat, which added to the disparity of the picture. McClellan appeared grand—Lincoln looked ludicrous.

The image was not lost entirely to the men who watched them along the way, but it was not the inferiority of the President's horse or horsemanship that struck those who looked closely enough to see the man. It was the careworn and exhausted face that most wrote home about.

A courier caught up with the group about five miles out of Harper's Ferry.

"A message from General Lee, sir."

McClellan made a deliberate effort to pull away from Lincoln to let it be known that this was obviously military business and should not concern him.

Maj. General A. P. Hill, of the C. S. Army, who had charge of the arrangements connected with the paroling of the prisoners at Harper's Ferry on the 15th ultimo, permitted General White to have the use of 27 wagons and teams to carry the private baggage of the officers to some point convenient for transportation.

It was agreed to between these officers that these wagons and teams should be returned within our lines at Winchester in a few days, or, if that place should be in the hands of the United States forces, then to the nearest Confederate post. I think it proper to make known to you the above agreement, in order that some arrangements may be made for the return of the wagons and teams.

I am, most respectfully, your obedient servant,

Robert E. Lee
General, Commanding

McClellan considered the document significantly longer than was necessary and returned it to the courier.

"Pass this along to General Porter. Tell him that I am indisposed to handle it at the moment and that he should take the necessary actions."

Only then did McClellan return to Lincoln's side. The general offered no explanation and the President requested none.

Once they arrived at Sharpsburg, Lincoln rode on out to visit the wounded and to see the battlefield. He visited with Barton Mitchell, who was still bedded in a barn, but was soon to be on his way home, and he visited with Israel Richardson, who was still being cared for at the Pry house and who, all knew, would never see home again. Lincoln then rode over the battlefield from the Dunker Church to the sunken road. It was not a pleasant tour.

Two weeks following the battle, the carcasses of the horses continued to burn. He saw a pig chewing on a human arm that still wore a blue sleeve. His tour guide, furnished by McClellan, did little to soften the effect.

"They used to call this Hog Trough Road, Mr. President, but now it's called The Bloody Lane. They pulled almost a thousand dead Rebels out of here."

"That must have been a beautiful farm before the war came here."

"Yes, sir. That's the Mumma farm. They've been here for generations, they tell us, but the old man still speaks German. He wanted us to pay for his house, but we didn't burn it—the Rebels did, so we told him to talk to them. He put up such a fuss that the quartermaster offered him a few hundred dollars if he would sign a loyalty oath, but he kept saying something about his religion wouldn't let him sign any oath other than to God or something. So the poor old guy is back where he started. He's gonna have to get his money from Ol' Jeff Davis."

The tour continued to Burnside's Bridge. As Lincoln passed the Rohrbach house, he heard a small voice ask, "Who is that tall man, Mommy?" and he turned and saw a drawn and pale, tired and dirty woman who looked to be well along into her pregnancy, holding the hand of an equally dirty but pretty little girl. "That's the President, Ada. That's Mr. Lincoln." The President nodded at the pair and rode on across the now famous Burnside's Bridge and on up the hill to where the 400 Georgians had held 12,000 Yankees at bay. Jane Mumma watched the great man ride away, and when she could see him no longer she led Ada back inside the house.

"Mary, Mary—did you see him? Did you see the President?"

The house slave turned away from the window and looked down at Ada and said, "Yes, chile, I did. I surely did see him."

"Why are you crying?"

OCTOBER 3RD

Gideon Welles heard the excited voice of the Treasury Secretary in the outer chambers of his office and rolled his eyes back in his head. Chase's visits never brought good news and were almost always a sign of some fresh intrigue within the cabinet.

Chase stormed into the office unannounced.

"Do you know where the President is?"

"And a very good morning to you as well, Mr. Chase, and no, I was not informed of his whereabouts. I assume that he has gone to Sharpsburg, but it is only an assumption."

"We have it on very good authority that that is precisely where he is. Hobnobbing with his friends, the generals and doing God-only-knows what kind of damage without us there to advise him. I have never seen Stanton so angry."

Welles again used his favorite tactic and remained silent through Chase's pause, waiting for him to continue.

As though informing Welles of a death in the family, Chase lowered his tone and bowed his head. "Edwin has prepared a letter of resignation."

Welles showed no reaction whatsoever. He continued his tactic of silence. Chase hated it when the Navy Secretary did that, but there was no defense for it, so he continued.

"If Stanton goes, I go. And for that matter, I believe that we all should go with him. The President apparently does not require our services. He is going to do whatever he pleases whenever he pleases without so much as a consultation. Stanton has presented me with $45 million in bills run up by the army, and I have absolutely no way of paying them. The army spends money, sir, and that is all they do. And the President allows it. He retains McClellan and Buell and all the others and pays them to do nothing. He pays us, for that matter, to do nothing as well, and Secretary Stanton believes that it is time to make a stand."

"Mr. Chase. The constant disagreements between Mr. Stanton and the generals must inevitably work disastrously. I have foreseen this for some time as I am sure have you and everyone else involved. You are apparently stunned by Mr. Stanton's threatened resignation, but I am not. Things cannot long continue as they are. Sooner or later, he or the generals or the whole must go.

"As to your argument for some kind of mass resignation, it simply does not follow that if one must leave then all must follow." Chase tried not to let his exasperation with the Navy Secretary show on his face. Welles had never been a part of the team and never would be. He knows nothing of politics, nothing of power, he is an addle-brained old clown. This would be a worthless trip and Chase had told Stanton that before he ever left to come here. Best to let the slow-minded old idiot say his piece though.

"If it is best for the country that all should go, then certainly all should leave without hesitation or delay, but I do not admire combinations among officials. I do not think it advisable that we should all make our actions dependent on the movements or the difficulties of the Secretary of War, who, like all of us, has embarrassments, and might not himself be exempt from error." Welles's associate stepped into the doorway and Welles waved him away. He had just gotten up his head of steam and had no intention of slowing down for anyone or anything.

"There are many things in the administration that we all wish were different. This Chiriquí scheme that the President finds so dear—the plan to deport all freed slaves to Costa Rica in return for their freedom— is appalling. It is nothing more than a business scam designed to provide cheap labor for the coal miners down there, and it is my department that will be compelled to buy the coal, if indeed there is any coal to buy, and foot the bill for the whole deplorable scheme. In short, Mr. Chase, if I should resign it will be over *that* issue, and not as a result of anything that Mr. Stanton does!"

The President spent Friday reviewing the troops of several corps and patiently posing for pictures. A Mr. Alexander Gardner had been on the field since the nineteenth photographing the aftermath of the battle. He represented Mr. Mathew Brady's firm, and the President was familiar with Brady, so he patiently posed as several photographs were taken of him with large groups of Union officers. He found time to visit privately with several generals, but did not press them regarding the conduct of the battle. He talked politics and personal matters and told some of his favorite stories from his lawyering days. He visited with the wounded soldiers of both armies.

OCTOBER 4TH

Early in the day, as the sleeping army awoke and began to ignite its breakfast fires, Lincoln and his friend Ozias Hatch stood where McClellan had stood during the battle, on the back lawn of the Pry house, and looked out over the field. The President was quiet and thoughtful. For three days he watched the army as the army watched him. He saw some respect for him or for his office, but mostly he saw just the usual gawking that he had become accustomed to. He also noticed the different way the men had of looking at McClellan. These men still loved their general.

Lincoln waved a long arm and bone-thin hand over the army that lay below them and asked, quite oddly it seemed to Hatch, "What is all this?"

"The Army of the Potomac."

"No, Hatch. No, this is General McClellan's bodyguard."

In this frame of mind, the President of the United States presented himself at McClellan's headquarters tent and awaited an audience. An American flag covered one table like a cloth and on the ground under it lay stacks of Confederate battle flags and trophies. Lincoln was left to ponder these while he waited for the Young Napoleon to invite him in. Finally, and for the first time ever, Lincoln and McClellan sat together alone.

"I am sure you understand, General, that I did not come here to relieve you of your duties. That I could have done with a letter. I believe you to be the most qualified man for the job and that is why you are here. You and your men fought well on this field—the entire nation is proud of you. The entire nation, though, is asking 'What next?' You appear to me, and to many, to be overcautious in your movements. Every detail must be exactly right in order for you to move, and you and I both know, sir, that every detail will never be exactly right. I am most anxious for this army to pursue the Rebels, General, and I must know what stands in the way."

"First, Mr. President, I appreciate your kind words. To the question, I hope that you have been informed that I am in communication with the War Department, often explaining to them my difficulties here. To summarize them briefly for you, though, we suffered over twelve thousand casualties here, and more at South Mountain. My veteran regiments are used up and need replenishing. My new regiments are far too green and in need of training. The men of General Pope's old army are still showing bad habits and signs of demoralization. A crossing now would be making the very same mistake Lee made in coming to this place—it would place us in a position of having to fight a battle with the river at our backs. Our supplies are far too slow in arriving even here, so much so that I cannot imagine supplying this army deep into Virginia before the bridges at Harper's Ferry are reconstructed. Progress is being made in all of these areas. Contraband workers are being sent from Washington to assist with the bridges and the expenses have been approved, but the work is just beginning. It will not be long, Mr. President, before we are ready, but it would be unwise for us to move before such a time as we are certain that we will be adequately supplied. I must always remember, sir, that a loss at this juncture could well result in the end of the Republic."

"And a victory at this juncture could well result in the end of the war. I need your word, General, that you will move as soon as is practicable. The weather is soon to turn bad and both armies will report to winter quarters. The war could be won by then."

"Or lost."

Lincoln sighed deeply and moved on. "And now to another issue—the Emancipation Proclamation." McClellan reacted physically as the old familiar electric shock ran from his head to his shoulder, but the soldier in him showed not so much as a blink. "I understand that you oppose it on political grounds," Lincoln continued. "I appreciate and respect that position. But as a military commander . . . what are your intentions?"

"I have given the matter a great deal of thought, and you must know that I believe that this document will serve only to prolong the war. Any hope that we may have had of reaching a negotiated settlement is gone, probably forever. The South will now have to be conquered completely."

He wanted to go on and accuse the President of malfeasance of office. He wanted to lay at Lincoln's door the bodies of all of the young men, North and South, who would die as the war became war of conquest. The thought of resignation flashed through his mind, as this was the perfect place and time to make his stand. He thought of demanding the resignations of Stanton and Halleck, but at this moment he took his eyes off the President and glanced out the tent flaps at the trophies of war gathered round him and saw the movement of his men just outside and in that instant he couldn't risk it. He couldn't give it up. He loved it all too dearly. "But you have asked my intentions as a soldier, and as a soldier I have come to the simplest of conclusions. I *am* a soldier, and you are my commanding officer. I shall view the document as an order and obey it as I would any other. It must be as simple as that. I do not have to agree, I must only obey . . ." Then he added, in the most ominous voice he could muster, ". . . for as long as I am in the service. Which brings us to the question that I have for you. I know that pressure is being brought to bear for you to replace me . . ."

"Do not worry yourself about that. As you just pointed out, I, and I alone, am the Commander in Chief. It was my decision alone to give you this command and it will be my decision alone to remove you from it."

"I want to believe that, sir, but the pressures of Washington politics can be great."

"The powers of my office are greater. Do your job, George, and you will command this army forever. When may I count on you to cross into Virginia?"

"I will work up a plan in the next day or so and will move when I am reasonably certain of success." Lincoln said nothing, but pulled himself up even taller and gave McClellan a look that said, Be more specific.

McClellan tried to wait out the President, but he could not. "It will be soon."

The insane asylum in Washington had been converted into a hospital, and there were some who found it hugely appropriate that it was in this building that Fightin' Joe Hooker recuperated from his wound. Chase had been to visit before and, along with his beautiful daughter, had become a regular at Hooker's bedside.

"Mr. Secretary, were it not for you and Miss Kate I would die here from boredom."

"It is always a pleasure to meet with our gallant heroes," he responded with a smile. Smiling was something that almost hurt Chase's face. It required the use of seldom-used muscles. "But you must know that I am here with a purpose this time, General."

Hooker smiled as well as it came into his mind that Salmon P. Chase *always* has a purpose. But Hooker could appreciate that. These two men were both ultimately ambitious and whatever the task, noble or not, self-interest was always their highest priority.

"I believe that General McClellan's days are numbered—I'm sure this does not take you by surprise."

"It does not." Simply spoken. Hooker was not about to hoist sails without testing the wind.

"Let me ask you this, sir. What is your stand on the Emancipation Proclamation?"

Hooker considered his response for less than a second. In actuality it mattered not a whit to the general one way or the other, but if command of the Army of the Potomac rested on his answer, he knew immediately what his position should be.

"I'm for it."

Chase smiled again. "Very well, sir. If the President should ask anyone other than Seward"—these words dripped with sarcasm—"then I shall recommend you."

Now Hooker smiled as well. "Should it happen you'll have the fightingest general this nation has ever known. I'll promise you that."

"I know that we will."

But as Chase started to leave, Hooker decided to throw up some defensive lines. "You may have some difficulties with Halleck though."

"Halleck? Why?"

"He thinks I owe him eight hundred dollars."

"Wonderful," Chase said. "Simply wonderful."

CHAPTER 20

NOT AN HOUR
SHALL BE LOST

OCTOBER 5TH

Gideon Welles ran into the President quite by chance as Lincoln returned from Sharpsburg. Welles knew from the nature of the President's greeting that he was again in good spirits. Lincoln loved and respected the man, but the white beard attached to a cheap wig never failed to make Lincoln smile.

"Noah—we have good news from the West at least. Rosecrans has repulsed a Rebel attempt to retake Corinth, and Buell, at long last, is moving against them in Kentucky."

"Excellent, sir . . . and in the East?"

Welles saw the confidence leave the President's face. "The news there is the same as always. McClellan tells me that he is making plans to move, but I saw no signs of it. He assures me that it will be soon, but . . ." Lincoln shook his head and shrugged his shoulders. "I will tell you this, Gideon: the only way that he can succeed as a politician is to succeed as a general. This puts me in the awkward position of encouraging him into a position from which he can defeat me two years from now. The shiny side of that coin, though, is that if he does succeed as a general and brings a proper ending to this war, then I shall be happy for both the general and the nation. Illinois is lovely in the fall."

"If all of that is true, sir, then I believe that you have nothing to fear from him." Welles heard Stanton's words coming from his own mouth and decided that enough had been said on the issue of McClellan. "It is good news from the West, however. Hopefully some gains will be made in both departments before the roads close . . . and the polls open."

Lincoln smiled and nodded and saluted "Father Neptune" on his way, but the Navy Secretary's parting words remained with him. ". . . *And the polls open.*"

Lincoln had omitted this thought from his essay. Might McClellan's procrastination be entirely politically motivated? Might he deliberately be waiting until after the elections so as not to place the administration in too good a light? A victory now in the East would be very helpful to the Republican congressional and gubernatorial candidates come November. Perhaps McClellan's position is equally as awkward as my own. If he performs well now, then it is I who benefit immediately, while his reward waits in the far too distant future. Lincoln shook his head. *It is all too complicated,* he thought. It is all too hard.

October 6th

The President was very kind toward me personally," McClellan told Marcy. "He told me he was convinced that I was the best general in the country. I really think he does feel very kindly toward me personally."

"And what are your intentions regarding his proclamations?"

"Well, obviously I have discussed the issue with him and left no doubt in his mind how strongly I feel about the issue. But I have also discussed the matter with Mr. Aspinwall and others, and all seem convinced that I should continue to perform my duties as a soldier and leave the politics, for the moment, to the politicians and the voters, and leave the army out of it."

"The army are voters."

McClellan beamed at the thought. "Right you are, sir! I shall prepare an order that reminds them of their obligations as soldiers, *and* as voters." McClellan laughed. "We may gain from this little fiasco yet."

"But the meeting with the President went well."

"Yes, I think so. I think it went very well indeed."

* * *

The more Lincoln thought about his meeting with McClellan, the more angry and frustrated he became. "It will be soon" was all he had been able to get out of him. "Soon." Well, "soon" means something different to McClellan than it does to every other man in this world. The President was disappointed with himself as well. He had gone there to "prod" the army out of Maryland. *"Pry" is a better word,* he thought. "Pleading" is what he ended up doing. Again. Timid. Always too timid face-to-face. Getting McClellan to move was like trying to pull an oak up by the roots.

The more he stewed on it, the angrier he became at himself. The more he considered the possibility that McClellan might be deliberately procrastinating for the sake of his party—not wanting to risk a victory so close to November—the more he thought that it might actually be a deliberate design.

Finally, he became so angry with his own timidity that he marched directly to Halleck's office and stormed in the door, giving orders.

"I want you to wire McClellan. This very minute."

Stanton, who was down the hall, heard the commotion and hurried into the room. The President didn't even acknowledge his arrival.

"Tell him that I . . . no WE . . . ORDER him to move south. NOW! He must cross the river and engage the enemy while the roads are still passable."

Halleck sat behind the desk, totally taken aback by Lincoln's outburst. Lincoln grabbed a pencil off the desk, handed it to the general and pointed to a piece of paper. "Write! Tell him that if he crosses the river between the enemy and the capital that we will provide him with thirty thousand men— if he chooses another route he will get only twelve thousand."

Stanton was only slightly less perturbed with Lincoln now than he was when he left for Sharpsburg. He smelled a wonderful "I told you so" opportunity and couldn't resist.

"What excuse did he conjure up this time?"

"Now he can't move until Harper's Ferry is reconstructed from the ground up." Lincoln was so worked up that his breath came in pants. "So tell him this as well. Tell him that no orders will be given for permanent bridges at Harper's Ferry until his plan of attack is presented and approved!"

There. Done. Politics be damned. He looked at Stanton and was further irritated by the self-satisfied, arrogant grin. Smug little bastard.
"And tell him that the orders come from me and that we are all three in
agreement. Send it now."

Stanton had to duck out of the way as the President charged out of
the room.

McClellan's Triumph!

The cover of *Harper's Weekly* greeted New Yorkers on this day with its
long-awaited etchings of the Battle of Antietam! The cover drawing was
of McClellan's triumphant ride into Frederick, with liberated Marylanders showering him with flowers and adoringly touching him and his
terrified-looking horse. A beautiful woman handed him her baby, hoping
for a touch or a kiss.

Harper's never provided very much in the way of news. The news was
three weeks to a month old by the time *Harper's* got around to publishing it. But *Harper's* had pictures! Drawings by battlefield artists etched in
wood and printed on paper for consumption by the masses.

George Smalley was no less anxious to get his hands on this weeks'
Harper's than any other New Yorker, but more for amusement than edi-
fication. After all, he had been there. He knew what it looked like, and he
couldn't wait to see *Harper's* rendition of the great conquest. They
always pictured a bold general on horseback, risking life and limb to lead
the Grand Army of the Republic into glorious battle. Flags were always
unfurled and the boys in blue stood strong in powerful and unbending
ranks and files, firing into the ghostly figures of distant rebels. Each contained an obligatory wounded soldier, but no blood, no mayhem, no
anguish, no death. Captions added insult to injury. "McClellan to the
rescue" and "Burnside holds the hill" were Smalley's personal favorites.

If these poor people—these poor oblivious people—only knew, Smalley
thought. If they could only see for themselves.

OCTOBER 8TH

Fewer than twenty-five miles from Sharpsburg, in Winchester, Virginia, Lee and his army waited and watched. Under the care and feeding of the home guard, they recuperated from their wounds and recovered from their "Confederate disease," the severe diarrhea that had plagued them throughout the Maryland campaign. The stragglers returned to their units and new troops provided by the various states joined up with the Army of Northern Virginia. Their numbers and bellies swelled, and many became restless and ready for another fight. Jeb Stuart was more restless than most and picked up his old habit of waiting around outside of General Lee's tent in the hope of a new and glamorous assignment.

Lee's Assistant Adjutant, Colonel Taylor, entered the general's tent with his usual casual approach. It was his duty to protect Lee from all but the most demanding of correspondences and to keep him posted on the vital matters of day-to-day operations while in camp. Today he brought the general his mail and watched as Lee attacked it like a hungry man would a plate of beans until he found precisely what he was looking for. Like all soldiers, his first priority at mail call was to get the news from home.

"Two new regiments arrived today, sir," Taylor reported as Lee opened and read the letter. "One from Georgia and one from Alabama. To whom should they be assigned?"

"I beg your pardon, Colonel. What was the question?"

"Two new regiments, sir. To whom should they be assigned?"

"Oh, yes." Lee took in a deep breath, obviously distracted. "Both to General Hood, I suppose, but . . . Yes. Both to General Hood if General Longstreet has no objections."

"Very well, sir."

Taylor turned and left the tent, but had not gone far before he remembered another matter that required the general's attention. A message had arrived from across the lines from General Fitz-John Porter regarding some wagons being returned by the Yankees. He pulled open the tent flap and entered, again unannounced, to find Robert E. Lee still standing, but bent down over his desk with the letter still in his hand. The general lifted his head only slightly, but enough for Taylor to see the tears. Lee tried to speak, but could not take a breath without sobbing. He tried desperately to regain his composure for the benefit of his guest, but the tears continued to pour from the proud brown eyes of Robert E. Lee. Taylor stepped forward to offer some help, but did not have a notion what to do or say.

"General . . . ?" Taylor had never felt so helpless.

Lee tried to speak again, but still could not, so he handed the letter to the colonel.

"*My dear General Lee, It is my sad responsibility to report to you that our worst fears have been realized, and our beloved Annie has succumbed to the fever that she so bravely combated . . .*"

Taylor looked up at his general and felt more helpless now than ever.

"Annie," Lee whispered. "Our . . ."

Taylor finally pulled Lee's chair around and the general gratefully accepted it. He sat by his table and put his head down in his folded arms and wept.

"I'll call for the boys."

Lee only nodded and Taylor went out in search of Rooney and young Robert.

At drought-plagued Perryville, Kentucky Rebs and Yanks came together in a fight over water. Not states' rights. Not slavery. Water. Nine thousand Rebels poured out of the woods and into General Buell's left flank. A diversion kept the majority of Buell's 55,000 men in place while their flank was turned and pushed back away from the creek. As darkness fell on Perryville, Kentucky, the Union army in the West slept thirsty again.

As darkness fell on Winchester, Virginia, every unit in Lee's army touched a torch to a bonfire to light Annie Lee's way to heaven.

OCTOBER 9TH

The Kentucky air was so still that the dawn revealed a huge orange sun, magnified and painted by the dust of battle that still hung in the air from the night before. What the dawn did *not* reveal was a single

Rebel soldier. Confederate General Braxton Bragg thanked his stars that he had survived the day and, frankly, got the hell out of there, leaving Perryville and its precious water to the Yankees.

Buell called the Rebel movement a "retreat." Bragg called it a "withdrawal."

Buell pursued, cautiously and from a distance, but at least the army in the West was going somewhere. Lincoln compared his two armies. One a tortoise, the other a tree.

Trying to ignore his broken heart, Lee forgot his broken wrist and painfully slammed his fist down on a tabletop and shouted, "I have had enough of this! Nothing is being served here but the vanities of two proud men!" Stonewall Jackson and A. P. Hill both recoiled in shock. Neither had ever heard General Lee shout in anger, or, for that matter, express anger in any way. "There is absolutely nothing to be gained from this by the army, and both of you—in fact all three of us—are at this very moment neglecting our duties by dealing with this petty question instead of seeing to our men!" All he wanted to do was get out of this room, put this issue behind him and grieve for his poor dead little girl. His body had to remain in this room, but his heart and his soul were where they should be—with his grieving wife and his perfect child. As the two proud generals stood aghast at Lee's outburst, the commander had only a short moment of silence to visit his family in his thoughts.

Tomorrow the coffin lid will be placed over Annie's beautiful face forever. He tried not to picture it, but could not keep the dreadful images from entering his mind. Mary watching as our perfect child is lowered into the earth. She will be hysterical with uncontrollable and inconsolable grief. And tomorrow I will still be here, mediating a petty dispute between two vain and arrogant soldiers. Duty. Honor.

The meeting was in its fourth hour and nothing was close to being resolved. The two men simply hated each other and nothing could be done about it. They remained standing at opposite ends of the table, where they had stood for the entire time firing charges and countercharges back and forth at each other in a grand verbal artillery duel that showed no signs of slowing. They glared at each other the entire time while directing their salvos to Lee. "If he had . . ." "He knew . . ." For four hours neither man had directed a single remark to the other.

"I could not agree with you more, General Lee," Hill said. "But I refuse to become another Dick Garnett! Another fine general whose career and reputation is soiled forever on the whim of a madman!"

The reference to Garnett alone was enough to send Jackson into a rage. His face reddened, his jaw clenched and his hands shook as he reached for his gloves, only one angry motion away from a duel to the death.

"*Silence!*"

Then, in a calm voice Lee said, "He who has been the most aggrieved can be the most magnanimous and make the first overtures of peace." It was all that Lee could say. It was all that he intended to say. He stood back and waited for the more gallant of the two to respond. A full minute passed without a sound and Lee would have sworn that neither general so much as blinked.

"I stand by my original decision, gentlemen. The matter is noted. Return to your commands and I wish to hear no more on the matter." Without looking at either, Lee retrieved his hat and left the room. On the porch of the house he waited for Traveller to be brought around—and for the sound of gunshots as Hill and Jackson remained together in the parlor. He was relieved when Hill ran past him like a shot and returned to his division.

With all of this on his mind, along with the unserved grief at the loss of Annie, Lee was happy to see Jeb Stuart step out of the shadows and onto the porch.

"General?"

"Yes, General. What is it?"

"General, we are fully prepared to depart at first light in accordance with your orders."

OCTOBER 10TH

At dawn on Friday, Jeb Stuart and 1,800 handpicked mounted troopers splashed across the Potomac at a run and returned to Maryland. By noon he was in Pennsylvania. By nightfall Chambersburg, twenty miles to McClellan's rear, fell to the Rebel cavalry without a shot.

CARROUSEL HORSES

OCTOBER **11**TH

he only citizen of Chambersburg prepared for a Confederate attack was the town banker, who emptied the vault and skedaddled at the first sign of trouble. Jeb Stuart was further disappointed to find that his primary objective, a bridge over which ran the vital B & O Railroad, was constructed of steel and could be neither cut nor burned. But it was not wholly a sad morning for Stuart and his troopers. They found the town store well stocked with shoes. Several hundred sick and wounded Federal soldiers being housed in the town were captured and paroled. The proud and hardworking farmers of southern Pennsylvania worked with the finest, strongest, largest draft horses any of these Southern cavalrymen had ever seen. They were so large that the animals had to be captured along with their collars because the Rebels did not have any that were large enough to fit. There was also a Union army warehouse in the town with 5,000 rifles and a generous supply of nice, new, warm blue overcoats. It was a rainy morning and the coats fit well.

Parked next to the train depot stood a line of fully loaded wagons with the letters C.S.A. clearly branded into the sideboards.

"And where did these come from?" Stuart asked a local citizen.

"A Colonel Davis captured them just before the big battle down in Maryland and he brought them here. They've been here ever since."

Stuart smiled and made a note to inform Longstreet that his missing stores had been located—and destroyed. "Burn them and burn everything of military use that can't be easily and quickly carried. It's time to move on."

The troopers fell in with their mounts facing west, to return by the way they had come, but to the surprise of everyone, Stuart ordered them about, eastbound.

Stuart knew his own reputation as well as anyone, and he was fully aware that a dark side tarnished the bright. Another successful circumnavigation of the Union army would add to the shine, but a failed attempt might tarnish it forever. It could be seen as a reckless adventure undertaken for vanity's sake, especially if Stuart himself was not around to defend it. As they left town Jeb ordered Captain Blackford forward to ride with him.

"Blackford, I want to explain my motives to you for taking this lower route, and if I should fall before reaching Virginia, I want you to vindicate my memory." They rode on for a moment in silence while Stuart composed his logic. "First, we passed within a mile of six regiments from Cox's corps between Williamsport and Darksville. They will have been notified of our presence and the fords near there will be heavily guarded. Farther down the Potomac the Yankees may *not* have been alerted. The fords will be guarded, but they will be guarded against a crossing *out* of Virginia and not into it. They will have their backs to us. They probably do not expect a crossing there, and the least expected action is almost always the best."

Nothing concerned Stuart more than his gallant and untarnished reputation. He had to make absolutely certain that Blackford understood every detail of his plan and why he selected it. Every detail. "I understand the greater distance will wear down the troops and provide the Yankees with additional time to prepare, but I am ready to take those chances rather than face Cox at Darksville. I further understand the large numbers that McClellan has garrisoned at Harper's Ferry will be nearby, but if we move quickly and carefully we can cross before they know we're there. Do you understand, sir, and do you appreciate the reasoning?"

"I do, sir." Blackford did understand, and he did appreciate the reasoning, but he also understood, maybe for the first time, the seriousness of the situation as it stood. An army nearing 100,000 men stood between this tiny marauding band and the safety of home. There was a very good chance that a great many, and possibly even all, would fall before they could get back to Virginia.

"If the contingency you spoke of arises and I survive you, I shall certainly see that your motives are understood."

"Rebel cavalry is reported to our rear, sir. As far north as Chambersburg."

"Who is it? Is it Stuart?"

"That is what we understand, General."

McClellan splashed his cup of coffee against a tree.

"Damn that man!" He angrily saluted the courier away and turned to Marcy.

"Stuart came close to ruining my career down on the Peninsula, joyriding around my army. The press made that inconsequential little jaunt look like another Bull Run! It *will not* happen again!"

As Stuart anticipated, Jacob Cox's entire corps prepared to move out at a moment's notice. Complete regiments waited in boxcars as the engines maintained full steam so that they could roll instantly the moment Stuart made his position known. The soldiers who pulled this duty fought for the spots nearest the open doors to gain some relief from the steambox heat and the horse-barn smell. For hours on end they stood crammed into these cattle cars and the only men permitted to leave were carried out, half dead from dehydration or asphyxiation. The trains waited on the tracks near Hancock, Pennsylvania, forty miles *west* of Chambersburg. McClellan also ordered Pleasonton's cavalry out in pursuit of the raiding party and, contrary to Stuart's expectations, all units posted along a hundred-mile front were placed on the lookout for James Ewell Brown Stuart.

Once the orders went out, first by telegraph and then by couriers, McClellan was content that Stuart was as good as captured. He lighted a cigar and decided it was time to boast ever so slightly to the big shots in Washington. "I have given every order necessary to insure the capture or destruction of these forces, and I hope we may be able to teach them a lesson they will not soon forget." Unable to pass up an opportunity to protect himself against disaster, regardless of the odds in his favor, he could not resist adding, "The great difficulty we labor under is the want of Cavalry, as many of our horses are overworked and unserviceable."

While McClellan and his army nervously watched for enemy cavalry, Stuart rode at a trot around them. He approached a college town in southern Pennsylvania where he had heard a shoe factory worked, and he feigned an approach there, just in case anybody was watching—which they weren't—only to turn south and east again, away from Gettysburg and on to Emmitsburg.

The morning rain had done Stuart a favor in that the roads were damp, and the 1,800 troopers leading 1,200 stolen horses did not raise a dust cloud that could alert the Yankees to their movements. Later the rain might work against him if he found the Potomac swollen and unfordable. For the moment though, it worked to his advantage. Without a stop the column continued at a trot throughout the day and into the night, slowing to a walk only on occasion to rest the animals.

By nightfall they reached Emmitsburg, still not halfway to their selected fords. The troopers looked hopefully to Stuart, thinking that an overnight bivouac would soon be ordered. No such order was given. No such order was considered. The men could not even sleep in the saddle because of the pace, and their horses were wet and frothing. Neither Stuart nor Skylark, his favored horse for such missions, showed any signs of tiring as Friday ended and Saturday began.

OCTOBER 12TH

They rode through Woodsborough and Liberty, New London and New Market without so much as a sign of a single Union soldier. It was Stuart's habit to ride ahead for a while and then halt and watch as his men paraded by. He saw a turnoff that he remembered fondly and pulled to the side to await the arrival of Captain Blackford and the rest of his staff.

"Do you remember this road?" Stuart asked.

Blackford smiled. "I surely do, General. It's the cutoff to Urbana. I'll tell you what, General. That was one hell of a night."

Both men sat for a while looking down the dark wagon trail with thoughts of a grand dance, a gallant skirmish and an heroic return to the festivities of the evening. Finally, Stuart simply could not resist.

"Blackford—how would you like to see 'the New York Rebel' tonight?"

The captain smiled so brightly he beamed even in the darkness. "I should be delighted." The two men laughed like college boys off to pull a prank and spurred their horses down the trail to Urbana.

With no effort at all, Captain Blackford located the home where his escort from the dance stayed with relatives while she attended school. Like all of the other homes in town, the house was dark and quiet. True to the form of a Rebel cavalryman, the captain gave no thought to timidity and pounded heavily on the door. An upstairs window opened and a frightened female voice asked, "Who is there?"

"General Stuart and his staff."

The window opened wider and "the New York Rebel" peered out and saw the unmistakable form of Jeb Stuart, complete with cape and plume and recognizable even in the dark. The coy young lady played her role well and attempted a delaying tactic to allow the other ladies of the house to dress.

"Who did you say it was?"

"General Stuart and his staff—come down and open the door."

Following the soft whispers and giggles of the ladies came the harsh mechanical sounds of bolts and locks. The New York Rebel rushed instantly into the arms of her dashing young captain while the other girls pranced around the man called "Beauty."

Young ladies in moonlight are difficult to leave, but one half of one hour was all that these men could afford. On the road back to catch up with the column, Blackford told Stuart that in addition to a wonderful time, he had gathered some information as well. "There are four available crossings to our front and they are guarded by as many as five thousand men under the command of General Stoneman. She does not know if they have been alerted to our approach."

"My, but she is a lovely thing, isn't she?"

Blackford smiled again. "That she is, sir. That she is."

"What is her name, anyway?"

"Her *name*?" Blackford blushed. "I don't even know."

By the time Stuart and Blackford caught up to their columns it was 7:00 A.M. and they had narrowed the distance between themselves and Virginia to a scant twelve miles. After twenty-four solid hours in the saddle, these would be a hellish twelve miles, filled, no doubt, with Union troops. Stuart knew that he could not power his way across. His men were too few and too tired. He couldn't do it strong—he had to do it smart.

He selected as his target an eleven-mile stretch of river across which cut four separate fords, supposing that the Federal guards would be thinly spread among them. His greatest fear during the approach to the river was that they might be seen by spotters on the heights of Sugar Loaf Mountain, and it was a fear well founded. At 7:40 A.M. a message was wigwagged from the Sugar Loaf semaphore station. "We can see heavy bodies of troops near Hyattstown."

One of Stuart's guides remembered the lay of the land and knew of a cutoff from the main roads toward the crossing point known as White's Ford—the very spot where Lee's army had crossed into Maryland a long month before. The side road ran through a stand of woods that might offer the troopers some protection from prying eyes. Certain that they could not put another mile behind them without falling from their horses, the men were astounded when Stuart ordered them to a gallop, as though hoping to attract attention, which was exactly what Jeb had in mind at this point. The main road led directly to Edward's Ferry, and a report that the Rebels were moving that way might even draw men away from White's. They could then, at the last moment, make the turn through the forest and bolt across the two-mile stretch to the Potomac and into Virginia.

They reached the cutoff without incident and slowed back to a trot upon entering the woods. They had almost cleared the forest when they were, at last, approached by a detachment of Federal cavalry. The Rebels still wore their new blue overcoats, and continued to ride slowly and calmly into the oncoming and unsuspecting Yankee horsemen.

"Sabers only," Stuart ordered. He smiled. A real, honest-to-God, genuine sabers-drawn cavalry charge. He spurred Skylark to a run and shouted, "CHARGE!"

The stunned Yankees put up a short but frenzied fight before falling back beyond the woods and to the protection of a ridge line, where they dismounted and began to lay down fire on the advancing Rebels. Rooney Lee's sharpshooters dismounted and returned the fire while two pieces of horse artillery came forward to help in the cause. The Yankees found themselves pinned down, and Stuart ordered the remainder of his troops to continue forward, protected by the ridge, to a road that stretched just two more miles to White's Ford—just two more miles to Virginia.

Major John Pelham commanded the guns here, as he had on Nicodemus Hill at Antietam, and at the Second Battle of Manassas. God, how Stuart loved this child genius. He situated his guns in such a way that the Yankee cavalrymen could not so much as raise their heads, and so that any approach by Federal reinforcements could easily be slowed as well. Stuart and Pelham stayed with the guns as Rooney Lee went forward to conduct the crossing. Arriving at the river Lee made a discovery not at all to his liking. Union infantry held a strong defensive position along the rim of an abandoned quarry that overlooked the ford and all of its approaches. Lee saw no artillery, but that was the only good news. He had no idea how many troops might be there and knew only that they held a position strong enough to destroy any party that might attempt a crossing.

Lee stood on a hill looking down on the river, and up at the Yankees. As he considered his unhappy options, Captain Blackford came forward with more bad news.

"General Stuart sends his regards, sir, and orders that you gain control of the ford and make your crossing with all possible speed."

"Tell General Stuart that the crossing point is heavily guarded and that his presence is required here before any movement can be ordered."

Blackford thought he knew what Stuart's response would be, but rode back over the two miles to the ridge where Stuart and Pelham continued to hold the Yankee cavalry at bay. In the time that Blackford was gone, Lee determined his only possible course of action. He would attack the Union position front and right flank and hope and pray that the action would keep them occupied long enough to get a few hundred troopers and one of his guns across the Potomac, where they could fire back across the river and into the Federal rear. If the plan were successful the casualties would be high. If it failed . . .

"General Stuart begs to report, sir, that he is occupied and cannot abandon his current position. He instructs that you, sir, *must* force a crossing. He further instructs that at no point should the horses be allowed to halt amidstreams to take water, thereby creating an obstacle. They must be pushed on through and cannot be watered until we are all safely on the other side. He wishes to add, sir, that he is concerned for the rear guard. Four couriers have been dispatched to locate Colonel Butler, but thus far none has returned."

Lee didn't bat an eye, but returned his attention to the Yankees above him.

"Courier!"

"Sir!"

Lee took a piece of paper and a pencil from his saddlebag and wrote a lengthy note, which he folded and handed to the courier.

"Ride forward under a white flag and instruct the enemy's pickets to give this document to their commanding officer. Ride."

Blackford looked puzzled. Rooney Lee smiled.

"It's a demand for their unconditional surrender." He shrugged. "I gave them fifteen minutes to respond."

At 11:00 A.M. the signal station on Sugar Loaf Mountain received a response to the message they had sent almost three and a half hours before: "Were the troops you reported wearing blue or gray?"

They responded instantly: "Some wore blue, most wore gray."

At the top of the quarry, a Union captain read Rooney Lee's message as the sounds of battle continued in the distance. If the Rebs could afford to do battle on two fronts at the same time, they must be here in significant numbers. His line of defense along the quarry's tow road numbered fewer than two hundred men. He knew as well as Lee how well positioned he was, but positioning is one thing and arithmetic is another. He saw no need to surrender, but he also saw no need to invite trouble.

Lee looked at his pocket watch for the twentieth time in fifteen minutes, and then again a minute after that. He snapped it shut and ordered his men to mount up and to prepare for their sure-to-be-costly assault.

"Sir, look!" a young lieutenant shouted, pointing to the Yankee positions.

Lee raised his glasses and smiled broadly. He saw the boys in blue move out from their splendid position at right shoulder shift and on the double-quick. The boys in gray, at long last, plunged again into the Potomac's cool waters and established positions on the Virginia side to offer cover for those who were soon to follow.

Breaking off the engagement with the Yankees still pinned on the ridge, Stuart and Pelham hightailed it down the two miles to White's Ford and under the protection of Lee's small guns.

Captain Blackford waited for Stuart on the Maryland side.

"Blackford—we are going to lose our rear guard! I have yet to hear from him or from any of the couriers I have sent to call him in and the enemy is closing in on us from above and below."

"Let me try it, General."

Stuart hesitated, but only for an instant before he put out his hand to his young friend. "All right. If we don't meet again, good-bye, old fellow."

The general saluted the captain and Blackford turned his horse, Magic, back into the face of the enemy and rode off in search of the six hundred missing troopers. Stuart shouted after him, "Tell Butler if he can't get through, to strike back into Pennsylvania and try to get back through western Virginia. Tell him to come at a gallop!"

While McClellan was waiting for word of Stuart's capture, his war with Washington went on unabated. At 3:30 P.M. he wired Halleck once again that the Army of the Potomac suffered from "a great deficiency of shoes & other indispensable supplies." Placing the blame for the lack of effort by his army squarely where it belonged—in Washington—he added, *"Unless some measures are taken to insure the prompt forwarding of these supplies there will necessarily be a corresponding delay in getting the Army ready to move, as the men cannot march without shoes. Everything has been done that can be done at these Head Qtrs to accomplish the desired result."*

Lincoln's temper had a long, slow fuse, but it had burned for three maddening weeks. He could not shake from his memory George Smalley's newspaper account of the Battle of Antietam that had appeared in the *Tribune*: "... *If not wholly a victory tonight, I believe it is a prelude to victory tomorrow* ..." Two dozen tomorrows had come and gone and in that time Lincoln had seen the battlefield for himself and knew that the *Tribune* reporter was right. Lee's army had been corralled and was ready for the slaughter, and yet had strolled safely back into Virginia. Adding to Lincoln's misery was his disconcerting belief that this dismal history was repeating itself, even now, in Kentucky!

"For God's sake, send this man some shoes! Send him horses, send him tents, send him as many men as can be found. Put an end to these eternal excuses before the nation is lost for the lack of shoes!"

Stanton had never heard the President yell before, and his right hand went immediately to his beard, which he tugged like it had never been tugged before. He wanted to remind the President that a million boots and a trillion horses would probably not be enough for the traitor McClellan. He wanted to remind the President of the reports that the Confederate army routinely marched without shoes and slept without tents, but he lost his nerve and his audience at the same time as Lincoln bolted out of the telegraph office and back to the Executive Mansion.

Captain Blackford rode more than three miles before he came upon Matthew Butler and his six-hundred-man rear guard. They were drawn up across the main road in anticipation of an assault from Pleasonton's cavalry, which at last appeared on the scene.

"The ford has been breached, sir, and General Stuart orders you to come up at a gallop."

Butler looked behind him and saw a cloud of dust rising beyond the bend and he clearly heard hoofbeats.

"Limber the gun! Mount up."

With some difficulty, the Pennsylvania draft horses were hitched to the gun and its caisson, and after what seemed an eternity to Captain Blackford, the Rebels finally rode south. They made the cutoff and went through the forest. As they rode out the other side General Butler saw white smoke rising from the banks of the Potomac and called the column to a halt. He heard cannon fire to the front, and hoofbeats, even closer now, to the rear.

"Wonderful. Artillery ahead of me and cavalry behind."

"Sir, your artillery piece is slowing us down. General Stuart ordered us forward at a gallop. If I may recommend, sir, the gun may have to be sacrificed."

"Not if there's any way on God's earth I can save it!"

General Butler wheeled his horse around behind the huge plow-pullers, which apparently failed to sense the urgency of the situation, slapped one of the beasts on the hindquarters with his saber while yelling and cursing and firing his pistol in the air. Suddenly the animals understood and broke into a run that would have put veteran cannon-pullers to shame.

When White's Ford came finally into view, Blackford saw one Rebel gun on the Maryland side of the river, and the young Major Pelham standing calmly alongside directing fire at Stoneman's Yankees and again holding them in place.

At a full gallop and with sabers drawn, Stuart's rear guard finally poured across the Potomac. The three guns posted on the Virginia side opened fire over the heads of their brothers-in-arms to offer Pelham time to limber and cross.

When the last man set foot back in Virginia, a cheer rose up over the noise of the cannon fire. After thirty-four hours in the saddle the troopers whooped and hollered and laughed like crazy men. The entire expedition had cost Stuart and the Confederacy one man killed, and two men wounded.

"Well, Jeb," Blackford said, "I'll be damned if we didn't do it again."

Stuart laughed and remembered "Cadet" Hartstuff's words from the last time they had spoken, way back at Cedar Mountain. *"It goes well,"* Stuart's old classmate had said, *"but it could go better if you would quit circling our armies like a bunch of goddamned carrousel horses."*

"Like a bunch of goddamned carrousel horses," Stuart said aloud.

"I beg your pardon, sir."

"It was nothing, Captain Blackford. Just a remembrance."

WILL YOU PARDON ME
FOR ASKING . . . ?

October 13th

For once, Edwin Stanton had only to stand back and allow others to plead his case. Even the normally cautious and irritatingly rational Secretary of the Navy raised his voice. Gideon Welles was so distraught that *he* actually raised his voice.

"It is humiliating. Disgraceful. It is not a pleasant fact to know that we are clothing, mounting and subsisting not only *our* troops but the Rebels' also!"

"In both departments," Lincoln said, "McClellan's *and* Buell's, I cannot understand for an instant why we cannot march as the enemy marches, live as he lives and fight as he fights. McClellan insists that it is from a want of horses. Mr. Stanton—have you made the effort, as I instructed you yesterday, to provide the general with the horses he demands?"

"I met yesterday with General Meigs, the Quartermaster General, and he provided me with the following numbers: according to his figures, in the last four days alone, General McClellan has been sent 1,578 horses and 711 mules."

After a pause for effect, Stanton continued. "Is it not time, now, Mr. President, to make the necessary changes?" The Secretary of War waited for a reply and was surprised and encouraged when he received none. "Mr. McClellan has been humiliated, as Mr. Welles points out. Surely, in view of these circumstances, the political repercussions which I know concern you—concern us all—will be minimized."

Three weeks, Lincoln thought. *In only three more weeks the elections will be behind us and I will be free to act as I choose.*

"Gentlemen, as you speak of the upcoming elections, it reminds me that I have a meeting today with Mr. Wadsworth, who I hope will be the next governor of New York. If you will now excuse me . . ."

Behind Lincoln's back, Stanton closed his eyes, looked to the heavens and shook his head.

"How can I be expected to do the job they have sent me here to do when they continually deny me the tools required to do it properly?" McClellan was red-faced with anger and humiliation at the events of the last seventy-two hours.

"Stuart rode over ninety miles in twenty-four hours. This cannot be done without a change of horses. It is an incredible feat that Pleasonton was able to give him any pursuit at all pushing his animals over the same course without a change." McClellan grimaced as, just for a moment, a pain darted through his head like a bullet. But thank God, it was gone as quickly as it had come. "General Stoneman should have done a better job, but he has no fewer problems where he is. The distances and number of fords he has to protect with so few men is yet another impossible assignment. I cannot expect my enemies in Washington to understand, they are fools, and I truly believe that they *want* me to fail. It is the only possible explanation."

The President, along with his friend James Wadsworth, boarded a steamer to return to Washington after reviewing the troops in Arlington. All afternoon Wadsworth had been painfully aware of Lincoln's morose frame of mind. He tried to keep the conversation light and avoided bringing up the difficult issues until an opportunity presented itself, but the day was almost at its close, and he took advantage of a serene moment to press for information.

"What news is there of McClellan?"

After a thoughtful pause, "When I was a boy," Lincoln said without looking up, "we used to play a game called 'three times 'round and out.'" The President drew three circles in the deck dust with the tip of his umbrella. "Stuart has been 'round him twice. If he goes 'round him once more, McClellan will be out."

"Is there any hope at all that McClellan will move?"

Again, without looking up, Lincoln shook his head. "I am trying to bore with an auger too dull to take hold."

The President saw his friend off at the train station and then walked alone up Pennsylvania Avenue to the War Office. General Halleck held a dispatch in his hand and without a word offered it to Lincoln. By the exasperated expression on the general's face, Lincoln knew without looking who it was from and what it contained.

"I am too tired now to read, Henry. Please, just give me the high points."

Halleck lowered his spectacles and began.

"'The recent raid of Stuart, who, in spite of all the precautions I could take with the means at my disposal, went entirely around this Army, has shown most conclusively how greatly the service suffers from our deficiency in the Cavalry Arm . . .'"

Lincoln fell back into his customary chair in the corner and rubbed his eyes too hard. A bad habit. The man's face showed no expression whatsoever. Every movement was that of a man physically, mentally and emotionally exhausted.

"Please go on, General."

"He complains, sir, that the distances he must patrol are too great, and that the waters of the Potomac are so low that all fords are passable and must be watched. He is stretched too thin. Let's see. He goes on, 'Our Cavalry has been constantly occupied in scouting and reconnaissances and this severe labor has worked down the horses and rendered many of them unserviceable.'"

Lincoln leaped from his chair with such angry energy that Halleck instinctively took a defensive step backward.

"You tell General McClellan that I said if the enemy had more occupation *south* of the river, his cavalry would not be so likely to make raids *north* of it!"

Halleck was so astounded by the President's outburst that he stood slack-jawed and blinking, looking for all the world like the idiot McClellan claimed him to be.

Lincoln, with effort, calmed his voice and said, "You tell him that." He looked around the room and saw the three telegraph operators all looking back over their shoulders at him, each with very much the same wide-eyed, slack-jawed expression displayed by Halleck. It was so ludicrous a picture that it almost made him laugh—but he was just too angry.

He took advantage of the walk back to his office to rethink the situation, to calm his nerves and to resolve one more effort to persuade McClellan to move. Back at his desk, he composed a letter.

You remember my speaking to you of what I called your over-cautiousness. Are you not over-cautious when you assume that you cannot do what the enemy is constantly doing? Should you not claim to be at least his equal in prowess, and act upon the claim? As I understand, you telegraphed General Halleck that you cannot subsist your army at Winchester unless the railroad from Harper's Ferry to that point be put in working order. But the enemy does now subsist his army at Winchester, at a distance nearly twice as great from railroad transportation as you would have to do . . . I certainly should be pleased for you to have the advantage of the railroad from Harper's Ferry to Winchester, but it wastes all the remainder of the autumn to give it to you, and in fact ignores the question of time, which cannot and must not be ignored . . .

You are now nearer to Richmond than the enemy is by the route you can and he must take. Why can you not reach there before him, unless you admit that he is more than your equal on the march? His route is the arc of a circle, while yours is the chord. It is all easy if our troops march as well as the enemy, and it is unmanly to say they cannot do it. This letter is in no sense an order.

OCTOBER 16TH

As the Rebel army "withdrew" from Perryville, Kentucky, their column was so long that the vanguard preceded the rear guard by no fewer than eight hours. They kicked up such mountains of dry Kentucky dust and dirt that their progress was easily measured from miles away. Buell's cavalry nipped at the rattles of this fifty-mile-long snake, but his efforts only spurred the serpent forward, deeper into Kentucky and closer to Tennessee.

Crossing the hills would be difficult enough, but after the hills came "the Barrens." The maps described this land as "sparsely vegetated." In the drought of '62, the Barrens became a desert, and on Thursday, October 16th, Kirby Smith's 6,000 Rebels set out to cross it. Don Carlos Buell, with 16,000 men, refused to follow.

The Quartermaster General reported to the General in Chief that according to official records, and deducting the losses from Second Bull Run, South Mountain and Antietam, the Army of the Potomac had at its disposal 31,000 serviceable horses and mules.

OCTOBER 17TH–26TH

H enry, the Northern states have apparently all turned to quicksilver, and not a man can move through it."

Halleck sat quietly and waited for the President to resume. Lincoln raised a document, which he held in his left hand. "General Buell has determined on his own that Nashville is threatened, even though we have no indications of it, and he has turned his army west, leaving eastern Tennessee uncontested to the enemy . . ." He then raised up another piece of paper. "And McClellan has promised me faithfully that he will move 'the moment my men are shod and my cavalry are sufficiently renovated to be available.' He has been under *orders* to move, General— *direct* orders from the President of the United States—for over *ten* days—ever since I returned from Sharpsburg! I left the decision as to the route of the movement to him, but he is *ordered* to move! I swear to you I believe he is waiting for the elections in the hope that we shall be weakened here to the extent that we will become absolutely powerless. We have already lost seats in Pennsylvania—but what he does not understand is that because of him and Buell, we are powerless now! General Buell even issues us a dare: '. . . the present time is perhaps as convenient as any for making any change that may be thought proper in the command of this army.' I am sorely tempted, General Halleck, to take him up on his most generous offer."

"General Buell is exercising his prerogative, Mr. President, as the commander in the field, to direct his forces as he sees fit. He suggests that the enemy is falling back on his lines of supply, while we must carry ours. He believes further, and this is a point that requires serious consideration, that an incursion into eastern Tennessee will result in the enemy bringing all of his forces—even those currently occupied in Virginia—against whatever force attempts it. It should not, therefore, be entered into lightly and without adequate numbers to hold against such a response. Let me also point out, sir, that General Buell has his army on the move, and a correction issued from here, should you find it appropriate, will probably be instantly obeyed."

"Then order it, General Halleck. Order Buell to continue his pursuit of the enemy into eastern Tennessee and to claim it for the Union! One more delay, my friend, and your friend will find himself fighting Indians with General Pope! And continue to do what can be done to assure that General McClellan has all that he needs. I want there to be no doubt that all was done from here that could be done."

Halleck's wire to Buell borrowed liberally from Lincoln's arsenal of logic, up to and including the posing of the question *"Why can we not march as he marches, live as he lives and fight as he fights unless we admit the inferiority of our troops and of our generals?"*

The Great Broadway of New York City celebrated this Monday morning as it did every workday. Ladies with parasols strolled the avenue to enjoy the sights and take note of the latest fashions. The bankers and shopkeepers went about their business generally without a thought of war or of death. Many strolled past the studios of Mathew Brady with only a vague notice of the hand-lettered sign in the window that read "The Dead of Antietam," but a few brave souls entered to spend an hour or so out of the sun while quenching a morbid thirst. Soon the word began to spread, and the lines began to form. The photographs taken by Alexander Gardner shortly after the battle were displayed for public viewing and, of course, for sale. The elegant people of New York City, until this moment, were untouched and unthreatened by war. It was generally the poor people who wept at the casualty reports. Only as they viewed Gardner's work did the faceless news reports and casualty lists become real young men and boys lying dead in ditches and fields. These were nothing like the *Harper's* drawings of gallant, flag-waving men mounting a glorious and bloodless charge. On this Monday afternoon the people of New York learned the brutal truth. On this day they walked among the dead and saw the carnage for themselves.

The images Alexander Gardner brought them were neither gallant nor glorious, and while they were all Confederate dead, they were dead young Americans nonetheless. By the time Gardner and his team of Brady-sponsored photographers had arrived at Antietam, two days after the fight, most of the Union dead had been laid to rest, while the Rebels had lain only in the sun. The bodies were bloated and rigid. Death contortions froze them in gruesome poses with their mouths open or their arms outstretched or with their clothing ripped open to expose their gruesome abdominal wounds. The entire country knew the geography by now, and the place names were common knowledge, but Gardner ripped them from the viewer's vague imagination and gave them form and features—the Miller Farm, The Bloody Lane and Burnside's Bridge. The shell-pocked Dunker Church lay in the distance behind half a dozen lifeless and barefooted Southern cannoneers. And there were the Johnsons, father and son, laid out for all to see in the sunken road, like so much rubbish waiting to be hauled away. Those with the courage to look closely saw the blood that stained the earth where it had recently formed a ghastly, stagnant creek. A young boy lay under a tree, curled up knees-to-chest, and might have been a carefree sleeping child but for the streak of black blood that stained his beautiful, girlish face.

"Mr. Brady has done something to bring home to us the terrible reality and earnestness of war," *The New York Times* reported. "If he has not brought bodies and laid them in our door yards and along streets, he has done something very like it."

A reporter from the *Tribune* stopped by to view the exhibit as well. He should have written a review for his paper but he didn't. He couldn't. George Smalley had seen enough.

The "Peace" Democrats in New York City found a silent ally in the gruesome images from Mr. Gardner's camera.

In the days that followed, the finger-pointing from Washington to Maryland and back again became almost lethal. The Quartermaster General showed records of 9,354 horses being forwarded to McClellan—McClellan showed receipts for 1,964.

The Quartermaster General assured the government that adequate supplies of shoes had been shipped—McClellan said the shoes were all too big.

On the 22nd, Buell politely explained to the government that he had no objection to marching against eastern Tennessee, but thought it appropriate to point out the difficulties involved in such a grand campaign. He reminded Halleck that the enemy could easily concentrate his troops there; that it would require 80,000 men to take and hold it; and that half of all of the army's necessities would have to be hauled from Nashville, which must first be secured. He told his General in Chief that the railroads from Nashville must first be rebuilt, reopened and protected.

Then, failing to note the rhetorical nature of Lincoln's question, he addressed the issue of "the inferiority of our troops and of our generals . . ."

The spirit of the Rebellion enforces a subordination and patient submission to privation and want which public sentiment renders absolutely impossible among our troops. To make matters worse on our side, the death penalty for any offense whatever is put beyond the power of the commanders of the armies, where it is placed in every other army in the world. The sooner this is remedied the better for our country. It is absolutely certain that from these causes, and from these alone, the discipline of the Rebel army is superior to ours.

On October 24th, Abraham Lincoln fired Don Carlos Buell and placed Major General W. S. Rosecrans in command of the Army of the Ohio.

On October 25th, McClellan forwarded to Halleck, for his information and without comment, a report from the First Massachusetts Cavalry complaining that his mounts were, among other things, "sore-tongued and broken down from fatigue and want of flesh."

Halleck read the dispatch and gave it to the President. Lincoln's hand began to shake and his cheeks reddened as he read.

"Send this to General McClellan," Lincoln snapped to a telegrapher. "I have just read your dispatch about sore-tongued and fatigued horses. Will you pardon me for asking what the horses of your army have *done* since the Battle of Antietam that fatigues *anything*?"

McClellan's reply was almost as short. He patiently explained to the novice-general in Washington that his cavalry had begun the Maryland campaign already worn down from its difficult duty on the Peninsula, and had, since that time, engaged in two major battles, chased Stuart around a 90-mile circle and patrolled 150 miles of Potomac shoreline for over a month. "If any instance can be found where overworked cavalry has performed more labor than mine since the battle of Antietam, I am not conscious of it."

General Marcy saw the danger and saw it as his double-duty to alert his commanding officer and his son-in-law of the rapidly falling ax. They leaned that night against a split-rail fence overlooking the field where the First Corps camped.

"George, Buell is gone, and if I read this correctly, so is the President's patience. I believe, and I have no reason to believe this beyond my own intuition, that he is waiting only for the elections to be over to have your head."

"Then so be it, sir! I have said before that it is a matter of total indifference to me. I should actually prefer to be a free man than to submit to this from men whom I know to be my inferiors socially, intellectually and morally! Our President is nothing more than a great, tall gorilla."

Marcy waited a long while in silence and in the hope that George's temper would cool. When he thought the time was right, he nodded out toward the men in the field. "And what of them then, George? What will happen to your army then?"

He watched as his daughter's husband looked out over the field where a thousand campfires burned, and neither man spoke for a very long time.

On Sunday, October 26th, almost six weeks after the Battle of Antietam, the Army of the Potomac slowly and cautiously began to move south, across the river from which it took its name, and back into Virginia at last.

CHAPTER 23

BY DIRECTION
OF THE PRESIDENT

NOVEMBER 4TH

Tuesday, November 4th, 1862, was election day in New York, forty-eight days after the Battle of Antietam, and nine days after the movement began, the Army of the Potomac crossed its last man into Virginia.

The move was not made without volumes of complaining dispatches that continued to plead for more horses and men and clothing. Some even took the form of threats, making certain that in the event of disaster the blame would fall on Washington, where it belonged, and not with the general commanding.

Edwin Stanton remained in a constant state of agitation. The President refused to acknowledge the proper chain of command and continually dealt directly with the officers in the field without so much as a consultation with the Secretary of War. To the secretary's way of thinking, all communications directed to the field, and specifically to McClellan, should be originated by himself and ordered by Halleck. Direct orders issued by the President were nothing more than improper meddling by the Chief Executive in the affairs of the War Department. Since Lincoln's arrogant and unannounced visit to Sharpsburg, the Secretary of

War had barely spoken with the President. He knew that nothing would be done until after the elections at any rate, so he bit his tongue and tugged his beard for more than a month while he looked forward only to this day. When the President began today's cabinet meeting with the reading of his private letter to McClellan written almost three weeks before, a letter of which Stanton had no knowledge until this very moment, the volcano that was Stanton erupted for all to see.

"General Halleck is hamstrung, sir, by your constant direct communications with General McClellan. He does not consider himself responsible for the movements or deficiencies of the Army of the Potomac—he has been forced to yield those responsibilities to you. And I, whose responsibility it is to oversee all war-related operations, have been left out entirely! General McClellan has refused to obey direct orders issued, again, from you and only through Halleck. We have absolutely no control over this man, and it appears that neither the General in Chief nor the Secretary of War has the authority to remove him as should have been done months ago!"

Stanton took his first difficult breath, and Lincoln jumped in before the irate secretary could resume his tirade.

"None of what you have said is correct, Mr. Stanton. General Halleck is, should be and will continue to be responsible. I have told him that I would at any time relieve General McClellan should he require it, and that I would assume full responsibility for such a decision."

"Then I urge you, sir, to assume that responsibility now. The elections will be done today, we have reports of heavy artillery fire indicating that another major battle may at last be imminent. General McClellan *must* be removed."

Abraham Lincoln abhorred face-to-face confrontations and was so adept at avoiding them that he had little practice in managing them. He was stunned at the very idea that a member of his cabinet would challenge him so in front of all of the others. In spite of the fact that he had every intention of replacing McClellan, he was now at a loss as to what to do next. An announcement at this moment would appear to be a capitulation, and Stanton would become ever more unbearable. The silence was uncomfortable to all as the two men glared at each other across the table.

The Postmaster General tried to calm the situation, but in so doing, he left no doubt that McClellan was now friendless in this room.

"We must consider with whom the general would be replaced should that decision be made. Perhaps General Halleck himself should assume the command."

This comment certainly drew attention away from the Secretary of War, but it brought with it no new confidence in Postmaster General Blair.

"That is entirely out of the question, General Blair. I am of the opinion that General Halleck would be an indifferent general in the field." The President was still angry at Stanton and chose to take out that anger on Halleck. "General Halleck shirks responsibility in his *present* position, he is a moral coward and is worth but little except as a critic and director of operations!" He spoke all of those words directly at Stanton and very quickly regretted the venomous tone they took.

"General Halleck is an intelligent and educated man—but he is no commander. I must say, at this time, however, that this is not a matter to be decided by a committee, no matter how august that committee may be." He looked again directly and sternly into Stanton's angry eyes. "And while the matter is under serious and constant consideration, and the views of all of you *and* General Halleck weigh heavily in the matter, the decision as to when to dismiss General McClellan and with whom he shall be replaced, is entirely mine. And now, gentlemen, if we may move on."

In the absence of the army, the Rohrbachs and the Mummas and all of their Sharpsburg neighbors were left to rebuild their lives on their own. Not a cow or a chicken had been left behind.

In the Rohrbach house Jane Mumma lay in the same bed where Henry Kingsbury and Isaac Rodman and a hundred others had died, and there she fought to give life, but the pretty little mother had not enough strength left in her to sustain even one life, much less give birth to another.

Neither mother nor child survived.

Mary walked slowly down the hill to the Antietam Creek, where Ada played while she waited to see her new brother or sister. The house slave watched Ada throw rocks into the water for a few minutes while she tried to figure out how to tell the child that her mother was dead. While she watched she cried and wondered if the misery would end.

It was not Stanton's tirade against McClellan that haunted Lincoln's rest that night, nor was it the abandonment of Little Mac by his last friend in the government, Montgomery Blair, who had not only failed to come to McClellan's defense, but who had suggested a possible replacement. No, it was none of that. It was geography. It was the locations—the return addresses—that headed all of McClellan's dispatches. Lincoln learned more from those than he did from the contents. He moved from Sharpsburg to Pleasant Valley and from there to Berlin, Maryland, where he remained for five full days. Finally, only two days ago, the headquarters moved into Purcellville, Virginia, and today the heading read "Middleburg." Lincoln charted the army's progress by these place names, and the progress he charted was slow, and cautious, and totally without purpose.

The President got out from his bed, pulled his trousers on under his nightshirt, and headed for his office. He could think better there. Along the way, he knocked on John Hay's door; he wanted to share this moment with someone.

He reread the copy of his October 13th letter and though it specifically said, "This letter is in no sense an order," it was, nonetheless, a test. The point had been made that McClellan was closer to Richmond than was Lee—that Lee's route to the Rebel capital was the "arc of a circle," while McClellan's was "the chord." The postmarks on McClellan's reports indicated that he had determined to follow the "arc," and that implied strongly to the President that the Young Napoleon had no intentions of engaging the enemy on any ground where the outcome of the entire conflict might quickly be determined. He remembered Major Key and his "fight 'em to a draw" philosophy. The President had long since decided that if McClellan was not on his way to Richmond, then he would be on his way out.

Hay arrived looking every bit as disheveled as Lincoln; both in their nightshirts and thoroughly ungroomed.

Lincoln placed another clean sheet of paper on his desk and he wrote, "By direction of the President it is ordered that Major General McClellan be relieved from the command of the Army of the Potomac; and that Major General Burnside take command of that Army."

He slid the document across the desk for Hay to read. "There," he said. "At last it is done."

Even after all this time, Hay was mildly surprised, and said nothing.

"What are your thoughts, John?"

"The same as yours I would imagine, sir. Glad that it's finally over, concern over Burnside's ability and how it will be received by the officer corps."

"Ah, yes. The 'officer corps.'" Lincoln suddenly beamed. "Give it back."

The President took the document, dipped his pin and added, "Also that Major-General Fitz-John Porter be relieved from the command of the corps he now commands in said army, and that Major General Hooker take command of said corps. General Porter to immediately report in person to the Adjutant General of the Army, in this city."

"There," Lincoln said. "That should douse that little fire before it ignites."

"Well, sir, your War Secretary will be a very happy man."

"Yes, he will." Lincoln once again handed the paper to Hay. "Take this to him first thing in the morning." He turned and started back to his chambers, but then he stopped short. He turned back to Hay and suddenly his entire face beamed with mischief. "No," he said. "Don't take it to Stanton. Take it to Halleck instead."

As the first snow of the winter fell softly on the nation's capital, Lincoln slipped back under his covers where he slept quite well.

NOVEMBER 5TH

Of course, Halleck brought the orders immediately to Stanton's attention. Lincoln knew that he would, but his message to the power-hungry War Secretary had been sent and received.

Stanton sent for the Adjutant General, General C. P. Buckingham, and, with glee in his eye, he handed him the President's order.

"This is a situation which must be handled delicately, General. I want you to deliver this yourself. It must come from the highest-ranking officer possible to carry the full weight of the President's office. But there are other reasons of which you should be made aware." He paused for dramatic effect and pretended to consider his choice of words. In actuality, this was a well-rehearsed speech that he had been waiting for months to deliver.

"General Burnside has been offered this position on several previous occasions, and he has refused it. Prior to notifying McClellan, we must be certain that Burnside is standing by and ready to accept command. You must go to him first, before you see McClellan. If Burnside refuses, pledge him to secrecy and return here. If he accepts, take him with you when you serve the papers on 'the young Napoleon.'" The secretary's voice took a gleeful and gloating tone at the mention of McClellan's *nom de guerre*. The only fly in this ointment was that Stanton could not be there to serve the papers himself. "No one is to know why you are there. Members of his staff are fanatically devoted to him and any rumor of your purpose could incite them to prevent you from doing your duty."

Buckingham thought this was an unreasonable fear, but Stanton always thought the worst about McClellan and prepared for it. Buckingham was more amused than surprised.

"If all goes well, wire us immediately, or have Burnside do it. But I warn you to have a fresh horse saddled up and standing by. There have been rumors—from respected sources—for over a year, that McClellan would prefer a march on Washington to relinquishing his command. He might very well attempt to become an American Cromwell by marching 'his' army against this town." Now Buckingham *was* surprised. One of the two, Stanton or McClellan, had lost his senses. The general just didn't know which.

"If there is any indication of that, you must mount and ride like all hell back here. Notify us along the way if you can, but get word here so that preparations can be made. Do you understand?"

Buckingham could not speak. He had never considered the idea that any such thing might be possible, and did not know whether to question the secretary's sanity or his own. He could only nod and wait for further instructions.

"The President wishes to speak with you before you leave, and is expecting you now at the mansion."

Buckingham saluted and, slightly dazed by what he had been told, left for his meeting with Lincoln.

Stanton splashed an ample amount of his favorite cologne in his hands and perfumed his beard and smiled as he watched the general go. "Alert the town's garrisons to be prepared for an attack, Henry. Say no more than that, other than to warn them that the enemy may be approaching from the north."

Halleck nodded and turned to leave the room, but Stanton stopped him.

"There's one more thing, Henry. We are going to court-martial Fitz-John Porter, and you and I are going to select the board ourselves. There will be no chance, and hear me well on this, General, there will be *no chance* that this man will win an acquittal." He paused for effect, but only briefly. "Do you understand me on this, General?"

NOVEMBER 7TH

Buckingham dusted the snow from his shoulders and knocked on the door of Ambrose Burnside's headquarters. Burnside recognized him immediately and just as quickly he knew that the time had come. The wait was over.

"I have orders for you, General, from the President."

Burnside read over the dispatch as a formality—knowing full well what it said, but praying that it would not.

"The President is making a dreadful mistake, here, General. General McClellan has the full respect of his army, and, frankly, I am not nearly so qualified as George. I've told Mr. Lincoln so." He felt tears welling up in his eyes and turned away. "You must return to Washington and inform the President . . ." *Inform him of what. He's heard all the arguments. I've promised both the President and myself that I would accept, back before Antietam. Remember Antietam.*

Buckingham took advantage of Burnside's pause. "The President begs me to remind you of your previous meeting in which you encouraged him to give McClellan another opportunity. He told me to remind you that at that meeting you assured the President that, should this offer be tendered again, you would accept. The President also told me to inform you that should you continue to refuse, then the command will be offered immediately to General Hooker."

"Hooker?"

"That is correct, sir. General Hooker has healed nicely from his wounds and is available for duty."

A deep sigh was Burnside's only response.

"The Secretary of War has instructed me that you should accompany me as I deliver the orders to General McClellan."

"Must I?"

"Those are my orders, sir."

The final numbers from the elections reached the President's desk, and they weren't happy ones for Mr. Lincoln and his party. In the House of Representatives, the Democrats gained thirty-six seats, but not all were "Peace" Democrats and the Republicans maintained their majority. Wadsworth in New York failed to gain the governorship of that key state in spite of all of Lincoln's efforts.

"I feel like a boy who stubbed his toe on the way to see his girl," he said while reading the somber news. "He was too big to cry, but it hurt too much to laugh."

It was a two-hour ride in near-blizzard conditions from Burnside's head-quarters to McClellan's, and the two men arrived tired, cold and hungry. They knocked on McClellan's door and interrupted him during his nightly ritual of letter writing to Mary Ellen. The moment he saw the two men together, brushing the snow from their greatcoats, he knew, as Burnside had known, the nature of their business. He remembered his father-in-law's words from a week or two before when Marcy had said, "I believe that he is waiting only for the elections to be over to have your head." There was no need for him to read any of the documentation but protocol demanded it nonetheless.

A rush of emotions ran through the general's mind as the deed was finally done. Stanton and Halleck—the "Gorilla"—Mary Ellen will be devastated—Burnside *et tu?*—the men—the poor leaderless men—my God, what do they have ahead of them—refuse the order—accept the order—do not show defeat—move the army, now, tonight to Washington and with the army at your back demand the dismissal of Stanton and Halleck. The Rubicon. All of these voices at once battled for dominance in his thoughts, but only one broke away. The only one that was ever a real possibility. Very quickly it was only the good soldier's voice that could be heard.

Standing bolt upright, almost at attention, McClellan maintained a casual and expressionless demeanor. He looked at Burnside, but Burnside could not look back. McClellan's heart went out to poor Old Burn. No one knew better than Burnside himself how inadequate he was for the job, and McClellan could see that his old friend fought back tears. Whether it was out of fear of losing their twenty-year friendship or just out of fear alone McClellan could not tell, but he knew that Burnside was in a terrible state.

Buckingham and Burnside waited an interminable time for McClellan's reply—Buckingham afraid that McClellan would refuse the order, and Burnside afraid he would accept. McClellan actually enjoyed their discomfort and stretched it out longer than necessary. Finally, in a full but casual voice he said, "Well, Burnside, I turn the command over to you."

"I'm sorry, George. I want you to know that I in no way sought this . . ."

"Quiet, Burn. I know that. I know very well who is responsible, and I know even better that it was none of your doing. To be frank, sirs, I am almost glad that the agony is over—at least for me." He looked once more at the order. "I am ordered to Trenton to await further orders, but if there is anything that I can do, Burn, to assist in the transition, I shall be more than happy to do so."

"Obviously I need your help, Mac. If you could remain here for a few days, to bring me up to date on the army's disposition and to—how shall I say it?—encourage the men to my . . . aid. I need that from you Mac—and so do they."

"Of course, Burn. And now if you will excuse me, sirs, I was in the process of writing a letter to my wife, and I now have something of interest to tell her."

NOVEMBER 11TH

The most difficult part of the last few days for McClellan had been the meetings with the men, the common soldiers who had grown from a being a rabble in arms into a veteran army under his tutelage. He could see in their eyes the anguish with which they accepted the news.

He wrote a farewell message to the army, and a letter of consolation to Mary Burnside to assure her of "the cordial feeling existing between Burn & myself. He is as sorry to assume command as I am to give it up."

Last night a gigantic log fire had been set before his headquarters tent and members of the officer corps invited to the obligatory "Hail & Farewell."

"You cannot leave us, George," he heard from more than just a few of them. "In a one day's march, we can set this straight."

Each and every time his response was the same. "We have only to obey orders."

But it was this Saturday morning that was the saddest of all. At the town of Warrenton, George B. McClellan rode before his final review of the troops. For three miles, from the camps to the train station, the blue army lined the way. Cheers rose up as he approached. So deafening was the sound that it spooked many veteran horses that were accustomed to the sounds of battle. Gray-bearded veterans cried as he passed and McClellan himself struggled to maintain his composure. Once aboard the train his farewell message was read to those close enough to hear, and finally the engine built its steam and prepared to roll out to Washington and to points beyond.

Caught up in the frenzy of the moment, several hundred men rushed forward and threw their weapons down across the tracks while three of them uncoupled the cars from the engine. It soon reached the point where McClellan himself had to quell the disturbance.

"I appreciate your motives, but I cannot condone actions not becoming to soldiers. As soldiers we have only to obey orders," he told the men as he had told his officers earlier. "Obey General Burnside as you have obeyed me, and all will be well. Farewell, men, and I shall see you again."

The Army of the Potomac came to attention and silently saluted as the train pulled out from Warrenton Station.

"You handled that well, George . . ." Marcy said as they settled down into their private car, ". . . or should I say, 'Mr. President?'"

McClellan smiled and lighted a cigar.

"General Lee, sir."

"Yes, Colonel."

"We have confirmation, sir. General McClellan has been relieved."

"And with whom has he been replaced?"

"Reports indicate that it is General Burnside, sir."

Lee looked around the tent at Longstreet, Jackson and Stuart, all of whom were smiling.

"I fear they may continue to make these changes till they find someone whom I don't understand."

He walked over to the map table, and the other generals followed. He stood for a while in thought.

"General McClellan was relieved not due to incompetence but due to inactivity. That means that General Burnside will be coming after us quickly and perhaps recklessly."

Another long period of silence passed before he continued.

"Well, General Longstreet, it looks as though you will finally get your wish."

"And what wish is that, General?"

"I distinctly remember you saying to me, 'I wish we could just let the Yankees come to us,' and that is precisely what I intend to do."

Longstreet smiled. He remembered the occasion quite well now. He remembered well enough to know that Lee had deleted the "damned," but that wasn't all that brought on his smile. He knew now that he would have the opportunity to prove that a defensive battle plan would win more battles than any number of reckless assaults. *Let's keep the army all together for once*, he thought.

"We shall cross the Rappahannock and invite him to attack us somewhere along this line . . ." Lee drew the line on the map with his finger and looked up as everyone else looked down. ". . . Winchester, Culpeper or maybe even here—at Fredericksburg."

AFTERWORD

I hope you enjoyed To Make Men Free. *I researched this topic for three years before I ever set a word to paper and I assure you that I have done my very best to maintain a high level of historical accuracy.*

I will deal here with some of the broader points that may require some additional historical context.

THE BLACK LEADERSHIP MEETING: Yes, like virtually everything else in *To Make Men Free*, this August 14th meeting actually occurred. It is well known to historians but generally skipped over in undergraduate textbooks. I am sure that a great many modern-day readers are appalled by the language and attitude of President Lincoln toward these men, but we must all remember that Lincoln was a nineteenth-century man, and even a great many abolitionists would have agreed with him in those days. I was extraordinarily careful in writing this section so as not to suggest anything beyond the facts. Rest assured that the words contained in quotation marks are all Abraham Lincoln's words—not mine. (Donald, David Herbert. *Lincoln*. New York: Simon & Schuster, 1995, page 367.)

THE WILSON MUTINY: Regarding the plot to get Joe Hooker to assume command of the army at Antietam, there are obviously only two accounts, both written years after the war. Smalley does not name Wilson in his article ("Chapters in Journalism." *Harper's New Monthly*, August 1894) either because he had forgotten the man's name or because it was an act of mutiny, and Wilson was by then a revered hero. Wilson's account is so self-aggrandizing and improbable that I simply choose to believe Smalley. (Wilson, James H. *Under the Old Flag*. New York: D. Appleton, 1912.)

THE MCCLELLAN COUP: Most historians will argue that no proof exists that this plan ever got far beyond the "camp talk" level. But coups by their very nature don't leave paper trails. Generals Hooker and Porter wrote very public letters stating that a temporary dictatorship was the only way the war could ever be won. These are not exactly private soldiers or young lieutenants whining around a campfire. It is almost solely from Jacob Cox's recollections that the events of the September 27th meeting are taken. (Cox, Jacob B. *Military Reminiscences of the Civil War*. New York: Scribner's, 1900.) The fact that this meeting occurred at all tells us that a plan was being considered. The well-substantiated fact that McClellan was discussing in high circles what his "response" to a direct order should be, borders on treason in and of itself. As a military man he had only two options—obey or resign. Apparently a third option was on the table somewhere. President Lincoln's comment to Ozias Hatch on the Antietam battlefield referring to the Army of the Potomac as "McClellan's bodyguard" certainly implies that Mr. Lincoln took this "idle talk" very seriously. The fact that Secretary Stanton ordered the Washington garrison on full alert following the dismissal of McClellan is further evidence that the government considered it to be a very real threat. The fact that Lincoln chose the order dismissing McClellan as the proper time and vehicle to order the arrest of Fitz-John Porter, I believe, was a shot across the bow of the officer corps of the Army of the Potomac, warning them to obey orders or face charges.

CHARACTER NOTES

For those of you who are not as familiar with Civil War history as others, I will follow up on some of the lives (and deaths) of the persons you have gotten to know through these pages. I will omit the obvious (Lincoln and Lee), but what is "obvious" to the eagle is "obscure" to the sparrow, so I hope the Civil War enthusiast will forgive me for reducing the careers of the famous and infamous to a single paragraph.

CLARA BARTON: Ms. Barton went on to found the American Red Cross. Because of her actions on September 17, 1862, Sharpsburg claims to be the "birthplace" of that organization.

AMBROSE BURNSIDE: General Burnside did in fact yield to the pressure and attacked General Lee's army at Fredericksburg, Virginia. Wave after wave of Union soldiers attacked entrenched lines protected by massed artillery. It was the Union's worst defeat of the entire war. The Irish Brigade was virtually decimated there. After repulsing the oddly similar Pickett's Charge at Gettysburg, Meagher's men began chanting, "Fredericksburg . . . Fredericksburg . . ."

SALMON CHASE: In 1864, Lincoln accepted Chase's resignation because they had reached a point of "mutual embarrassment" in their official relations. Nevertheless, when Roger Taney died in October of that year, Lincoln appointed Chase Chief Justice of the United States Supreme Court.

KYD DOUGLAS: Kyd Douglas survived the war and wrote a memoir entitled *I Rode with Stonewall.* Civil War enthusiasts lovingly call it "Stonewall Rode with Me," but it is nonetheless required reading and I obviously leaned heavily on his anecdotal account. As for his friend Joel Westbrook, this is the only entirely fictional significant character in the book. Douglas often refers to "a friend," but leaves him nameless.

JOHN GIBBON: His famous Black Hat Brigade went on to become one of the Union's most respected units of the war. It was the first Union infantry unit to arrive on the field at Gettysburg and its tradition is carried on today under the name of The Iron Brigade.

JOHN BROWN GORDON: General Gordon survived the war and was the man who surrendered the Army of Northern Virginia at Appomattox Courthouse.

HENRY HALLECK: One of the most maligned persons in American history, Halleck's reputation went from "Old Brains" before the war to "Old Wooden Head" during. His ineptness may be the only thing on which McClellan and the Lincoln administration agreed.

WINFIELD SCOTT HANCOCK: General Hancock advanced to Corps Commander and received the brunt of Pickett's Charge at Gettysburg. Urged to dismount on that day he replied, "Sometimes a Corps Commander's life does not matter." Shortly thereafter he was severely wounded, but survived.

GEORGE L. HARTSTUFF: Brave and well respected, General Hartstuff had a bad habit of getting shot. He continued to serve in combat roles even after receiving severe wounds at Antietam. He retired in 1871 and died less than three years later from an infection of his very first wound suffered at the hands of the Seminoles.

JOHN HAY: If he did nothing else, the country would owe a debt of gratitude to Hay for retrieving Lincoln's essay on God and slavery from the presidential trashbin.

AMBROSE POWELL (A.P.) HILL: A. P. Hill was killed at the Battle of Petersburg only days before the surrender of the Army of Northern Virginia.

JOHN BELL HOOD: Hood lost the use of his arm at Gettysburg and a leg at Chickamauga, and yet returned very quickly to command the Confederate forces at the Battle of Atlanta.

JOSEPH HOOKER: Hooker followed Burnside as Commander of the Army of the Potomac and was outflanked in a masterful maneuver by Jackson at Chancellorsville. Normally bold and brash as a corps commander, he seems to have lost his nerve in higher command. After the defeat he reportedly said, "I just lost faith in Joe Hooker."

THOMAS (STONEWALL) JACKSON: Wounded by "friendly fire" at the Battle of Chancellorsville, he died of complications resulting from the amputation of his left arm. One of the great unanswerable questions of American history is, "What if Lee had had Stonewall at Gettysburg?"

D. R. (NEIGHBOR) JONES: Neighbor Jones died in January of 1863 "of a broken heart."

JAMES LONGSTREET: A man before his times, his defensive tactics won acceptance and were widely applied in WWI. He was reviled in the South after the war and ultimately became the scapegoat for questioning Lee's tactics at the Battle of Gettysburg.

GEORGE B. McCLELLAN: McClellan did run against Lincoln in the election of 1864. The army was allowed to vote absentee—and voted for Lincoln. The Young Napoleon went on to serve as governor of New Jersey. While "McClellan bashing" has become a bit of a parlor game among Civil War enthusiasts, the general was correct about a great many things. He was right when he suggested that the Emancipation Proclamation would do nothing to hasten the end of the war but would rather prolong it, and convert it into "a war of total conquest."

THOMAS FRANCIS MEAGHER: General Meagher was much more Irish than American, and after the Irish Brigade was disbanded, he attempted to resign from the service entirely. His resignation was not accepted and he finished the war serving under William Tecumseh Sherman. He survived the war and was appointed acting governor of Montana, and during a drinking spree he fell off of a steamboat and drowned.

MITCHELL AND BLOSS: Both survived the war, but their personal battle over who found the lost dispatch raged on for both of their lives.

ADA MUMMA: This little girl's story is gathered from her recollections that she set down many years later, and may be faulty according to historians. Samuel Mumma may not have been in Sharpsburg during the battle, and may not have spoken German. My thanks to Wilmer Mumma for publishing her work. The Mumma family still resides in Sharpsburg.

THE NEW YORK REBEL: Unfortunately for us all, her name and all else about her remains unknown to history.

JOHN POPE: The bombastic General Pope was sent west to deal with the Indian uprisings. After successful campaigns against Cochise and Geronimo, he set himself up for further public ridicule by recommending humane treatment for Native Americans.

FITZ-JOHN PORTER: Fitz-John Porter was relieved of command in November of 1862 and brought up on charges, leveled against him by General Pope, of disloyalty, disobedience and misconduct in the face of the enemy. He was tried by a commission "packed" by Edwin Stanton with anti-McClellan favorites, found guilty and discharged from the army. Sixteen years later another commission vindicated him, and in 1886, President Grover Cleveland reinstated his name on the roll of honorably discharged veterans.

JOHN RICKETTS: General Ricketts was appointed to serve on the Porter court-martial, which cost him politically. He didn't return to service until late in the war, but saw significant action at Monocacy River and in General Phil Sheridan's Shenandoah campaign, where he was wounded at Cedar Mountain.

GEORGE SMALLEY: George Smalley's battlefield report was reprinted in virtually every major Northern newspaper. He went on to become an editor at the *Tribune* and from there a foreign correspondent based in London. He claims to have been the first newsman ever to send a transatlantic telegram. He also covered the Crimean War.

EDWIN STANTON: Stanton is credited with the famous quotation following the Lincoln assassination, "Now he belongs to the ages." He agreed to stay on with the Johnson administration, but was eventually fired by the new President. Some contend that it was this firing that inspired the Republicans in Congress to go along with impeachment proceedings against Johnson.

JEB STUART: While much has been said about Stuart's being "missing" in the approach to Gettysburg, I can't help but wonder if a clandestine side trip to Urbana might not be a possible explanation. Stuart was mortally wounded at the Battle of Yellow Tavern on May 11, 1864.

EDWIN SUMNER: "Bull" Sumner participated at the Battle of Fredericksburg and after that defeat he refused to serve under Hooker's command. He was transferred to the Department of Missouri but he died en route.

GIDEON WELLES: Most historians don't think as highly of Welles as I do, but he was a man of high principles and served his country well. He continued in his post as Secretary of the Navy through the Andrew Johnson administration.

JAMES WILSON: Wilson, who dabbled briefly in mutiny at Antietam, went on to become one of General Grant's best cavalry commanders. He also saw action in the Spanish-American War and retired a highly respected major general. One point of literary license: Wilson didn't actually arrive in Washington until September 5th. While Smalley refers to him as a lieutenant at Antietam, records indicate he had been promoted to major by then.

PRIMARY SOURCES

While this is far from a complete bibliography, these are the works I relied upon most heavily while researching To Make Men Free.

Andrews, J. Cutler. *The North Reports the Civil War*. University of Pittsburgh Press, 1955.

Donald, David Herbert. *Lincoln*. New York: Simon & Schuster, 1995.

Douglas, Henry Kyd. *I Rode with Stonewall*. Chapel Hill: University of North Carolina Press, 1940.

Freeman, Douglas Southall. *Lee's Lieutenants*. New York: Scribner's, 1978.

Gibbon, John B. *Personal Recollections of the Civil War*. New York: Putnam's, 1928.

Hay, John. *Lincoln and the Civil War*. Tyler Dennett, ed. New York: Dodd, Mead, 1939.

Johnson, Robert, and Clarence Buel, eds. *Battles & Leaders of the Civil War*. New York: Century, 1887.

Longstreet, James. *From Manassas to Appomattox*. Philadelphia: Lippincott, 1896.

Marvel, William. *Burnside*. Chapel Hill: University of North Carolina Press, 1991.

Murfin, James V. *The Gleam of Bayonets*. Baton Rouge: Louisiana State University Press, 1965.

Priest, John Michael. *Antietam: The Soldier's Battle*. Shippenberg, Pa.: White Mane, 1989.

Sears, Stephen W. *Landscape Turned Red, The Battle of Antietam*. New York: Warner Books, 1983.

———. *George B. McClellan: The Young Napoleon*. New York: Ticknor & Fields, 1988.

———, ed. *The Civil War Papers of George B. McClellan*. New York: Ticknor & Fields, 1989.

Smalley, George. *The New York Tribune*. New York Historical Society collection.

Stackpole, Edward J. *From Cedar Mountain to Antietam*. Harrisburg, Pa.: Stackpole Books, 1993.

Welles, Gideon. *Diary of Gideon Welles*. Howard K. Beale, ed. New York: Norton, 1960.

ON REVOLUTION

"It is in the nature of revolution, the overturning of an existing order, that at its inception a very small number of people are involved. The process in fact, begins with one person and an idea, an idea that persuades a second, then a third and a fourth, and gathers force until the idea is successfully contradicted, absorbed into conventional wisdom, or actually turns the world upside down. A revolution requires not only ammunition, but also weapons and men willing to use them and willing to be slain in the battle. In an intellectual revolution, there must be ideas and advocates willing to challenge an entire profession, the establishment itself, willing to spend their reputations and careers in spreading the idea through deeds as well as words."

Jude Wanniski, 1936-2005
The Way the World Works, (Touchstone Books, 1978)

THE FOUR YEAR
CAREER®
FREEDOM EDITION

HOW TO MAKE YOUR DREAMS OF FUN
AND FINANCIAL FREEDOM COME TRUE

OR NOT ...

By
RICHARD BLISS BROOKE

ISBN 978-0-9766411-6-2
Published by High Performance People, L.L.C.
1875 North Lakewood Drive
Coeur d'Alene, ID 83814
Telephone 855.480.3585, Fax 888.665.8485
Printed in the United States of America

This book is intended to be a fair and honest view of the Network Marketing Income model. Network Marketing is just one name for a form of distribution of a product or service. The core profession has been historically called Direct Sales, whereby a person directly sells a product or service to others outside of a retail establishment. Direct Sales has been a profession for thousands of years. In fact, it is the original method of sales and business. Network Marketing is a more modern term to describe a more modern form of compensating sales reps for not only selling the product but also inviting others to sell with them. In 1945, California Vitamins, a direct sales company selling Nutrilite vitamins, changed a simple traditional rule allowing all sales reps to recruit other sales reps and earn a commission on their sales ... and the sales of many generations of sales reps below them. Network Marketing is also referred to as Multi-level Marketing, Referral Marketing and Social Marketing. It takes many forms and exists in many sales channels including the Internet and even retail establishments. Occasionally the classic pyramid scheme masquerades as a Network Marketing company. The differences are clear and easy to discern and the guidelines are detailed in chapter two. The Network Marketing profession produces at least 30 billion in annual sales by 10 million US-based direct sellers.

AN INTRODUCTION FROM RICHARD BROOKE

As the author of this book I am biased. In 1977 I had my own four year career under my belt at Foster Farms, the single largest chicken processing plant in the world. With only 36 years to go I changed course and at the age of 22, I joined the ranks of the Network Marketing profession. It took me three years to make a living at it. I quit 100 times my first year and watched thousands quit who joined before, during, and after me.

Then I figured something out—and three years later I had 30,000 active partners building the business with me. Sure people still failed and quit but 30,000 people stuck with it. I was earning $40,000 a month in 1983 at the age of 28. I have earned millions since and have coached tens of thousands to earn $500 to $5,000 to $50,000 a month and more.

I figured out how to make Network Marketing work. So have a lot of other people.

Thirty-six years later, I have seen thousands of companies come and go and hundreds of thousands of hopeful Distributors quit before they made it … or maybe they would have never made it. I have seen our profession dirty its pants with its own greed, selfishness, immaturity and general lack of character within its leaders. I have heard all the rational experiences and factoids about how and why this profession is the scourge of the earth. Many of those perspectives are right on, well deserved and make total sense.

I have also seen that, for those people who "figure it out," their lives are forever enriched financially, physically, emotionally and spiritually. Some would say that it's not fair that only a few people create the success they wanted in Network Marketing. I would say that everyone who "takes a look" at Network Marketing as a part-time income or a significant wealth building alternative has the same opportunity to succeed. Life is not fair if you define fairness as "everyone wins." My mentors never promised me life would be fair. They just promised me it would "be." The rest was up to me.

In 2012, had I stuck it out, I would have been retiring from Foster Farms. That's not a bad thing, just different. I loved the people there and even enjoyed the work.

Instead, I have traveled to every state in our union at least twice, to every province and territory of Canada and to over 20 fascinating countries (including my favorite, Cuba, three times). I've built incredible relationships with thousands of people from all over the world and had incredible successes, as well as my share of mind-bending failures. My favorite people in the world are still my high school buddies and my favorite places in the world are still where I call home, which is Coeur d'Alene, Idaho and Carmel, California. I am grateful to be able to clearly make the distinction between my life as it is and what it would have been had I stayed at Foster Farms.

I suppose a person can figure out how something won't work or figure out how it will. Either way, each attitude is a self-fulfilling prophecy.

Success

In March 1992, *SUCCESS* magazine featured the Network Marketing industry's skyrocketing success as its lead story. It was the first time a mainstream publication had done so in the industry's 50-year history. That is your favorite chicken chopper turned CEO, Richard Bliss Brooke, in the middle picture. (You can read about how they picked him in *Mach II With Your Hair On Fire*.) It outsold every issue in the 100-year history of the magazine.

Richard Bliss Brooke has been a full-time Network Marketing professional since 1977. He is a former member of the Board of Directors of the Direct Selling Association, a senior member of the DSA Ethics Committee, as well as:

- Author of *The Four Year Career* and *Mach II With Your Hair On Fire, The Art of Vision and Self-Motivation*
- Owner of a Network Marketing company founded in 1984
- Industry Expert and Advocate
- Motivational Seminar Leader
- Ontological Coach

v

CONTENTS

CHAPTER 1

A Four Year Career vs. A Forty Year Career?

Security is mostly a superstition. It does not exist in nature, nor do the children of men as a whole experience it. Avoiding danger is no safer in the long run than outright exposure. Life is either a daring adventure, or nothing.

— Helen Keller

A Four Year Career vs. A Forty Year Career?

The 40/40/40 Plan

Since the dawn of the Industrial Revolution, over 250 years ago, the idea of a career has been to: work (at least) 40 hours a week for 40 years for 40% of what was never enough for the first 40 years.

The mandated path for most of us was:

1. Get a good education … a four year degree is your ticket.
2. Get a good job with a big company … with lots of benefits.
3. Work it for 40 years to retire and enjoy the Golden Years.

Things have changed a lot since then. Your "company" is more likely to file bankruptcy to avoid paying your retirement than it is to honor it. Even states, counties and cities are starting to face the fact that they over promised and can't deliver and are filing bankruptcy to ditch their retirement and health care obligations. And even if the retirement is there … even if your 401k is not a 201c, there is rarely enough income from this model to have a grand ol' time in your Golden Years. Most people just hunker down and run out the clock. I don't know, maybe they think this is a trial run and they get another shot at it.

Investing in Your Future

Tech companies today are paying kids … 16–20 year olds, to "pass on college" and get in here and create products with us *now*.

All things being equal, college is still smarter than no college. But some kids are figuring out if they invest those four full–time years towards their business ideas and talents, they can end up hiring a lot of college graduates. Think Bill Gates, Steve Jobs, and Larry Ellison … they all quit college to launch their empires.

Most young adults following the college model do end up well trained to get a job, but are also well saddled with tens to hundreds of thousands in debt. This debt that cannot be discharged in bankruptcy, it can rarely be renegotiated and most people are ill–afforded to pay it off. And since most people in their 30s and 40s are not even in the career they majored in, the debt they are carrying is a depressing load.

For sure if you are intent on becoming a doctor, lawyer, engineer or CPA the more education you get, probably the better. But there are viable options for those that choose to consider them. The cheese has been moved.

Not only has the cheese moved, it has been cut up in a lot of different pieces and placed in different places. There is a big piece of it over here in Network Marketing.

The Four Year Career Alternative

The Four Year career is simply a Network Marketing plan and as such is not a guarantee. It is just a model to consider and study … perhaps engage in, believe in and "graduate" four years later with no debt and a significant Asset Income that could provide freedom of choice for the rest of your life.

Most people do not build a Network Marketing empire in four years and enjoy a fabulous life from then on.

But they could. This book is about the "could." Just the could. If you take from this that it is a promise you are misreading the words and intent. There are no guarantees. Just ask all the graduates still looking for a job that pays more than $50 thousand a year.

First we need to understand it ... not from rumor, not from Uncle Bob and his train wreck in Network Marketing 20 years ago. But understand the facts, just like we understand how succeeding at getting a job works.

Then we need to find something about the process that appeals to us. Maybe it is the upside to earn a king's ransom, maybe it is the freedom to work from home, maybe the flexibility to choose your own schedule, maybe to live/work from anywhere you choose or maybe it is the spiritual, leadership, communication and relationship building skills you will learn. You must have a really good reason to take a road less traveled, otherwise it is too dark and scary.

Lastly, you need to learn to believe that it will work for you and those you offer it to. This takes time but it is the most important aspect of "figuring it out." **Belief does not come from success. Success comes from belief.**

The rules most of us grew up with have consistently been thrown out the window over the past 30 years. Loyalty to one particular job no longer provides security. A four-year degree might get you a job, but that's about it. The average person today will change jobs seven to ten times in their lifetime.

Saving and investing won't start to happen for most people until their kids are out of college—when most adults are well into their fifties. Starting to invest at age 50 only leaves about 20 years for accumulation. As we can clearly see from the compounding chart on the next page, it is not so important how much you invest, but for *how long* you invest.

Take a close look at the compounding chart for a reality check. Invest $500 a month at 7% from age 30 to 70 and you will have over $1.2 million. That Asset will pay you $84,000 a year for life at 7%. How much would you need to invest to end up with the same amount if you wait until you are 50?

In order to achieve the same cash value in only 20 years (starting at age 50 through age 70), your required monthly investment is nearly $2,500!

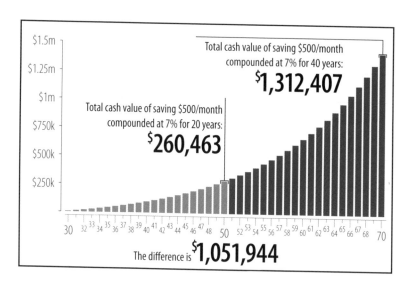

And notice I used a 7% return. That is quite a generous assumption. What are you earning on your investments on average since you started investing? 7%, 10% or 2%?

The Investment Strategy

What about investment strategies? The models for us to choose from have traditionally been real estate and equities.

Liquid Investments/Equities

Most of us probably do this to some extent. We take what we can or will out of our paychecks, after paying taxes and all of our bills. If we are fortunate and/or frugal, we might end up with 10% to invest … perhaps $500 to $1,000 a month. For many people it's just the opposite … they are going in debt $500 to $1,000 a month and are just "hoping" something will change. Which group are you? Who do you know in the latter group? What are their options for "change"?

The save and invest system does work when we work it. We need to invest consistently, every month, and we need to invest in ways that produce at least an aggressive return over time, such as 7%. Anyone of us who started doing this from our first working years would end up with a sizable nest egg. For those who waited, the results are less favorable. And equities can go from 100% to zero overnight if you pick the wrong investment such as Enron, Global Crossings, MCI, AIG, Bear Stearns, Washington Mutual, IndyMac, Goldman Sachs, Kodak, Hostess, General Motors, SAAB, American Airlines, MF Global, Borders, Solyndra, Lehman Brothers, Delta Airlines, WorldCom, Inc., etc.

Real Estate

Many of us gain most of our net worth through the payments we make over time on our own home. This works because we must pay someone for a place to live; therefore we are consistent with the investment. In higher-end markets and any waterfront community, historically the return is much more than 7%. However, we have also seen market corrections that have dropped real estate values by up to 50% even in those coveted California and Florida markets.

The Challenge

For most people who consider these strategies, it is deciding what to invest in and, more importantly, where to get the money to invest. These strategies work great if you have the extra $1,000 a month to invest every month without fail for 25 years.

And unfortunately, the downturns in the markets rarely give notice. Those that even do it for a living are, for the most part, completely caught off guard. Those of us that invest as a necessity are caught in the landslide.

WHY NETWORK MARKETING?

Far better it is to dare mighty things, to win glorious triumphs, even though checkered by failure, than to take rank with those poor spirits who neither enjoy much nor suffer much, because they live in the gray twilight that knows neither victory nor defeat.

— THEODORE ROOSEVELT

WHY NETWORK MARKETING?

There is a third strategy that anyone can employ to build extraordinary wealth and financial freedom, regardless of age, experience, education, income level or social status: Asset Income from Network Marketing.

A Network Marketing Income Offers Huge Advantages

1. You can build it part-time, any time.
2. You can build it from anywhere, any city, any virtual office.
3. You can launch it for $500 to $1,000.
4. You are "in business" for yourself, but not *by* yourself, meaning your host company will do all the heavy investing and lifting from product development, legal ground work, customer service, data processing, banking, sales training, marketing, branding and even social media.
5. Your business partners ... those above you in the network in terms of seniority and linage have a vested interest in your success. Somewhere in your team, someone is making it work and they want more than anything to teach and motivate you to make it work for you.
6. You can create enough tax deductions alone each year to make it worthwhile.
7. You can learn it while you earn it. You can create cash flow your first month.
8. You can earn an extra $500, $1,000, $5,000 or more a month—every month—to invest in the traditional options of real estate and equities.
9. And because with time and success your income will be produced for you by hundreds, perhaps even thousands, of others each pursuing their own success creating a asset

income … that means it could go on forever regardless of whether you are working hard at it or not. A pure asset income creates an asset … or net worth.

The asset value of your Network Marketing income will be approximately 200 times your monthly income. If you are earning $5,000 a month in Residual Asset Income, and you can rely on it continuing, your Asset Income could be worth $1 million.

How much would you have to earn to invest enough to build $1 million in real estate or equities? How long would it take? How much would you have to sacrifice in your *lifestyle* to do it?

It is 200 times easier to build your net worth all three ways, using your Network Marketing income to fund the other two options. And you can get to your target net worth in five to ten years, versus it taking your whole lifetime.

Yeah, But Why Network Marketing? Let's Start With a Couple of Simple Facts
Fact #1:
It's legal.

In the U.S. and around the world in over 70 countries, Network Marketing has been legally used for product distribution and compensating Distributors for more than 60 years.

During this time, Network Marketing has repeatedly been upheld by the federal and state courts as a legal distribution and compensation method, when the following legal guidelines are followed:

1. The main objective of the business is selling viable products or services at a market driven price. Meaning, there is a market for the product from consumers absent of the financial opportunity. The test is simple. Would you or do you have customers that are buying this product without any connection to the Network Marketing financial opportunity? Is it a real product at a market driven price or is the product a shill in a money game?

2. Potential incomes can't be promised. Even hypothetical incomes can't be inferred without the appropriate disclaimers. This is not an even playing field with the rest of the business world … even lotteries get to hype us into thinking we might win millions (better chance of getting stuck by lightening). But beware of Network Marketing companies that hype the income without transparency.

3. Distributors are not paid for the act of recruiting others (head hunting fees). Income has to come entirely from the sale of products.

There are many products or services that Distributors will be "customers" for as long as there is a financial opportunity to go with it. The means justify the end. Unfortunately, when all the shine wears off, no one continues to use the product. This is a pyramid scheme. The true test of a legitimate Network Marketing company is whether most of the product is sold to consumers who are not earning any commissions or royalties from the opportunity. Most Network Marketing Distributors start out pursuing the income opportunity but once they give up they settle in to being a customer. Most companies' total sales are made up of these "wholesale" customers. Maybe they sell enough to get "theirs for free." This is easily 70% of most Network Marketing sales forces. They don't have any sales reps on their team. They are just using the product. They are customers. The other 30% is made up of those earning a few hundred to a few thousand a month.

The concept attracts very dynamic promoters—some are ethical, some not. Many Network Marketing companies have crossed the line legally and have been the subject of negative media, as well as civil and criminal penalties. However, I also seem to have been reading in the last few years about the banking and investment industry, the oil industry and the drug industry being indicted, prosecuted, fined, and sometimes executives imprisoned. Such is the nature of free enterprise in the wild, wild West.

Fact #2:
Most companies fail, some succeed.

There are an estimated 2,000 Network Marketing firms distributing over $30 billion a year in goods and services in the U.S. alone. Most Network Marketing companies do not succeed. Most restaurants do not. Most dry cleaners do not. Most companies we went to work for just out of college or high school have already failed.

And some do succeed. Herbalife, Mary Kay Cosmetics, Forever Living Products, Nu Skin and Usana are multi-billion dollar brands and have been in business and growing steadily for 30 to 60 years. Hundreds of other companies sell between $10 million and $1 billion a year through millions of independent brand representatives.

This is the nature of free markets and enterprise.

Fact #3:
Most Distributors give up long before they could have succeeded.

Some rare individual Distributors have earned and enjoyed long-standing Asset Royalty Income fortunes of $1 million or more per year, for years. Some elite business builders after investing 5 to 10 years earn $25,000 to $100,000 a month. Many more earn from $1,000 to $10,000 a month. And the masses earn a few hundred.

And all of the above are those that did not quit.

Most individuals who pursue building a Network Marketing business, give up before they see the level of success for which they hoped.

The average Network Marketer never creates enough success to warrant doing anything beyond buying product at wholesale. The fact is, people with average ambition, commitment, and effort usually don't do well in a business like Network Marketing.

Is that the fault of the system or the individual? Both, I think. Network Marketing is not easy. Who do you know that is right now looking to get involved in Network Marketing? No one, unless they are already involved.

We obviously shed light on our misunderstood profession for enough people that 175,000 a week join one of our companies … people that never thought they would … given who they thought we were. *We are not entirely our reputation.*

We have a long way to go in educating the public and treating the public with respect and honor before there will be a public demand for our profession. That is one of the intentions of this book.

To be successful, one must have a high level of personal confidence, love talking to people, be comfortable creating new relationships every day, be coachable and most importantly be a proud ambassador of the Network Marketing profession.

Fact #4:
WE are a major player in the global economy and we are growing!

The Network Marketing method of marketing as an industry has grown 17 out of the last 20 years, including over 90% in just the past 10 years. A staggering *$110 billion* worth of goods and services are sold worldwide each year in this industry.

The Top 12 Billion Dollar Network Marketing Companies: 2011 Revenue

$12 billion

$10 billion

$3 billion

$2.9 billion

$3.5 billion

$2.5 billion

$2.3 billion

$2.2 billion

$1.7 billion

$1.5 billion

$1.3 billion

$1.3 billion

Each week, about 475,000 people worldwide become sales representatives for one of these companies. That's *175,000 each week* in the U.S. alone.

There are 15 million Americans and 67 million people worldwide who participate at some level in this concept.

Twenty-five years ago there were no books written on the subject of Network Marketing. Now there are dozens ... some have sold millions of copies. Fifteen years ago no mainstream magazines or newspapers or television shows had featured the positive uplifting opportunity of Network Marketing. Now there are hundreds of examples. Ten years ago there were virtually no "thought leaders" who endorsed our profession. Now many of them do.

There are thousands of companies and millions of sales representatives ... each looking to build their team. This idea's time has come. And it is about to explode ... in a good way.

It Works

The bottom line is, Network Marketing works and has worked to build extra—to extraordinary—individual wealth for more than 60 years. Some of the smartest people in the world are taking advantage of it.

 Paul Zane Pilzer, World-Renowned Economist and Best-Selling Author of *The Next Millionaires*

"From 2006 to 2016, there will be 10 million new millionaires in the U.S. alone ... many emerging from Direct Selling."

Robert T. Kiyosaki, Author of *Rich Dad Poor Dad* and *The Business of the 21st Century*

"… Direct Selling gives people the opportunity, with very low risk and very low financial commitment to build their own income—generating assets and acquiring great wealth."

Stephen Covey, Author of *The Seven Habits of Highly Effective People*

"Network Marketing has come of age. It's undeniable that it has become a way to entrepreneurship and independence for millions of people."

Bill Clinton, Former U.S. President

"You strengthen our country and our economy not just by striving for your own success but by offering opportunity to others …"

Tony Blair, Former British Prime Minister

"[Network Marketing is] a tremendous contribution to the overall prosperity of the economy."

David Bach, Author of the New York Times Bestseller, *The Automatic Millionaire*

> "… you don't need to create a business plan or create a product. You only need to find a reputable company, one that you trust, that offers a product or service you believe in and can get passionate about."

Tom Peters, Legendary Management Expert and Author of *In Search of Excellence* and *The Circle of Innovation*

> "… the first truly revolutionary shift in marketing since the advent of 'modern' marketing at P&G and the Harvard Business School 50 to 75 years ago."

Zig Ziglar, Legendary Author and Motivational Speaker

> "… a home-based business offers enormous benefits, including elimination of travel, time savings, expense reduction, freedom of schedule, and the opportunity to make your family your priority as you set your goals."

Jim Collins, Author of *Built to Last* and *Good to Great*

> "… how the best organizations of the future might run – in the spirit of partnership and freedom, not ownership and control."

Seth Godin, Best-Selling Author of *Permission Marketing*, *Unleashing the Ideavirus* and *Purple Cow*

> "What works is delivering personal, relevant messages to people who care about something remarkable. Direct Sellers are in the best position to do this."

Donald Trump, Billionaire Businessman and Owner of the Trump Network

> "Direct Selling is actually one of the oldest, most respected business models in the world and has stood the test of time."

Ray Chambers, Entrepreneur, Philanthropist, Humanitarian and Owner of Princess House

> "The Direct Selling business model is one that can level the playing field and close the gap between the haves and have-nots."

Roger Barnett, New York Investment Banker, Multi-Billionaire and Owner of Shaklee

> "… best-kept secret of the business world."

Warren Buffet, Billionaire Investor and Owner of three Direct Selling/Network Marketing companies

"The best investment Berkshire Hathaway ever made."

Network Marketing
Myths

Every man takes the limits of his own field
of vision for the limits of the world.

— Arthur Schopenhauer

Network Marketing Myths

Myth #1:
Getting in on the ground floor is the best way to success in a Network Marketing Company.

The truth is, it is the worst time to join. Most companies, including Network Marketing companies, go out of business in their first five years. Of course, no company is going to tell you that in their promotional materials. Everyone involved at the start of any company hopes it will succeed.

Another risk with a new company is that no company has its best foot forward early on. It takes years to develop competent, experienced staff, reliable procedures and efficient services.

The best time to join a Network Marketing company is when it is at least five years old, or backed by a larger company. By then, it has demonstrated a commitment and ability to:

- Grow ethically.
- Stay in business.
- Honor its Distributors and customers.

And yet, this allows you the opportunity to get involved with the company before they are so well-known that everyone has either already given them a try, or decided they aren't interested.

Now of course if everyone adhered to this sage advice, none of us would be here. To the pioneers and courageous (the risk-takers) come both the thrill of victory and the agony of defeat. The ground floor is not for the faint of heart.

Myth #2:
Network Marketing is an opportunity for someone who is not doing well financially to make some money—maybe even a lot of money.

Unfortunately, many of the success stories have perpetuated this myth with a rags-to-riches theme. Although there are enough people to substantiate the myth, it is still a myth.

The same skills it takes to succeed in any marketing business are required in Network Marketing:

- You must be assertive.
- You must have confidence.
- You must be dynamic in your ability to express yourself.
- You must have enough resources to propel yourself through the challenges.

Those resources should include working capital, contacts, time, discipline and a positive, crystal-clear vision of where you intend to go with your business—whether it is easy or not.

The truth is that many people who are struggling financially are doing so for a number of reasons, including low self-esteem and/or lack of the basic skills and preparation that allow one to succeed in anything. Network Marketing is a powerful and dynamic economic model, but not so powerful that it can overcome peoples' lack of readiness or persistence.

The fact is that the people who are already successful in whatever they do, tend to also succeed in Network Marketing. The great part is, they are apt to do better financially in Network Marketing because the economic dynamics are so powerful. Successful people are rarely in a profession where they can earn on the leverage of thousands of other people. Real estate agents, teachers, coaches, medical professionals, counselors, small business owners, beauty professionals and physical fitness professionals may be stellar performers in their domain but how do they create the opportunity to earn on the efforts of thousands of others in their same profession? Here they can.

Myth #3:
Network Marketers succeed by being in the right place at the right time.

Network Marketing is a business; it is not a hobby, a game, a scheme, a deal or something in which to dabble. People who treat it lightly do not succeed. People who treat it as a new career, a profession and a business have a reasonable opportunity to make it pay off very well. Professionals who treat it as a Wealth Building Art to be "mastered" eventually can earn a yacht-load of money. Most people invite a few people to look and then quit. Those who master it invite a few people every day for a year or two and in that "practice" they hone the art of listening more than talking, interpret rejection in a learning way, and learn how to craft their offer in such a way that someone actually WANTS to hear more. Just like any worthwhile career it takes time, patience and repetition.

Myth #4:
The way Network Marketing works is the "Big Guys" make all their money off the "Little Guys."

The "big guys, little guys" myth is usually perpetuated by people who define fairness as "everyone gets the same benefit, regardless of their contributions." That is how socialism works, not how Network Marketing works.

In Network Marketing, the people who attract, train and motivate the most salespeople earn the most money. Period.

There are basically three levels of participation:

Wholesale Customer
This is someone who gets involved just to use the products and buy them at the lowest cost. This often requires a little higher minimum order and an annual renewal fee, very much like being a member of Costco. (Who can go in to Costco without actually spending more money?) Many Distributors end up just being wholesale customers after pursuing the income opportunity and deciding it is not for them.

Retailer
A Retailer is a Distributor who focuses their efforts on just selling the products. In many cases they do not understand the income opportunity well enough to sell it.

A retailer will earn 20% to 50% commission on their own personal sales, and the upper limit of their income will usually be in the hundreds of dollars a month.

Network Marketing Leader

A Network Marketing leader is someone who is a customer, a retailer and an inviter. They understand the business model well enough to know the best upside is in getting geometric progression to work for them so they are always inviting others to look ... just look at the opportunity.

A Network Marketing leader may enroll as many as 100 people to build with them over their career. Out of those, most will just use the product; some will retail it, and a few will actually do what the Network Marketing leader did by enrolling others.

To be a successful Network Marketing leader, one must be able to enroll lots of people to sell with them, and they must be able to train and motivate the group to continue growing. The better one is in these roles, the more money one will earn.

In simple terms, if a person sells a little and enrolls just a few people, they will earn far less than someone who sells a lot and enrolls, motivates and trains a group that grows. That's basic capitalism, which most North Americans consider quite fair.

Myth #5:
You have to use your friends and family to make any money in Network Marketing.

The truth is, you do not and you should not. Your friends and family should only become a part of your business if it serves them to do so. If it serves them—if they see an opportunity for themselves just like you did—then they are not being used, they are being served. If you do not believe your opportunity can serve them, do not offer it to them.

An opportunity that truly inspires *you* will most likely inspire them as well. Offer it to them. If they say no, respect and honor their viewpoint and do not make a nuisance of yourself.

Myth #6:
If Network Marketing really worked, everyone would get involved and the market would be saturated.

The truth is, although this is mathematically possible, history has proven that saturation is not an issue. There are many companies you will see featured in this book that have been in business for 30 to 50 years doing billions a year in business with millions of sales reps. Yet you are not one of them. Nor are 298 million people in the U.S. and 6.9 billion people worldwide.

Plus you might consider a great leader who personally sponsored 12 people 2,000 years ago. They have all been recruiting via weekly opportunity meetings and one-on-one for all of those 2,000 years. And yet most of the world does not subscribe to their program.

4

TRADITIONAL SALES VS. NETWORK MARKETING

Many people fear nothing more terribly than to take a position which stands out sharply and clearly from the prevailing opinion. The tendency of most is to adopt a view that is so ambiguous that it will include everything and so popular that it will include everybody...

— MARTIN LUTHER KING, JR.

Traditional Sales vs. Network Marketing

Most of us grew up with a traditional selling paradigm. It sounds like this ... if you have the opportunity to earn money with a product, what you are supposed to do is sell a lot of product. The more you sell, the more money you earn. Right?

In the Traditional Selling Paradigm, if you had a goal of selling $1 million worth of product a month, you might hire 100 full-time, professional salespeople to work for you, giving them each a territory and a quota of $10,000 in sales per month. If they couldn't meet that quota, of course, you would fire them and find other salespeople who could. And you would keep hiring and firing (forever) seeking to find the 100 who would consistently meet your quota. (And if you didn't own the company, the owners would fire you if you didn't.)

While Network Marketing is a form of selling, there are some very important distinctions. As a Network Marketer, you would use a very different *paradigm* to achieve the same $1 million in sales.

Instead of full-time professional salespeople with terrifying quotas, Network Marketing is based on satisfied customers, most of whom do not like to sell but are happy to tell others about the products they, themselves, use. These customers are not full-time or part-time employees. They are some-time, independent volunteers with no quotas and no protected territories. They "work" *when they feel like it*.

Network Marketing is not about personally selling a lot of product, although some Distributors do. It is about **using** and **recommending** the product and, IF you see and believe in the wealth building model of geometric progression, finding a lot of others to do the same.

The differences between **Salespeople** and **Network Marketing People** are:

Sales	vs.	Network Marketing
Full-time	vs.	Some Time
Salespeople	vs.	Customers
Employees	vs.	Volunteers
Quotas	vs.	Incentives
Protected Territories	vs.	No Territories

To Sell $1,000,000:

100 Salespeople each sell $10,000 = $1,000,000	vs.	10,000 Volunteers each sell $100 = $1,000,000

Network Marketing is simply a lot of people "selling" a little bit *each*.

CHAPTER  5

How It Works

Nothing worthwhile really ever comes easily. Work, continuous work and hard work, is the only way you will accomplish results that last. Whatever you want in life, you must give up something to get it. The greater the value, the greater the sacrifice required of you.

There's a price to pay if you want to make things better, a price to pay for just leaving things as they are. The highway to success is a toll road. Everything has a price.

— Unknown

There Are Three Basic Activities Required To Create Your Own Four Year Career

1. Use …

First, become your own best customer. USE all of your company's products in as many ways as possible, discovering as many benefits and success stories as possible. Create your own best product story. You will want to be able to tell people exactly what this product did for you that made you want to use it forever and share it with others. The more powerful your own story, the more impact you will have in recommending the product to others—and most importantly you won't be "selling" it, you will just be telling your story.

2. Recommend …

This is where most people think they have to sell the product. It's better to see yourself just recommending it, like you would a good movie or restaurant. You listen to the people around you … listen to their problems. And when someone shares a problem your product can solve, just tell them your story. Let them decide if it is right for them. If you recommend a great Italian place and the person says, "I don't like Italian," then the conversation is probably over. If they say, "That place is too expensive," you just let it go as their opinion. You don't argue, right? Don't sell or argue with customers either. Just recommend it. If it is a fit, perfect. If not, let it go. This is how successful Network Marketers establish lots of customers over time and move lots of product without making a nuisance of themselves.

3. Invite "Just to Take a Look"

Inviting people is like recommending the product, only you are inviting them to "just take a look" at the income opportunity. The best way to do this is with a tool like a CD, DVD, brochure or website. Those who master inviting, eventually master The Four Year Career.

Again, this is not selling, convincing or arguing. People are either ready in their life right now to look at new options or they are not. Arguing with them about whether they have time, the money to get started or whether they are good at selling is a waste of time and energy. (Although it is fun to "let" someone "sell" you hard on why they can't sell.)

You may not have as great of an income story to tell your prospects as you do your product story. That is what your "upline" partners are for. Tell their stories. There are just a couple keys to being an effective inviter:

1. Be convinced yourself ... in your product, your company and The Four Year Career. Your conviction should show up as enthusiasm, confidence, peace, patience, acceptance, love and leadership.
2. Be interesting. Not by what you say, what you drive, or how you hype but by being *interested* ... interested in them. Ask curiosity questions and **LISTEN**. You will be amazed at how interesting people are ... their lives, their families, their careers, their heartaches and their dreams. In this process they will either tell you exactly what is missing in their lives that your invite may help solve ... or they won't. Invite those that reveal their own opportunity.

CHAPTER

6

FOUR CORNERSTONES OF
THE FOUR YEAR CAREER

The American Pioneers HAD to become successful entrepreneurs
… the Native Americans wouldn't hire them.

— RICHARD BLISS BROOKE

Four Cornerstones of
The Four Year Career

Below is a model of The Four Year Career. Each person represented is a Sales Leader meaning they are doing all three activities in the last chapter.

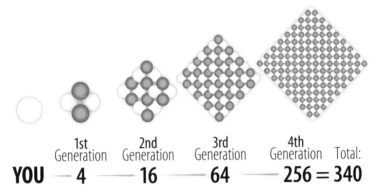

	1st Generation	2nd Generation	3rd Generation	4th Generation	Total:
YOU —	**4** —	**16** —	**64** —	**256**	**= 340**

You enroll 4 (who each enroll 4)

for 16 (who each enroll 4)

for 64 (who each enroll 4) for 256

Each of you uses and recommends just an average of $100 a month in products for $34,000 in monthly sales. Earning an average of 10% on each generation of sales for an Asset Income of $3,410 a month.

The Four Cornerstones:

1. The People
2. Product Sales
3. Your Asset Income
4. The Asset Value

The First Cornerstone is The People

Network Marketing is a lot of people selling a little bit each. Remember the example of Traditional Sales where the goal was to sell $1 million a month in products? Hire 100 superstars and give them a $10,000 a month quota. 100 times $10,000 is $1 million. In Network Marketing, you swap the numbers: 10,000 "anybody" volunteers each using and selling a little bit each.

So the question is how do we get 10,000 people ... or even 1,000?

Two laws allow us to gather 1,000 people. The first was written by the creators for the Network Marketing concept who said, in essence: "Anyone can, and should sponsor others." This allows the second law: Geometric Progression.

This is How The Rich Get Richer and The Poor Get Poor

If you had $1 million today to invest at 10%:

- In 7 years, you would have $2 million.
- In 14 years, you would have $4 million.
- In 21 years, you would have $8 million.

With $8 million at 10% you would be earning $800,000 a year in interest alone. Eventually, whether it is at $800 thousand a year or $2 million a year, you tire of spending it (on assets that do not appreciate).

In many "old money" families, this investment compounding has gone on for so many generations, they can't possibly spend all the interest income produced. They are on autopilot to just keep getting richer.

- *Geometric Progression is to Network Marketing what compounding is to wealth building.*
- The question is, how do you get 1,000 people to be "recommending for you?"
- The answer is, you don't. You just get a few … like four, and lead them to do the same.

The path to gathering one thousand, two thousand or thirty thousand people to "sell for you" in Network Marketing is geometric progression. This is made possible by the Rule of Law in Network Marketing … that everyone regardless of rank or time involved is encouraged to invite and enroll others. If you have been involved for one day you are encouraged to invite and enroll others. This is the same if you have been involved for 10 years and are earning

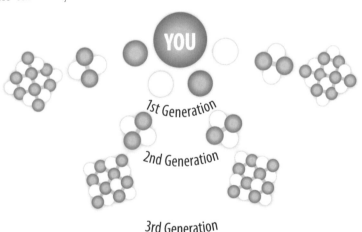

Note: No Network Marketer's organization looks exactly like this one. This is merely an illustration of a mathematical formula that shows the dynamic and potential available. There is no way to control how many, or how few, people any one Distributor will sponsor.

$10,000 a month. Everyone enrolls new sales representatives. This creates the compounding impact.

You enroll four who each enroll four who each enroll four, etc. 1 – 4 – 16 – 64 – 256 – 1,024 and so on.

It's Not Nearly as Easy as It Appears on Paper.

This progression can quickly be overwhelming. But your role in Network Marketing is just to get the first four – not the whole bunch. Focus your attention on just the first four. And in actuality you may build in units of 2 or 3 depending on your particular compensation model … the same concept holds true.

The key to understanding the geometric opportunity lies in a simple question you can ask yourself:

> *"If you really, really wanted to,* could you find four people, anywhere in North America, to do this? Before you answer— let's define "do this."

"Doing this"… or a Sales Leader is:

1. Using the products.
2. Recommending the products to others in need/want.
3. Inviting others to "Just take a look."

So I ask you again. If you really, really wanted to, could you find four say in the next 4 to 6 months?

Now if you are not sure, what if I told you I would give you $5,000 for each of them … $20,000 cash if you get four in the next four months. Then could you? Would you?

Most people would answer yes. The reason is, if they really "wanted to," anything like this is doable. Getting four people to make a fortune is not THAT hard to do.

If you answered YES … lock in on that YES; it is the key to believing you can get 10,000. Why? Because if you believe you will get four … and they are four who are "doing it"… then they also will be "standing" in the same question. Will they get four? If you are not sure … ask them. And what is usually the result of someone really, really wanting to do something—but more importantly—believing they will do it and being in action doing it? It eventually gets done.

Now remember, I am typing this on my laptop. Creating it in actual, real-life human production requires more than just simple keystrokes.

Perhaps you are "getting it" right now. Perhaps you need to let it rest or doodle it on a notepad … $1 – 2 – 4 – 8$, $1 – 3 – 9 – 27$, $1 – 4 – 16 – 64$, $1 – 5 – 25 – 125$.

This is how geometric progression will work for you. One person each believing they will get four creates … You $– 4 – 16 – 64 – 256 – 1,024 – 4096$ and so on.

The Second Cornerstone is Product Sales

Compared to the rest of the Cornerstones, people are the most important and most challenging aspect to understand, believe in and execute. Product Sales, however, are not. In a legitimate Network Marketing business, the brand representatives are very satisfied customers … one could even say evangelical. They love the product. They love it so much they open their mind to becoming a Network Marketer and recommending it.

Some will ask after seeing all the geometric progression of recruiting … "well if everyone is recruiting who will sell the product?" I like to let people think for a moment about what they just asked. The answer is Grant's Tomb obvious. Everyone is selling the product. And the more people we have

selling it the more we sell. We just don't worry about how much any one representative sells.

The average Network Marketer might only personally use and sell $100–$300 a month. There will always be exceptions. There are people who sell thousands a month. But as long as the product is compelling, the Distributors will sell it … or more accurately recommend it. Sales are simply created by the Distributors using and offering products. So if you have 2,000 representatives each averaging $200 a month in consumption and sales, your business generates $400,000 a month in sales. That pretty much answers that. Period.

The Third Cornerstone is Asset Income

This is the easiest Cornerstone to understand and believe. Every Network Marketing company has a compensation plan that pays you on most, if not all, of the many generations of representatives in your group. This is the percent of sales volume you will earn on each generation of brand representatives.

Each company is very creative to incentivize (yes, this is now a word) certain business building behaviors. The bottom line is you can expect to earn between 5% and 10% on the sales of most of your organization and even a small percent on all of it providing you qualify to earn at the deepest generations. This gives you Royalty Income. If your sales are $400,000 a month, you are earning between $20,000 and $40,000 a month. Basic math class.

The Fourth Cornerstone is The Asset Aspect of Your Income and The Asset Value

If you continue to use the theoretical model of four who sponsor four, etc., then at some point perhaps around year two or three, 256 people would fill your fourth generation of Distributors. This would result in a total of 340 people in your Network Marketing organization.

If each of those Distributors use and recommend just $200 of product per month, there would be 340 people selling a total of $68,000 worth of product monthly.

If you're paid an average royalty of 10% on that $68,000, your monthly check would be $6,800.

If you could count on it continuing long after you were done building it then it is deemed residual and will have a corresponding asset value. $6,800 a month for example is worth about $1,200,000.

Examples of other income producing assets would be real estate, dividend producing stocks, patent and copyright royalties. All of these can be appraised for a value based on their income history and future income prospects.

Think about it. What is your home worth? If you own it, what could you rent it for? If you are renting, you already know. If your home is worth $250,000 you might rent it for $1,500 a month or a 7% annual return on the owner's investment.

Although you cannot sell a Distributorship for $1,200,000 that earns $6,800 a month (far too easy for one to build on their own), it is worth that to you as an asset.

So how do you know it will be residual?

The Answer ... Is In The Numbers

Look closely at the generations diagram that follows. Which generation earns you the most income? Obviously, it is the fourth generation, which has four times as many people in it as the third generation before it. In fact, more than 75% of your group's sales volume—and therefore, over 75% of your earnings—are from your fourth generation Distributors.

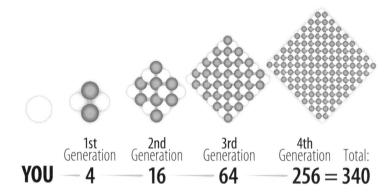

YOU	1st Generation 4	2nd Generation 16	3rd Generation 64	4th Generation 256	Total: = 340

In this scenario, however, we are showing your fourth generation sales leaders as just getting started in the business. As sales leaders "doing it" they are inviting others to have a look, but they have not yet enrolled anyone themselves according to the diagram as we do not show a fifth generation.

When each fourth generation Distributor gets their four, you would have added 1,024 new Distributors to your fifth generation. At $200 per Distributor in sales, and with a 5% royalty, that translates into an additional $204,800 in sales and an additional $10,240 in monthly earnings for you.

THIS ONE PIECE OF THE PUZZLE PULLS IT ALL TOGETHER.

WHEN YOU UNDERSTAND THIS PIECE, YOU ARE LIKELY TO "GET IT" AND START TO UNDERSTAND THE POSSIBILITIES OF THE FOUR YEAR CAREER.

Everyone we have shown thus far in this hypothetical plan is what we call a Sales Leader. We have shown that each one gets four. In

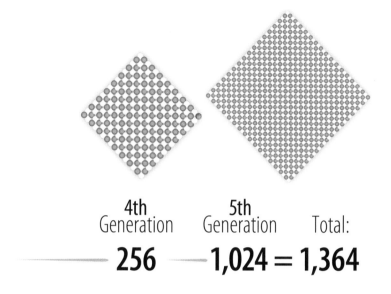

4th
Generation

5th
Generation

Total:

256 — **1,024 = 1,364**

order to get four to actually "do this" or be a Sales Leader, each Sales Leader will have enrolled many more than just four. Your first four are not likely to be "the four." Each Sales Leader will likely enroll 20–100 people in order to get their own four Sales Leaders. The point is that in The Four Year Career we only show Sales Leaders … they are not the best of the best, just the best of the rest. They didn't quit. They are doing it.

So calculate what happens to your "asset" income when they each get their own four … it grows by 400%. The definition of Asset Income is that it just remains static … that it never grows at all. So your asset income is designed to grow … *geometrically.*

So what about all the Non-Sales Leaders? What about the majority of new Distributors who did not end up "doing it." Some quit and never continue even using the product. Some give up on the income opportunity but remain loyal customers. Some sell a little and some even enroll a few people here and there. But they are not Sales Leaders and NONE of them are shown in this plan. If you add them back in ...

Adding them back in is more than an exercise in mind blowing ... it is actually reality. Four years from now if you build your Four Year Career, you will have more sales from customers and retailers as a total group than from sales leaders ... far more.

CHAPTER 7

THE ASSET VALUE

If we don't change our direction we're
likely to end up where we're headed.

— CHINESE PROVERB

THE ASSET VALUE

Build your network right and its sales and your income should flow long after you have anything to do with actively managing or growing it. That does not mean you ignore it or fail to nurture it. When we build or buy something that produces income without working it daily, it becomes an asset worth money in proportion to the income it produces.

Although you cannot sell a Distributorship for $1,200,000 that earns $6,800 a month (far too easy for one to build on their own), it nonetheless is worth that to you as an asset.

In pursuing financial security or more from life, people tend to pursue real estate investments or stocks (which require money to invest). These investments require time to produce enough income to provide security. Imagine or calculate how long, and at what rate of investment, it would require to amass $1 million in real estate.

	1st Generation	2nd Generation	3rd Generation	4th Generation	Total:
YOU —	4 —	16 —	64 —	256 =	340

$200 sales each x 340 people = $68,000

If each person has $200 in sales, that's 340 people earning a total sales of $68,000. You could earn an average of 10%* on all of it per month:

$68,000 x 10%* = $6,800 a month = $1,200,000 Asset Value

$6,800 a month for example is worth about $1,200,000 at a 7% annualized return over the course of 10 years.

*Industry average.

Not your residence, but rental real estate. It could easily take a lifetime of sacrifice, risk and management. And $1 million in real estate might earn you $5,000 a month.

Compare that to investing $1,000 once and only 10-20 hours a week for four to five years to earn the same asset income with an asset value of $1,200,000. Which is more appealing and more achievable to you? Yeah, us too.

Now take it a step further and think about a powerful Three-Prong Approach. You are building an Asset Income in Network Marketing while at the same time investing $1,000 a month, then $2,000, $3,000 and ultimately $5,000 a month in real estate, stocks, bonds, etc.

Network Marketing can actually give you access, the keys to the vault, in the other net worth-building investment models. Now your "extra few thousand a month" is worth a great deal more.

CHAPTER 8

MOMENTUM

Insanity: Doing the same thing over and over again
and expecting different results.

— ALBERT EINSTEIN

Momentum

Launching a Network Marketing sales group is much like pushing a car over a very slight hill. Imagine that you ran out of gas as you were driving up a hill. At the top of the hill the road becomes flat for some period of time and then slightly descends to the bottom of the hill where there is a gas station. Your mission is to get out of the car, get it rolling up the slight hill, to the top, and keep it going on the flat section until you crest the hill. Then you hop in and ride it to riches.

This is the same. In the beginning, you will exert the most amount of effort promoting the product and enrolling new people for the least amount of return. Once you get things rolling it will take less effort to keep them rolling but you must still keep pushing to keep it going. Once you hit "momentum" you just hop in and ride the wave.

Momentum happens at different times in different companies. You will know it when you are in it. You will not be able to keep up with the help requests people have for you and your group will be on fire.

Think of it like starting out pushing a Smart Car up the hill, having it turn into a Cadillac at the top and a Ferrari at the downhill crest.

It is the low return on effort in the beginning that leads most people to give up. They do not have the Vision and Belief in the payoffs on the other side.

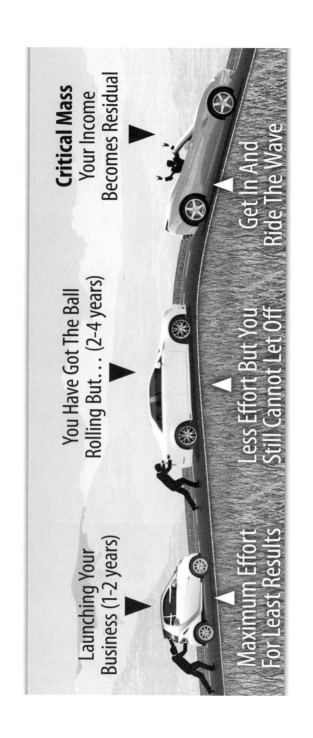

Launching Your
Business (1-2 years)

You Have Got The Ball
Rolling But... (2-4 years)

Critical Mass
Your Income
Becomes Residual

Maximum Effort
For Least Results

Less Effort But You
Still Cannot Let Off

Get In And
Ride The Wave

Another way to look at the growth of your group is to look at the Penny a Day chart. If it took a lot of effort to double that penny, given the return on investment of effort, most people would quit. Even half way through the month it is only worth $163.84! Yet if you understand the power of geometric progression and compounding then you KNOW if you keep doubling it, that little penny is worth over $5 million at the end of the month.

Day 1	$0.01	Day 16	$327.68
Day 2	$0.02	Day 17	$655.36
Day 3	$0.04	Day 18	$1,310.72
Day 4	$0.08	Day 19	$2,621.44
Day 5	$0.16	Day 20	$5,242.88
Day 6	$0.32	Day 21	$10,485.76
Day 7	$0.64	Day 22	$20,971.52
Day 8	$1.28	Day 23	$41,943.04
Day 9	$2.56	Day 24	$83,886.08
Day 10	$5.12	Day 25	$167,772.16
Day 11	$10.24	Day 26	$335,544.32
Day 12	$20.48	Day 27	$671,088.64
Day 13	$40.96	Day 28	$1,342,177.28
Day 14	$81.92	Day 29	$2,684,354.56
Day 15	$163.84	Day 30	$5,368,709.12

After 30 days, 1 penny becomes over 5 million dollars!

CHAPTER 9

THE RENAISSANCE OF THE FAMILY & COMMUNITY

It's what you learn after you know it all that really counts.

— COACH JOHN WOODEN

THE RENAISSANCE OF THE FAMILY & COMMUNITY

Yes, it is true that building a sales organization of on-fire volunteers is still a challenge. However, it is being done, and in a powerful way. The biggest challenge is in erasing people's negative beliefs and biases about the Network Marketing concept and replacing them with what those of us who have already done it know to be true. And, it's coming … one day soon, world consciousness will shift and many people—perhaps most people—will in some way be a part of this dynamic, wealth-building industry.

Opportunity appreciation is not the only factor fueling the future of Network Marketing. It is also fueled by people's basic need to connect with others, to be a part of something bigger than themselves, and to have a sense of community.

Most of us know all too well that the family has disintegrated in many segments of our country. Since family is the foundation of neighborhoods and communities, they too have been compromised. Most of the industrialized world is deeply entrenched in the rat race—parents with full-time careers, day care, career advancement, soccer, music lessons, e-mail, social media, cell phones, mania— payments, payments and more payments. Some of us are winning the race, but it has been said, "We are still rats!"

Today, people are longing for a return to a real, safe, relaxed time of freedom and soulful connection with others. People want to play together, pray together, get to really know each other, and most importantly, to be known by others.

We want to improve ourselves, to have more pride in ourselves, to love and respect ourselves. We are hungry for guidance and support that will help us grow to be more powerful, more generous and more self-assured. Anyone who has come full circle can tell you that these are the things that bring true happiness.

Achieving financial success and status are wonderful, especially if the alternative is being financially strapped to a life of despair. I think we'd all be better off rich, but money is relative—the more you have, the more you think you need.

Or, as it has been said, "Money is relative. The more money you have, the more relatives you have." There is a point, however, where we must have the wisdom to know when enough is enough.

This return to basic human values in business is a subtle, yet powerful, force driving the Network Marketing industry.

These are the qualities that will endear you to your family and to the community you create:

Patience	Honesty	Forthrightness
Generosity	Integrity	Leadership
Open-mindedness	Authenticity	Love
Cooperation	Courage	Listening

Network Marketing may offer the most dynamic environment within which we can develop our spirituality, and manage our humanity at the same time. It may just be the most exciting leadership and character development program you have ever imagined ... often times disguised as skin care, nutrition and fitness products.

Are you up for that?

WHAT TO LOOK FOR IN A NETWORK MARKETING COMPANY

A building has integrity just like a man. And just as seldom.

— AYN RAND

What To Look For In A Network Marketing Company

1. Product

You must find a product or service you absolutely love:

- Something you would buy forever, regardless of whether or not you are a Distributor.
- Something you can recommend to others without reservation.

If you have to try to feel this way about the product, let it go. It will not work for you long term. Less important (but still vital) is that the product or service is consumable, which means that the customer will want to reorder it regularly.

Look at the list of billion dollar companies and look at what kinds of products they sell. Ask yourself ... will this product really be relevant 25 years from now? Will it be in demand? Will it still be able to be competitively priced? Technology and service products are challenged here, as are commodities. Pick your product line with an eye on the long-term. How long-term? How long do you want to get paid? I prefer forever.

2. The Company

You must be proud of and trust the company: your "mothership" and its leaders. They are your partners in product development, legal and financial issues, human resources, customer service, product development, order fulfillment, data processing, international expansion, public relations, ethics and culture. They are crucial to your long-term success.

Imagine working hard for two or three years to build a solid Network Marketing group, then having the company go out of business or embarrass you and your group so badly that everyone wants to quit.

Do your homework. Study the ownership and management of the company. Study the product's actual performance with customers. Study the compensation plan so you know ahead of time that it is something that will motivate and reward you. Most people spend more time analyzing a $50 Network Marketing product for purchase than they do on the company when they decide to jump in and stake their reputation on it. Measure twice, cut once.

3. Your Upline

These are the people above you in your line of sponsorship. They will be partnering with you, training you and supporting you. You will be spending countless hours with them. They may be in your home, and you in theirs. *You may be earning them a lot of money.* You must at least like them. Preferably you will love, honor and respect them.

Look for people who are dedicated, loyal, focused, positive, committed, generous and successful And most importantly, once you choose your sponsor and upline, listen to them. Follow their lead. Get trained by them. Be coachable. They can only be successful if you are successful.

4. Follow Your Intuition,
Feeling For a Fit of Your Values

You're encouraged to use this book as the beginning of your Network Marketing education. Be a student. Do your homework. Start by talking frankly with whomever had the Vision and courage to give you this book.

If you can, find the right product, company and people for you. If you can't, keep looking. Don't settle by copping out or by looking for reasons why it won't work. Instead, look with the intention of finding the right match—no matter how long it takes or what it requires of you.

When you find a company to call home, build your empire. Don't be deterred by challenges and setbacks; even dumb mistakes your company may make. Stick with them through thick and thin. Your life and the lives of thousands may be enriched. The world is waiting …

FREEDOM EDITION SUCCESS STORIES

The following stories feature people who perhaps may be much like you. Certainly in their beginning they didn't understand or necessarily believe in the promise of Network Marketing. And as you will read most were not instant successes. Many of them have the same story as most people who get involved during their first few months or even years ... "This doesn't work!"

Yet if you can reflect on the examples of duplication, compounding and the car over the hill, it might help you make sense of these massive success stories. This is a much bigger opportunity than most people believe. And that is The Promise of Network Marketing ... that it's just an opportunity. What you do with it is up to you.

DONNY ANDERSON

DESOTO, TEXAS
TOTAL FREEDOM!

Donny Anderson knows the value of setting goals, planning, focusing, committing and taking action. Those traits coupled with hard work have allowed him to move through the management ranks of a major corporation and become a Vice President, where he managed a division that covered the Western Hemisphere. Eventually, Donny grew tired of airports and boardrooms and left his cushy, corner office to become an entrepreneur.

Donny had found financial success in various methods of business but ultimately found financial and time-freedom through Network Marketing.

Donny realized that if he ever wanted to create time-freedom and financial freedom, he had to be the employer and not an employee. Next, he and his wife, Susan, were drawn to the franchise world because of the track record they had seen, and they purchased a total of three franchises. While this business model afforded Donny and Susan a better lifestyle than the traditional JOB, he was still tied down to a hectic schedule and had a $75,000 per month overhead cost, as well as 70+ employees.

Approximately ten years ago, a friend approached Donny and Susan wanting to share a Network Marketing business that would create a passive residual income. The residual income part of the business intrigued Donny greatly. You see, Donny and Susan had enjoyed great success in the business world, but had no solid retirement plan. The way Donny saw it, the residual income could be their ticket to retirement when the time came.

Donny got involved with Network Marketing and became a student of the business quickly. Within the first 12 months of his new business, he had created a 6-figure passive residual income … the retirement plan was unfolding just as he had imagined.

Donny has introduced 49 people to his Network Marketing business and those have turned into over 65,000 reps with tens of thousands of customers on the team. Donny will be quick to give credit to his team for the massive success they have had.

Donny and Susan believe that total freedom includes two elements:
1. A passive residual income that exceeds your monthly expenses
2. Becoming debt free

"That, my friends, is total freedom," Donny says. Today, Donny and Susan's mission is to teach and help others create life-changing residual income and become debt free as he and Susan have.

Donny is so grateful that he was willing to look at the information when his friend called, and more importantly, to get involved.

RANDALL & MICHELLE BLACKMON

Randall and Michelle always had big dreams and were able to fulfill them through their Network Marketing opportunity, and they now have over 6,500 in their organization!

Randall and Michelle are your typical American family ... hard working with big dreams and a burning desire to be successful. Like most they were taught to go to college, make good grades and get a good job. Michelle worked as an accountant in Corporate America for over 20 years but soon realized that her time was not her own and that she could not obtain her ideal work schedule of 10 am to 2 pm. Randall, a former employee of a major package delivery company and high school basketball coach, woke up one day and realized they were nowhere near their dreams and goals of financial freedom.

Michelle's family was filled with self-employed individuals including her dad, grandmother and several uncles. Randall's grandfather and several of his uncles were entrepreneurs as well. So the idea of owning their own business appealed to the both of them. However, they couldn't decide on what to do and they noticed that none of their family members had the time freedom they wanted.

So why Network Marketing? Michelle, being an accountant, was very reluctant to invest the family savings in a traditional business and realized Network Marketing ("NWM") just made sense because of it's a low start-up investment and it can be built on your free-time. Michelle accepted a friends' invitation to attend a business presentation. That was the start of their Network Marketing career. Randall was very supportive but wanted nothing to do with her newly found Network Marketing opportunity (in the beginning).

Randall eventually came around and began to get involved. But 7 years and $30,000 in credit card debt later, the couple was now even further away from the goal of financial freedom. Now what do we do they thought. They so desperately wanted and needed another stream of income but Michelle was very skeptical and afraid of another NWM failure. After some serious soul searching they found themselves thinking, "what if our kids found out we quit and gave up on our dreams? Do we really want to settle for that old broken 40/40/40 Rat Race Plan?" They made a decision to get back in the game, and finally found the right NWM business for them.

"Freedom isn't free and getting it won't be easy, I do promise it's VERY well worth it" says Michelle. Today they live the financially free lifestyle they have always dreamed of. They've personally sponsored 88 independent business owners and have nearly 6,500 people on their team.

MARK & LA DOHN DEAN

Mark and La Dohn enjoy their time-freedom to be together and give back to their community, which they have accomplished through Network Marketing with their organization of over 75,000 people!

Mark and La Dohn understand the power of residual income. After 20 years working for the "other guys" and building *their* dreams, Mark decided it was time to build his *own* dreams. The first few businesses were not a huge success and certainly did not offer residual income. While owning a small car dealership with his best friend, Mark realized that he did not own the business, the business "owned" him. As the years passed, his health was deteriorating due to stress and the credit cards were mounting. One day a customer shared Network Marketing with him. Soon after, he closed the car dealership and entered the profession full-time.

Not only has the industry rewarded Mark financially, the biggest blessing of all has been marrying his wife, La Dohn, three years into the business.

La Dohn had been a restaurateur for five years, and then experienced a financially rewarding real estate career for 12. Both fields devoured her health and time. She knew residual income was the only way to create a future she could again dream about. She loves being able to spend uncommon time with Mark and Duke, their Shih-Tzu, without the pressures of a common career.

Now they work the business together and are able to set their own schedules. Their new lifestyle created a path for them to realize a successful and happy marriage, and it has opened up opportunities to have the time to volunteer in their church and community.

They have grown their organization to over 75,000 people, turning their initial $300 investment into millions. Ever since the second year in the business, they have been enjoying a six-figure residual income and are among the top income earners in their multi-billion dollar company.

Today, the Deans enjoy their days together. Mark says, "I love getting up early in the morning to enjoy quiet time and setting my own schedule." They both cherish volunteering at their church and Mark enjoys teaching a Bible Study at an assisted living facility.

Whether they are actively working or not, they always keep their ears open for people looking for additional time or money. Mark says, "You know, those people are everywhere. It's a blessing to be able to help others turn their lives around just as Network Marketing did for us so many years ago. The Lord has blessed us beyond measure. Now comes the most fun part of all … we get to give back!"

TREY & SALLY DYER

After just 12 months, they were able to retire Trey from his two jobs and now are top 10 income earners with tens of thousands of customers.

Sally's initial prospect in her first-time Network Marketing business was her toughest—mainly because she was trying to recruit Trey, her husband. Sally had been approached by her aunt about the business and thought it would be perfect for Trey, but he was skeptical. It took her a couple of months of working the business part-time before Trey agreed to sit down and take a look.

"She seemed to be having fun," says Trey. "She wasn't spending too much time working it and she had already made some bonus checks." The small amount of time that Sally was spending working her business caught Trey's attention. He finally decided to take a look.

Sally and Trey were born and raised in typical small towns in west Texas. They grew up just a few miles apart, fell in love, got married and still live in the small community Trey grew up in. They have a son, Joshua, who was 4 when Sally was approached with a Network Marketing opportunity. After working 15 years in their body shop, Trey had taken on a second job and was working 60 to 80 hours a week to make ends meet and pay down debt. "My goal was to get Trey home," Sally says. "I wanted him to be able to be there as Joshua grew up."

Trey got excited when he saw the business plan at a company event. Although he didn't understand all the details, he did understand the leverage that they could create. Trey and Sally teamed up and went to work putting in a little time every day.

Their business took off and in just 12 months they accomplished their goal. Trey was able to retire from both jobs after having built a six-figure income. The next year, they became top 10 income earners with their company. The Dyers still live on a ranch in that same small town, but their lives are very different. They are full-time parents while getting paid every month on tens of thousands of customers.

"We go to baseball games, basketball games, play golf, take vacations and do just about anything we want on the spur of the moment these days," Trey says. "I'm so thankful Sally stuck it out early on." "I love our life!" Sally says, smiling! "Having the time to spend with the ones you love is a wonderful feeling."

STEVE FISHER

After growing up in Florida, Steve Fisher hired on with American Airlines at the young age of 19. Not having a college degree, Steve started out as a baggage handler in Dallas, TX, enduring the hot Texas summers and cold winters. He eventually became a manager for American at the DFW Airport and ultimately became a Sr. Analyst of Airport Operations in their corporate offices.

After spending years climbing the corporate ladder, he was laid off the Wednesday before Christmas of 2004. He realized he wanted his life to be different. He wanted something more. He wanted to own his time.

Steve has been a leader in the Network Marketing Profession for over 20 years and has literally inspired hundreds of thousands of people to change their lives and their financial futures through the message of residual income and true success.

Steve was introduced to residual income through Network Marketing and his life has never been the same. He saw a way to attain the freedom he was looking for. It made total sense and he's never looked back. Since then he has built one of the largest teams in Network Marketing and has earned millions. He is a very sought after speaker, coach, and trainer. Steve is also the author of the Amazon Best-Selling book, *Residual Millionaire*.

Steve currently travels the world helping and teaching people how to reach their full potential, how to create residual income that provides true freedom, and how to live the lives they were created to live. Steve says, "I'm amazed at how many people live lives they never intended to live, doing something they don't want to do, with people they don't want to do it with! There's a better way... it's Network Marketing!"

He and his wife, Diane, live in Colleyville, TX and have been married for 25 years. They have three daughters and a son-in-law and are living the life of their dreams.

SUSAN FISHER

BEDFORD, TEXAS
RETIRED IO YEARS EARLY!

After taking a look at her brother's Network Marketing opportunity, Susan realized that it could be her ticket to retirement, and after just two years was able to retire and be credit card debt free!

Susan Fisher grew up in Florida knowing she wanted to teach and coach tennis. Her drive and competitive spirit blossomed while playing tennis at the collegiate level. Soon after beginning her first teaching and coaching position, the administrative staff witnessed her leadership qualities and encouraged her to pursue a postgraduate degree. Susan relocated to Texas, completed her Master of Education degree, and worked as a high school assistant principal. She had her heart set on becoming a principal and sharing her love of students and learning with others. Susan thoroughly enjoyed five years working as a middle school principal and three years working as a high school principal.

Steve Fisher, Susan's brother, came to her house one weekend and shared with her an opportunity of how she could get involved with a business and earn a passive residual income. Steve painted a vivid picture of what Susan's life could look like if she would begin to carve time out of her busy schedule. Steve also challenged Susan to look at her retirement plan to determine if she could live on that income comfortably. After dissecting and studying what she would make after retirement, Susan simply put her head down and went to work building her residual income empire.

After two short years of building her business, she had the blessing and privilege of retiring ten years early. She was also afforded the benefit of becoming free of credit card debt. What a gift it has been for Susan to retire ten years early and to have NO credit card debt! Susan was able to achieve time-freedom and flexibility of time, as well as a tremendous amount of financial freedom.

Today, the former high school principal is able to continue using her educational skills through teaching others about residual income in order to achieve their dreams. Susan states, "There are many great blessings in this business; however, the greatest joy of all is working alongside my brother, Steve Fisher."

TERRI HATCH

Terri initially saw Network Marketing as an opportunity to earn extra income on the side, but now it is her family's sole income and her team has grown to over 7,500, leading her to become a top money earner!

Based in Pilot Point, Texas, Terri Hatch was a Sales and Marketing Representative with a Fortune 500 company when she was approached with the opportunity to see the business plan in her current Network Marketing company. She had been with that company for over 20 years and had always expected to retire with the company.

Terri and her husband have two children, one of whom had a medical condition that required monthly maintenance, but was getting to the age insurance coverage was ending. She saw the networking marketing opportunity as an answer to prayer and joined to earn $500 extra per month to enhance financing healthcare for her daughter. Both children were in college, so she also saw it as a means to fund their college education and prevent student loan debt. She truly felt she had no time to participate on a large scale because of the long working hours and family commitments.

At the time, Terri was confident of the stability and longevity of the Fortune 500 company she worked with and was looking forward to retiring. The shocking truth was the company was sold and all employees were without a job. It was just five weeks before Terri could have retired with 25 years of service and a retirement income. Three months later, the company her husband worked with filed Chapter 7 and he too was now unemployed. What had been a dual income family was now depending solely on what she had called Plan B. Her Network Marketing business was no longer a Plan B or a means to an end ... it was their sole income. "Networking has been a financial blessing for my family and has given me great confidence in our future," she says.

An accidental call to a wrong number became the right number to catapult her business to great heights. Thanks to that one call, her team grew well over 7,500 associates. "I never expected to fall in love with the business and just have so much fun," says Terri. She feels people are put in your path for a reason and we owe it to them to share our business. Today she is a top money earner, leading a growing team of thousands of associates and truly wants to help others attain the same success. She is excited to see the opportunity deliver more than she ever dreamed possible and develop true, long-term residual income. Relationships she has established through networking marketing have become an extended family to her, one that she truly cherishes.

RANDY HEDGE

By working a couple of days a week, Randy was able to build an income that not only replaced what he had, but well surpassed it!

Based in DeQueen, Arkansas, Randy Hedge was a single dad and a former insurance broker when he got involved in his current Network Marketing company. Today, he is a top money earner, leading a growing team of over 35,000 in Texas, Georgia, Pennsylvania, Maryland, Missouri, and the District of Columbia.

"I'd always been chasing passive income," says Randy, "whether it was with the ranch, rental properties or insurance." In the mid-nineties, Randy was doing well running a couple of insurance businesses, along with his cattle operation, when another insurance broker told him about a Network Marketing company.

"More and more people know they need a plan B," he says. "There are many great companies now that have legitimized Network Marketing. Unfortunately, it still has some baggage, but so does the medical profession and real estate. Name any profession and there are jokes and snide comments about it. The beauty of networking is it's the only career I know where a person, regardless of education, background, or even ability, can find success if they're willing to learn and work. Unfortunately, many people aren't willing to pay the price for whatever it is they want to accomplish. To be a good husband takes work. To be a good dad, you have to work at it, and you're going to fail. I fail miserably every day at everything I do, but I just keep trying."

Randy believes Network Marketing will be the answer for a growing number of people he sees who have been squeezed out of the middle class and are struggling.

When Randy married his soul mate Marcie in 2006, he made the commitment to never be away from his family for more than three or four days at a time. Extensive travel while building his previous business took a toll on his first marriage, and going through the loss of a business and a marriage made him reprioritize. What was one of the most difficult times in his life became one of the biggest blessings, because it allowed him to understand and protect what's most important to him.

By working a couple of days a week, Randy was able to build an income that not only replaced what he had, but well surpassed it. For the first time he truly experienced time and financial freedom. It's just been an amazing ride ever since.

JERRY & MONICA SCRIBNER

Jerry and Monica started their Network Marketing business to help eliminate their debt. They did just that as well fund both daughters' college educations, and they are now helping hundreds of others do the same!

Jerry Scribner knows the value of personal development. As a young man growing up in central Michigan, he wanted more than anything to be a professional athlete. Jerry dreamed of playing for his beloved Detroit Tigers, Lions, or Pistons and becoming a champion. Jerry had a lot of heart and refused to give up, but had normal talent. His sports career ended in high school. Always the dreamer, he set out to be a millionaire by age 30; it didn't happen. So Jerry went to college at age 31 and entered corporate America. Over the years his dreams diminished and he "settled" for an average job, home, debts, and life.

In 2007, a friend asked Jerry to watch a short online video regarding Network Marketing. At the time, Jerry had a lot of credit card debt and no money saved for college for his daughters. The timing was right and he was open to "taking a look."

It made sense and Jerry launched his business on a spare time basis in April 2007.

The first thing Jerry's friend did was send him a personal development CD by Jim Rohn. That single act of kindness propelled Jerry to seek his own journey of personal responsibility. Jerry became a devout reader of personal development books.

Over the next nine months, working a 50-60 hour week at his regular job, Jerry would ask people to "just take a look." He would meet people for breakfast, at lunch, and after work. In December 2007, they paid off all credit card and car loan debt. They have since saved enough to fully fund both daughters' college education without taking on more debt.

In a little over seven years, Jerry has personally sponsored over 80 friends and has built a team of over 7,000 reps that have enrolled tens of thousands of customers. Jerry has been blessed to have met many great people who have become a part of his networking business.

Because of the success of the people in his networking "community," Jerry and his wife Monica and their two daughters, have lived a blessed life. His "purpose" is to help families totally eliminate debt from their lives. "We had serious economic needs when we found our Networking business," Jerry says. Jerry considers himself a normal guy who focused on studying the success of others. Today he continues to build his networking "community," teaches people how to get rid of debt, and shares the personal development principles that have enriched his life.

MICHELLE & LOUIS MIORI

Michelle and Louis had a powerful "Why" and were able to turn that drive into a successful organization of over 7,000 associates.

Michelle Miori and her husband, Louis, have an incredible story of building their business with integrity. They were introduced to Network Marketing by their son's football coach. Louis was a pastor at a very large church in the Houston area and Michelle was a sales executive for a printing company at the time. They simply went to see the presentation as a favor to their son's football coach because he had recently visited their church.

They had a feeling it was a Network Marketing presentation and they were fully prepared to say no. However, when they saw how they could create passive, residual income, they knew they had to do it! They had three kids and, therefore, three college tuitions to pay for! This "why" drove them to build their business and find ways around, through, and over the inevitable obstacles that would get in their way.

You see, Louis made a commitment early in their business that he was not going to build their Network Marketing business through their church. He wanted to keep the two separate. So they began building their business through their contacts outside the church on a part-time basis, but with full-time persistence. They were blown away as their team grew to over 7,000 associates. Louis remained a pastor at the same church, but Michelle was able to quit her sales job and go full-time in their Network Marketing business and has become a sought-after speaker and trainer.

Michelle tells it this way, "The things I love most in life are spending time with family and friends and helping people. I used to have very little time to do these things. Now, thanks to the monthly residual income our Network Marketing business provides, I am able to spend MOST of my time doing exactly these things!" Network Marketing has allowed Michelle to buy back her time while helping her family financially at the same time. Her three children are now out of college and grown and as she and Louis have become "empty-nesters.' Thanks to Network Marketing and residual income, "empty" is the last thing their nest will ever be as they both invest their time, money and lives into helping many people not only in their spiritual journey, but also in their journey to financial freedom.

PRESLEY SWAGERTY

Presley Swagerty began with the humblest of roots before transforming into a true American success story. He is a self-made multi-millionaire, world-renowned networker, well-respected businessman, success coach, speaker and author. Presley grew up with his mom in an impoverished area of Dallas and, in his formative years, used basketball as an anchor to keep him on the right track in life.

He earned his bachelor's degree in history and math and then became a successful high school basketball coach over a 16-year career. Along the way, he earned the fitting nickname of "Coach," a title he proudly wears today as he continues mentoring and coaching thousands of people to take the next step toward living their dreams.

After coaching, Presley developed into one of the world's leading

After a 16-year career as a high school basketball coach, Presley developed into one of the world's leading networkers, building an organization of over 250,000 independent associates and over 1 million customers.

networkers, building a distributor force of over 250,000 independent associates and enrolling over 1,000,000 customers.

Coach lives out his personal motto of "Be, Do and Have More," as he motivates and equips people around the world to do the same. The secret to success is not where one is raised, as Coach's story proves; it is the drive and motivation that exists within an individual to get to whatever the next desired level might be. This is a frequently delivered message, complete with instructional how-tos, when Coach speaks as a keynote presenter at workshops and major national conferences to audiences of thousands.

Coach's straight-from-the-heart, high-energy, passionate message motivates and engages audiences to step into their greatness, providing them with the motivation to take the next steps toward living their dreams. His charisma, warmth, and sense of humor have affected thousands upon thousands of lives.

In addition to his networking business, Presley is a successful businessman with a vast and varied portfolio. He is a major shareholder for Global Innovation, where he serves on the board of directors. He also owns a real estate company, Swagerty Investments, a record label, Circle S Records, and a music publishing company, Delta Pearl Publishing.

Coach and his wife, Jeanie, live in Flower Mound, Texas. They have two successful, grown children, SaraBeth and Jordan, who have displayed the same desire to succeed as their dad. SaraBeth is a rapidly rising star in the country music industry and just released her second CD, Obsessive. Jordan is a talented, professional baseball pitcher for the St. Louis Cardinals.

THE FOUR YEAR CAREER VISION

The Four Year Career is now a standard paradigm for Ethical Network Marketing and Financial Freedom. It is an alternative to a four year college education or an add-on strategy for those fortunate enough to have a higher learning degree. The Four Year Career is catalyst for the profession of Leadership, and the Arts of Listening, Public Speaking, Ontological Coaching, Accountability, Vision and Self-Motivation, and Authenticity.

Ethical Network Marketing is now clearly known and accepted by the media, the public and government agencies as a means to build wealth. All proceeds from The Four Year Career messages are contributed to fund the production of a future mainstream documentary film. Just watching this film once will change a person's views, beliefs and life strategy forever.

Join the Tribe and Enjoy the Ride.

DARING GREATLY

"It is not the critic who counts: not the man who points out how the strong man stumbles or where the doer of deeds could have done better. The credit belongs to the man who is actually in the arena, whose face is marred by dust and sweat and blood, who strives valiantly, who errs and comes up short again and again, because there is no effort without error or shortcoming, but who knows the great enthusiasms, the great devotions, who spends himself for a worthy cause; who, at the best, knows, in the end, the triumph of high achievement, and who, at the worst, if he fails, at least he fails while daring greatly, so that his place shall never be with those cold and timid souls who knew neither victory nor defeat."

Theodore Roosevelt, 1858-1919
From the speech, Citizenship in a Republic, (Sorbonne, Paris; April 23, 1910)

THE MASTER GAME

"Seek, above all, for a game worth playing. Such is the advice of the oracle to modern man. Having found the game, play it with intensity—play as if your life and sanity depended on it (they do depend upon it). Follow the example of the French existentialists and flourish a banner bearing the word "engagement." Though nothing means anything and all roads are marked "No Exit," yet move as if your movements had some purpose. If life does not seem to offer a game worth playing, then invent one. For it must be clear, even to the most clouded intelligence, that any game is better than no game."

Robert S. DeRopp, 1913-1987
The Master Game, (Delacorte Press, 1968)

BLISS BUSINESS

Richard is also the author of *Mach II With Your Hair On Fire*. This powerful work connects the Law of Attraction with the Laws of Action, teaching you exactly how to think, how to speak, how to feel and how to act in order to manifest your wildest Visions.

"I found a copy of *Mach II* at a friend's house. I read and loved it. So much of what the great athletes do to accomplish the impossible is done though visualization. Richard captures exactly how it works, why it works, and how anyone can use it to do great things in their life. Richard has a unique way of telling the story so we all really get it! I highly recommend this book to anyone wanting to master their own motivation and accomplishments."

John Elway
Super Bowl MVP & NFL Hall of Fame Quarterback

"Congratulations! Congratulations! Congratulations! Congratulations! Congratulations! I just read your *Mach II* book, and it is a masterpiece … head and shoulders above the rest of the motivation books I have read."

Harvey Mackay
Chairman & Founder, MackayMitchell

"In this accelerated economy you have to travel at *Mach II*. This book teaches you how to do it in an omni-effective and fun way."

Mark Victor Hansen
Co-creator, #1 New York Times Best-Selling series Chicken Soup for the Soul and Co-author, The One Minute Millionaire

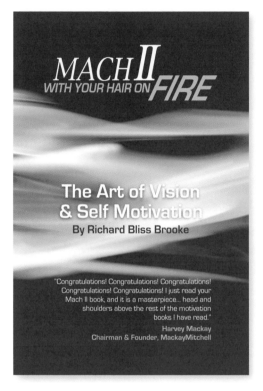

"Absolutely incredible!"
John Addison
Co-CEO, Primerica

"I love *Mach II With Your Hair On Fire*. I could tell when I read the book that Richard has a passion for changing people's lives. I respect Richard and his work and thank him for who he is and the difference and impact he's making in people's lives and businesses."

Les Brown
Motivational Speaker

Richard would love to hear your stories of how this work has impacted your life or business. You can reach Richard at 855.480.3585 or RB@BlissBusiness.com.

You can order *The Four Year Career* (in either book, audio, and/or video formats) and *Mach II With Your Hair On Fire* at BlissBusiness.com.

BLISSBUSINESS.COM

To buy more copies of this book, go to BlissBusiness.com/FreedomEdition. Richard's site is designed to inspire and provide practical tools that will nurture your success and help you achieve your personal and business goals. Richard taps 30 years of experience as a visionary leader, trainer and coach to lead you on a journey of self-fulfillment, personal freedom and financial independence.

AT BLISSBUSINESS.COM YOU WILL FIND:

- FREE monthly **blog subscription** – Sign up to receive Richard's latest training and send to your friends with a click of your mouse.

- FREE access for downloading dozens of archived **training articles, audios, videos, PowerPoints and books** to your computer and/or iPod!

- FREE **real-time quizzes** that assess your skill level and give you on-the-spot feedback.

- FREE access to Richard himself! Ask your questions and/or **request a guest appearance** on your next group training call.

- Huge discounts for bulk orders only available on BlissBusiness.com.

- **Books, CDs and software** available to order. Get your whole team using them!

- Dates and locations of Richard's next **Vision workshop, seminar or retreat.**

- A brief bio that will leave you eager to read the rest of Richard's story in Mach II With Your Hair On Fire.

- Dozens of endorsements hailing the virtues of Richard's tools and trainings.

- A photo gallery that will inspire you to create a lifestyle of choice for yourself!

"If you are committed to extraordinary success, Richard Brooke's information on Vision and Self-Motivation is some of the best you will find anywhere. Richard is a great example of what a person can do with the right information … plus, he understands the importance of sharing."

Bob Proctor
Author of best-selling book, You Were Born Rich